UPPERCUT

A JOHN MILTON THRILLER

MARK DAWSON

PART I

1

———

Lilly Moon reached into her jacket and touched the butt of her suppressed pistol, just to reassure herself that it was still there. It was midnight, and the harbour was quiet, at least when compared to the bustle of daylight hours. The full moon cast a soft light, picking out the silhouettes of houseboats and *shikaras*—traditional Kashmiri wooden vessels—as they bobbed gently in the water. The faint outlines of the Himalayas were visible in the distance, their snow-capped peaks bathed in silver. Dal Lake was breathtaking, but Lilly and the others had not travelled here to enjoy the view. This wasn't a vacation.

This was business.

The lake was nestled in the heart of Srinagar, the summer capital of Jammu and Kashmir. It was fringed by the mountains, stretched all the way across ten square miles and was divided into four distinct basins, each boasting its own distinct character and charm. The team had arrived in the city this morning after a long journey and had gone to work as soon as they arrived. One and Two had posed as backpackers and scouted the harbour. They hadn't seen

John Milton but had confirmed that the signal from his mobile phone was still pinging from inside the houseboat. They had spent the afternoon tweaking their plan with the benefit of the on-the-ground intelligence, and now, cloaked by the dark, they were ready to put it into action.

Two months had passed since the attack in New Delhi. All of Group Fifteen—including Lilly—had been set the goal of finding Milton, but, so far, there had been no sign of him. They all knew he was adept at disappearing, and that he had managed to stay ahead of the Group when they had searched for him after his attempt to leave years earlier. Milton was good, but—as they had been reminded by the team from Group Three that was also engaged in the search for him—he'd been found back then, and he would be found now, too.

It would take only one mistake, and they would be onto him.

It was just a question of time.

The Group facility at Brize Norton had been put on alert. There was always an aircraft ready to leave within minutes of Milton being found, and they had flown out of the facility yesterday evening as soon as it was confirmed he was here.

Lilly was on edge, and everything around her seemed amplified: the sound of the water lapping against the wooden pilings was a little louder; the air felt cooler; the freshness of the lake's water mixed with the fragrance of night-blooming flowers and woodsmoke seemed more intense, drifting through the air as houseboat owners kept themselves warm with traditional *bukharis*.

Lilly crept ahead. There were four houseboats moored to the jetty, and Milton's mobile phone was pinging from the last one on the right.

A nightjar's call echoed across the lake. Lilly closed her eyes for a moment and listened: she heard the murmur of voices from the last houseboat before the jetty, the creaking of the wooden planks underfoot, the wash of water against the hulls of the boats.

She heard the crackle of static in the earbud that she had pressed into her ear.

"Alpha to Group," said Number One. "Comms check. Out."

The other members of the detail—the surviving Group Fifteen agents—radioed back that they could hear her clearly.

Lilly was Number Six now but didn't feel the seniority that would usually have come with that designation. To rise from Twelve would usually have taken years, but her ascent had been rocketed by the deaths of the agents in Krasnodar and New Delhi. She had been a member of the team sent to rescue Control from Otto Sommer but had returned to London to report that Milton—who had also been on the detail—had sold them out. She had reported that everyone else had been murdered and that she had escaped only by dint of good fortune.

That wasn't what had happened at all—not even close— but she'd needed a fall guy, and Milton, with his chequered past, was the perfect candidate.

Lilly had been persuasive, and, so far, she was confident that her story had been bought. There were just two loose ends: Control and Milton.

They both knew what she had done.

Lilly wasn't concerned about Control. Sommer had reported that she was in Siberia, and, while she was trapped there, she offered no threat.

Milton, though, was another matter. He was in the wind,

and Lilly knew enough about his history to know that he wouldn't stay quiet; he had an irritating sense of right and wrong and would come after her for what she had done. Lilly's daughter, Lola, was at home, and the prospect of a Group Fifteen agent—let alone an agent like Milton— running free while holding a grudge had been the source of many sleepless nights.

Milton was good at disappearing. He had managed that successfully before, vanishing for months despite the best efforts of the Firm to find him. They had expected something similar this time, too, until Group Three had found the SIGINT that said he was in Kashmir. A police report had been filed following a brawl between a Western tourist and two local men who had tried to mug him. The Westerner had been arrested and processed; the name he gave them was false, but he couldn't fake his mugshot and prints. The analysts pulled the file, crosschecked the prints with Group records and confirmed that it was Milton. They dug in some more and identified the mobile phone he had been using.

They were able to track it to the houseboat that lay ahead of them now.

The radio squelched again. "Alpha to Bravo. Confirm you're ready to breach. Out."

Two looked over at Lilly.

Lilly nodded.

"Bravo to Alpha," he said. "Ready to breach. Out."

"Alpha to Bravo—Roger that. On my mark. Out."

They had split into two groups: Alpha and Bravo. Alpha was One, Four and Five, and they had stolen a tender and were out on the water where they had an unobstructed view of the houseboat. Five had put a small drone into the air and was using that for overhead coverage. The three of them would be well placed should Milton manage to evade the breaching party by throwing himself into the lake. He could try to swim clear, but he wouldn't get far.

Lilly was in Bravo Group, and, together with Two and Three, was responsible for boarding the boat.

"Alpha to Bravo," the radio buzzed. "You have a green light to proceed. Weapons free. Say again, weapons free. Out."

Lilly drew her pistol, held it in both hands and trained it on the back of the houseboat. Three drew her pistol and came up to stand alongside her. Two stepped onto the small wooden platform that wrapped around the exterior of the vessel, and Lilly followed, with Three staying on the platform to provide cover and to ensure that Milton would have nowhere to run if he somehow managed to come this way.

The houseboat had a simple, hinged door. An iron handle was used to secure it, with a series of decorative wooden slats to allow for natural light and ventilation. Two carefully turned the handle; the door was unlocked, and he pulled it back and stepped inside.

Lilly followed. The interior was a blend of traditional Kashmiri craftsmanship and modern convenience. The living area was small, with seating arranged around a low wooden table. Handwoven carpets and rugs covered the floor, and the walls were hung with local tapestries. Windows in the sides of the houseboat offered views of the lake and the surrounding landscape; Lilly caught a glimpse of the tender out on the water.

Two cleared the room and gestured that he was going to go forward. The boat tapered to a corridor with a bathroom to the left. Two crept ahead silently and stopped at the door to clear the tiny room beyond. He gestured that it was empty and pointed to the last remaining door. Lilly stepped around him and advanced. The orders that they had been given were clear: the preference was to bring Milton back to London for questioning, but were that to prove impractical, they had clearance to take him out. Lilly had no interest in having him provide his version of what had happened in Krasnodar, she would refute it, and she thought her word was more likely to be believed than his, but why take the chance? She had decided during the flight to New Delhi that she would see him reach for a weapon—whether one was there or not—and remove him as a threat to her and her daughter once and for all.

She stepped up to the door and took a breath. Her heart was hammering in her chest, and she could feel the sweat slick on her skin. The door wasn't closed, so she pushed it far enough ajar that she could look inside. The bedroom was just large enough for a bed. Lilly raised the pistol and aimed, her finger tightening on the trigger.

She stepped forward.

The bed was empty.

A phone had been left on the pillow. A cable ran from it into a large rucksack.

"Shit," she muttered. "*Shit!*"

Two stepped alongside, saw the phone and rucksack and froze.

Lilly's earpiece crackled. "Alpha to Bravo—send SITREP. Out."

"Bravo to Alpha," said Two. "The target is not here. Say again: target is not here. He's left a trap—could be a bomb. Out."

"Get out," One said. "Get out now."

Lilly stepped back, her heel catching against Two's toe.

And then the phone rang.

2

John Milton watched the feed on the laptop screen as the two agents opened the bedroom door.

"Here we go," said Ziggy Penn.

Ziggy had bought the phone and rigged it to spoof the IMEI number of Milton's device, using it to bait a trap that had lured Group Fifteen halfway across the world. The phone was powered by a 5,000 mAh power bank with enough juice to keep it running for three days, more than sufficient for it to be live when they arrived. It was set up so the device's camera broadcast to the cloud, giving them the ability to confirm that the bait had indeed been taken.

Milton feared the Group would come after him again but had wanted to be sure. Ziggy suggested the plan and had then taken great pleasure in putting it together: faking the police report that Milton had been arrested; leaving enough breadcrumbs for his erstwhile colleagues from Group Three to follow; even going as far as sending Milton into the office on the dock to hire the houseboat and ensuring his likeness was captured on the security camera behind the desk.

"Recognise either of them?"

Milton laid a finger on the screen. "That's her."

The woman looked down into the camera almost as if she knew she was being watched.

The woman who had betrayed the others in Krasnodar.

The woman who might as well have lined them up on the ground and killed them herself.

"Ready?" Ziggy said.

Milton had given thought to taking her out. It would have been easy. He *could've* followed through on his threat, built a simple bomb, turned the phone into a trigger and blown her to bits. He had decided against it. A bomb would be messy and would do collateral damage. He didn't want to kill the other agents, either, but, more to the point, he needed her alive. She'd implicated him for the massacre in Krasnodar, and there were only ever going to be two ways that he would be able to stop the Group from coming after him.

First way: find out where she lived, identify her vulnerabilities and then use them to make her confess.

Or, second: find the only other witness to what had happened and have *her* correct the record. But Control was in the custody of a Russian psychopath who could have stashed her anywhere.

The first way was the only way.

"Do it."

Ziggy tapped return to activate a command he had written in advance.

The phone rang.

Both agents had started to back away, but now they froze. The fear on their faces turned to confusion as they were not obliterated and realised that something else was at play.

The male agent picked up the phone.

"Milton?"

"That's right. Put on Number Twelve, please."

"What?"

"I want to speak to her—put her on."

Milton heard muttered conversation and then a female voice.

"Yes?"

"I just remembered," Milton said. "You're not Twelve anymore, are you? You would've made quite a jump after what you did. Are you working for them now? Who is it? Sommer or the FSB?"

"What are you talking about?"

He had hoped she might forget herself and confess, but she wasn't that gauche.

"What do you want, Milton?"

"I'm not in the mood to play games. I'm going to give you a chance to come clean and tell London what happened. You should give very strong consideration to doing that."

"Or what?"

"I'm not just going to sit here and wait for you to find me. I'll come for you."

"I'm not afraid."

"You should be. Your *face* when the phone rang—you should've seen it. You thought I'd left a bomb, didn't you? The thing is, though, I could've done that. I thought about it. Or I could find where you live. I could find where your *daughter* lives. And you know the best thing? You know how good I am at this. You'd never see me coming."

"Threaten me all you like. You—"

"Tell them what you did," he cut over her. "Confess, or we can discuss it face to face. But you won't like that *half* as much."

She started to respond, but Milton ended the call. He leaned back in his chair, laced his fingers, and cracked his knuckles.

"*That* went well." Ziggy unplugged the laptop and packed it away. "What are you going to do now?"

Milton stood and went over to the tiny cupboard in the corner of his hotel room. He opened the doors and took out his chef's whites. "I'm going to go to work. My shift starts in ten minutes. Are you still good for tonight?"

"I am if you are."

"He's still on holiday?"

"I told you—he's away all week."

"Perfect. I finish at ten."

Milton opened the door, told Ziggy he'd see him later and waited for him to leave. He went over to the miserly window that looked down onto the roof of the kitchen, the foul-smelling bins and the car park beyond, then looked up and out onto the rooftops of Dublin. He could see the Spire and, beyond that, the twin red-and-white striped chimneys of the defunct Poolbeg Power Station. He had arrived in the city three days ago and, thinking that he might stay for a week or two, had found a kitchen job that he could use to replenish his funds.

He thought of the houseboat, thousands of miles away, and the agents inside it right now. He was ahead of them for the moment, but that wouldn't last. He knew how to drop off the radar and had done it before, for months, but it had only ever been temporary. Today had made something very clear to him: Twelve, or whatever her number was now, had told the Group that he had betrayed them, and the Group unequivocally believed her. As far as London was concerned, the blood of the agents who had died in Russia was on his hands. They were looking for him, and they were willing to mount an operation on foreign soil to get to him.

They'd keep coming until they found him, and eventually, they would.

Milton needed exculpation before that happened. That was why he was here. He'd asked Ziggy to dig into Twelve's history, and he had found more than enough for Milton to be getting on with. She was separated from her husband, but Milton knew he could still be useful: they shared custody of her daughter, Lola, and that made him a vulnerability that Milton could exploit.

The man—a multimillionaire from the sale of his business—owned a large house outside the city.

Milton was going to pay it a visit and see what he could find.

3

Maria stared at Morrison as she tried to pull the lapels of her blouse closer together. His eyes had drifted down to her chest even as he was chastising her for yet another manufactured irritation. She was used to him by now, but that didn't mean he didn't disgust her.

Não brinque comigo, seu pervertido. The denunciation caught on the tip of her tongue. He might not have understood exactly what she was saying, had she said it, but he would've got the gist of it. And annoying as it was, Maria *really* needed this job.

She knew he'd taken her aside just so he could ogle her. The heat of the kitchen could kill a horse, yet she'd found herself putting on ever thicker tights and longer skirts, and buttoning up her blouse as far as it would go. It was nothing new to her. There was a hierarchy in the hotel, and it hadn't taken her long to recognise it and her place in it. The local staff had it easiest; the owners were two brothers of dubious reputation from Dublin, and they showed a leniency towards their countrymen that didn't extend to any of the others; next were the Europeans; beneath them came everyone else. Maria was Brazilian and at the top of this lowest caste. The Poles and Czechs and, most recently, the Ukrainians had it worst of all. She'd seen colleagues from Eastern Europe dismissed for no reason, and those who stayed were treated to the most ignominious tasks involving bleach and porcelain.

Morrison pointed at her. "Maria? *Hello?*"

"Yes?"

"Are you listening? You're not listening."

"I am."

"Have you got it?"

"I've got it."

"Right. Well, good—make sure it isn't left like that again."

Maria knew that all it would take to give herself an easier life would be to allow him a little flattery or the occasional warm look. But she couldn't bring herself to do it. The Poles in the hotel called him a '*maje,*' while the Irish called him an '*eejit.*' It made her smile to know that she and her closest friends—from Bulgaria, East Timor and Poland—had five university degrees between them. Morrison had a diploma in food hygiene that must have taken him all of three months to earn and of which, for some strange reason, he was inordinately proud. He referred to his qualifications and experience often as his finger trailed along the countertops and the hoods above the ovens, examining them for dust and other evidence of incompetence.

Still, it gave them all something to chuckle about on their nights off, gathered in one of their rooms, drinking spirits pilfered from the kitchen or from bottles of wine left unfinished at functions. They had a laugh at his expense as they sat around and shared stories about the places that they had worked and the incompetents who had been their bosses.

Morrison was finished now and, his eyebrow raised, turned and strutted away. The others glanced over with eye rolls of ridicule at his lack of self-awareness. She smiled back at them. The admonishment made no difference to her whatsoever.

One of the orderlies—a man called Luca with a degree in criminal justice—came over to her. "He is like bull today."

"I ignored most of it, to be honest."

"It is this function. It must be very big deal to make him so...?"

"Pathetic?"

"Worried."

Maria noticed that one of the chefs was listening to their conversation. It was the new guy; he had started in the kitchen yesterday and had barely said a word to anyone. She had the impression that he saw everything and yet said nothing. He was handsome too, in a rugged, worldly sort of way. He was in his late middle age but looked very fit. He had a scar across his face that lent him a little edge.

"They are all worried," Luca went on. "I spoke to Pavel. He is telling me they are thinking about bringing in security people."

"Why would they do that?"

Luca shrugged. "No idea. But it must be very big deal."

He went back to his mop and bucket. Maria looked over at the new chef again. He looked back at her and then down at the lump of pastry he had been kneading. Something about his self-assuredness caught her attention. She wondered whether he might like to join them tonight for a drink in her room. She tried to remember his name.

Eric, she thought.

Was that it?

One of the others had asked him, and that was what she thought he had said. The name was ugly and old-fashioned. It didn't suit him.

His eyes did, though. They were the iciest blue that she had ever seen.

I'll ask him if he wants to come, she thought. *And I won't fasten too many buttons if he says yes.*

4

Billy Gallagher watched as his son, Charlie, wrestled his opponent to the mat, slithered around and tried to apply a choke. Charlie's trainer, Jackie Garner, called out instructions from the apron, but it was obvious that Charlie was having trouble securing the hold. This was Charlie's final sparring session before the big fight, and Billy had hoped to see him performing a little more impressively than this. It wasn't just because the fight was so close, nor even that his opponent, Danny Farley, was so heavily favoured that bookies were offering ridiculous odds to get action going for Charlie; it was because Billy had brought along Frank Rickard with the hope that Charlie would put on a show.

And that *wasn't* happening.

"Come on, Charlie," Jackie called.

"I'm trying," Charlie grunted.

"Secure the underhook!"

"I'm *trying*."

Billy didn't know the name of the sparring partner, but wasn't impressed with him; surely he must've been told that he was there so that Charlie could show off? He was fighting hard to prevent Charlie from applying the choke, tucking his chin to protect his windpipe and then grabbing at Charlie's wrist and pushing up to maintain space.

Billy looked over at Rickard. "He's a slippery bastard."

"What's that?"

Billy pointed. "Look at how sweaty he is. Charlie can't get a grip on him. His hands are sliding off."

Rickard chuckled. "You're not telling me he's only got a ground game when his opponent *isn't* sweating, are you? Because, I have to tell you, pretty much *everyone* sweats when the lights are on 'em."

"That's not what I meant." Billy could feel his cheeks reddening from both anger and embarrassment, but he managed to stop himself from saying anything he might regret. He turned back to the ring instead. "Come on, Charlie. Finish!"

Charlie slid around until he was on top of his opponent, pinning his legs beneath him as he sat on his chest. The other man tried to squirm and buck his hips, but Charlie's weight and pressure were too much and left him with no room for manoeuvre. Charlie raised his fists like hammers and rained down a barrage of punishing blows, targeting the head and body. The other man's face contorted with pain as he tried to shield himself from the onslaught. Sprays of sweat flew into the air with each new blow.

The referee stepped in. "We're done."

Charlie either didn't hear him or paid him no attention. He continued to fire out rights and lefts, powerful hooks that caught his opponent on the side of the head, and, when he raised his guard, landed in his ribs. Charlie wore him down until he had him battered and bloodied and gasping for air.

"Charlie—" the referee said.

"Fuck's sake!" Jackie yelled, stepping through the ropes. "That's enough."

Charlie looked up, blinking the sweat out of his eyes as he held his father's gaze. Charlie had always been a needy boy, always craving his father's approval and, when he couldn't get that, his attention. Billy was not a sentimental man, but, despite that, he had found it endearing when Charlie had been small. But Charlie was a grown man now, trying to make a career for himself as a fighter, and that kind of weakness would do him no favours. Charlie was still looking at Billy as he got back to his feet, blood on his gloves and on the canvas, but Billy knew not to pander to him. Charlie had embarrassed himself, and, more importantly, he had embarrassed *him*. Billy was put in mind of an old family pet they'd had, long since dead, who would come over for a stroke after doing a shit in the middle of the living room carpet.

Rickard had taken out his phone and was scrolling through his messages.

Billy was almost afraid of the question that he knew he'd have to ask. "So? What do you think?"

Rickard dropped the phone back into his pocket. "I don't know, Billy."

"Meaning?"

"Meaning I've got to be honest—that wasn't the best show I've ever seen."

Rickard was one of the most influential agents in mixed martial arts. He was a native New Yorker, and the brashness of the city, together with his own chutzpah, had lent him a personality that was as much his defining characteristic as the sunglasses that never left his face.

Billy scrambled for an excuse. "He's got half his attention on Saturday night."

"You really think that'd make any difference?"

"You don't *know* Farley's going to win."

Rickard gave him a look of pity. "Come *on*. We do. You do, too, if you're honest about it. You've gotta face facts: your boy's good, but he just ain't good enough."

Billy clenched his fists so hard his nails dug into his palms. "I don't agree."

"That's your prerogative, but it doesn't change the facts. They don't build those buildings in Vegas because they don't know how to pick a winner. Charlie's a decent local scrapper, but someone like Farley is a step up in class."

"'A decent local scrapper'?"

"It's the truth."

"Fuck you."

Rickard spread his hands. "Let's not fall out over this."

"Then don't insult my boy."

"I'm not insulting him. I've been doing this a while. I've looked at his fights, and I've watched him train. You put him in the ring against second-division opponents and he'll knock 'em all out all day long and look good doing it. But put him in with proper fighters—anyone he'd fight in America, and definitely someone like Farley—and we both know he's going to get himself embarrassed. He doesn't have the chin. And his ground game... well, come on, we just saw that, and it was a joke. He doesn't have one—sweat or no sweat."

"That's just your opinion."

"No, Billy, it's not. It's a fact. You're biased—course you are. It's understandable. But I can't afford to be. This is business for me."

"And it's not for *me*?"

"It's *family*. He's your *son*. I know you've invested a lot into his training, but it wasn't done objectively. You couldn't be *less* objective. You used to be a fighter yourself, didn't you?"

"Years ago."

"And you didn't get anywhere."

"I didn't, because—"

"The reason doesn't matter," he cut over him. "You didn't get anywhere, so maybe this is you trying to find success vicariously, through him."

Billy clenched his jaw and ground down on his teeth. No one ever interrupted him, and certainly no one spoke to him like this.

"I might as well put my cards on the table," Rickard said. "I've been speaking to the Dillons about Farley." Billy started to speak, but Rickard stalled him with a raised hand. "It'll be better if you hear it from me. Farley is a real talent—he's the best pure striker I've seen since McGregor, and I can see him absolutely tearing it up when he gets to America. The Dillons offered him to me, and I said yes. I'm going to represent him and take him to Vegas. We're signing the contract at the weigh-in tomorrow."

"Assuming he beats Charlie."

"He'll beat Charlie. He could beat him with one arm tied behind his back. You know it, and I know it."

"So, all this—coming here, abusing my hospitality—it was all just leading me on?"

"Don't get your panties in a bunch. I told you—this is business. It's not personal."

"It *wasn't*," Billy said. "But you just made it personal."

Billy squared up to him. Rickard wasn't imposing, and, even though he was decades younger, Billy knew he'd be able to take him. He wanted to do it—wanted to drive his fist into his perfect American teeth and ruin his Hollywood smile—but, before he could even close his fist, Rickard's muscle stepped up and put an arm out. Rickard wasn't impressive, but his bodyguard was: well over six feet tall, with broad shoulders and muscles that tested the limits of his tailored suit.

"Easy," Rickard said.

Billy put his face inches away from the bodyguard's, then stepped back. "Get out."

"Think about it, Billy," Rickard said. "You'll thank me. Do you really want to put your boy in the octagon with someone really good? He's going to get battered tomorrow. If you've got any compassion, you'll see that's the last time. Find him a job in your operation. You'd be doing him a favour."

"You patronising piece of shit. Get *out*."

5

Milton knew he was being watched. He had a feeling for it, a sixth sense that had developed over the course of his career and then in the time he had spent on the run afterwards. He'd been trained to be aware of his surroundings and—especially—to note anyone who might be paying him a little *too* much attention. His back was to the woman, but he could see her reflection in the stainless-steel hood of the oven. He'd noticed her twirling her hair, waiting for him to turn around and look at her. He did now, reaching back for the bottle of disinfectant that he'd left on the prep table. She smiled, and, a little awkwardly, he did the same. She finished up and left.

It had been a busy session. There had been fifteen of them, all working flat out to start the prep for the function scheduled on Friday. Milton had worked on the caviar. That was no everyday requirement, the Southside Hotel was top end for Dublin, but he doubted that the kitchen would normally have seen such a large amount of such an expensive ingredient. It was to be used with smoked salmon and dill-flecked crème fraiche on designer mini-pizzas that were surely only on the menu to make a statement. Milton might have been able to justify it if the caviar had been the more affordable farmed sturgeon or salmon roe, but it wasn't; instead, it contained genuine Beluga from the Caspian Sea. A copy of the invoice had been stapled to the side of the box, and Milton had looked at it and shaken his head in bemusement; the 100g tins cost more than €700, and there were fifty of them. Thirty-five grand just for caviar? It was lunacy.

It wasn't just the caviar that spoke of extravagance. The fish was king salmon that cost €70 per pound, and they had taken delivery of two large specimens that Milton guessed must have tipped the scales at fifty pounds apiece. He had watched the orderlies load hundreds of bottles of Laurent-Perrier Cuvée 'Grand Siècle' Brut Champagne into the enormous fridges. The instructions for the event stipulated that each table was to be supplied with two bottles, and Milton had heard the discussions about the need to take a delivery of extra ice buckets to facilitate the extravagance.

Whoever was paying for the festivities was rich and not afraid to spend big to make an impression.

Milton made the pizza dough, following a recipe that he'd been taught years before: he put the flour into a food processor and slowly drizzled in a mixture of olive oil, honey and salt. He made balls with the dough and transferred them all to one of the fridges to chill until he was ready to use them. He then chopped a handful of chives to add to the dough when he rolled it out. It had taken him three hours, and now he was finally finished, he just had to clean up and clock off.

He was the last man standing. He wiped his hands on his whites, flicked off the lights and headed up the stairs.

The woman was waiting on the landing.

"Oh," Milton said. "Hello."

She smiled and put out a hand. "I'm Maria."

Milton shook it.

"You're Eric?"

"That's right."

He stepped around her and climbed the stairs.

"Long night," she said.

Milton stopped and turned, resting one hand on the banister.

"Lots to do," he replied, looking down at her from a few steps above.

"He seems worried about the event. Morrison, I mean. He's nervous."

"There's a lot of money being spent. Do you know what it's all about?"

"I have no idea," she said. "I asked, but they say it is private."

Milton had already noted her accent. "What part of Brazil are you from?"

She smiled with pleasure. "Many people think I am Spanish." He noticed the subtle but playful tilt of her head, the flick of her hair. "I am from Rio. Have you been there?"

"I have."

"What did you think?"

Milton had found plenty of trouble in that city's *favela* but wasn't about to mention it to a civilian. "Loud and busy," he said instead. "And hot. Very hot."

Milton was happy to bring the conversation to an end, but perhaps emboldened by his interest in her background, she hurried to fill the silence. "We are having drinks in my room tonight. We have wine and some chips. Some music, you know? Is fun. Want to come?"

"That's very kind of you."

"Are you going up to your room now?"

"I am."

"And me."

She climbed the stairs to where he was standing, and they continued up together.

"Where did you work before coming here?" she asked him.

"All over the place."

"In Dublin?"

"No."

"Ireland?"

He made an affirmative noise, hoping that she might take the hint while trying not to be unfriendly. They reached the landing. Milton moved ahead of her to push the door and hold it open. She smiled in appreciation, and a slight spring in her step suggested she had interpreted the gesture as hopeful. The corridor beyond the door was much less impressive than those used by the guests below. The carpet was threadbare, and the paint on the walls flaked from neglect. The heating was off, and the temperature was frigid.

"The others will be here soon," she said. "My room is number ten."

"Thank you," Milton said, "but I'm really tired. I think I'm going to go straight to bed."

She smiled to hide her disappointment. "Just for twenty minutes? A drink?"

He paused at the door to his room. "Not tonight. But thanks for asking."

"I understand. Maybe another time."

"Maybe," he said. "Have a good night."

He fished his key from his pocket, but she lingered, looking at the floor. There was silence for a moment before she looked up.

"My friends do not always come." She shrugged a little.

Milton felt the need to offer her something. "I don't drink," he said, hoping the explanation would allow him the chance to escape without hurting her feelings. "I try to stay away from places where people are drinking. It's better for me."

"Oh," she said, flustered. "Maybe, some time, with no wine."

"Maybe. Good night, Maria."

"Good night, Eric."

Milton heard her walk away as he slid the key into the lock and warned himself not to look back at her in case their eyes met and she took a hint he was loath to offer.

He stepped inside and pressed the door closed behind him.

Better find a meeting soon, he thought.

He changed out of his whites and took a shower. The communal bathroom was small and unpleasant, but the water was hot, and he needed to scrub the grime and sweat from his skin. He stood there for five minutes until he finally felt clean, then reached out for a towel and wrapped it around his waist. A message was waiting for him when he returned to his room.

>> *Gravediggers, 10pm.*

He pulled on his jeans and a T-shirt, laced up his boots and retrieved his leather jacket from the hook on the back of the door. He went out onto the landing, concerned for a moment that he might bump into Maria and have to explain why he was going out when he had told her that he was going to bed. She wasn't there, but he could hear the sound of music from the room at the end of the corridor.

Definitely get to a meeting, he told himself.

The conversation with Frank Rickard was twenty minutes ago, and Billy Gallagher was still seething. Billy had been revered in certain parts of Dublin for years, and no one who valued having all of their teeth in their mouth would've spoken to him like that. Billy knew the reason for Rickard's braggadocio: part of it was his background, and the fact he had his tame gorilla with him; the rest was because he had aligned himself with the Dillons, and was working under the assumption that their association would protect him.

There'd been a day, not so long ago, when no one would have come into Dublin to do business without paying homage to Billy. Finn Dillon would have known not to piss him off, but Finn Dillon was dead, and his fuckwit boys and their shrewish mother were in charge now. They'd never shown him the respect he was owed. The boys didn't care about the old traditions and values that governed the underworld, they were young and rich and reckless and stupid, and it was long past time that they learned the cost of their disregard.

Charlie finished his stretches and came over. "What was that all about?"

"What was what?"

He waved a hand vaguely. "You and that fella having a shouting match."

"'That fella,'" he said, "was Frank Rickard."

Charlie's eyebrows kinked up. "The agent?"

"Yes," he said. "The agent. I asked him to come and watch you. I thought it might've helped us get him on the team, but then you made that stiff you were sparring with look like Jon *fucking* Jones, and now he wouldn't piss on you if you were on fire."

"Why didn't you tell me he was coming?"

"Would it have made any difference?"

"I would've knocked him out. I only went to the mat because Jackie told me to."

"You don't like grappling?"

"You know it's not what I'm best at."

"What *are* you good at?"

He started to answer, but, seeing his father's expression, decided to hold his tongue.

Gallagher's blood was up. "He saw that shitshow and then laughed in my face. You know how he described you?" He didn't wait for an answer. "'A decent local scrapper.' He said I'd be doing you a favour if I got you out of the fight and put you to work in the crew. I thought he was saying that to get a rise out of me, but the more I think about it, the more it sounds like a good idea. Because I'll tell you something, son: you need a killer instinct to make it in the fight game, and you don't have it. You just *don't*."

Billy knew he was being hard on him, but maybe tough love was what Charlie needed. The fight was still down for Saturday night, and the best way for him to be able to get back at the Dillons was for Charlie to upset Farley. It didn't matter what Rickard had said; Billy knew enough about fighters to know that Danny Farley was not the dead cert that he'd been made out to be. His striking was impressive, but everyone knew he'd never taken a proper shot. Charlie was never going to beat him on the mat, but that wasn't the game plan. His boy was as thick as mince, but he had a right-handed uppercut that could lay out a man fifty pounds heavier; he only needed one lucky punch and Rickard would have to eat his words.

But that wouldn't be enough to satisfy Billy. Not now, not after what he'd said to him and the way that he'd said it. Billy waited until Charlie went into the changing room to shower and then gestured over to where his consigliere, Gerry Kelly, was standing. The two men had been childhood friends and had been involved in the business together for years. Kelly had fulfilled many roles—from enforcer to marital counsellor to advisor—and was the man Billy trusted above all others. He had a violent temper, but, despite that, he was a savvy businessman who had often been involved in negotiations with rivals and politicians, and his ability to read people and situations had always been a quality that Billy valued.

"Didn't go well with Rickard?"

"Did you hear?"

"Some of it."

"I'm not having him talk to me like that—*disrespecting* me."

"What do you think?"

"I think the Dillons have done a number on us," Billy said.

"He's going with them?"

Billy nodded. "What were we offering him?"

"Ten points lifetime."

"Maybe they went higher."

"Maybe," Kelly mused. "Maybe he thinks Farley's the better shot."

Billy clenched his fists. "If he won't work with us, he's not working with them."

"How are you going to stop him?"

Billy snorted. "You think I've gone soft?"

Kelly paused, then nodded his understanding. "No, Billy. Of course I don't think that. But are you sure? He always goes around with his muscle, and he'll be more careful now than he was before."

"We know where he's going to be on Friday night."

"At the hotel."

"That's right. At Dillon's table."

Kelly shook his head. "It'll be locked down tighter than a nun's drawers."

"I know that."

"You know what else I heard? They block-booked the whole place so there'll be no guests other than those they've vetted, they'll have guards on all the doors, and they've hired one of those scanners they use at airports to make sure no one's carrying. They're not taking chances."

"And there'll still be a way to get it done."

"Go on, then," Kelly said. "Let's hear it."

"I was thinking—maybe we give this to Mahoney."

Kelly gave an appreciative nod. "Mahoney would be perfect."

"He owes me."

"So he does."

"Give him a call. Get him to come over for a chat."

"When?"

"No reason to wait. Tell him I want to see him tonight."

Shay Dillon watched as Danny Farley worked the heavy bag, his fists slamming into the canvas with impacts that echoed around the room. He started firing out right-left-right combinations: the first right was into the ribs, the left drew the defence down, and the next right was aimed at the chin. Each punch echoed through the gym, each one a note in a brutal syncopation.

Shay was no expert, but he knew talent when he saw it, and Farley had it in spades. Shay watched as he circled the bag, his movements smooth and fluid. His muscles bulged with each punch, the power starting in his shoulders and then detonating down his arms and through his fists. He unleashed a flurry of jabs and hooks, tattooing the bag with a rat-tat-tat that started at rib height and ended with a cross that would have been strong enough to knock out a horse.

The fight was one that could make or break Farley's career. Shay couldn't help but feel confident. Farley had been training hard, and it showed.

Shay's brother, Colm, was standing on one side. Frank

Rickard, the New Yorker who had agreed to represent Farley, was standing on the other.

Colm turned to Rickard. "What do you think?"

"I think he's a machine. Look at him—there's not an ounce of fat on him anywhere."

"You reckon it's too late?"

"For what?"

"To put a bit more on him."

Shay exhaled. "How much have you got on now?"

"Two hundred."

"Two *hundred*?"

"Yeah," Colm said. "And now I'm thinking maybe I'll double it."

"You'd be a mug," Shay answered. "What are the odds now?"

"Last I heard?" Rickard offered. "Two to one."

"Odds-*on*," Shay added. "What's the point?"

"I could lay out another hundred and get a hundred and fifty back when he puts that arrogant fucker on his backside. It's free money."

Shay breathed in, taking a moment to frame his response. His brother was many things—intimidating, brutal, effective when it came to the more unpleasant tasks that went hand in hand with running their business—but he wasn't the sharpest tool in the box.

"It might be free money," he said patiently, "but let's just say, for the sake of argument, that Gallagher gets lucky."

"That uppercut," Rickard said with a nod. "He might be a douche, but we know he's got that in his locker, at least. Nasty."

"Exactly," Shay said. "And that's all it'll take—one lucky punch. He lands it, he puts Danny down, and you've just lost the hundred."

"I know how betting works. I—"

Shay spoke over him, masking his impatience with a smile. "That's not how we make money out of this." He turned to Rickard. "Right?"

"*Right*. We get him through this fight and make sure he gets the tilt at the title like they've promised, and *then* you coin it in. Anything extra you make tonight is gonna look like chump change."

"Fifty-fifty," Shay said. "Every dollar he makes, we take half."

Colm smirked over at Rickard. "And he takes twenty per cent of that."

"I do," Rickard said, "but I grow the pot so there's more for everyone. If he's as good as we think he is, we make millions. I'm serious, guys. *Millions*." He looked at his watch. "Shit—I'd better go. I'm supposed to be having drinks with a couple of contacts at the network. You promised me a couple of tickets for the weigh-in? It'd be good to have them there, make a fuss of them."

"No problem," Shay said. "Colm can get them on the list. We'll need their names so we can check they are who they say they are."

"You can't trust me?"

"No offence, but we hardly know you. I'm sure it'd be fine, but I'm not in the business of taking chances."

Rickard started for the door, then paused. "That reminds me. I went to see Billy Gallagher before I came over here."

Shay raised an eyebrow. "And?"

"And I told him some home truths about how his boy doesn't have a future in the game and how I'm hitching my wagon to Danny."

"You told him that?"

"There's no point in putting it off. In my experience, you

lead a man on and then pull the rug out from under him and he's liable to be a whole lot angrier than if you set him straight as early as you can. That all being said, it *did* get a little heated. He's an angry old bastard. He got right up in my face."

Shay bit down on his lip.

"What?" Rickard said. "You're not worried about him, are you?"

"He's a dinosaur, but he's been around the block a hundred times, and he's not the type of fella you'd want to underestimate."

"That's why we've got security," Colm said. "There's no need to worry. We've got it sorted."

Shay nodded, aware that it would do them no good at all to rock the boat. "The hotel will be locked down tight. It'll be fine."

"I know it will," Rickard said. "You two have delivered everything you promised, and I'm not about to let Gallagher spoil the mood." He made to go, then stopped for a second time. "Oh—one more thing. I saw Charlie sparring, and it was awful. Horrible. He's got that big punch, but that's it. You should have a word with Farley's trainer and tell him to get your boy to put him on the mat. Get him in an arm bar and I'll bet you dollars to doughnuts he squeals like a little piggy the moment he applies even a *tiny* amount of torque." He grabbed his jacket. "See you both at the weigh-in."

8

The meeting with Michael Mahoney was arranged to take place in their usual spot: a lay-by on the road heading out of Kilshane Cross. It was inconvenient to have to head out there at this time of night, but Billy had always been careful that this kind of assignation took place at a location that was unlikely to be observed. Whatever—he had his driver, Maynard, and there were worse things he could have done than spend an hour in the back of his ice-white Rolls-Royce Ghost. The car was an extravagance he would never have allowed himself as a younger man. It was obscenely expensive and ostentatious and altogether *not* the car that a man wary of police attention would have chosen. But Billy was older now, he was rich enough that the expense was a trifle, and he had built up legitimate businesses that paid enough to put a Roller within reach. The fact that those businesses were fronts, established to wash his illicit earnings, was beside the point. Another benefit of age was a more relaxed attitude to risk. He wouldn't be here forever, and if a man with his advantages couldn't indulge in the odd little luxuries, then who could?

Maynard slowed the car. "We're here, sir."

They rolled to a stop, the lights of the Ghost picking out Mahoney's battered old Volvo. Billy waited and watched as Mahoney got out, holding a hand up to shield his eyes from the glare of the high beams, then made his way down the lay-by until he was alongside the car. Maynard pressed a button on the console, a motor hummed, the door opened, and Mahoney lowered himself into the back next to Billy.

"Evening," he said.

Billy glanced over at Mahoney. His face was weathered and lined, with a small scar above his left eyebrow that spoke to a history of physical altercations. His hair was short and neatly trimmed, with just a hint of grey at the temples. He was dressed casually tonight in jeans and a T-shirt.

"I've got something for you," Billy said. "It's outside of our usual retainer, so there'll be a nice little bump for you."

"Go on."

"Do you know about the fight on Saturday?"

"Between your boy and Danny Farley? Yes. Course. Talk of the town."

"What about the weigh-in?"

"Friday at the Southside. What do you want me to do?"

"There's a man," Billy said. "A sports agent. He's a big deal—he's got the swing to take a fighter and send them to the top. He can set up the right fights, negotiate endorsements with the right companies, make TV deals with the right platforms. That kind of help is indispensable if you want to make it, especially in the States."

"What about him?"

"He had a choice about who he was going to represent: Charlie or Farley."

"And he chose Farley?"

"He did. That would've been difficult enough, but he didn't handle it the right way. I've been in this business long enough to earn respect when I'm spoken to—that's right, isn't it, Maynard?"

"Absolutely," Maynard said.

"Too right," Mahoney echoed.

"This man is American," Billy went on, "so I suppose you could give him a little leeway on account of natural brashness, maybe a little more for not doing his research on who I am and what I've done, but, even with that taken into account, even if I was being generous—if I gave him the benefit of the doubt—even if I did all of that, you can't help but be left with the impression that he took a very big fucking liberty. And, that all being said, I've decided it's not the sort of big fucking liberty that I can ignore. You know what it's like, Michael—you let someone behave that way and, before you know it, *everyone* behaves that way. Something's got to be done."

"And that's where I come in?"

"It is."

"What, then? Rough him up?"

"No. I want you to kill him."

Mahoney paused and sucked on his teeth. "Shit, Billy."

"You've done it before."

"I know, but this sounds different. Kenny Ward was a junkie who might as well have had a needle hanging out of his arm. Topping him so it didn't come back to me or you was easy. And Pete McDonald was a nonce who had it coming."

"Brookman?"

"Practically dead anyway. This, though? It'll take more than a 'little bump.'"

Billy heard his reluctance and ignored it. "There's something else—I want it done at the weigh-in."

Mahoney shook his head. "You're having a laugh. No way. There's a reason they're doing it in the hotel—the two of them won't admit it, but I know for a fact they're shitting themselves that you're getting ready to come after them after what happened to..." He stopped.

"After what happened to my boy."

"Exactly. They know it, and they'll have their boys crawling all over the place. Why does it have to be there?"

"Because both of those little gobshites will be at the same table as the man I want you to kill. We're going to use him to remind them that I'm not the sort of fella who'll just sit back with his thumb up his arse while ungrateful little shites like them take advantage. And, yes, you're right—I *am* going to come after them, and I want them to know it."

Mahoney breathed in and out, then shook his head. "I'm sorry, Billy. I wouldn't even know where to start with something like that. You could pay me a hundred grand, and it still wouldn't be worth the risk."

Billy had expected resistance and had decided that he wasn't going to accept it. "I'm not asking, Michael—I'm *telling*. I want it done, and I want *you* to do it."

"Please... Think about it for a minute—isn't the work I do for you worth something?"

"You know it is."

"So, if I do this and I end up getting nicked... what then? No more work."

"So, see that you're *not* caught. It's as simple as that."

Mahoney slumped back in the upholstered seat. He knew Billy well enough to know that it was unwise to turn him down when he had his mind made up.

Billy punched him on the shoulder. "Don't look so

concerned. I'm not expecting you to pull the trigger your-self. I just want you to oversee it."

He frowned. "What does that mean? You want me to arrange it?"

"You remember Mickey Flannagan?"

"Yes. Street dealer. Got nicked for possession and sent down."

"And did five years. He got out six months ago. His parole officer helped him find a kitchen job. I bet you can't guess where?"

"The Southside?"

Billy smiled. "The security won't pay any attention to the staff. We just need to make sure he's suitably motivated and has everything he needs to get it done."

"You want me to scare him? You'd be better for that, Billy."

"Probably, but what about if he gets nicked? What if they offer to go easier on him if he spills the beans on who told him to do it? I don't want him to be tempted to point the finger in my direction."

"They'll *know*, Billy. They're not stupid."

"There's knowing, and then there's proving. I need a middleman between him and me." He put a hand on Mahoney's shoulder. "I couldn't think of anyone better suited than you."

Mahoney's face fell; he knew he was trapped. He'd been taking money from Billy for so long that it had got to the stage where it was almost impossible for him to say no. The favour that Billy had done him in the early days had been paid back long ago, but, despite that, the fear of what Billy could do with it still hung over him. Mahoney had been out drinking with a girl and had driven her home. He was pissed, and the car went off the road at Stacummy Lane and ended up in the Liffey. Mahoney had managed to swim clear, but the girl was not so lucky. Mahoney had gone to Billy to beg for his help, and Billy had agreed. He made sure the car was recovered by a firm he could manipulate, persuaded the only witness to the crash that he hadn't, after all, seen anything, and saw that there was no other evidence that could be traced back to Mahoney.

It had been a lot of work, and it had cost Billy plenty in cash laid out and favours called in. But it had been worth it. Mahoney was a useful tool—perhaps his *most* useful—and had paid back the investment many times over. And on this? Billy agreed with him: giving him the job *was* risky. But there were ways to insulate him from exposure. And even if those failed, Billy trusted Mahoney to keep his mouth shut. He had too much to lose, apart from the fact that he knew from experience what happened to the grasses and the families of grasses who set themselves against him.

"All right," Mahoney said. "Give me Flannagan's address. I'll go and speak to him."

"Good show. Maynard?"

The driver reached across to the passenger seat, collected a bundle wrapped in a cloth, and handed it back to Mahoney. He put the bundle on his lap and peeled back the corners, revealing a pistol and a loaded magazine.

9

Milton took an Uber to the Glasnevin district of the city. The Gravediggers was near to the National Botanic Gardens, Milton had visited the pub on his previous visit to Dublin, but he had been drinking then, and much of what had happened that evening had been lost in a flood of Guinness. The place was famous, reputed to have been run by eight generations of the Kavanagh family since the 1830s. It was next to the Glasnevin Cemetery, and a much-cherished local rumour had it that there was a secret hatch in the cemetery wall that allowed gravediggers to slake their thirsts during their working days.

The driver turned onto St Teresa's Road, skirted Prospect Square and reached the pub. The exterior was traditional and unassuming, with a simple red-brick façade and a modest wooden sign above the entrance with an illustration of a man digging a grave. Milton thanked the driver and got out, then pushed the door and went inside. It was a resolutely traditional place, without the accoutrements that other pubs deployed to attract credulous tourists. There was no singing, no dancing, and not a television in sight. The atmosphere buzzed with conversation—some sober, much not—and Milton found himself looking at the pumps behind the weathered wooden bar with a wistful longing that he knew was dangerous.

Ziggy had found a table at an alcove in the back of the taproom.

"You couldn't have thought of somewhere to meet where it's not all about alcohol?"

Ziggy put his hand to his forehead. "I didn't think. Are you going to be all right?"

"I'm sure I'll survive." Milton pointed to Ziggy's empty glass. "Want another?"

"Are you sure?"

"I can buy you a drink without falling off the wagon."

Milton went to the bar, ordered a pint of Guinness for Ziggy and an orange juice for himself, and then returned to the table.

He had asked Ziggy to dig out everything he could find about Number Twelve, the agent who had betrayed him—and the others—in Krasnodar. The same agent had then made an attempt on his life in New Delhi. Ziggy had done his best to put together a dossier, but there was only so much that he could do. She was a Group Fifteen agent, and, despite the fact that he still had access to the relevant servers at the Firm, the most pertinent information on her was inaccessible. Milton remembered what it had been like when he had been active: the most sensitive information was kept on air-gapped servers that were themselves locked away in a secure vault that only those with the very highest security clearances could access.

Ziggy had been inventive. He'd used footage from the hotel in New Delhi to isolate an image of her and, using that, had identified her as Lilly Moon. He dug into her background for anything that hadn't been suppressed: her father had been a decorated Coldstream Guards officer, and her mother had worked in the Houses of Parliament as a researcher. Ziggy found references to a military career, but the files had been scrubbed; standard operating procedure when someone was transferred to the Group. Details on her personal life were patchy, too, but he had been able to find details on her estranged husband, James, including his address: a large house in one of the swankier parts of Dublin.

"So," Ziggy said, "I've checked and double-checked. He's definitely not at home."

He took out a tablet from his bag and put it on the table. He woke the screen, navigated to Facebook, selected the profile for James Moon and spun the tablet around so that Milton could look at it. He saw a series of photographs showing Moon and a woman together with a young girl.

Ziggy put his finger on the man. "There's James." He tapped the woman. "And that's his girlfriend, Eve." He tapped the young girl. "And I *think* that's Lola, his daughter with Lilly."

"Where are they?"

"Disneyland Paris. They got there three days ago, and the hotel has them there for another week."

"You're sure about that?"

"The hotel computer took about five seconds to access. I could give you the suite they're staying in and how much they spent at dinner last night if that'd be helpful."

"And the house is *definitely* empty?"

"He has IP-enabled cameras inside and outside, so I checked them to see. The cleaner went in yesterday morning, but that's it. There's no one there."

"You can switch off the cameras?"

He scoffed. "*Please.*"

"What about alarms?"

"A decent system, but..." He shrugged. "Just tell me when you want it off and it'll be off."

"Have you got the gear?"

Ziggy nodded down to the rucksack at his feet. "It's all there. When do you want to do it?"

"I don't see any reason to wait. Tonight?"

Ziggy gestured to his pint. "Can I finish this first?"

Milton sipped his orange juice, put it down on the table and stood. "I need you sober. I'll buy you one to make up for that later."

10

The Dillons had arranged for Danny Farley to be trained by Paddy Coffey. He was one of the most respected trainers in Ireland and hadn't come cheap. His retainer was ten thousand euros a month, and, because Colm had messed up and let slip how much they wanted him, he'd been able to negotiate a point on Farley's earnings for the next twelve months on top of that. Shay had been furious when he found out, but, given that getting Coffey on the team was essential, he'd held his nose and agreed.

Coffey was watching Farley on the speed bag with his arms folded and his usual expression—a frown of dissatisfaction—on his face.

"All right," he barked out. "That's enough showboating. Thirty minutes in the ring."

"Seriously, Paddy?"

"You're not concentrating. I want you to think about not getting hit." He clapped his hands. "Ross? Get your gloves on and get in there with him."

Farley gave the bag a final punch and went over to the

ring. He vaulted onto the apron, slipped between the ropes and warmed up, his movements quick and fluid. Ross was one of the sparring partners Shay had paid for, and, this time, chosen specifically for his size. Farley fought as a middleweight, usually tipping the scales at around one hundred and eighty-five pounds; Ross was a light-heavy, with an advantage of a good twenty pounds and three inches in height. Coffey had explained that it would be good for Farley to get experience with fighters of different styles and sizes, and Ross offered something that he wouldn't normally see.

Coffey clambered up the stairs to the apron. "All right, lads. Away you go."

Ross was no slouch, a seasoned fighter with a record of his own, but Farley was undeterred. He circled the ring, his eyes locked on his opponent, waiting for the right moment. He began to dance around the slower man, both of them trading jabs and hooks and probing kicks, testing each other's defences. Ross was lead-footed, but Farley moved like a panther; his footwork was smooth and graceful, and, once he had his range, his strikes landed with unerring accuracy. Dillon could see the strategy in Farley's movements, the way he was analysing Ross's responses, looking for weaknesses to exploit.

It didn't take long. Farley cracked jabs through Ross's lazy guard, goading him into coming forward. Ross lunged ahead with a clumsy punch. Farley dodged to the side and grabbed Ross's arm as he did so. He twisted the arm behind Ross's back, locking it in an arm bar, and took them both down to the mat. He applied pressure as Ross struggled to break free. Farley had the hold cinched in tight, and there was no escape. He wrenched the arm, and Ross cried out in pain.

"All right," Coffey said. "That's enough."

Farley was beneath Ross, but he looked over at Shay and Colm and gave a wink. He yanked harder, hyperextending the elbow and popping it out of the joint.

Ross screamed and slapped his hand against Farley's leg.

"Break," Coffey shouted. "He tapped out. *Break!*"

Farley released the hold and slithered out from beneath Ross's body. He looked down at his fallen opponent and smirked. "Sorry. Didn't hear."

Coffey was angry, but rather than tear a strip out of Farley in front of the Dillons, he went over to tend to Ross.

Shay and Colm met Farley by the steps.

"You're ready," Colm said, clapping him on the back.

Farley grinned back, his eyes shining with excitement. "I'm going to fuck him up."

Coffey joined them, a frown darkening his face. "What *was* that?"

Farley stopped. "What was what?"

"You had him beat. He tapped."

"I didn't feel anything."

"Don't be a dick, Danny. You mess around like that, eventually you'll fall on your face. You think someone like Rodriguez will let you do that to him? McCallister? Ronnie Thompson?"

"Line them up, Paddy. I'll knock 'em down."

Coffey sighed. "We'll see. Get your shoes on and meet me outside."

"What?"

"Three miles. You're a pound over. We need to get it off for the weigh-in."

"I'm *right* on the weight," Farley protested.

"Shoes on, Danny."

"And it's late. Look at the time! It's gone ten!"

"Outside in five minutes or it'll be six miles."

Farley frowned in frustration, hopped down from the apron and made his way to the changing room.

"Give him a break," Colm said.

Coffey snorted. "Why? Go easy on him now, let him develop bad habits, it'll come back and bite him on the arse. I've been doing this awhile, lads, and I've seen this kind of thing happen before. You get someone with lots of potential and allow him to develop a bad attitude and it'll all go to shit."

Colm looked ready to protest, but Shay spoke up first. "That's why we hired you. Just as long as he's ready for the fight, I don't care."

"He's ready," Coffey said. "Gallagher doesn't have a chance. Danny will batter him."

"What about after that?"

"After Gallagher? It'll get more challenging." Coffey was cagey as ever when it came to making the bigger predictions.

"But? If you had to bet? Can he beat the Americans?"

"He's the best clean striker I've ever seen. I don't care who you are—he gets that right hand firing, you get hit, you go down. The attitude, though? That's going to be a problem unless we can get it out of him."

Shay was prepared to give himself a little credit for what they'd been able to achieve. Farley had been just another scrapper off the estate, but he'd seen something in him that had persuaded him to give him a spot on the crew. He'd put him on the door of Pulse in Temple Bar, and it had been in the club, after closing one night two years ago, that he had seen just how dangerous Farley could be. Two lads from Ballymun had had a tilt at a girl Farley was chasing and hadn't seen the good sense in backing off when he warned them off. They'd waited outside and gone for him, two on one, and Farley had put them both down with two shots.

The brothers had watched Charlie Gallagher doing well, and, with the goal of poking a thumb in Billy Gallagher's eye, they'd pulled Farley off the door and paid for training with Coffey. When Farley had knocked out his first six opponents in quick succession, they had started to wonder if they hadn't aimed a little too low. Coffey had agreed, and they'd drawn up an agreement: the Dillons would fund Farley's expenses—full-time training, medical, travel, management and promotion, insurance and equipment—and, in return, they would be cut into all of his future winnings. Fifty-fifty. Upfront costs set off against the potential earnings Farley stood to make.

Farley emerged from the changing room as the two of them made their way across the gym to the door. Shay glanced over to him, nodded in acknowledgement, and turned away.

"I've sent you my invoice for the next six weeks," Coffey said.

"Colm will sort you out," Shay said.

They all went outside. Farley limbered up while Coffey wheeled his bicycle out of the lobby. They set off, Farley on foot and Coffey trailing behind.

Shay was confident. Fight night was going to be *special*. It was the start of Farley's ascent to the top, but more important than that and the money they stood to make was the humiliation of Billy Gallagher. The bitter old fucker had never got over what had happened to his boy and had been threatening payback for months.

Fine.

Shay had been forced to tread carefully ever since, and, although he'd come to accept that as the price of doing business, he wasn't going to let Gallagher think he was scared. Danny knocking out Gallagher's *other* son would be the perfect message: Shay wasn't going anywhere, and if Gallagher had a problem with that, he should put up or shut up.

11

Ziggy's hire car was parked outside.

Milton went around to the driver's side. "Keys."

"I can drive."

"You've been drinking. Keys."

Ziggy muttered something under his breath, reached into his pocket and tossed over the keys. "Fine."

Milton got in the car. The seats were covered in crumbs, and the floor mats were smeared with mud. The dashboard and console were cluttered with food wrappers, and empty Coke bottles had been tossed into the footwell.

"Look at the state of this," Milton said. "How long have you had it?"

"A couple of days."

"You made this mess in a *couple* of days?"

"I've spent a lot of time in it," he protested.

"It smells."

"I dropped a kebab last night. Probably didn't do a particularly thorough job cleaning it up."

Milton eyed him. "Have you been sleeping here?"

He shrugged. "May have done."

"You're doing me a favour with all this," Milton said. "Get a hotel. I'll pay."

Ziggy waved a hand as he reached out to close the door. "This is fine."

Milton started the engine and pulled away from the kerb. "You're an animal."

ZIGGY PROGRAMMED the satnav with the address, and Milton followed the directions, sending them around the city's ring road and then down through Ballymount and Sandyford towards the coast. Killiney was a suburb known for its views of the Irish Sea and the Wicklow Mountains and had long been a popular destination for local commuters with pockets deep enough to afford the inflated prices. Milton looked left and right and saw rows of elegant Victorian and Edwardian houses lit by the streetlights, flanked by the upscale restaurants, cafés and boutiques that served the neighbourhood.

The satnav directed them to Saint George's Avenue.

"It's at the end," Ziggy said. "We can park and walk the rest of the way."

Milton pulled over and got out. Ziggy collected his bag, slung it over his shoulder and started up the slope.

"It's expensive," Ziggy said. "The beach is a five-minute walk. The views from his place are crazy. It looks right out over the bay."

"How much was it?"

"Eight million."

Milton raised his eyebrows in surprise.

"I told you he was rich."

They climbed for another five minutes until they

reached James Moon's property. It was at the top of the hill, hidden behind high granite walls. A cobbled walkway led to what Milton suspected was a bin store, and, as he continued down the slope, he reached a set of iron gates. The property was built into the hill, with the drive on the other side of the gates climbing around in a gentle left-hand curve.

"Cameras?"

Ziggy nodded. "All off." He pointed down the slope. "There's another entrance down there. It's better."

They set off again. The road was narrow, with enough space for a single car to pass, and not the sort of place that would be much used by pedestrians. They came to the property's second entrance, two black wooden gates set between substantial granite piers.

"Alarms?"

"Off."

Milton went to the wooden gates and, after checking that the road was clear in both directions, jumped up so that he could get a grip on them. He held his weight for a moment before using the box that housed the intercom as a foothold. He lodged the toe of his right boot against it and then boosted himself up so that he could get his left leg over the gate. He slithered over it and dropped down on the other side, waiting a moment to assess his surroundings.

The gardens were minimal and uncluttered, with square lawns bisected by gravel paths. The house had been built as a low pavilion, with a second storey set back behind the first so that it masked the sense of height.

Ziggy clambered up the gate and balanced on the top, a leg straddling each side.

"Here," he said, breathing hard. He held out the bag. "Take this."

Milton reached up and took it and helped Ziggy to slide down.

"Which door to get in?"

Ziggy looked, then pointed. "There. See where the two wings meet?"

"Yes."

"There's a door there—it leads onto the foyer."

Milton led the way, taking them across the garden by way of the lawns rather than crunching over the gravel. He reached the door and waited, listening for any noise that might suggest the house was occupied. There was nothing.

"I told you," Ziggy said. "They're not here."

Milton knelt down so that he could get a better look at the lock. It was substantial and looked as if it might be magnetic. That was awkward. Milton knew enough about magnetic locks to know the key would have a complex shape, and that, coupled with the magnetic element, would make it an extremely difficult lock to pick.

He looked back, but Ziggy already had his phone in his hand. He touched the screen, and, after a second, the lock buzzed and disengaged.

"Voila," Ziggy said. "That's an expensive IP-enabled lock, but it's no good if someone can get into the back end."

He was fishing for compliments, as usual. Milton was not minded to pander to him, but on the basis that he was going to need him to be on his A-game while he was inside, he decided to play along. "Well done."

Milton started into the house and quickly saw that Ziggy's assessment of it had been correct: no expense had been spared. The hall comprised solid oiled oak boards and led into a double living room.

"We need the study," Ziggy said. "This way."

Milton followed him deeper into the house, eventually

reaching a room decked out with curved cabinetry and full-length windows that overlooked the grounds. Ziggy unslung the rucksack from his shoulders and set it down on the desk. He opened it and took out a small device about the size of his thumb, with two ethernet plugs at either end: a data tap. Ziggy opened the cupboards one by one until he found the router, then turned it around so that he could get to the ports on the back. He disconnected one of the ethernet cables, inserted the tap and then reconnected the cable so that the jack was plugged directly into it.

"Let me just check."

Ziggy took out his laptop and set it up on the desk. Milton looked around the room while he waited. There was a top-of-the-line Mac on the desk. The curved shelving was vast, the space taken up by a handful of books and ornaments that looked as if they had been selected by an interior designer rather than for any practical benefit. There was a homogeneity to the selections—an Asian influence, with elephants and Buddhist iconography—that was so perfect as to feel forced. Milton started to build up a picture of James Moon and what that might tell him about his real quarry. Why was Lilly Moon, the mother of a young child, engaged in such a dangerous role—an assassin for Group Fifteen—when her ex-husband was so obviously wealthy? Milton wondered about that, about the circumstances that had led to the breakup of their marriage and how those might have shaped her.

"I'm good," Ziggy said. "It's working."

Milton took one last look around the room, checked that everything was as he had found it, and led the way back through the lounge to the front door. He went outside, closed it and, even before he could tell Ziggy he could lock it, heard the same buzz as before and the sound of the bolt sliding home. Milton took a moment to allow his eyes to adjust to the darkness and then set off across the lawn to the gate, Ziggy a few steps behind him.

"That should be all we need," Ziggy said. "We own his network now. Anything that goes through it—email, calls, video from his cameras, whatever—we'll be able to see it. His server, too. I'll be able to dig around and see if there's anything interesting."

They reached the gate. Milton confirmed that it was quiet on the other side, helped Ziggy up and over it and then followed himself.

12

It was just before midnight when they finally got back to the hotel.

"Thank you," Milton said to Ziggy.

"I'll run a search on his server," he said. "What am I looking for?"

"Anything about Lilly Moon—her address, especially."

"You're serious about going to see her?"

"I don't have much choice if I want to get myself out of the mess she put me in."

"There is the other way," Ziggy said.

"Finding Control? I wouldn't even know where to start looking."

"I told you," he said. "Leave that to me. I've got a couple of ideas."

"Be careful. What we did in Kashmir would've annoyed them, and they'll double down on finding me now. You need to remember that—we both do."

"I'd be surprised if they even remember I exist."

Milton stared at him. "How much have you pissed them off over the years?"

"A bit."

"A *lot*."

"I'm still small fry."

"And I'm not. And if they think you're helping me, you'll get the kind of file I used to work on. You don't need me to spell out what that'll mean."

Ziggy smiled and raised both hands in surrender. "I know—be careful. I will."

Milton bid him good night and watched as he drove away. It was late, and Milton was tired.

He needed to get to sleep.

PART II

14

Lilly Moon crossed and uncrossed her legs, trying to master the nervous anticipation of what the next hour would hold. She'd received the summons as they flew back to London last night, and had been so anxious about it that she hadn't been able to sleep. The message suggested she was being called in for a debrief, but Lilly always had a fear in the back of her mind that there would come a time when she would have to account for the things that she had done.

Returning to London after what had happened in Krasnodar and then New Delhi had been difficult. There had been time to work on her lie, but living it was a challenge that went beyond what was required of Group agents who used a false identity when going about their work. The debriefing sessions, conducted in the basement *oubliettes* of the Group's building, had lasted for hours. They had asked her the same questions over and over and over again, picking up on the most infinitesimal variations and probing them for weaknesses. There had been the suggestion of administrative leave, but that had been put to one side by the fact that Lilly's perfidy had seen half of the Group's active agents killed and its commanding officer abducted. It would also likely have led to the end of her career. There were always new recruits ready to be deployed to fill the shoes of agents killed or incapacitated, but that anticipated a modest rate of attrition rather than the replacement of fifty per cent of the Group's strength in one go. Lilly had stuck through necessity, and she meant to underline the good sense of that decision by finding and ending John Milton.

It would demonstrate her worth as an agent, but would also secure her future in more fundamental ways: Milton could testify to her betrayal.

The light above the door switched from red to green.

The man at the desk glanced up at the light, then over to her. "You can go in."

Lilly stood and made her way inside. The room beyond was large, with broad windows offering a wide view of the Thames. It was light and airy, with a dove-grey Wilton carpet. An old hearth sat beneath a large marble mantelpiece, and a central table bore a bowl of flowers and served two club chairs. Lilly had been in the same room before, her first visit had seen her meet the woman who had recruited her, but she was gone now—buried in a Siberian gulag— and her place taken by the man sitting behind the desk.

"Sit down," he said.

Lilly did. She felt her heart pounding in her chest and clasped her hands in her lap to stop herself from fidgeting.

"Thank you for coming, Number Six."

"Of course, sir. How can I help?"

"I thought I'd better introduce myself. Control's been missing for some time, and, while we're still looking for her, we need someone in place to oversee the Group. That will be me—I'm Acting Control until she's found, so you'll be reporting directly to me."

The man, though not dressed in uniform, gave off an impression that suggested a career in the military. He was of average height and carried himself with an air of quiet confidence. His features were sharp and angular, with deep-set eyes that were a piercing grey. His short dark hair was perfectly groomed, and his clean-shaven face suggested discipline. His clothing was civilian—a well-fitted suit, a crisply ironed shirt, a conservative tie—but there was a punctiliousness about the way he wore it that again suggested the military.

"I think we should get to business. I've read the briefing from yesterday—our intelligence was faulty, and we've wasted your time. I'm aware that you are due some R and R, but that's going to have to wait."

"Is this about Milton?"

"It is. We might have made a breakthrough. We've always suspected he was receiving help from a former Group Two analyst." He handed her a piece of paper with a photograph of a man on it: he had a thatch of thick and unruly ginger hair, as stiff as wire wool, pallid skin, and eyes that seemed to bulge from their sockets. "That's Ziggy Penn. He's been out almost as long as Milton, and we've seen evidence suggesting that he's maintained access to Firm servers. He's usually careful, but it seems that he let his guard down. We had a stroke of luck."

Control handed her another printout. This one showed a still from a security camera that looked as if it had been taken at an airport. The camera looked down on a queue of travellers waiting at a carousel for their suitcases.

Lilly saw Ziggy Penn. "Where is this?"

"Dublin. Two days ago. Penn arrived via an Aer Lingus

flight from Dubai. We've gone back and confirmed his movements before that. He flew to Dubai from New Delhi. He was in Srinagar before that."

"He helped Milton set us up?"

"That would certainly appear to be the case."

She felt sick. "Why is he in Dublin?"

"I think you can probably guess."

"My ex-husband?"

"I understand he lives in Dublin."

"He does. You think this is about him?"

"Group Three identified a possible unauthorised breach of our servers just before you went to Srinagar and just before Penn arrived in Dublin. They're investigating the possibility that he left himself a backdoor in the event that he wanted to maintain access."

"What was he looking for?"

"You," he said.

"He didn't find anything?"

"Your personal details? No, of course not—those are sealed. Your ex-husband, though? There's security on that, but it's not as tight. It'd be child's play for someone like Penn."

"How would he know we were married?"

"Were you masked in New Delhi?"

"No," she said.

"Penn would probably have been able to get a still of you from there. It's easy from that point—he runs an image search and finds something that identifies your ex. We scrub as much from the internet as we can when an agent joins the Group, but there are always things we don't find. If you're good enough and you know where to look... you can always find the breadcrumbs left behind."

"What about Milton? Do you think he's there, too?"

"We've checked arrivals into Dublin, and we haven't seen anything. But that could be because he's more cautious than Penn. I think we have to assume either that he *is* there and we haven't found him yet, or that he's on his way. Of course, it could be a coincidence that Penn is in Dublin, but, given the context, we can't assume that. You're the only surviving witness to what he did in Krasnodar. We don't have any idea how Milton's mind works, but it might be that he sees you as a vulnerability."

Lilly thought of Lola. She was with Jimmy on holiday. "My daughter..."

Control looked at her. "I was going to ask you about her —she's in Paris with your ex-husband?"

She hadn't mentioned the holiday to anyone; she reminded herself that the Group kept a close eye on its agents and, apparently, their dependents. "At Disneyland. The plan is for her to stay with him for a week afterwards."

"I've already sent Four and Five. They'll be staying in the room opposite your ex-husband and your daughter. I have a local asset keeping an eye on them until they get there. Nothing will happen to them."

"Thank you, sir." She paused. "Can I ask how this affects me?"

"Operationally? That's what I wanted to talk to you about. The way I see it, I have two choices: consider you compromised and transfer you out of the Group, or put you back in the field."

"I don't want to be pulled."

"I don't want that, either. I've read your file, and I know what happened in Krasnodar and New Delhi. You did good work—you've just been unfortunate."

"Thank you."

"Plus, on top of that, we're short-handed, and you've got

skin in the game. Some of my predecessors might have seen that as a reason to get you out of the line of fire, but I don't agree. It'll be a motive for you to make sure we get to him. You're committed. That's helpful."

"So, I go to Dublin?"

"Yes. Not alone, though—with One, Two and Three. Milton's been underestimated before, and I'm not going to make the same mistake."

"And when we get there?"

"You set up and wait."

She realised what he was suggesting.

"Using my daughter as bait?"

"That's an emotive way to describe it, but... yes. I suppose so." He leaned back in his chair. "We can't warn them. Milton is very good at this—he'll smell a rat if there's any suggestion that your ex-husband has changed his plans without an obvious reason, and, if that happens, he's gone. Getting a lead on him again will be difficult. It took *months* the first time he bolted before they tracked him to Mexico. We need him to think that we have no idea where he is or what he's doing."

"But it's my *daughter*, sir."

"And we will be watching her, as well as your ex-husband. There won't be a moment when they're left alone, and every remaining Group agent is going to be in the field. Remember, we don't know whether Milton is in Ireland yet, or whether he's coming at all. But if he *does* come to Dublin, you'll be waiting for him in force—and he won't know you're there. The last thing you want is to have someone like him in the wind, to not know where he is or what he might do. You'll always be looking over your shoulder, and if I think your identity has been compromised, I won't have any choice but to take you out of the Group. You'd be given a new name and a new life in New Zealand or Australia or somewhere Milton won't find you. This, right now—*this* will be the best chance we get to take him out. And, of course, when we do that..." Control shrugged. "The threat will be over. You won't need to worry about him anymore."

She stopped to let that sink in. She couldn't do anything that would risk her being removed from the Group. She had promised Otto Sommer she would provide him with intelligence in return for the money she needed to get her daughter back. The bargain depended upon the value she could deliver, and if she was sent away, that value disappeared. She would have more to worry about then than just John Milton.

"Six?"

"I understand, sir."

"Good."

"Will you tell the others?"

"About your connection to Dublin?" He shook his head. "No. That would compromise you. I don't think it's necessary—we don't need to tell them *why* Milton might be headed there, just that he is."

"I agree."

"Excellent." He got to his feet and clapped his hands. "Group Eight has prepared a new legend for you. Pick up your passport on the way out."

She stood.

"When do we leave?"

"Now—there's a car downstairs waiting to take you to Brize."

15

Mahoney parked his patrol car at the end of the street where he could watch the comings and goings into and out of the bail hostel where Mickey Flannagan was staying. He had printed out Flannagan's record, together with one of the litany of mugshots that he had accumulated over the course of his long criminal career, and had propped the sheet of paper up between the dashboard and the windscreen. He referred back to it as he watched, waiting for Flannagan to emerge so he could get to the hotel to start his shift.

Mahoney had spoken to Flannagan's parole officer, and she had confirmed that he was living here in Ringsend and working the evening shift at the Southside. She said he was expected to be in the kitchen at four o'clock. Mahoney guessed it would take him an hour on the bus to get to the hotel from here, and, given the time was ten to three, he would have to be leaving in the next few minutes.

He unwrapped a packet of Polos and popped one in his mouth just as the door of the hostel opened and a man stepped outside. Mahoney looked up at the printout and the photograph—a man in his late fifties, shaven-headed, with large ears and a bulbous nose—and compared it to the man who was walking along the path toward the bus stop.

It was Flannagan.

Mahoney opened the door, stepped onto the pavement and blocked the way ahead.

"Mickey?"

Flannagan saw Mahoney's uniform and froze. "What?"

"Can I have a word?"

"No," he said. "I've got to get to work. And I haven't done anything wrong."

"I know you haven't. I'd still like to talk to you. And you'll want to hear what I have to say."

"I can't afford to be late."

"I'll give you a lift. Get in."

Mahoney put Flannagan in the back of the car and set off.

He looked into the mirror. "Not your first time in the back."

"I've gone straight now," Flannagan said. "No more nonsense."

"Is that so?"

"I mean it. Ask my PO—she'll tell you. I've been clocking in on time every day since they took me on. My work's good, too. Ask my manager if you don't believe me."

"I'm not here about that—I don't care."

"So, what do you want?"

"How's your boy?"

He glanced up into the rear-view again to gauge Flannagan's reaction. "What?"

"Harry—got himself into a bit of a mess, hasn't he?"

Flannagan glared back at him. "It's all bollocks. He

didn't do anything wrong. What they're saying about him—none of it's true."

"You would say that, wouldn't you—being his dad and that. Confident a jury will agree with you?"

"He didn't—"

"He's got form for beating people up, Mickey. He only just got out for kicking the shit out of that lad in Temple Bar. Pretty stupid of him to put himself in the same situation again. He got lucky then—eighteen months for what he did. He could easily have had twice that. He could've got five years. But this time *and* with a knife? The jury says he's guilty, and the judge's going to throw the book at him. Five years is getting off easy. Seven or eight years is more likely, more if the judge gets out of bed the wrong side."

They crossed the Liffey on the Tom Clarke Bridge and continued north.

"What's this got to do with you?"

Mahoney looked back in the mirror again. "I might be able to help him."

"That right?"

"What if I said that I could make sure the knife disappeared?"

"How are you going to do that?"

"It's in the evidence room at the nick. You don't think things go missing every now and again? What do you think the prosecution's case will look like without it? They need it. What happens if it's not there? Just *think* about the song and dance the defence will be able to make. They'll be able to question the integrity of the entire investigation. 'If the police lost something as important as the knife, what else might they have lost?' See where I'm coming from?"

Flannagan narrowed his eyes. "Why would you do that?"

"There's something I need in return. You scratch my

back and all that. There's an event tomorrow night at the Southside."

"I know—the weigh-in for the fight."

"Are you working it?"

"*Everyone*'s working. It's the Dillons—it's a big deal. They've pulled out all the stops."

"One of the guests there needs to go away. I want you to make it happen."

"Go away? You mean…"

"You know exactly what I mean—he needs to be shot."

"Piss off," he said. "You heard what I said? It's the *Dillons*. They've booked the whole place, and they're bringing their lads for security. You think anyone would do something as stupid as shoot someone at their event?"

"Most people wouldn't," Mahoney said. "But you've got a lot to gain and nothing to lose."

"What does that mean?"

"Your boy, for one. And I know about your cancer, too."

"I…" He stopped.

"It's not like it's a secret. You used it for mitigation the last time you went down. How long do you have left?"

Flannagan paused, perhaps wondering whether he should answer. "Six months."

"So what does it matter what happens to you? You're a dead man anyway. Do this, though, and the six months will be a lot better than they would be otherwise. I'll make sure you get out of the country with enough money to set your-self up in Spain or South America or somewhere else where the weather's better than it is here. You get to die on a sunny beach, and your boy doesn't spend the best years of his life in some shitty cell in Mountjoy."

Mahoney flicked the indicator and turned onto Drumcondra Road. He looked up in the mirror and saw that Flannagan was looking out of the window.

"Well?"

"Who's going away?"

"His name's Rickard."

"Never heard of him."

"No reason you would. He's American. An agent or something. I don't know, and I don't care. He just needs to go."

Flannagan paused again. "Who wants him gone?"

"Doesn't matter. Are you going to do it or not?"

"I don't know."

Mahoney tightened his grip on the wheel. "Let me rephrase that—you *are* going to do it. What I just said—that was me being reasonable. I'd much rather we did it like that, but there's another way. I can get rid of the knife and make Harry's legal problems go away, or I could see to it that someone turns up who'll testify that they *saw* what happened. That kind of witness? It'll *guarantee* the jury sends him down. Or maybe something's found in your room at the hostel. What happens if they find pills or coke? What if they think you're dealing again? They'll send you straight back inside." He glanced up and saw the hate burning in Flannagan's eyes. "I don't *want* to do that. I'd rather see you sunning yourself on a beach next week with Harry's case fucked up beyond all recognition. But that's up to you."

Mahoney wasn't sure which way it would go, but, as he looked in the mirror, he saw the fight drain out of Flannagan's expression. There was an angry resignation now, an acceptance that he had found himself tied up so that all his room to manoeuvre was gone. He really did have only one choice: agree to the proposal and secure his son's future, or refuse and condemn himself and his boy to more time inside.

"There'll be security there," he said.

"You're staff. And you used to work for them, didn't you? Why would they be suspicious?"

"I won't be able to get a gun inside. They've got a scanner on the door."

"Even now?"

"They put it in yesterday."

"What do the guests think about that?"

"There aren't any guests. It's closed. The last guests left this morning."

Mahoney drummed his fingers on the wheel. "Fine. I'll find a way."

"I haven't said I'll do it yet."

Mahoney pulled over a hundred yards before they got to the turning for the hotel. He didn't want anyone seeing Flannagan getting out of his car.

"You'll do it," he said. "I'll pick you up tomorrow, same time. We'll run through what's going to happen."

Flannagan eyeballed him. He didn't respond, but reached for the door handle only to find that it was still locked.

"Open this bloody door."

Mahoney pressed the button on the dash to release the lock, and Flannagan opened the door and got outside. He set off for the hotel at a brisk walk and never looked back.

16

L illy was transferred from London to the Group's facility at RAF Brize Norton in a government car. The driver waited at the wire-mesh gates and then, after their details had been verified, drove inside. There was a Gulfstream on the apron. The ground crew were fuelling it from a mobile bowser, and the captain was making her final visual checks.

The driver headed toward the administrative building, where they would wait for their flight to be ready. Lilly looked at the plain-looking structure and thought back to when they had all gathered inside before going to Krasnodar. She still could not believe how precipitously things had changed since then. Number Two had been the catalyst and his constant harassment the trigger. His refusal to accept that their brief flirtation was a mistake had led him to blackmail her, and when that had failed, he'd turned to the threat of violence. He'd put Lola at risk, and, backed into a corner and with nowhere to go, Lilly had acted instinctively: she shot him. It was a moment of helpless rage, but it had promised to put an end to everything: her career, the possibility of fighting Jimmy for custody, and—given that it had taken place in a Russian facility run by Otto Sommer and the Unit—her life.

She'd been left with no other choice: she had sold herself to Sommer.

Lilly got out of the car and crossed over to the building. Four other agents were waiting in the ready room. The toll in Krasnodar had been heavy and had necessitated a radical reordering of the hierarchy: Lilly had gone from Number Twelve to Number Six. Number Three—a slender Black woman who never said much—had been promoted to Number One, with Five moving to Two, and so on. The two missing agents—Four and Five—were in France to take up surveillance on Jimmy and Lola while they were away on holiday.

Lilly looked from agent to agent and saw able, experienced operators who would not be under any illusions about the challenge ahead. The Group had failed in New Delhi, and that chastening experience was not one that they were ready to repeat. Four agents to go after Milton's friend —and Milton, if he was there—ought to be more than enough.

One glanced over at Lilly. "Wheels up in thirty minutes."

"What about gear?"

"We'll pick it up there," she said. She collected a tablet and held it out so that Lilly could take it. "There's been an update. You'll need to be familiar with it by the time we land."

17

M ahoney turned onto Seven Oaks and waited for a minibus to pull out before driving all the way down to the hotel. Cars were parked nose-to-tail on the side of the road and in bays; he found a space, reversed his patrol car into it and switched off the engine.

He had gone to the Brazen Head for a drink and had ended up necking three pints with three chasers and now, two hours later, he was a little drunk. He'd needed a stiffener because he was nervous. The Dillons. *Jesus.* Mahoney knew all about them. Their father, Finn, had been a well-known local figure, and despite a reputation as something of a scallywag, he had died with a reputation for philanthropy and the affection of those who knew him. He'd built a shipping business that involved the import of all manner of cargo into the country: flatpack furniture from Sweden, circuit boards from Taiwan, wines from France, spice from India. Shay and Colm had taken over the business when Finn topped himself, and had quickly seen the potential it offered: an existing transportation network with experience in bringing goods across the border. The police and the customs officers knew it, too, but the brothers were too smart for them, and no one had ever been able to lay a glove on them. They had funded the purchase and the refurbishment of the Southside with the money they made from the drugs they sold.

And they weren't just smart; they were *vicious*. Mahoney was wary of them, and it was only because Billy paid him so well that he was here at all.

He had a good view of the entrance from here and could see that what Flannagan had said was true: an airport scanner had been installed inside the door, and the two men and a woman who had just climbed the steps to the door were being told they would have to pass through it. He watched as the woman and then the two men emptied their pockets into plastic trays before walking beneath the arch.

The booze and the nerves made Mahoney feel bilious, but he tried to ignore it. There was something he needed to do, and he would just sweat on it until it was done; he needed to get it over with. He opened the glovebox, took out the pistol that Gallagher had given him, and tucked it under his stab vest. He hadn't been told that the security would be as thorough as this, nor that it would have been put in place this far ahead of the weigh-in. He'd intended to rely on his uniform and standing to get him inside, and, as he reflected on the change in circumstances, he decided that his strategy need not change.

He opened the door, stepped out and crossed over the road. He climbed the steps and waited as one of the doormen opened the door for him.

"Afternoon, sir. Is everything all right?"

"We had a call," he said.

"For what?"

"Theft from a guest's room. A watch and a sum of money."

"I don't know anything about that."

"I'm just telling you what I've been told." Mahoney pointed at the scanner. "What's all that about?"

"There's an event at the weekend."

"Want me to go through it?"

"Please."

Mahoney indicated the handcuffs on his belt. "I'll set it off."

"Don't worry. I think we can trust you."

The scanner was a stainless-steel arch, around seven feet tall from top to bottom, with a control panel on one side. LED lights on both sides of the arch shone red or green depending upon whether the scanner revealed anything that needed additional investigation when a guest passed through. Mahoney walked through the machine, and, just as he had expected, it bleeped angrily at him. He couldn't help the instinctive feeling of guilt and tried to mask it with a shake of his head and a wry chuckle. He gestured down at his belt. "Told you. You sure you don't need me to take it off?"

The man shook his head. "You're fine. In you go."

He went to the front desk. The receptionist was an embodiment of the hotel's newly elevated status: dressed impeccably in a crisp white shirt and black waistcoat with a little pop of colour from his scarlet bow tie.

"Hello, sir. How can I help?"

"We've had a call from someone who said he'd been staying here. He says five hundred euros was stolen from his room last night."

The receptionist frowned with concern. "Really? We haven't had a report of that."

"He only found out when he got to the airport."

"And he called you rather than speaking to us?"

"I didn't speak to him, obviously, but I understand he was angry and wanted us to look into it."

"What's his name?"

"Mr. Walsh."

"Okay. Let me have a look and see what I can find."

"While you're doing that—which way's the bathroom?"

"Oh," the man said. "Of course." He pointed. "Down there, first on the left."

Mahoney crossed the marble floor to the corridor that ended with the lifts that took guests to their rooms on the floors above. There was a bathroom before that, and Mahoney went inside. He took a moment to check that the cubicles were vacant, then made his way to the one at the end of the line. He closed the door and locked it.

He lowered the toilet seat and climbed onto it, reached up to the ceiling and pressed at the panels with his fingertips until he found the one that was loose. He lifted the panel from the metal framework that supported it, sliding it away and to the side. He reached into his stab vest for the gun, drew it out and placed it in the cavity, leaving it on top of the next tile along. He scrabbled for the edge of the loose tile, carefully slid it back and settled it in place once more.

He lowered himself down to the floor and took a moment to gather himself. He suddenly—and shamefully—felt sick. The burger he'd had for lunch from Pete Welbeck's van had been disgusting, that and the booze were swirling around in his stomach, and the nerves just set it all off. He lifted the lid of the toilet and knelt down next to it, holding his head above the porcelain, and voided his guts. His body heaved, and the splash of the vomit echoed loudly off the cubicle walls.

Stop being so pathetic. Pull yourself together.

He stood up, made sure that none of the sick had splashed back onto his stab vest, and straightened it out. He flushed the toilet, unlocked the door to the cubicle and stepped back outside.

18

Milton had found a meeting to help him clear his head. There was a lot going on, and he needed a peaceful hour to disengage from it all. He had known that he would find it there, as he almost always did. The meeting had focused on acceptance. The secretary explained how it was a critical part of recovery to accept that their lives had become unmanageable and that they needed help. He went on to suggest that it was also about accepting themselves and their past mistakes, learning from them, and moving forward. It was just what Milton needed to hear, and, rather than sharing, he sat in his customary place at the back of the church hall and soaked it all up.

He walked back to the hotel, and as he arrived, the guards behind the scanner regarded him with sour hostility. He put his phone and keys in the box, passed through the machine without sounding the alarm and was allowed to continue without question.

He needed the bathroom and diverted there before going up to his room. He opened the door, went inside and relieved himself, staring at a framed poster for Guinness from the 1950s that had been fixed to the wall above the urinal. He finished and went over to the sink to wash his hands. As he reached for one of the towels from the stack next to the sink, he heard the sound of someone being sick in one of the cubicles.

Milton dried his hands, dropped the towel into the bin and was about to leave when the door of the last cubicle in the line opened. A uniformed police officer emerged: he was middle-aged, rugged, with an imposing physicality and a strong, broad-shouldered build. His face was weathered and carved with deep creases and lines.

He saw Milton and glowered at him. "What?"

"Sorry?"

"What are you staring at?"

The man had dark eyes beneath heavy brows, and his prominent nose was crooked, suggesting previous breaks that had not been properly set. His lips were thin and cruel.

"Are you all right? I heard you—"

"Mind your own business, pal."

The man's aggression was unwarranted and unusual, but Milton wasn't bothered by it. Rather than get into an argument that could escalate, Milton raised his hands and stepped back.

"Okay—fine. Take it easy."

The man eyed Milton for a moment longer, then feigned submission and looked away. Without a word, he went to the sink and rinsed out his mouth, then walked to the door and stepped back into the corridor.

19

Mahoney ignored the man from the bathroom and went back to the front desk. The same receptionist was waiting there.

"I'm a bit confused," he said. "I looked through the system for the last week, and we haven't had a Mr. Walsh staying here."

"Are you sure?"

"Completely. Do you have any other information?"

"No. That was all I was given."

The man spread his arms helplessly. "I don't know what to suggest."

Mahoney shook his head, feigning irritation. "I know what's happened."

"You do?"

"It's a crank. Someone's called up to cause mischief. I've seen it before. It might be as stupid as another hotel looking to make trouble for you. I think we can chalk this one up to experience—sorry for wasting your time."

"No, it's fine," the man said with a smile. "I'm sorry *your* time was wasted."

Mahoney said goodbye, walked back to the exit and eyed the guards as he waited for the door to be opened. He recognised one of the men: his name was Keith or Keir or Karl, and he was a bruiser from the Dillons' crew. He hadn't had any dealings with him before, but he remembered his face from a briefing that had been delivered by officers from the Drugs and Organised Crime Bureau. There had been a presentation, and the slides had been distributed afterwards; Mahoney had printed it out and sold it to Billy for a little extra on the side.

He stepped outside and drew in a big gulp of fresh air. He could still taste the vomit in his mouth. He thought of the man in the bathroom and chided himself for his angry response; it was the kind of thing that would stick in the mind. It couldn't be helped, though; what was done was done. Flannagan would get the pistol when he needed it, and, once it was gone, it wouldn't matter what the man saw or thought he saw.

Mahoney went back to his patrol car, opened the door and slumped down into the seat. He thought about his relationship with Billy and wondered—not for the first time—whether now might be the time to say he was finished. He was paid peanuts by the police, and the extra money was welcome, but he couldn't help but wonder whether the juice was worth the squeeze. The nights cursed with hours when he couldn't sleep, the ulcers he'd had six months ago, the headaches that felt like an elastic band was fitted around his forehead, squeezing and squeezing... the stress was a serious problem, and he knew what caused it. But, on the other hand, his tastes had grown more expensive, and his lifestyle more lavish, and he would lose all of that if he called it quits. And more than that, would Billy even *let* him walk? Mahoney was good at what he did; he warned Billy of police interest, made evidence disappear, intimidated witnesses. He'd killed for him, too. Billy might think him too valuable to lose, and that was without even considering how he would feel about how much Mahoney knew about his business.

He started the engine.

He'd earned enough over the years to buy himself a little *finca* on the skirts of Panama's Baru volcano, and he had been building up enough money to ensure that he wouldn't have to work when he got over there. He had just about half of what he had originally budgeted, but perhaps that would be enough. The other half would do him no good at all if he was arrested.

It'd do him even less good if he were dead.

He pulled out, drumming his fingers on the wheel.

Yes, he thought. *Why not?* See this job through to the end and then go. All good things came to an end eventually, and maybe his time here had run out.

20

The hotel was closed to guests, but the kitchen was surprisingly busy as Milton punched in for the evening's service. It was loud: the clanging of pots and pans, the sharp hiss of steam escaping from pressure cookers, the hum of the industrial fridges. The sous-chefs barked orders to the line cooks, voices echoing off the stainless-steel walls. The smell was unmistakeable and immediately cast Milton back to all the other kitchens he'd worked in since leaving the Group: grilled meat, sautéed vegetables, baked bread. There were pungent spices—garlic, ginger, and cumin—and the strong odour of frying oil from the deep-fryers, leading to a slightly greasy atmosphere.

The head chef—a Hungarian named Ernő—saw Milton and came over to him. "We're going to be busy."

"I thought the restaurant was closed. Wasn't this just prep for the event?"

"Change of plan. The owners want to have dinner with their guests."

"How many?"

"Fifty."

"Where's the menu?"

Ernő reached over to the counter behind him and collected a printout that had already been stained with a wet ring from something that had been stood on it. Milton scanned it and saw—again—that no expense had been spared. It all looked bespoke and expensive, with each dish requiring careful attention.

Milton looked up. "What courses do you want me to do?"

Ernő stabbed his finger on the paper three times. "The risotto, the duck and the soufflé."

The truffle-infused risotto was one of half a dozen starters, with pan-seared duck breast the most appetising of the mains. "Fine."

"Service in three hours."

"I'll get started."

The others were working hard, too. Many of them were foreign, with a contingent of minimum-wage Eastern Europeans bolstering the Spaniards and Italians and Irish who, when taken together, formed a decent crew. There was Miguel from Barcelona, mid-thirties and with a megawatt smile that made him look like a movie star; Ivan was Polish and the recipient of multiple warnings that he was not to smoke while he was in the kitchen; Francois was from a Parisian *banlieue rouge*, a card-carrying communist who didn't miss an opportunity to decry the nouveaux riches while ignoring the fact that the extortionately priced food he prepared for them paid for his pleasant apartment in the Southside.

The air was thick with the aroma of the dishes being prepared. Along with the notes of simmering garlic and onions, Milton picked up the tantalising odours of roasting meats and sweet, fresh pastries. He breathed in deeply, taking a moment to savour the smells and the energy that fizzed in the air, before he set about his work.

He checked his *mise en place*, surveying the neatly arranged ingredients: bright, crisp vegetables; cuts of prime meat; fresh herbs; a rainbow of spices, each set in its designated place. Everything was placed in a logical order; he found his knife and got to work. He began the preparation of the main course, trimming and seasoning the duck breasts. The sound of the knife as it struck the board was rhythmic, almost therapeutic. He set the meat aside to marinate, then busied himself with the risotto, preparing a stock that he would simmer until it was rich and thick. That done, he moved on to the tray of chocolate soufflés. He filled the ramekins, the rich, dark mixture a stark contrast to the crisp white of the ceramic. The smell of the chocolate was intoxicating, and he found his mouth watering as he anticipated the moment they would rise in the oven, their tops cracking to reveal the molten centres.

Milton was in perpetual motion, his hands and mind never resting. It was chaotically busy, but despite the noise and the heat and the pressure, he found the serenity he usually felt. It was the same kind of release he attained when he was out running; there was no time for his mind to dwell on the past or to indulge the guilt that was liable to swamp him at other times.

Ernő came over to his station. "Okay?"

"Prep's all done," Milton said, wiping his hands on the towel that was tucked into his belt. "I'm going to take a quick break before we get started."

Ernő said that was fine, and continued along the line to check that the rest of the menu was on track.

Milton checked that his cigarettes were in his pocket and left the kitchen.

21

H e made his way to the door at the back of the hotel that the staff were encouraged to use. It opened out onto a densely wooded area that separated the hotel from the businesses to the north and lent the area a darkly sylvan aspect.

Three men were smoking next to the door. Milton recognised two of them: a bellboy named Declan and a pot washer named Padraig. Declan was a Dubliner who had been proud to announce that he was the third in his family to work at the hotel. Milton found him a little bombastic, but he didn't know how long he would be in the city, and it was always useful to have friends with the benefit of local knowledge. Padraig was young—just sixteen or seventeen— and had told Milton the last time the two of them had shared a smoke together that this was his first job after leaving school. He was a sweet boy who was trying hard to fit in with his older colleagues.

"Evening," Milton said.

Declan turned. "Evening."

"Evening," Padraig said with a smile.

Declan turned to the third man. "Do you know Marcus?"

"We haven't met," Milton said.

"Marcus—this is Eric."

Milton shook his hand. "What do you do here?"

"Night duty manager."

Marcus had a well-groomed beard and wore a black suit with a matching tie.

"Eric works in the kitchen," Padraig offered.

"I haven't seen you before," Marcus said.

"I've not been here long."

Marcus chuckled. "Just in time for the function. Bad timing."

"Why do you say that?"

"It's a big deal," Marcus said. "Management are on edge."

"I noticed."

"Pete was shitting himself this morning. They're spending a fortune."

"Dinner tonight's not cheap," Milton said.

"And they booked out the whole hotel," Declan said. "I was trying to work out how much that'd cost."

"Thousands," Marcus said. "Plus their own security—have you seen out the front?"

"The organisers own the hotel?" Milton said.

"The Dillons," Declan said. "You met them yet?"

Milton shook his head.

Declan paused, as if wondering how much it would be wise to say.

"They're gangsters," Padraig answered for him.

Marcus glared at him. "Are you stupid? Don't talk about them like that."

"They're not here, are they? And it's the truth. They are. Everyone knows it."

Milton could see that Marcus was uncomfortable discussing the Dillons in front of him and made a show of looking at his watch.

Declan noticed. "We keeping you?"

"They're sitting down soon—I'd better get back."

"A few of us are going up to Maria's room tonight," Padraig said. "You should come."

"I don't know," Milton said. "You've all got twenty years on me."

"Don't tell me you won't want a drink after you've knocked off. Come and hang out for twenty minutes. You know what Maria can be like."

"*Relentless*," Declan said. "If she knows you're in your room, she won't stop until you've given in and come and had a drink. I find it's best just to accept it."

"Noted," Milton said. "Maybe I'll see you later."

22

The adrenaline rush of the evening's service gave way to a sense of relief and accomplishment now that everything was done. The food they'd sent out had been excellent, and most of the plates had come back clean. There had been a couple of complaints—a steak not cooked to a diner's liking, a delay in service—but that wasn't unusual, and each had been handled with professionalism.

"Well done," Ernő said. "Good work. Clean up and then go and get some sleep. We'll be busier tomorrow."

The team worked in unison, scrubbing down surfaces and washing utensils. Despite the long hours and the pressure of service, there was a sense of satisfaction in seeing the kitchen clean and quiet. Milton's body ached, and his feet throbbed, but a successful service made it worthwhile.

He and Padraig were just scraping off the hob when a man in an obviously expensive suit came in through the kitchen doors. There was nothing particularly memorable about how he looked, but there was something about him that stopped Milton short. He had a calm yet intense aspect that was unsettling.

"I just wanted to come in and say thanks," he said. "That was a bloody good meal."

Milton leaned against the counter next to Padraig and whispered, "Who's that?"

"Shay Dillon," Padraig whispered back.

"Who cooked the duck?"

Milton didn't want to take the praise, but Ernő pointed to him.

"You?" Dillon said.

Milton nodded.

"What's your name?"

"Eric."

"That's what I had," Dillon said. "The duck."

"How was it?"

"Bloody fantastic, mate. Best I've ever had."

Milton wiped his hands on the towel. "I'm glad."

Dillon grinned. "You want to watch out, Ernő. He'll be after your job if he keeps cooking like that."

Ernő smiled, obviously unsure how he was expected to react.

Dillon noticed his discomfort. "I'm pulling your leg. Thanks again, all of you, and good luck for tomorrow. We've got nine hundred coming. You're going to be even busier."

He went over to Ernő, put a hand on his shoulder and turned him away from the others.

Milton and Padraig continued to clean the hob.

"He doesn't seem so bad," Padraig said.

Milton said that he agreed, although he had seen something in Dillon that belied his friendliness. His hearty laughter echoed in the room, but his eyes held an icy glint that his apparently warm smile never quite reached. There was a predatory aspect to him, an edge hidden behind the avuncular façade. Milton recognised some of it in himself.

M ilton stepped out of the elevator and made his way down the corridor to his door. He took out his key and stopped; he could hear the sounds of music and conversation from Maria's room. He opened his door and slipped inside before anyone could see that he was there. He took off his jacket and his boots and wondered whether he should have a shower. He knew he would appreciate it, but the showers were in the communal bathroom, and he didn't want to advertise the fact that he was up and about. He didn't dislike Maria—far from it—but he wanted to read his book and then get to sleep.

He concluded that it would be better to shower in the morning and went over to his tiny basin, picked up his toothbrush and squeezed out a line of paste. He had just started brushing when there came a knock at the door.

"Eric?"

He stared at his reflection in the dusty mirror.

"Eric?"

Milton sighed.

The knock came again. "Eric—are you awake?"

He rinsed out his mouth, dropped the toothbrush in its glass and went to open the door.

Maria was in the corridor.

"Hello," Milton said.

"It's not too late, is it?"

Milton shrugged. "It's quite—"

"I heard you coming back. I thought you might like to have a quick drink with us?"

"I told you," he said patiently. "I don't drink."

"I know—I remembered. So I went down to the bar and got a bottle of lemonade. That's all right, isn't it? We have chips, dips, fags and music."

"I'm tired. I'd be awful company."

She reached out a hand and snagged his wrist. "Come on. Don't be so *boring!* Half an hour. You can't hide in your room all the time. Have a drink and a chat, and then I promise I'll leave you alone."

"Half an hour?"

"Half an hour."

"And then I can go to bed?"

She smiled at him. "Promise."

"Fine."

PART III

M aria led the way back to her room. The door was ajar, and as he went inside, Milton saw that there were three people waiting for them: Declan from front of house, Padraig from the kitchen and a woman he hadn't met before.

Maria put her hand on his shoulder. "This is Eric."

The woman got up and put out a hand. "I'm Louisa. From reception."

"Nice to meet you."

Milton looked around. Maria's room was identical in size to his, but, in contrast, she'd made the effort to personalise it. There was a floral duvet cover on the bed and a small vase of sweet-smelling flowers on the bedside table. The door of the wardrobe was slightly ajar, revealing neatly organised clothing. There was a framed photo of four smiling women on the wall, two of them bearing enough of a resemblance to Maria for Milton to suspect they were her mother and sister. Music was being played from a laptop hooked up to a Bluetooth speaker. Milton didn't recognise the song; his tastes were marooned in the eighties and nineties, and—

with the grim realisation that it made him sound like a grandfather—this felt altogether *too* contemporary for him.

Padraig pointed to the nest of beer bottles that they were trying to keep cool in the basin.

"Want one?"

"Eric doesn't drink," Maria said, bustling into the room and stepping around Milton. She went to a carrier bag next to the bed and pulled out a bottle of lemonade and a plastic cup. She smiled at him. "Here."

"You don't drink?" Louisa said.

Milton smiled with as much forbearance as he could manage. "I don't."

"Why?"

"It doesn't agree with me."

"Leave him alone," Maria said, filling the plastic cup. "He doesn't have to drink if he doesn't want to."

Louisa mumbled something about it being strange, but, after a knowing look from Maria, she held up her bottle of beer for a toast. Maria gave Milton the cup, and he touched it to the bottle, then to Maria's bottle, and tried to work out a way to extricate himself from the room without causing offence. The four of them were all young—younger than him, anyway—and he felt out of place. He tried to guess Maria's age, but although she was older than the others, it didn't matter; the idea of any kind of relationship with her was foolish and didn't deserve even a moment's thought. He was only planning on being in Dublin for a week—two weeks at the outside—and then he was going to move on. There was no question that she was attractive, but Milton was not about to hurt her because he was too weak to listen to his conscience. Alcoholism came hand in hand with self-ishness and narcissism, and he valued his sobriety enough not to unleash his demons. And, more importantly, being with him had never been safe for anyone; it was even more perilous now given his knowledge, without doubt, that the Group was coming for him again. The risk to Ziggy was one thing—Ziggy knew the situation and how to minimise his exposure—but Milton wasn't about to put anyone else in harm's way.

Louisa finished her beer and took another from the bag. "Maria says you're a traveller?"

"That's as good a description as any."

"Where do you travel?"

"All over."

"Never feel like putting down roots?"

"Not really interested in that."

Louisa looked over at Maria with pretend mournfulness.

Maria blushed, and Milton decided—again—that he would leave as soon as he could.

Declan changed the subject. "Earlier, outside—you were asking about the Dillons."

Maria was evidently glad that the conversation had gone in another direction. "The owners?"

He nodded.

Milton sat down. "No one seemed to know much about them."

"No one likes to gossip," he said, then grinned. "But I've had a beer, so..." He emphasised his point by finishing his bottle and getting another. "My old man's in the Gardaí. He talks about them all the time. They're bad news."

"How?"

"The way my dad tells it, they used to be legitimate. There are two brothers now—Shay and Colm—who took over the family business when their old man died. He was a bit of a rascal, by all accounts, but an angel compared to them. He told me all kinds of things about them—they're into guns and ammunition, and there was that container full of immigrants from Vietnam that was supposed to be connected to them." He turned to the others. "Remember that?"

"They suffocated," Maria said.

Declan nodded. "What was it? Twenty dead?"

"Twenty-three."

"Jesus," Padraig muttered.

"They found them in the back of the container when the truck was stopped."

Milton's instincts were aroused. "So what's the deal with tomorrow?"

"It's to do with the fight this weekend," Padraig said.

Milton had seen posters about that. "The MMA fight?"

"That's it. Danny Farley—he's their boy."

"Related?"

"No. They sponsor him."

"Is he any good?"

"Very. You know why he got his nickname?"

"I don't even know what his nickname is."

"'Relentless.' He never stops. He comes on at you, again and again, until he knocks you out or gets you to tap."

"Or until someone knocks *him* out," Milton said.

Declan shook his head. "Hasn't happened yet."

"Tomorrow's the weigh-in," Declan said. "My dad says the Dillons are trying to get into the fight game."

The music stopped. Louisa looked to Milton and then gestured over to the laptop. "You choose."

"I doubt you'd like the kind of music I listen to."

"One way to find out."

Milton went over to the laptop and saw that Spotify was open. He went to the search bar, found a Madchester playlist and selected 'Movin' On Up.'

Louisa took a moment to recognise it, then nodded in time with the beat. "See?" she said. "This is a classic."

"Vintage," Padraig said. "Stone Roses?"

"Primal Scream," Milton corrected him.

"Vintage?" Maria said. "What does that mean?"

"Old," Declan offered.

"Not *that* old," Milton said before looking at the album and seeing that it had been released more than thirty years earlier. "Okay. Quite old."

"I like it," Maria said, trying to dig Milton out of his hole.

Milton drank the rest of his lemonade and dropped the cup into the bin.

Maria noticed. "Another?"

"No, thanks. It's late, and I'm tired. It's going to be busy tomorrow"—he checked himself—"sorry, *today*, and I need to get my sleep." He knew he sounded pathetic, but he didn't care. He stood and gave her the warmest smile he could manage. "Thanks for the drink and the invitation."

"You'll come next time?"

"I'd love to," Milton said, knowing that he would have plenty of time to think of an excuse he could stick to before then.

25

Milton rose before his alarm and, after reaching out for his phone, saw that it was just before five. He'd got to sleep as soon as he lay down, but that was only four hours ago; he would have liked a little more, but he knew there was no prospect of getting back to sleep now. It was going to be a busy day, and he was going to have to rely on caffeine to get him through it.

He waited until he was properly awake and then slid out of bed. He washed, splashing his face with cold water, then stretched out his muscles before putting on his shorts and singlet and lacing up the cheap running shoes he had bought when he had arrived in Dublin. He opened the door gently so as not to disturb the other members of staff with rooms on the fourth floor and crept outside, heading for the stairwell.

He climbed down to the ground floor and then stopped and turned, placing his toes on the tread of the second-last step with his heels levered downwards so that he could stretch out his calf muscles. He stood on one leg and brought his right knee up to his chest, pulling it to work his quad, and then repeated it for his left. Satisfied, he turned and walked to the foyer, where the staff were setting up the dining room for breakfast service. Milton's shift wasn't due to start until after the sausages had been fried and the eggs flipped, and he hoped the crew would leave the kitchen in better shape than had been the case yesterday. Milton had heard from others that the early shift was jaded and lacked motivation, not to mention having a slovenly attitude that Milton would not have stood for had he been in charge.

The night duty manager, Marcus, was behind the desk. He saw Milton and made his way over to intercept him.

"You're up early."

"Like to get a run in before procrastination gets the better of me."

"God bless your energy. Pleasant morning for it, all the same."

Milton looked to the front doors and the body scanner. A guard was lounging on a plastic seat that had been placed next to it.

"How long's he been there?"

"All night," Marcus replied. "Not said a word to me."

Milton walked over to the man. "Morning."

He looked up with a sour expression on his face. "What do you want?"

"I'm going for a run. You'll be here when I get back?"

"Maybe."

"I work here," Milton said.

"So?"

Milton took a breath: he wasn't sure if the man was being deliberately obtuse or if he really was this stupid. "I just want to make sure that I don't have any trouble getting back inside."

"You work here," the man said. "Why would you?"

Milton turned away from him, pushed open the doors and walked out into the chill of the morning. He put in his earbuds, shuffled through the playlists on his phone—eventually settling for a compilation of New Wave standards—and pressed play. The percussive beginning to Bauhaus's 'Bela Lugosi's Dead' started up. The ominous bassline kicked in; Milton started the stopwatch on his watch and set off.

The streets were quiet, although that wouldn't last. Milton began easily, allowing his legs to find their own pace and slowly putting heat into his muscles. He wasn't as young as he once was, and although he was still easily fit enough to run ten miles a day, he was determined not to injure himself by pushing the pace too soon.

Milton turned south with Peter Murphy's lugubrious baritone in his ears. He made his way through the affluent areas and headed for the river, a line that divided the city in more ways than one. The south side was affluent: the men and women dressed well, the stores offered trivial fripperies, and the hotels were expensive. The streets were lined with trees, the architecture was often elegant Georgian, and the cars parked up included the most upscale German marques. He crossed the water by way of the Samuel Beckett Bridge, followed the Liffey for ten minutes and then crossed back by way of the Ha'penny Bridge. He started east again until he reached O'Connell Street. It was working class, with a gritty urban vibe. Milton had known that it had a reputation for being more diverse and vibrant, and that had quickly been borne out during his first run. The area was waking up now, with bleary-eyed tradespeople unloading vans for shop refits, traders rolling up shutters and stock deliveries underway.

"T'bacca?"

Milton smiled at the man who had called out to him, both of them enjoying the ironic suggestion. He had seen the same market trader yesterday, and the gnarled Dubliner had said the same thing to him then. His stall was crammed with boxes of what Milton assumed were hooky cigarettes.

"Maybe tomorrow," Milton said.

"Sure you're out of puff anyway!" the man called after him.

Milton took care to place his feet carefully on the slick cobblestones. A horse-drawn cart laden with fruit caught his attention, and he followed it to an open-air market wedged between wider streets where McDonald's and Subway occupied the prime real estate.

A woman was setting up a stall selling shoes. "Howareye, Usain?" she shouted at him.

He only realised now what she meant: she was making a wry joke at his expense, comparing his running to that of the immeasurably faster Jamaican.

"Banana?" another woman cried out from behind her fruit and veg stall. She barely had a tooth in her head yet made herself heard clearly enough. "Great potassium for all yer runnin'!"

Milton quickened his stride to take him onto Parnell Street and farther north to Our Lady's Park. He found an empty bench and took a moment to catch his breath.

He took out his phone and called Ziggy.

"What?" he mumbled.

"Morning to you, too."

"What time is it?" He paused, and Milton could hear the sound of him grumbling. "It's half past seven! I was asleep."

"Think of how much you'll be able to do today now you're awake."

"What do you want?"

"Anything useful yet?"

"I haven't looked."

"But it's working?"

"Course it is. I ran a script, and we've got control of his network. I'll keep an eye on it."

"And you'll let me know what you find?"

"I will. What are you doing?"

"Running. Why?"

"You sound out of breath."

"That's what happens when you exercise."

"You're getting old."

"You're still in bed, Ziggy."

"There's a difference," he said. "I never said I was fit."

"Call me when you find something."

He ended the call, started the music again and continued north along Drumcondra Road to bring him back to the hotel.

26

M ilton hit stop on his watch as he turned into the car park once more, ninety minutes after he had left it. He found a bench and, with his foot wedged against it, lowered his head and bent down to stretch out his hamstring. He switched legs and, as he dipped down to stretch again, saw two large black vans pull up. The side doors rolled back, and Milton watched as six men emerged, three from each. They all had hair cropped short, some wore heavy rings on their fingers, and all wore boots rather than shoes.

Milton shook out his legs as the men made their way into the lobby. He wiped his brow and, rather than move around the back of the building to enter through the staff door, used the main entrance again.

Marcus had come around the desk to attend the men. "Can I help you, lads?"

One of them turned to him. "Security. We're here for the weigh-in."

"I don't have you getting here until later."

"Change of plan. We're here now."

Milton loitered on the other side of the scanner. The man spoke brusquely, without pleasantries, with the air of someone who expected his orders to be followed.

The man gestured to two of his colleagues. "Show these two to the door at the back."

"Why? That's just for staff."

"Just do what you're told, mate."

Marcus looked uncomfortable, but there wasn't much he could do. "I'll need to call my manager."

"No. You take the lads down to the back right now and stop pissing about."

He turned to the others and directed two of them to take up positions behind the scanner.

"Excuse me," Milton said. "I need to come through."

The man who had spoken to Marcus looked over at him. "Who are you?"

"I work in the kitchen. I spoke to the man who was here before I went out."

"You'll have to wait until we're set up."

"How long will that take?"

"The scanner's got a fault. Might be a while."

"Frisk me, then."

"No. You'll have to wait."

Milton took a breath, then walked through the scanner.

The man looked up, his mouth open in surprise or anger. "Did you hear what I said?"

"I did."

"And?"

"And I've got work to do. I'm not waiting outside while you sort yourself out."

The man came across the lobby and squared up to Milton.

"Get out, pal."

"No."

"What?"

"Are you hard of hearing?" Milton said. "*No.* I'm going up to my room, and then I'm going to start work."

"What did you say your name was?"

"I didn't."

"That's Eric," Marcus said. "He works—"

"Piss off," the man said. "I didn't ask you."

"You're not very good at this, are you?" Milton said. "Manners cost nothing, and they'll make your day *much* easier."

The man stood up to his full height. Milton was an inch or two taller, but the man was packed with muscle and was probably forty or fifty pounds heavier.

He stepped up into Milton's face. "What's your problem?"

The man levelled a stare at Milton, but Milton held his eye. There was an awkward moment, but Milton didn't mind that at all.

"You got some balls on you, mate."

"I do. And I'm not your mate."

The man looked over at the others and shook his head in feigned bemusement. His colleagues were watching, but their amusement became something else as they noticed a newcomer waiting outside.

"All right, lads?"

Milton turned and saw the man who had come into the kitchen to thank the staff last night.

"Mr. Dillon, I didn't know you were coming until later," said the first man.

"Couldn't sleep and wanted to check it all out. What's going on?"

"This fella was giving me lip."

Milton stepped to the side and turned back so that he could see Dillon properly.

Dillon cocked his head to the side. "I recognise you, don't I?"

"I work in the kitchen. You came in yesterday after your meal."

"You cooked the duck."

"I did."

Dillon turned to Milton's interlocutor. "What the *fuck*, Tommy? He's a bloody magician. What are you doing messing him about?"

"I didn't know who—"

"It's Eric," Dillon said. "Right?"

Milton nodded.

Dillon stepped closer and laid a hand on Milton's shoulder. "I'm sorry about this. Security is going to be tight today, but it looks like it's a little bit *too* enthusiastic. Tommy—say sorry for messing Eric around."

Milton turned back to the man and struggled to keep the smile from the corners of his lips.

"Sorry," Tommy muttered.

"Didn't catch that."

He said it a little louder: "Sorry."

"Be nice to the staff," Milton said. "They're not paid nearly enough to put up with bullshit from the likes of you."

He could've delivered his message a little more forcefully, but there was no point in making a scene that would just mean things were more difficult for everyone else. Milton held the man's eye for long enough to let him know that he wasn't intimidated, nodded his thanks to Dillon and gave Marcus a wink as he went by. He made his way to the stairs so that he could go up to his room and get changed for his shift.

27

The office of the Garda Síochána Ombudsman Commission was on Upper Abbey Street. It was on the first two floors of a plain modern block, opposite a coffee shop, a kebab house and a bare wall that had been scarred with graffiti and patches of lichen. A track ran outside the building, and Garda Eoin Lynch waited for a tram to rumble by on its way to O'Connell Street before crossing over. He had walked up and down the street for ten minutes as he had tried to marshal his confidence; he'd also watched for anyone who might have recognised him. The last thing he wanted was for a colleague to spot him going inside. The ombudsman was responsible for investigating complaints against the police, and Lynch's presence there could only really be for two reasons: either he was being investigated himself, or he was being asked to grass on someone else.

Neither conclusion would be any good for him.

Lynch thought of the letter in his pocket. The investigators had told him that they were working on an ongoing enquiry and that they were of the opinion that he might have information that would be of help. They had asked him politely to come in for an interview, but Lynch knew that he didn't have a choice in the matter. To refuse would be to encourage the question: why not? What did he have to hide?

The inside of the building was just as bland as the outside: an unmanned reception desk, a line of chairs, posters on the wall detailing initiatives that the ombudsman was involved in. Lynch went up to the desk, there was a button, and he pressed it, hearing the chime of a bell in a room nearby.

A woman emerged. "Morning."

"Good morning."

"You must be Garda Lynch."

"That's right," he said. "I'm here to see—"

"Elizabeth Collins," she said, putting out her hand. "That's me."

Lynch shook it. "I'm a little confused about how I can help. Your letter didn't say much."

"Didn't want it to. Much better to have a chat face to face in cases like these. Can be a bit delicate—I'm sure you can imagine."

"Absolutely."

"Right, then. Shall we get started?"

"Yes," he said. His mouth was dry. "Of course."

"This way, then. We're in the conference room."

Collins took Lynch to a room at the end of a corridor and gestured that he should take a seat at the table. A tray with a pot of coffee, two cups and a plate of biscuits had been left there, and, after asking whether he would like a coffee, she poured out two mugs and then sat down opposite him.

"So," she said, "when do you go on shift?"

"Two."

"Thanks for coming in. I appreciate it."

"It's no problem," he said. "What can I do for you?"

"I'd like to ask you some questions. I'm conducting an investigation at the moment, and I think you might be able to help."

"Not guilty," he said, hiding the flush of nervousness behind a poor attempt at a joke.

"Nothing to do with you," she said, smiling indulgently.

"*That's* a relief."

"It's your partner, actually. Sergeant Mahoney."

Lynch was about to respond but stopped; he felt as if he were about to be asked to make his way across a minefield.

"What I am about to tell you is part of an ongoing investigation," Collins said. "It's sensitive and confidential—I just need to make that clear."

"Of course."

"As far as we know, Mahoney doesn't know that we're looking into him."

"He hasn't said anything to me," Lynch said.

"Good. Things need to stay that way. It's too early to say whether we'll end up bringing a case against him, but, if we do, anything you might say that could tip him off wouldn't be looked upon in a positive light. I know you know that, but I have to say it. Okay?"

"I understand." He shuffled in a seat that suddenly felt uncomfortable. "What is it you're investigating?"

"We've established a board of inquiry in respect of Sergeant Mahoney in light of allegations that he might be in breach of the discipline regulations. In particular, we've received evidence that he has engaged in unethical practices, including the improper termination of penalty points for road traffic offences. We've been told that he's been involved in allowing preferential treatment and favouritism to certain individuals, potentially compromising his own integrity and that of the Gardaí."

"Who told you that?"

She smiled. "You know better than to ask that."

"Sorry—yes, of course."

"So? What do you know?"

He shrugged. "Nothing."

"He's never mentioned anything before?"

"About penalty points? What's the allegation—that he's waiving them?"

She nodded. "That's what we've been told."

"What—once or twice? There could be a reason for that."

"Unfortunately not. We've found more than a hundred instances where points were cancelled from different accounts. All of them emanated from the IP address of the Pearse Street station."

"Different accounts?"

"Most of the logins were through the credentials of retired officers. It's a glitch—the credentials should've been cancelled when they left, but the admin was sloppy, and they weren't. Has he ever mentioned that he knew anything about that?"

"I don't think so," Lynch said.

"You don't *think* so?"

"No. He hasn't."

"What about his attitude?"

"Jaded."

"Do you think that's to do with his demotion?"

Lynch had heard about that from scuttlebutt in the

locker room: Mahoney had been knocked back from inspector after allegations of incompetence at a siege involving a man with mental health problems. It had been Mahoney's responsibility to make critical decisions, including the order to bring in armed police to resolve the crisis. The man had been shot and killed, and Mahoney had been criticised for ignoring reasonable requests that might have made it easier to resolve the situation.

"He doesn't really talk about it," Lynch said.

Collins leaned back and laced her fingers on the table. "Have you seen anything that you think might be relevant to an investigation into Mahoney? Anything at all?"

He paused, trying to give the impression that he was thinking back for any instances that might be helpful. There *were* examples, of course, and plenty of them: free food and drink from restauranteurs and landlords that Mahoney should never have accepted; valuable items he had confiscated from criminals that were reported as 'lost'; an assault that he squashed for no reason other than his friendship with the suspect. There was also the matter of the very nice new apartment that Mahoney had moved into six months ago; he had explained it away as a bequest from a dead aunt, but Lynch had never really believed that. He'd always known that Mahoney had a flexible attitude to discipline, but that didn't mean that he was prepared to grass him up to the ombudsman.

"I'm sorry," he said. "I really can't think of anything."

She nodded. "Not a problem. Thanks again for coming in, and, if you do think of something that you think might be useful, please do let me know." She reached into a pocket and withdrew a business card, laying it on the table. "I know you know, but I have to make it clear: if something comes to light later on that you knew about now and didn't mention, there can be penalties for you, too."

"I do know that," he said, picking up the card and tapping it with his finger. "If I can think of anything, I'll let you know."

"Thank you. Let me show you out."

28

L ow's 'I Could Live in Hope' was playing in his earbuds when Milton woke up from an afternoon nap. He showered and then made himself a strong cup of coffee to prepare himself for the shift ahead. He put on the set of whites that the hotel had provided, slid his feet into the rubber-soled clogs and pushed a packet of cigarettes and his lighter into the hip pocket of his trousers. He finished the coffee and went down to the kitchen.

He pushed open the double doors and stepped inside. It was hot, with the radiant heat from the stoves heavy in the air, and he felt himself start to sweat. The kitchen was already alive with activity; the cooks were busy preparing the food while waiting staff wove in and out, collecting the plates and cutlery that they would need to dress the tables.

Milton was five minutes early, and, as he started to work, the others gradually arrived. Milton looked up as Maria came through the door; she noticed that he was looking at her and raised a hand in shy greeting. Milton gave her a smile and turned his attention back to cleaning the four-burner stove, a task that had not been done to his satisfaction after the breakfast service.

Ernő came in from the restaurant with the hotel manager. Ernő was fine, but the manager—an officious Dubliner called Morrison who had nothing but disdain for his staff—was a different matter altogether.

Ernő clapped his hands together.

"Pay attention," he bellowed, waiting for silence. "We're going to be busy today—*really* busy—and I need you all to be on top of your games. We've got nine hundred people coming this afternoon, and they haven't spared any expense. We need to put out nine hundred plates of *perfect* food. I'm going to be on the pass, and nothing goes into the restaurant unless I'm happy it is the best we can make it. Is that all understood?"

The others responded with a "Yes, chef," that, if reasonably enthusiastic now, would become wearier and more resentful the longer the day went on.

"Today is important," Morrison said, taking over. "This event is for the owners of the hotel. I'm not going to stand for anything other than the best."

"Yes, sir," the staff replied as one.

Morrison stood by the door, arms folded, watching them. Ernő clapped his hands and told them to get back to work. Milton took out the ingredients that he was going to need. He was in charge of the smoked trout croquettes. Ernő had asked him whether he had prepared anything like that before, and he had lied and said that he had; he'd only got the job on the back of an inflated CV, and he knew that a cook with the experience he had claimed would not have had any problems with the dish. He was blagging, but that was fine; he'd found a video on YouTube that had showed the precise steps that he would need to follow, and he started preparing the fish.

It took him an hour, but, when he was done, he was pleased. He carefully positioned the lemon slices and seaweed to give it an attractive garnish and took a moment to check it.

"Looks good."

It was Maria.

"Thanks," Milton said.

"For the fridge?"

"Yes, please."

She picked up the platter and transferred it to one of the big industrial units that would chill it until it was ready to be served.

Morrison was becoming a dreadful irritant. He snarled and barked at the staff for no reason that Milton could discern other than to demonstrate his authority. Milton watched him strut along the lines as he worked on the next items on his list: opening oysters and clams and depositing them on serving platters, rolling smoked salmon and carving Guinness wheaten bread onto tiny timber boards embossed with the hotel's name.

Morrison tore a strip out of Ivan for some perceived error before moving on to glare down at Maria.

"What are they?" he said, pointing at her shoes.

"My trainers?"

"Do you think they're suitable?"

"They're more comfortable during prep. I change them before service."

"You'll have time for a break before service?"

"I..."

He mocked her hesitation. "I... I... I... What? Time for a break? Are you serious?"

Milton put down his knife. "That's enough."

Morrison turned. "What did you say?"

"I said that's enough. Have you worked in a kitchen before?"

"What?"

"Have you ever worked in a kitchen before? Not what you do now—whatever that is—but actually *worked*, on a station."

"Of course I have," he spluttered with an indignation that told Milton—and everyone else who was eavesdropping on the conversation—that he hadn't.

"She's wearing trainers because they're more comfortable when you're on your feet for hours and—"

"I don't care if she's comfortable or not." Morrison spoke over him. "I—"

Milton spoke over *him*. "And because you don't want people slipping on these tiles before service. You'll be down on staff, and the union lawyers would make mincemeat of you when they sue." He shrugged. "Trainers are a much better choice."

"What's your name?" He turned to Ernő. "What's his name?"

"Eric," the Hungarian said.

Morrison turned back. "And what's any of that got to do with you, *Eric*?"

Milton shrugged again, opening an oyster with the tip of his knife. "You've set some ambitious targets for service. If we lose anyone, we won't hit those targets. It'd be a shame if the reason the Dillons complain is that you were throwing your weight around about something irrelevant, all because you were trying to make a point."

Morrison's indignation wasn't faked this time.

He squared up to Milton; Milton held his eye and

watched as his aggression melted away like an ice cube on a sunny day, to be replaced by uncertainty.

"Mind your business," Morrison muttered. He turned away immediately, evidently desperate to draw the exchange to a close.

Maria looked over at him and mouthed her thanks. Morrison shouldered the swing doors open and stormed outside. Milton heard him shouting at some other unfortunate in the restaurant. The chatter in the kitchen resumed. Milton glanced up and saw that Ernő was looking at him with an amused smile. The big Hungarian acknowledged him with a nod and then returned to ensuring that stock levels were sufficient for the rest of the day.

Padraig—the young pot washer who had been at the party in Maria's room last night—idled over. "You've got some balls."

"Not really."

"He'll give you your cards for that."

"I'll get another job."

Padraig chuckled at Milton's insouciance. "Fair play to you, though. He's a tit. As thick as manure but only half as useful."

Milton smiled.

29

The kitchen staff were all on the same contract, and they were all entitled to two fifteen-minute breaks every shift. Milton finished his prep and followed Padraig out to the back. The doors were not normally guarded, but Milton saw that two of the guards from this morning had taken up position and were now insisting that anyone who wanted to go out had to agree to being frisked when they were ready to come back inside. Milton was impressed by their thoroughness and did not demur as he was searched before making his way back to the kitchen.

The waiting staff were taking ice buckets out to the tables, and Milton offered to help. He picked up two buckets and took them into the facility that was being used for the event. The hotel had plenty of capacity for occasions like this: the wing of the building that was used for conferences contained four separate rooms that could all be combined for larger events. The sliding walls had been pushed back today to open up a space of perhaps seven thousand square feet. The tables were arranged around the room so that they all had a clear line of sight to the stage that had been erected at one side of the room. A long desk with eight chairs sat on the stage, high enough so that it was visible to everyone. The stage was flanked by two large screens that would show the proceedings, and a gleaming silver scale had been placed in front of the table. A banner had been fitted to the wall behind the stage with photographs of two men facing each other in an approximation of a fight with the words 'Farley' and 'Gallagher' emblazoned above them. A sentence —'Shay and Colm Dillon Welcome You to the Southside Hotel'—ran along the bottom of the banner.

"Shit," Padraig said. "It's bigger than I expected."

It was a large room, but the stage was substantial, and there wasn't that much distance between it and the nearest tables. Milton suspected that it would feel oppressive once seats had been taken and festivities commenced. It was incongruous, too: there were chandeliers overhead and art on the walls, and the tables had been dressed as if for a high-class dinner. Cage fighting was brutal; there was an obvious dichotomy between thinking about someone being beaten to a bloody pulp and enjoying caviar and champagne. Milton caught himself; was he being unfair? After all, he had been to the Mayfair Sporting Club in London and watched amateurs batter each other for the pleasure of an audience done up in black tie and ballgowns.

Padraig pointed to the banner. "You like that sort of thing?"

"I'm more of a boxing man. Can't say I've ever paid much attention to MMA."

"You've heard of Conor McGregor?"

"Of course."

"You know he's from Dublin?"

"I knew he was Irish."

"Born in Crumlin. Same as me."

Men and women had gathered in the lobby, and as Milton set down the second of the ice buckets, the doors were opened, and they were invited to come inside. There was a seating plan on an easel, and most of the guests found their tables on it before heading across the room to take their seats. Others went to the bar in the north-western corner of the room and ordered their first rounds of drinks.

"I wouldn't mind being out here when they bring the fighters out," Padraig said. "You think Morrison would let us?"

"Not a chance."

"Eric."

Milton turned. It was Maria.

"Thank you."

"What for?"

"For sticking up for me." Milton found that he couldn't look away from her enormous brown eyes. There was no point in trying to deny it: she *was* very attractive. "We have a word to describe men like Morrison," she said. "He is *filho da puta*."

Milton smiled. "I couldn't agree more."

"You speak Portuguese?"

"Enough to know when someone's been called a son of a bitch."

Her smile widened. "It is true. He is." She laid a hand on his arm. "Maybe you would like to watch a film later? I have many films on my laptop."

"Aren't you tired?"

"No—why?"

"The party last night," he said.

"Oh," she said. "It's fine. I slept late this morning. You'll come?"

Again, Milton was reluctant, but like the previous evening, he didn't want to disappoint her. "Let's have a chat after the shift is finished."

30

The heat washed over Milton again as he returned to the kitchen. There was an energy in the air: the more experienced members of staff knew that they would be mainlining adrenaline to get them through the next few hours, and the anticipation of the effort was infectious, taking in the greener chefs and all the others who swarmed around them. The waiting staff moved with a fluid choreography, alert for Ernő to tell them that they could take food through to the other room. There was a noisy symphony: the sizzle of grease in hot pans, knives slicing through vegetables, the bark of orders and instructions. There was chaos here, but it was controlled, and Milton felt a sense of calm despite it. He loved a busy service; for the next few hours he would be able to think of nothing else, and, once they were done, the high would be better than anything he had ever found in the bottom of a glass.

"Let's go," bellowed Ernő.

Milton took out the caviar-topped pizzas from the fridge. The delicate, glistening orbs sat on top of beds of thinly sliced smoked salmon, nestled on the crisp miniature bases. He remembered he hadn't eaten and was tempted to take one for himself, but that would have to wait until later. He picked up a small piping bag filled with crème fraiche and piped out a series of small, uniform dollops. The tangy cream would provide a contrast to the salty caviar and salmon. He added extra sprigs of dill for colour and freshness and then took them to the pass.

Ernő examined them.

"Good. Service!"

Milton went back to his bench and prepared the next pizza and then the next. He delivered each to the pass, where Ernő checked them and called for the waiting staff to get them next door. Milton slipped into the routine, his mind racing ahead of the thing that he was doing so that he was ready for what he needed to do next. He started to sweat, using his dishcloth to wipe his brow and, when that wasn't enough, running the cold tap into his cupped hands and dousing his face.

The doors to the conference room opened, and Morrison came through. His face was red. "I need more help."

Ernő straightened up from the platter he was wiping down. "What's wrong?"

"What's *wrong*? They're animals!"

Milton turned.

"One of them groped Lucia," Morrison said. "Paolo saw what happened and went to make sure she was okay, and he got decked. So now I'm down two—*she's* refusing to go back in there, and *he's* gone to hospital to get his bloody nose fixed."

Milton took off his apron. "I'll help."

Ernő frowned.

"I'm pretty much finished."

Morrison looked at him, no doubt thinking of the way Milton had chided him earlier; there was disdain in his face at first, but when it was obvious that no one else was ready to volunteer, it became resignation. "Fine. Go and see Barbara for your uniform. You'll need to hurry—we're miles behind."

Maria put up a hand. "And me."

"Whatever," Morrison said. "Go with him and get changed. And get a bloody move on."

———————

31

Colm Dillon took his seat and looked around, delighted—again—at what he saw. The hotel's conference space had been transformed for the evening, and although it had been eye-wateringly expensive, it was looking like money well spent. Crystal chandeliers hung overhead, and royal blue curtains, trimmed with gold, fell from ceiling to floor and dressed the expansive windows that flanked the room. They'd found a red carpet for the approach to the front doors, and the guests—once they had passed through the scanner—were greeted by hotel staff with champagne flutes on silver platters.

They'd spent a fortune on buying the hotel and then another fortune on doing it up. He had been resistant to the project, but his brother, Shay, had insisted; his justification was that it was a perfect vehicle to launder money, and, while that was true, Colm knew there was another reason. Their grandfather had opened the hotel in the 1950s, and their father had taken over after him, but he had been forced to sell it when people realised that the Irish economic 'miracle' was built on reckless lending to property developers and homebuyers. The boys had been young when the bank had sent the bailiffs to repossess the property, but they could both remember their father in tears and how it had been the start of a long decline that ended with him putting a gun in his mouth. Buying the hotel was a shrewd financial decision, but it was also an emotional one; it allowed them to right a wrong that had blighted their childhood. And it was a thumb in the eye to everyone who said that they'd never succeed.

Colm looked behind the stage and saw Harry Shillingford, the MC they'd hired for the night. He was on his phone, and when he noticed that Colm was watching, he raised his hand in acknowledgement.

Colm turned his attention back to the table. Frank Rickard, the agent they'd secured for Farley, was laughing at something on his phone. Colm's daughter, Cara, was lost in the game she was playing on her iPad.

"You'll need to put that away soon," he said.

She looked up from the screen, cocked her eyebrow, then looked back down again.

"*Cara.*"

She heard him and, without taking her attention away from whatever game she was playing, nodded. She rarely spoke. Colm and his first wife, Clare, had noticed it when she was little, and how she was so far behind the other children in her playgroup and in their circle of friends. They'd taken her to a doctor, and he had diagnosed her as autistic. Those difficult months had caused friction in their marriage: Clare was religious and had said that Cara had been afflicted as punishment for the crimes of her father. Colm had told Shay what she'd said, and he'd suggested Clare was selective in her condemnation, reminding him that she'd never before complained about her charmed life and how it was all made possible because of what the brothers had achieved.

It hadn't taken Colm long to accept his daughter's condition, and he didn't love her any less because of it; indeed, perhaps he loved her even more. She was a striking young girl with deep, expressive hazel eyes that held an ocean of thoughts. Although she rarely spoke, they didn't find it hard to understand one another. Her silence wasn't an absence of communication but rather a different language, a world of meaning expressed through her thoughtful gaze and occasional smile. Colm had tried hard to empathise with her, and the effort had borne fruit: each of his daughter's actions was rich with intent and painted a picture of her inner world for those patient enough to understand.

Rickard turned to Colm, putting a hand on his shoulder. "Where's your brother at?"

"He can't come. We've had a little bit of business that he needs to take care of."

"Shame. He'll be here for the fight, though?"

"Wouldn't miss it for the world."

Colm smiled, hiding his annoyance that Shay had ducked out. He'd told him that Rickard would expect to see him, but he couldn't be persuaded. They were expecting a shipment, and, thanks to a little concern about increased scrutiny at the dock, Shay had decided he needed to be at the warehouse just in case.

Whatever. Colm wanted a project to get his teeth into, and he quite fancied building a career as a fight promoter. He suspected that his brother's main interest in the fight was because it was a chance to thumb his nose at Billy Gallagher, but Colm had a much longer view of things. Putting Charlie Gallagher on his arse was the last thing Farley needed to do before being welcomed to the big leagues, and, once he was there—and once Colm was there with him—everything else became possible.

Colm leaned over so he could whisper in Cara's ear. "Two minutes and then that needs to go away."

She was busy building towers with flamethrowers and machine guns that cut through an advancing horde of zombies.

"Cara?"

She glanced over at him with a frown and gave him an exasperated nod that he recognised as 'Shut up, Dad. I know.'

32

The uniform room was in the basement of the hotel, sharing space with the laundry and near to the service entrance to make it convenient for staff coming on shift. The hotel staff laundry room exuded a functional and bustling atmosphere. Milton stepped inside and was greeted by the sound of humming machines and the rhythmic tumbling of dryers. The room was lit with bright fluorescent strips, and the air carried a distinct scent: a mixture of fresh detergent, the fragrance of fabric softener, and a hint of cleanliness that mingled with the gentle warmth that came off the machines. The room had sturdy stainless-steel tables and counters laden with piles of clean linens waiting to be folded and stacked. Shelves and racks lined the walls and held supplies: from detergent and fabric softener to bins of fresh towels and bed sheets, all ready to be restocked in the guest rooms above. Barbara—a septuagenarian from Rathmines who had worked at the hotel for more than thirty years—was putting newly laundered staff jackets onto a rail when Milton and then Maria arrived.

"How can I help the two of you?"

"They're short of waiting staff upstairs. We're helping out."

"But you need a change of clothes. Hold on there— shouldn't be a problem."

She sized Milton up with an experienced eye and, after considering him for a moment, went to one of the rails and picked out a black jacket, black trousers and a white shirt and handed them to him. "Try those on."

"Where?"

She shrugged. "We don't have anything fancy like a changing room," she said. "Don't worry. I'm too old for you, and your friend here can look the other way."

Milton caught Maria's eye, but as he paused, she gave him a wink and then turned her back. Milton took off his grubby whites and dropped them in the bin that Barbara used for dirty linen. There was a mirror on the wall that Maria was facing, and, too late, Milton saw that she was looking at him in the glass. She was smiling, and, helpless, Milton couldn't help but smile, too. He put on the trousers and did them up; they were a little loose but would have to do. He reached for the shirt and turned, realising too late that Barbara and Maria could see the tattoo of the winged angel across his shoulders.

"Jaysus," Barbara exclaimed.

Milton tore the plastic sheath from the shirt.

Barbara was still staring. "Where'd you get that?"

"Manila," Milton said. "Long time ago."

"Must've hurt like hell."

"Wouldn't know. I was drunk."

Maria frowned. "But you said—"

"Doing stupid things like that is one of the reasons I decided drinking wasn't for me."

He put the shirt on, buttoned it up and added the black

bow tie that Barbara gave him. He tried on the jacket, and although it was also a little large, when he turned to check his reflection, both Barbara and Maria nodded in satisfaction.

"Shoes," Barbara said, handing Milton a pair of polished black brogues.

Milton replaced his kitchen clogs with the brogues and checked his reflection one final time.

"You'll do," Maria said.

Barbara went to another rail and picked out a waitress's uniform. "Go on then," she said to Milton. "Away with you. Can't have you here when she's getting changed."

"I'm not—"

"Away with you," she said, dismissing his objection with a flick of her tar-stained fingers. "It's all right for the two of us to enjoy a little show, but you're old enough to be her father."

"Older brother," Maria suggested.

"Go on with you," Barbara said, putting her hands on his shoulders and guiding him to the door. "Go and get started. I'll send her upstairs as soon as she's done."

33

Mickey Flannagan checked his watch. It was almost time, and he needed to be on the move. He didn't want anyone to see him leave the kitchen. It wasn't because he was afraid of detection—that was unavoidable, given the number of cameras around the hotel and what he was going to do—but rather because he was on a tight schedule that did not have the elasticity to accommodate the delay if Ernő saw him and asked him where he was going.

He looked over to the pass and saw that the Hungarian's attention was on the food. He reached down to the counter and took a knife—just in case—before leaving through the door at the opposite end of the room.

He would much rather not have been doing what he had agreed to do, but he had no choice. His son was looking at spending the best years of his life in prison thanks to a momentary indiscretion, and Mahoney had promised to make that go away. Flannagan knew that he was agreeing to his own exile, but the promise of a good wedge of cash would allow him to fund six months in Spain. He had a couple of old Republican mates who were involved in smuggling fags, and they'd made him a standing offer to come and get involved whenever he wanted. He loved Dublin, but you couldn't argue that the weather was shitty for most of the year, and at least Malaga would give him the chance to top up his tan.

Flannagan followed the corridor to the public restroom nearest to the conference space. There was a man using one of the urinals, and Flannagan heard the sound of someone snorting a line from the cubicle he had been told he needed to use. He went to the sink and washed his hands.

The man from the urinal came over and took the sink next to him. "Get back to the kitchen, you lazy bastard."

He looked into the mirror to see whether the man was joking; he was drunk, his eyes barely focusing. He glanced down at himself and remembered that he was still wearing his whites.

The man staggered away without another word. The cubicle door opened, and a man and a woman emerged. The woman was much younger than her bronzed companion, wearing a dress that left little to the imagination. She saw that Flannagan was watching her in the mirror, tittered, and then wiped her nose with the edge of her hand. Her companion was considerably the worse for wear, and, arm in arm, the two of them wobbled out of the bathroom and disappeared outside.

Flannagan looked at his watch. He'd built in enough of a buffer to accommodate the odd delay, but now he needed to get going. He went into the cubicle the pair had just vacated and shut the door. He saw a white, powdery residue across the cistern, ignored it and stood on the seat. He reached up, pressed his fingers against the panel until he had raised it, and slid it over to the side. He reached into the cavity, feeling to the left until he found the gun that Mahoney had said would be there.

He looked at it: it was a 9mm pistol. Guns didn't frighten him; he had carried one as a matter of course when he was in Belfast and used it on more than one occasion. He removed the magazine, checked the rounds were loaded correctly, and pushed it back into place. He grasped the slide firmly, pulled it back and then released it, allowing it to move forward under spring tension. He performed a press check to confirm that the round had been correctly chambered, and, seeing the brass nestled in place, gently returned the slide to its forward position. He flipped the safety to the 'off' position and shoved the pistol inside his waistband, feeling the cool polymer frame against the small of his back.

He slid the loose panel back into place and stepped down. He pulled out his shirt and used the tails to hide the gun, then stepped back out of the cubicle.

There was a man waiting outside: the pot washer from the kitchen.

Flannagan couldn't remember his name. "Hello."

"What are you doing?"

Flannagan remembered the lad's name: Padraig. He smiled at him. "What do you mean?"

"Up in the ceiling."

Flannagan feigned confusion. "Sorry?"

"You took something down. I could see over the top of the cubicle."

He was young, probably not even out of his teens. Flannagan was already pushing at the edge of his schedule and couldn't be delayed any longer.

"The panel was loose," Flannagan said. "I thought it was going to fall down."

"Bollocks. You took something down."

Flannagan didn't have time to waste. "I'll show you," he said. "Go stand on the toilet."

Padraig stepped by him, and, as he did, Flannagan reached into his jacket and pulled out the knife he had taken from the kitchen. He stabbed him in the back, between the shoulder blades, then stabbed him again. He slumped forward, and Flannagan shoved him so that he fell into the cubicle, following him inside. He grabbed a fistful of the lad's hair in his left hand, yanked back to expose his throat, and then sliced the blade across and through his larynx. He shoved him so that he was all the way inside the cubicle and then closed the door.

Padraig gurgled horribly as Flannagan checked his reflection in the mirror. There was a splash of blood on his whites, but there was nothing else for it. The guests had been drinking for more than an hour, and most of them were likely on the way to getting pissed. He only had to get close enough to his target to pull the trigger, and he was confident that he would be able to do that without anyone thinking to stop him, blood or no blood. The pistol was invisible beneath the tails of his jacket, and although it was uncomfortable there, he would manage.

He took another moment to adjust it, and, with a nod—and a silent acknowledgement that he was doing the right thing—he turned and made his way to the door.

who had worked on the family business for years: Finnegan McCarthy, Connor O'Sullivan, Rory O'Neill, Brendan Walsh and Eamon Fitzgerald. Billy hadn't told any of them what he had arranged on the basis that the fewer people who knew, the less chance that someone might blab. The Dillons would guess who was responsible, but he didn't care about that. Rickard wasn't part of their crew, so they wouldn't take his capping as a reason to go to war. It wouldn't have mattered if they did, though; the Gallaghers and the Dillons had been in conflict ever since Billy's eldest son had choked to death on his own vomit after using a bad batch of heroin he'd bought from a dealer connected to them. If the brothers wanted to step up to him? He'd be waiting.

"Where's Rickard?" Billy said to Gerry. "Have you seen him?"

"Over there," Gerry said, nodding his head as discreetly as he could.

Billy got up on the pretext of reaching for one of the bottles of champagne and looked in the direction that Gerry had indicated. He saw the American sitting next to Colm Dillon at a table with some of the lads from his crew. There was a young girl there, too, who couldn't have been more than ten years old.

Gerry stood, too. "See him?"

"Yes. Who's the girl?"

"Colm Dillon's daughter."

"Shite."

"Want to call it off?"

Billy wondered whether he should, but his indecision didn't last long. He thought about his own lad and what had happened to him. After the boy's death, Billy had told the brothers to hand the dealer over so he could face justice, and they'd turned him down. They'd shown no compassion to him, so why should he show any to them? It was unfortunate that the girl was there, but it wasn't Billy's fault. What was she doing at an event like this anyway?

"No," he said. "Nothing changes."

35

M ilton climbed the stairs to the ground floor and went into the exhibition space. He noticed immediately that the atmosphere had become raucous. They'd cooked enough food for nine hundred guests, but it appeared that there were more than that. The room was awash with people, most had taken their seats, but there were plenty drifting between the tables. Milton could hear angry denunciations as the staff were chastised for being too slow with the drinks. The atmosphere thrummed with a buzzing note of tension.

Milton saw Morrison and picked a route around the perimeter so he could get to him.

"It's going to kick off," Morrison muttered.

"What do you need?"

He pointed to the bar. "Help with the drinks. They've fallen behind."

Milton went over, waiting for the flustered bartender to finish pouring the last of six pints. There were drinks lined up across the bar: pints, mostly, lager and Guinness, but also bottles of wine and champagne and glasses filled with colourful cocktails that Milton didn't recognise.

Milton signalled to get the bartender's attention. "Morrison sent me over to help."

"Take these," the bartender said, wedging the pint onto a tray with five others. "Table six." He pointed to a copy of the seating plan posted at the side of the bar.

Milton rested the tray on his left hand and turned away from the bar, waiting for a path in the crowd to clear and then walking as quickly as he dared into the conference area. He reached a junction between three tables where a clutch of men had gathered and had to step to the side to get around them; his attention was focused on avoiding them, and, because of that, he didn't notice the man to his left. He turned into him, the man's elbow catching the tray. Milton reached up with his right hand to try to save it, but it was no good; the glasses slid off and fell to the floor. They struck the parquet one after the other, shattering noisily and spilling their contents everywhere.

Milton turned back to the man who had bumped into him. He was looking down at his trousers in disgust. One of the glasses had splashed its contents over his shoe and up past his ankle.

"You clumsy twat."

Milton wanted to tell him that he needed to look where he was going but bit his tongue. "I'm sorry," he said instead.

Maria had seen what had happened and hurried over with a dustpan and brush, kitchen roll, and a black bin bag. She knelt down next to Milton so that she could help him clear away the broken glasses.

"It's so busy," she said quietly.

He knelt down, too. "Busier than it was supposed to be."

"How many do you think?"

"A thousand?"

"Isn't that against the rules? They can only have so many people in here."

"Not our problem. We just need to get through this service. Here—give me that."

Milton took the brush, swept the glass into a pile and then used the dustpan to scoop it into the bin bag. Maria sopped up the liquid with handfuls of kitchen roll. The guests swirled around them, occasionally giving the pair dirty looks and muttering that they were in the way. There were more men than women, Milton noted. The men wore suits, the quality varying from the obviously expensive to shiny fabric that could be had from Top Man for a couple of hundred euros. Some of the younger men had tattoos, and plenty sported physiques that suggested obsessive work in the gym: slim waists and muscles bulging through too-tight shirts and trousers. There were shaven heads and ostentatious jewellery: diamond ear studs, gold necklaces and chunky sovereign rings. The women wore vertiginous heels and short skirts, and Milton, still kneeling as they peacocked around him, studiously kept his eyes down rather than risking a look that might infringe upon what modesty they had left.

He finished and, with Maria, took the bag of debris to the bar. He dumped it in the bin and collected a fresh platter of pints. Maria picked up a bottle of wine, threaded the stems of four wine glasses between her fingers, and followed him back out into the crowd. The lights dimmed, and a man in a dinner jacket came out and climbed onto the stage.

Milton stepped around two older men in his way and saw a young girl, no more than nine or ten, standing beside one of them. The man was tall, and Milton saw that he bore a resemblance to her. The girl stood out because Milton hadn't seen any other children, because she was being ignored by the man and because she looked frightened. Milton paused to allow a third man to approach the man with the girl; the second man dipped his head in an unmistakably deferential fashion before offering his hand.

Milton moved on, reached the guests who had ordered the lager and set the pint glasses on the table.

"About time," one of the men slurred.

The man picked up his pint and, holding it up so the others could see, put it to his lips and made a show of draining it. He slammed the empty glass down on the table, wiped his lips with the back of his hand and stared up at Milton. "Go and get me another one, mate, and don't take so fucking *long* this time."

Milton had no intention of doing any such thing, but rather than tell him to go and get the next round himself, he managed a thin smile and went back to the bar. Maria had just emptied the dishwasher and was loading it with dirty glasses.

She saw him and shook her head. "There aren't enough of us."

"Not nearly. And no one's interested in the food. They just want to get drunk."

"The men are..." She paused. "My English isn't so good. We would say they are *pervertido*."

"What happened? Did they touch you?"

"No," she said. "It is all this." She turned her thumb and fingers into a yapping mouth. "'Do you want to come back to my room,' saying how pretty I am."

"Go back to the kitchen if they give you trouble."

She looked at him with an amused air. "You think this is the first time it happens to me? I've worked in hospitality for years. It happens all the time. And I can look after myself."

Milton felt heat in his cheeks. "I wasn't saying you—"

"I know you weren't. I'm teasing you."

The man on the stage tapped his microphone to make sure it was live.

"Here we go," Milton said, glad for the distraction.

"Ladies and gentlemen," the man announced, "my name is Harry Shillingford, and I'm your MC for tonight. Thank you for being with us for the weigh-in in advance of this weekend's bout between Danny 'Relentless' Farley and Charlie 'the Celtic Prince' Gallagher. I've got one thing to say before we get started." He cleared his throat. "Are you *ready*?" He paused and looked around, a look of theatrical disappointment on his face at the limp response. "Dublin—I said are you *ready*?"

Shillingford was answered this time with a loud, drunken cheer.

"Let's bring out our fighters," he said. "Introducing first, and fighting out of the red corner, he has a record of eighteen wins and just one defeat, with ten wins by knockout. Here is Charlie 'the Celtic Prince' Gallagher."

Music played—U2's 'Better than the Real Thing'—and Gallagher emerged from the door at the rear of the stage. He was lean and powerful, his skull shaven to a reflective sheen.

"And fighting out of the blue corner, with an amateur record of twenty fights and twenty victories, all by knockout... Danny 'Relentless' Farley."

Farley came out to a rap track that Milton didn't recognise, climbed the stairs to the stage and went straight over to where Gallagher was standing. He stepped right up to him and leaned in so close that there were just a handful of inches between them. His muscles were defined and toned, and his eyes, in contrast to Gallagher's, were bright and fierce under a mop of tousled brown hair.

"Charlie," Shillingford said, "we'll get started with you. Please step on the scales."

The crowd roared their approval. Gallagher's black robe billowed as he stepped up, his demeanour stoic. His coach patted his shoulder, whispering last-minute words of encouragement, and the robe was removed. Gallagher stood in tight-fitting black briefs and hopped up onto the scale.

"Let's see the weight," the MC said, bending down to check the scale. "Charlie Gallagher weighs in at eleven stone, two pounds and three ounces."

Gallagher flexed his muscles and winked at the crowd.

"Danny—up you come."

Milton watched as Gallagher stepped down and Farley took his place on the scale. A wave of applause and whistles filled the room. Farley's gaze remained fixed on the scale, his jaw set.

"Danny Farley weighs in at eleven stone, three pounds and five ounces."

Farley stepped down and went over to Gallagher again.

"You won't make it out of the first round," he said, his voice carrying over the open microphone.

Gallagher started to retort, but Farley shoved him in the chest and sent him stumbling back to the edge of the stage. He caught himself and came back at Farley, Shillingford stepping in between them with his hands outstretched to keep them both apart. Men from each fighter's entourage stepped up, too, hands pressed into the chests of the fighters.

"Spicy," Shillingford said, "but I'm not going to let you get it on now."

The crowd booed its disapproval. The corners of Farley's mouth curved into a smirk.

"No, no," Shillingford said. "We're going to save it for the octagon."

A man at the front stood up. "Let them fight!"

Shillingford grinned, aware that any extra edge that could be generated now would make the fight a more compelling prospect when it got underway.

He went over to Farley. "Danny—let's have a word with you first. This is a huge fight for your career. What does it mean to you?"

Farley took the microphone and pointed his free hand at Gallagher. "Harry, when we get in that ring, Charlie's going to come to a harsh realisation—disrespect, when it's aimed towards someone of my calibre and my skill, doesn't come without consequence. I'm going to give that man the beating of his life—Charlie, you're *dead* in the octagon, and I mean it!"

The crowd whooped.

"Danny Farley, ladies and gentlemen," Shillingford said as he crossed the stage to where Gallagher was waiting. "Charlie—you come into this bout on the back of a knockout in your last fight. What do those words mean to you, and what does tomorrow night mean to you?"

"It means nothing," he said. "It's noise. Make sure you get in your seat as soon as the fight starts, because Danny's going to be sat down on his arse the first time he gets to eat my uppercut."

36

Mickey Flannagan made his way into the big room where the weigh-in was taking place. He had looked in earlier, but it had been quiet then, and it was *far* from that now: there was a raucous crowd watching the two fighters as they posed and preened on the stage. No one paid him any attention as he slid around a group of women who had gathered at the door, and then plotted the easiest path to get to the table where Rickard was sitting. He'd already given thought as to how he would get out of the room once he had done what he had agreed to do, concluding that his best chance of escaping would be to use the staff door on the other side of the space. That led down into the basement, where the chairs and tables were stacked up when they were not in use; he'd be able to move quickly down there, using the stairs at the other side to get back onto the ground floor, where he would then be able to use the staff exit to get clear. He knew that the doors were guarded from when he had gone outside for a smoke, but he wasn't concerned about that now. The two men would surely hear the commotion and leave their posts to investigate. It wouldn't really matter if they stayed where they were, though; he'd still have the gun, and he wouldn't have a problem using it again.

The tables were arranged around two intersecting aisles that split the room into a cross; Flannagan reached the junction at the top of the room and turned onto the aisle that led to the stage. It was choked with guests who had stood up to get a better view of the action, and as Danny Farley pushed past the MC so that he could get right into Charlie Gallagher's face, more people stood in the hope that things were going to kick off.

Flannagan reached around to touch his fingers against the butt of the pistol. His thoughts swam amid a welter of sudden panic at his audacity and the odds that he would walk out of the room in one piece, but they were slippery and difficult to grasp and not strong enough to drown out the voice that told him he was doing the right thing, that he was doing this for his boy, that the question of whether he got away or not was irrelevant given the disease inside him that he was powerless to stop.

He set off for the stage.

37

Milton stepped between two tables, trying to negotiate a path through the men who had stood up from their chairs.

"Excuse me. Coming through."

One of the men turned to him, his face twisting into a sneer. "Go another way, you fecking maggot."

Milton stopped and held the man in his cold stare.

"What?" the man said. "You want to go? Go on, then. I'll fucking *burst* you, pal."

Milton felt the buzz of adrenaline that heralded violence but knew he didn't have the luxury of teaching the man his manners. He was in a room full of drunken locals, and they wouldn't take it kindly if a member of staff put one of their number on his back. Milton would end up getting his face put in and—more importantly—would probably end up arrested and processed. The Group had found him that way once before, and he had no desire to make it any easier for them to track him down now.

"Sorry," he said.

"Too fucking right you are. Now—piss off."

Milton reversed course and plotted another route back to the bar. He was halfway there when he saw a commotion at the main doors. A man in a red-speckled white shirt had just pushed himself between a man and a woman, and a drink had been spilt.

"Why are you just standing there?"

Milton turned: it was Morrison.

"There are drinks on the bar lined up three deep. Go and bloody deliver them."

Milton ignored him and watched the man as he continued towards the stage.

"What are you looking at?" Morrison said.

The man stopped and turned, and Milton got a glimpse of his face: it was one of the sous-chefs from the kitchen, a man who had always kept himself to himself and whose name Milton couldn't remember.

Milton pointed. "Who's that?"

Morrison looked and frowned. "Flannagan. He's not supposed to be in here."

"You didn't ask him to help out?"

"Looking like *that*? Of course I didn't."

Morrison turned away and, his face turning puce with anger, went to intercept Flannagan. He had a clearer path to the stage than Flannagan did and was able to cut him off just before he reached the VIP tables that were closest to the front. He blocked Flannagan's way and bawled at him, stabbing a finger into his chest to emphasise his point. Flannagan, who was half a head taller, looked down at him, but whatever it was that Morrison had told him to do, he didn't do it. The crowd parted, and Milton got a better view of the two of them: there was something in Flannagan's face—pinched, nervous tension—that Milton had seen before. He started toward the two of them, bumped against a woman and continued on, ignoring her complaint.

Morrison prodded Flannagan in the chest again, then grabbed his shoulder and tried to turn him. Flannagan shook his hand away, drew back his fist and punched him in the face. They were in a busy part of the room, and the guests reacted with exuberant hollers; the atmosphere had been wound tight all night, and it was obvious that something like this would happen. They might have been cheated when Gallagher and Farley's stage-managed confrontation had been thwarted, but perhaps this would do instead.

Morrison reached up to touch his bloodied nose.

Milton shouldered a man out of his way.

Flannagan reached around his body and grasped the butt of a pistol that he had hidden in the waistband of his trousers.

And Milton started to run.

38

Flannagan recognised Rickard from the picture that the policeman had shown him. He was sitting at a table of six, with Colm Dillon to his immediate left and four other men—none of whom Flannagan recognised —leaning in as the two men shared a conversation. The final seat at the table was taken by a young girl, she couldn't have been older than nine or ten, and she was engrossed in the tablet that was propped up in front of her.

Too late to stop now.

Flannagan raised the gun and aimed.

The girl looked up from her screen and saw him. She stared at him, her expression changing from confusion to realisation and then fear.

Flannagan blinked the sweat from his eyes.

Colm Dillon looked over at his daughter and then turned, following her gaze.

"*Gun!*"

Flannagan pulled the trigger.

Nothing happened.

Misfire.

The men at the table rose as one.

The girl froze.

Flannagan pulled the trigger again.

Nothing.

Misfire.

Dillon knocked over his chair as he spun around. He took a step to put himself between the gun and the girl.

Someone called Flannagan's name. He ignored it, stepped back, looked down at the gun, looked up again and saw Dillon coming right for him, aimed and pulled the trigger for a third time.

Flannagan heard the boom, always louder than he expected, and felt the jerk and the way the recoil ran up his arm all the way to his shoulder and his neck.

39

Milton darted left and then right, opening up a clear line of sight to the table Flannagan was heading toward: there were five men, none of whom Milton recognised, and a girl. The men were laughing and joking; the girl was watching something on an iPad.

Milton cursed as he saw Flannagan pull a gun. He sprinted, shouldering bystanders out of the way as he tried to close the distance to the table.

He was too far away.

Flannagan aimed down at a man sitting at the table, but the gun didn't fire. He looked at the gun, confused, then aimed it again.

"Flannagan!"

People turned at the sound of Milton's voice.

A man who had been sitting at the table rose and lumbered down the aisle towards Flannagan.

The pistol fired.

People screamed.

The bullet struck the man in the chest. He fell.

More screams, louder this time—panicked—and people started to move. Guests got up from their tables and scattered, crashing into one another, funnelling into the aisles as they tried to get away. Some of them clambered across the tables; there was a loud clatter of chairs overturning. Milton lost sight of Flannagan in the sudden scrum, stepped to the side and saw him again.

Flannagan raised the pistol again and fired a second shot.

The noise was deafening: the crack of the gunshot, hysterical screams, a heavy thud as a table was upended.

Milton ran faster. Two women staggered into his way; he barrelled through them, scattering them like ninepins.

Three men came at him, running for the exit, and Milton swerved left.

Flannagan was suddenly directly ahead. Milton lowered his shoulder and crashed into him with all his weight, toppling him over and sending them both to the floor. Flannagan tried to bring his pistol to bear, but Milton anticipated it; he reached up with his right hand and closed it around Flannagan's wrist, pressing it against the wooden floor as he struggled to get his legs on either side of his torso. Milton punched down with his left hand, but Flannagan jerked his head to the side, and Milton's knuckles scraped across his ear and struck the floor.

Flannagan was desperate. Milton tried again to get on top of him, saw that it would be too difficult and bent his left arm, driving his elbow down into Flannagan's face. His first attempt produced a glancing blow, but the second found its mark, and the point of his elbow crunched into Flannagan's mouth, pressing his upper lip into his teeth. Flannagan spat blood, then struggled even harder. He grunted with effort as he brought the gun up. He pulled the trigger, and a shot *thwipped* by Milton's cheek. The noise in the room faded out, and all he could hear was a high-pitched whine; the discharge was close to his ear, and it had deafened him. He felt the sting of the power burn on his cheek.

Flannagan grunted with effort and struggled to move his arm, and the gun, so he could fire into Milton's chest, but Milton had leverage and more strength; he pushed Flannagan's wrist back, forcing it as hard as he could to keep the muzzle pointing away from him. Milton looked down into the man's face and saw his expression change; the anger had become desperation and now resignation.

The man swiftly rotated his wrist, pushed the muzzle of the gun straight down onto his breast and pulled the trigger.

The strength went out of his body, and his arm fell to the side.

Milton disarmed him and tossed the weapon aside.

He stood now, carefully, and exhaled, the adrenaline buzzing, then assessed the situation. The lights over the stage were still flashing, strobes flickering on and off and lasers cutting red and green beams through clouds of dry ice. The guests were stampeding now, diverting to the fire exits on the other side of the room. Curtains had been ripped from the tall windows; one man managed to force the lock on one of them so that the window could be opened and used as a way out.

Milton looked to the left. A man was on the floor, blood already pooling on the parquet and his foot twitching. He saw the body of a second man slumped across the table with his arm hanging loose. Milton's eye was drawn down, beneath that table, to where a terrified face stared back at him.

The girl with the iPad.

She had reached for the foot of the man on the floor and was pulling at his shoe, as if trying to wake him. The man's leg had stopped jerking now; Milton knew death when he saw it.

The room was in chaos, and Milton swung his head left and right, looking for patterns in the sea of movement. He had no way of knowing whether Flannagan was the only shooter, or whether there might be others.

His gaze fell back on the girl under the table. He couldn't leave her here alone.

"Hello," he said, crouching down.

Her face was wet with tears.

"I'm going to make sure you're nice and safe." She looked up at him, her eyes brimming, and pointed at the man's body. "We're going to have to leave him there until the police come. The most important thing is to make sure nothing happens to you. I'll look after you—I promise. Is that all right?"

She looked at the man's motionless body and then back to Milton and nodded.

"Good girl. What's your name?"

She didn't reply.

"Tell me later. I'm going to pick you up, and then we're going to go somewhere safe. Can you put your arms around my neck?"

She nodded, and when Milton shuffled around, leaning toward her, she did as he asked.

"That's good. Now—close your eyes. We're going to move nice and fast. Are you ready?"

He put his left arm around her waist and took a breath.

He readied himself, counting down—three, two, one— and then stood, hoisting the girl and clutching her tight. She

meant that Flannagan ought to have been in place. Mahoney knew the plan was decent, but that if there was a weak link, then Flannagan was it. It ought to have been easy —get the gun, shoot the target, get out—but he was worried that something would go wrong.

Lynch returned with two paper bags and two cups.

"Here," he said, handing Mahoney one of the paper bags and setting the cups in the centre console drink-holders.

"Thanks."

Mahoney reached into the bag and took out the carton with the burger. He balanced that on the dash and started with his fries.

The radio squelched with an incoming message. "Control to all units, we have reports of an ongoing firearms incident at the Southside Hotel. Please respond immediately and proceed with caution. Armed backup and medical assistance are on the way. Over."

"Shit," Lynch said.

"Did she say firearms?"

"That's what I heard."

"So much for dinner."

Mahoney took a final mouthful of fries, then dumped the carton and the untouched burger back into the paper bag and dropped it onto the centre console. He started the engine, flicked the switch to turn on the lights and the siren, and set out.

41

Milton followed the stairs down to the basement. He went to the laundry room, where he had collected his uniform, and saw that Maria and a handful of the other staff from the kitchen had taken shelter. They were all frightened, speaking in tense whispers and looking up at the sound of Milton's approach with fearful eyes.

Ernő was there. "Is it still going on?"

"I don't know," Milton said. "Has anyone called the police?"

"I did."

Maria caught his eye, and he carried the girl over to her.

"What happened?" she said.

"I'm not sure."

She nodded to the girl; her arms were still wrapped around Milton's neck. "Who is she?"

"I think she's the daughter of..." He let the sentence drift rather than finish it in front of the girl, and Maria nodded that she understood. "We need to get her out of the way."

"Why? You don't think we're safe?"

"I don't know whether the shooter was on his own or whether there were others. It'll be safer upstairs."

"We can go to my room," she said.

"Would you be able to look after her until I'm sure it's over?"

"Of course."

Milton knelt down, gently lowering the girl until her feet were on the floor. "We're going to go upstairs," he told her. "And then my friend Maria is going to look after you for a few minutes. Is that okay?"

The girl blinked back tears, swallowed and gave a little nod.

Maria knelt down next to Milton and smiled at the girl. "That's good. What's your name?"

The girl pressed her lips together and wouldn't answer.

"She wouldn't tell me, either," Milton said.

Maria rose and offered the girl her hand. "There's a lift over here. It'll take us straight up to my room."

Milton told the others that if they had a room in the hotel, they should go to it, and if they didn't, they should stay here and lock the door and only open it to the police. Once he was happy that they understood, he led the way along the corridor to the elevator, checking left and right as they went. He pressed the button to summon the car, and they waited for it to descend. Milton was still on edge and made sure that he was standing in front of Maria and the girl as they waited. The bell chimed, and the doors parted; Milton was relieved to find the car was empty. He stepped to the side, put his arm out to hold the door and waited for Maria to lead the girl inside. Two others followed, leaving just enough space for him. He pressed the button for the fourth floor and stood between them and the door as the engine whirred and the car carried them up.

The staff corridor was quiet, although Milton could hear the sound of hushed conversation as he passed the room next to his. He went to the end of the corridor and waited as Maria took out her key card to unlock her door. She went in first, with the girl still holding her hand. Milton followed them in and gave the room a quick once-over to ensure that everything was as it should be.

"I'm going to go back downstairs," he said.

"Why?"

"To see if it's safe. Do you have your phone?"

She reached into her pocket and took out an old iPhone.

"I'll call you when I know it's okay to bring her down. What's your number?"

She recited it; Milton tapped it into his own phone and then called her so that she had his.

"I won't be long."

He left them and diverted to his own room. He took out his phone again and called Ziggy.

"Evening," he said.

Milton went to the window and looked down into the yard below. "You can still monitor police radio?"

"Of course. Why?"

"There's been a shooting at the hotel where I'm working."

"A shooting?" He stopped, and Milton could almost hear his mind working. "What did you do?"

"Nothing to do with me."

He sounded doubtful. "Really?"

"I was there, and I got to the shooter, but not before he shot two men. They're both dead. That's why I'm calling—I need to know what the police are saying."

"I think I've still got a receiver card in my bag," he said. "I'll need to fit it. Do you want anything in particular?"

"There was a young girl nearby when it happened. I've taken her out of the way until I can be sure it's safe. It'd help to know what they're saying now."

"Stand by."

Milton, still holding his phone, opened the door, went into the corridor and made his way to the stairs. There was a window that looked down onto the front of the hotel, and he could see the blue strobe from the lights on top of two patrol cars.

"You there?" Ziggy asked a couple of minutes later.

"I'm here."

"It's all they're talking about. You'll have half a dozen cars with you soon."

Milton looked outside as another patrol car pulled up. "They're already here. What are they saying?"

"They're confused. One just said they've got the scene under control, and another said he wasn't sure. Oh—stand by." He paused. "That was the dispatcher. They're searching the hotel, but they think it's over. They're saying there was a single shooter and that he's been taken out."

"Dead?"

"No—he's being taken to hospital now."

"Thanks." Milton started down the stairs.

"Need anything else?"

Milton thought. "Monitor it. The shooter was a man named Flannagan, but the names of the victims would be useful. And anything else that'll tell me what happened."

"Leave it to me."

42

M ilton reached the door to the public areas and paused, hearing voices—hushed and tense—but nothing else. He opened the door and then breathed out in relief; Ziggy's report of the police conversations had been accurate, and the immediate danger seemed to have passed.

The curtains in the conference room had been torn down, and Milton could see the blue lights from the waiting cars pulsing against the trees on the other side of the road. Four officers—three men and a woman—had secured the exterior, marking off the perimeter with crime scene tape and ushering bystanders to a safe distance. They moved with a sense of urgency, obviously aware of the potential for further danger and the importance of preserving evidence.

Morrison and two of the waiting staff were standing near the door to the kitchens. All three of them were in tears.

"What is it?" Milton said.

Morrison wiped his face. "Padraig."

Milton felt his stomach drop. "What happened?"

"They found him in the bathroom. Stabbed."

"Which bathroom?"

"Near the lobby. The police just found him. He'd been left in the cubicle with the door shut. He'd been stabbed, and his throat was cut. I... I don't know..."

He didn't finish the sentence. All of Morrison's self-important bluster was gone, and now he looked just like all the rest of them: white-faced with shock and fright.

Milton's fists clenched. He knew he ought to run—he ought to leave the girl with Maria, leave the hotel and put as much distance between himself and Dublin as possible—but he couldn't. He couldn't abandon the girl, and he wasn't prepared to let Padraig's death go without consequence. He hadn't been much more than a boy, and his life—all the experiences he might have had, the things he might have done—had been taken away from him.

Milton was exceptional at staying hidden, with just one weakness: his conscience. His recovery depended upon him making amends and, since those to whom he most needed to apologise were generally dead, he had his own version of the Steps whereby he made amends through bringing justice and helping others. It was the best way he had found to stay away from the pity and self-disgust that would lead him back to the bottle.

He tried to get an understanding of what might have happened. It was obvious that the organisers of the event—the Dillons—had been nervous: the security had at least *looked* thorough, with the scanner and the guards at the front door. They must have contemplated the possibility of something happening, but, however cautious they had been, it hadn't been enough.

Flannagan had been able to get around it.

But Flannagan? Why had he done it? Milton realised he knew next to nothing and would need to learn more.

Milton saw a uniformed officer and went over to him.

The man turned. "Evening, sir."

Milton looked at the badge on his lapel: LYNCH. His hair was dark brown, cut short and tousled and slightly messy. Expressive eyebrows arched over deep-set, hazel eyes. He had a strong jawline accentuated by a hint of stubble.

"Can I talk to you for a moment?" Milton said.

"What is it, sir?"

"I saw what happened. I was very close."

The officer paused. "Do you work here?"

"Yes. Usually in the kitchen."

"Usually?"

"I was helping at the bar."

"So you saw what happened?"

"A man called Flannagan went up to two of the guests to shoot them."

"And you saw all this?"

"I got to Flannagan just after he shot one of the men."

"How do you know his name?"

"He worked in the kitchen."

"You got to him—what does that mean?"

"We..." Milton paused, preferring to underplay his involvement, but knowing that was impossible. "I managed to get him to the floor. We were wrestling for his gun, and it went off." He pointed to his chest. "Here."

"He's on his way to the hospital." Lynch took out a notebook, flipped it open and started to write. "I'm definitely going to need you to give us a statement. What's your name?"

"Eric Blair."

"And where do you live?"

"At the hotel," Milton said. "Staff quarters."

"Where's that?"

Milton pointed upwards. "Fourth floor."

"Best if you go up to your room and stay there until we've got things under control. I'll come up and see you as soon as I can."

"There's something else. One of the men who was shot was with a young girl. I don't know for sure, but I think she might be his daughter. I took her out of the way after... after he was shot."

"Where is she now?"

"Upstairs. Would you be able to get someone to look after her?"

"Bring her down, and I'll make sure she's taken back to her folks."

43

The guests had been shepherded away from the hotel to the car park, and they were being asked to provide their details before being allowed to leave. Billy had been funnelled into the crowd, and now he was doing his best to be patient while the line slowly edged forward.

Gerry Kelly was alongside. "What do you want to do now?"

"Get home," he said. "We need to speak to the lads."

"I'll sort it out."

"*Everyone*," Billy said. "No exceptions. It's going to get messy."

They shuffled forward again; they were now just one from the front.

"Look," Kelly said, gesturing discreetly to the right.

A line of metal bollards demarked the boundary between the car park and Seven Oaks Road. A police car had parked there, and, as Billy looked, he saw Michael Mahoney inside. He gave a whistle, and, as Mahoney looked up, he made eye contact and indicated that he wanted to speak. Mahoney looked petrified; that was reasonable, given what had just happened.

The officer took the name of the man ahead of them, dismissed him and then beckoned Billy forward.

"Name?"

"Billy Gallagher."

The officer looked up from his notebook; there was recognition and trepidation on his face. "Don't need your address, do we?"

"I shouldn't think so."

"What about your man there?"

Kelly gave his name and address, and the officer added the details to his list.

"You two wouldn't have had anything to do with what happened tonight, would you?"

"Of course not," Billy said. "That was my lad onstage."

The officer bit his lip, then shook his head with rueful amusement. "Fine. Whatever. Don't be going anywhere for the next few days, will you? I've got a feeling the detectives will be wanting to have a word."

"They know where to find me." Billy stared at the man. "Are we good to go?"

"You are," he said. "On your way."

They walked on. Billy glanced over to the left and saw that Mahoney had got out of his vehicle and was making his way toward them.

Kelly noticed, too. "You sure this is a good idea?"

"I need to speak to him," said Billy.

"Here, though? There are police everywhere."

"Come on, now, Gerry. It's not going to be surprising to anyone if they see a policeman speaking to me, is it? Go and wait in the car. I won't be long."

Kelly walked on. Billy slowed down so Mahoney could catch him up.

Billy glanced back to make sure they were not attracting undue attention, and then lowered his voice to a hiss. "What the fuck happened?"

"Not now, Billy."

"Not now? Your monkey just shot Colm Dillon."

"*My* monkey?"

"The Dillons will know it was me. They'll know, and then fuck knows what happens next."

"I can't be seen talking to you."

"We're nearly finished. Shay Dillon and his mad mother and the rest of his mad family are going to come after us, and it's your fault."

"Billy—"

"Don't 'Billy' me. I'm not stupid—I always knew there was going to be a war, but it needed to be on my schedule, not theirs. Find a way to buy me the time to get ready. It's on you. You break it, *you* pay for it."

The blood ran out of Mahoney's face. "I'll try."

"Call me when you've got good news."

Billy walked off without a second look. He went to the Rolls-Royce and slid into the back seat. Kelly was up front, his phone pressed to his ear. He finished his call and dropped the phone in the cupholder.

"Everything okay?"

"Fine," Billy said. "Who was that?"

"Albert. He's calling around."

Albert was one of the lads. "Good," Billy said. "Set up a meet. We've got a lot to talk about."

44

Milton took the staff elevator back up to the fourth floor. He went to Maria's room and knocked.

"It's me," he said.

He heard the rattle as the door chain was removed.

The door swung open, and Maria looked out. "What's happening?"

"The police are downstairs. It's safe now."

She stepped aside so that Milton could come in. The girl was sitting on Maria's bed with her legs crossed.

"How is she?"

"She won't speak."

Milton lowered his voice. "I'm not surprised. She's just seen..." He stopped. "Never mind. She'll be in shock."

"There is one thing," Maria said. "I know her name."

"How?"

"There's a name tag sewn into the collar of her coat. I saw it when I brought her up here. Her name is Cara."

"That's a start."

She bit her lip anxiously. "But what do we do now?"

"The police want to speak to me. They'll want to speak to you, too."

She looked unhappy. "Really?"

"You saw what happened," he said. "We both did. We'll need to give them a statement."

She winced with discomfort. "I'd rather not."

"Why?"

She bit her lip again and looked away.

Milton guessed at the reason for her reluctance. "Are you here illegally?"

She nodded. "If I tell them, they could send me back to Brazil."

Milton frowned. "I wonder if there's a way we could avoid that."

"How?"

"They'll only want a statement if you tell them you saw what happened."

"What do I tell them?"

"You didn't see anything."

"I was in another room?"

"No," Milton said. "There's a camera above the bar, so the footage will show that you were there. We don't want them to find out that you're lying. Just tell them you didn't see anything—that'll be enough. It's not like there'll be a shortage of witnesses. They'll have hundreds to work through, and they won't give you a second look. This is a murder enquiry now—a triple murder. They won't be interested in looking at whether you should or shouldn't be here."

"A triple murder?"

Milton realised: he hadn't told her. "Padraig."

Her mouth fell open. "*No.*"

He lowered his voice. "He was stabbed. I'm guessing he disturbed Flannagan."

She blinked back tears. "He was... he was..."

"He was young," Milton finished, "and a nice guy."

Her voice caught in her throat. "It's not fair."

Life rarely is. "I know. But the police have a lot to go on. They'll find out what happened."

"What about Flannagan? He is dead?"

"No," Milton said. "He'll be in the hospital now. But that's good—he'll be punished for what he did, but the police will be able to question him to see if anyone else was involved."

"Jail? That's not punishment. He should be dead after what he did."

Milton didn't disagree, but let it go. "So—what are you going to say?"

"I didn't see anything."

"Good. And there's no need for you to come downstairs now. I can take the girl. If anyone asks, you're too scared to come out of your room."

She nodded.

"You've got my number if you need me, but I don't think you will." He went over and sat down on the bed next to the girl. "I'm going to take you downstairs again, Cara. The police are there, and they'll be able to look after you. They'll be able to get you back home. Is that okay?"

She looked to Maria with wide, fearful eyes.

"I'm going to stay here," Maria told her. "You'll be fine. Back home with your family in no time."

She nodded.

Maria went over to her, knelt down and wrapped her in a hug. "You're a very brave girl."

Milton waited until Maria disengaged herself. "Come on, then. Let's get going."

Milton led the way out of the room and waited for Cara to join him.

"Eric?"

He turned back. Maria was in the doorway. "Yes?"

"Come back and see me when you can?"

"I will."

He turned and, as he set off, felt the coolness of Cara's slender fingers as they slid into his hand.

45

ilton kept hold of the girl's hand as they descended in the lift; the numbers ticked down from three to two, and she squeezed a little harder. They reached the ground floor, and the doors parted. The girl didn't move.

Milton crouched down in front of her. "It's all right. I'm not going to leave you until the police have got you home again."

All the blood ran from her face, and she looked deathly pale.

Milton had no experience with kids. He wasn't paternal —never had been, not really—and he found it difficult to know what to say. "I expect you want to see your family?"

She gave a little dip of her head.

"Right, then. They'll pop you in a car and take you home."

She swallowed but nodded again and allowed Milton to lead her out of the elevator. Milton had no interest in taking her into the main room, where she might be able to see the body of the man he assumed was her father. Instead, he took her to the corridor where he had spoken to the officer and saw that he was still there. He was with a second officer, and the two of them made their way over to him.

"Mr. Blair," Lynch said, "this is my partner, Detective Sergeant Mahoney."

"Evening, sir," Mahoney said.

Milton looked at him a little longer and realised: he'd seen him before.

"I told him what you said to me," Lynch said. "This is the girl you mentioned?"

"That's right," Milton said, his eyes lingering on Mahoney as he tried to place him.

"What's her name?"

"Cara. She's not speaking, though—I think she's in shock."

"To be expected."

"What happens next?"

"DS Mahoney will take her back to the station and find out how to get her home, and then you and I can have a chat about your statement."

Cara tugged on Milton's hand. He looked down at her. Her wide, almond-shaped eyes seemed to double in size, and her lips quivered. What little colour had been left in her cheeks now drained away, leaving a ghostly pallor that made her look more vulnerable than ever.

"What is it?" Milton asked her.

She shook her head.

"I don't understand."

She tugged her hand away from Milton's and backed away.

Milton followed. "What is it?" he said quietly.

She nodded in the direction of the two officers. Her body language echoed the distress on her face. She clutched her hands tightly together, knuckles white with the force of her grip, and her shoulders hunched inward, as if she were trying to make herself even smaller.

"You know him?"

She nodded.

"The first one?"

She shook her head.

"The second one?"

She nodded.

She held her breath as she tried to maintain her composure, but failed; her lip quivered, her face crumpled, and her eyes filled with tears. Milton crouched down in front of her and was about to reach out a hand to stroke her arm when her eyes went even wider still.

"Come on then, darling," a voice said from behind them. "Let's get you home."

Milton stood and turned and saw that Mahoney was approaching, with Lynch behind.

Milton blocked his way. "You might need to give her a moment."

"I haven't got time for that."

"She's frightened."

"Course she is. Who wouldn't be after what happened to her? She doesn't need to be frightened now, though. We'll get her home."

"Could you find a female officer?"

Mahoney masked his irritation with a chuckle, but it was obvious. "Don't be so daft."

He approached Milton and tried to step around him.

Milton mirrored his movement, keeping Cara behind him.

"Find someone else. She's scared."

"Come on, Mr. Blair. Let me have a chat to her."

Mahoney stepped in the other direction, and Milton matched him again. It was only now that Mahoney was annoyed and his mask of avuncularity had slipped that Milton realised where he had seen him before: in the bathroom yesterday, coming out of the cubicle.

"Get out of the way, sir."

He put a hand out and grabbed Milton's shoulder. Milton's reaction was automatic and instinctive: he brought his right arm up and around in a clockwise circle, using the side of his forearm to knock into Mahoney's wrist. He pushed out with his left hand at the same time, the heel of his palm striking the policeman in the sternum and sending him stumbling back.

"Don't touch me," Milton warned.

Lynch had been watching, but now he came closer, too.

Mahoney reached for the can of CS gas holstered on his belt. "Step aside."

Milton wasn't prepared to do that, but, before he could say anything else, he saw frustration flash across Mahoney's face. Milton glanced back; Cara was running away down the corridor and back to the staff elevator.

Mahoney dodged around Milton and set off after her.

"Wait here, sir," Lynch said.

Milton didn't. He followed.

Cara reached the lift and pressed a finger against the button to call it, but Mahoney reached her before the car could arrive. He grabbed her upper arm and yanked, then wrapped an arm around her chest and hauled her back. The girl screamed and struggled, but Mahoney was much too strong for her and hoisted her up until her feet dangled off the floor.

Milton acted without thinking: his fists were already clenched, and he threw a straight right that caught

Mahoney on the side of the head. His legs buckled, and he bounced against the wall, the sudden impact causing the CS cannister—with the retaining strap already undone—to fall out of the holster and onto the ground.

Lynch grabbed Milton by the shoulder and hauled him backwards. Milton lost his balance, stumbled, then threw out another punch. Lynch took it on the chin, thudded into the wall and slid down onto his backside.

Milton swung back around just as Mahoney hit him; it was a stiff blow, and it landed against the side of his head. Milton saw stars, blinked them away, and felt Mahoney's hands on his shoulders. He came in close enough for Milton to smell the alcohol on his breath and see the beads of sweat on his brow. Milton butted him, his forehead crunching into the policeman's nose, the cartilage crumpling from the impact. Mahoney's grip on Milton's shoulders loosened, and Milton shrugged him off, elbowing him just above his right ear and putting him on the ground.

Milton heard movement from behind him and felt arms around his waist, dragging him down. Lynch was stronger than he looked, and he managed to twist Milton onto his back and sit on top of him, getting one knee up high enough to pin Milton's left arm to the ground. Milton reached out with his right hand, collected the gas cannister, then sprayed Lynch full in the face. It splashed over him, his face contorted, and his eyes started to stream.

Milton threw him off and got back to his feet.

Cara had backed away from the three of them. There was a mechanical clunk as the lift door opened and then closed again without her being able to embark. Milton went to her and, seeing the look of fear on her face as she continued to eye Mahoney, scooped her up again and jogged down the corridor. She must have been even more scared now than she had been before, but reassurance would have to wait.

As he moved, Milton joined the dots that connected Mahoney to whatever had happened; Flannagan must have got his weapon from somewhere, and, if Mahoney had been responsible for organising what was obviously a hit in a venue where security would be an issue, he would've hidden a weapon somewhere it could be easily reached.

Somewhere like a ceiling cavity in the bathroom.

And with Mahoney's suspicious behaviour last night, and his obvious interest in getting to the girl now, Milton couldn't avoid the conclusion that he was up to his ears in what had happened.

Milton couldn't trust him, and he couldn't trust the police.

The girl was in danger. He was going to have to get her somewhere safe while he worked out the angles that had put him, once again, in the middle of a situation he hadn't wanted, but couldn't avoid.

46

Mahoney was still dazed. The man had taken him by surprise and had butted him hard enough to make his head spin. His legs felt weak, and it was all he could manage to shove himself across the hall so that his back was pushed up against the wall. He looked down and saw blood over his uniform, and when he touched his fingers to his nostrils, they came back sopping red.

He closed his eyes. The man had been familiar. He had seen him before; but where?

He took a moment to gather himself and then, with one arm down by his side, levered himself back to his feet. The effort was dizzying, and he was only just able to stumble over to a chair and sit down.

"Jesus."

Mahoney blinked until his eyes came back into focus. It was Lynch. His eyes were streaming, and his nose was running. His skin prickled with a rash that started around his eyes and went all the way down to his neck.

"You okay?" Lynch said hoarsely.

Mahoney touched his nose again. "Fucker broke it." He pointed to Lynch's face. "You?"

"He got your CS," he said, trying to blink the residue out of his eyes. "Sprayed me with it. Who *was* he? He wasn't like that when I first spoke to him."

Mahoney groaned and tried to stand. The dizziness increased, and he slid back down again. He remembered where he had seen the man: he'd been in the bathroom after he'd left the pistol. He'd heard him throw up, and Mahoney had had a go at him.

Shit.

Shit.

What if the guy recognised him, too?

"What was that all about?" Lynch said. "You and the girl —you scared her."

Mahoney closed his eyes and tried to gather his thoughts. He couldn't very well tell Lynch what had happened without explaining why he wanted the girl. And if he told him *that*, everything would come falling down.

"Michael?"

"She wasn't listening to me. I told her to come, and she did the exact opposite. We can't have a kid running around in here."

"I don't know—maybe grabbing her like that wasn't the best way to get her to do what you wanted."

Mahoney felt his temper bubbling up, but took a moment and bit down on the retort he was tempted to deliver. He'd already messed up enough for one day, and the last thing he wanted to do now was give Lynch a reason to be suspicious.

Lynch didn't press. "Which way did they go?"

"Don't know," Mahoney said. "I was on my arse."

Lynch took his radio from his pocket. "I'll call it in."

Mahoney wanted the man found—he wanted him found *very* much—but not by anyone else. There was the potential for awkward questions about the girl, for a start, but what if he *did* remember their previous encounter? He could bring everything crashing down on him.

Lynch pressed the button to transmit. "Control, this is Lynch, badge number 5472. I've just been assaulted at the Southside Hotel. Suspect has fled the scene—we think with a young girl. Over."

"Copy that," the dispatcher replied. "Got a description of the suspect? Over."

"Control, the suspect is male, average height and build. Think he might be a waiter here. Dark hair, a scar across his cheek. Blue eyes—very blue. Over."

Mahoney shook his head to try to clear away the cobwebs. He knew he had acted impetuously, but he still thought he had done the right thing. Billy had been crystal clear: he wanted leverage over the Dillons. He wanted a pause so he could pursue his options—either prepare for war or sue for peace—and having the girl would've been enough to make that happen. It was a good strategy, but the man who had attacked him had ruined it.

He touched his face again and winced with the sudden stab of pain. Mahoney had no idea how the man was involved, other than the fact that he had put his nose in his business and made things *much* more difficult for him.

The two of them were going to have to have a little chat.

Mahoney just had to find him first.

47

Milton pushed open the doors to the kitchen and looked inside: it was empty. Pots and pans had been left on the stove tops, and the ovens were still on. He followed the corridor to the back door and stepped out. The guards were gone, as he had suspected. He ducked behind the big industrial bins and checked left and right: there was no one here at all. He needed to get away from the area as quickly as he could; the two officers he had put down wouldn't stay down for long, and once they realised he was gone, they'd rally the others to come and find him.

A van with the logo of a local laundry company was parked up at the goods entrance. It must have arrived before the attack; Milton was wondering about that as the driver got out, grinding a cigarette underneath his foot. He left his door open and the engine still running. He went around to the rear of the van and opened the doors, sorting through a collection of large cardboard boxes that had been stacked in the back.

"Come on," Milton said to Cara.

He took her hand and led her to the van, helping her to climb into the cab and then encouraging her to shuffle across to the passenger seat. The driver was still occupied with whatever he was doing at the back, and he didn't notice as Milton climbed inside. Milton put the van into first gear and stepped on the accelerator. The van jerked ahead; Milton heard the driver yell out an angry protest, but it made no difference. Milton bounced over the speed bump and swung the wheel, turning the van sharply onto the main road. The driver ran after them until he realised that it was futile; Milton caught a glimpse of him in the mirror, shaking his fist in impotent rage. The rear doors were still open, flapping about as Milton turned the wheel and headed east, and, although he knew they would attract attention, he wanted to be a little farther away from the hotel before he stopped to close them. He looked in the mirror and watched as a box fell out and bounced along behind them. Another followed it, and then a third, splitting open and spilling folded sheets across the road.

He looked over at Cara. "Are you okay?"

She swallowed and gave a little nod.

"Are you going to tell me why you were frightened of that policeman?"

She shook her head.

"It's okay. I don't trust him, either."

She swallowed again.

"I'm going to get you somewhere safe. We need to have a think about the best way of getting you home."

He saw a junction up ahead and turned left, spilling another two boxes, drove on for a quarter of a mile and then turned right onto a residential street. He pulled over, sliding the van behind another van that would obscure it from the main road, and switched off the engine. He told the girl to wait, got out and went around to the back. The cargo space was a mess, but Milton wasn't concerned about that. He closed the doors, took out his phone and dialled the number that Maria had given him.

"Hello?"

"It's me," he said.

"Where are you? You said you'd come back up to the room."

"It didn't work out the way I was hoping. Cara was scared—she recognised one of the officers, and then I did, too. I think he was involved with what happened."

"How can he be involved?"

"I don't know. But there's a lot we don't know. We don't know anything about Cara, either."

"We know she's a frightened little girl."

"Exactly—we do. And we have to trust her."

"Find another police officer?"

"I don't know if we can. Cara ran away. He went after her, and it got physical. She didn't want to go with him, and he tried to make her. I stopped him."

"Do I want to ask how you did that?"

"Probably not. But the police will take his word over mine, so I decided it would be best to get her out of the hotel. I'm also not sure who we can trust. I need to sit down and work it through."

"So, what now?"

"I need to get somewhere safe, and I don't have anywhere. I only arrived here last week."

"*I* don't have anywhere," she said.

"Do you know anyone who might be able to help?"

She didn't answer.

"Maria? I could take her to a bed and breakfast, but that wouldn't be ideal."

"Maybe," she conceded. "There might be somewhere you could go."

"Where?"

"Clondalkin," she said. "I lived there before I started work at the hotel."

Milton tried to remember his geography. Clondalkin was in the west of the city and was one of its more challenging districts.

"Can you find out?"

"How long would it be for?"

"Not long," Milton said. "Just until I've been able to work out how to get her back to her family."

"Okay." Maria paused. "But... I don't understand."

"What?"

"Why are you doing this? Why would you help her?"

"Because it's the right thing to do."

She was quiet again, and Milton knew she was weighing up what he had said; she was probably weighing *him* up, too. She didn't know him—not really—and what had happened in the hotel had been extraordinary. What he was saying now—that a policeman might have been involved in an attack that led to three deaths—would make things even more unsettling. He was asking a lot of her. He was trusting her, too; he didn't know her, and knew it was possible that she might go straight to the police. There was nothing he could do about that.

"It's Fifty Castle View Road. The key's under a brick next to the door."

48

Shay could feel his temper fraying. His second-in-command, Cillian Quinn, had just told him that Ronan McGrath was late and knew that his boss wouldn't take kindly to it.

"I don't *care* what he says," Shay said. "Tell him he needs to be here in ten minutes or else he can turn around, drive out of the city and never fucking come back!"

Shay didn't wait for a reply. He took his cigarettes and lighter from the desk and left his office. It was late, but the warehouse was busy and noisy: there was the clank and clang as one of the forklifts moved a pallet loaded with cardboard boxes; the shouts of the men as they struggled to make themselves heard; the rumble of a diesel engine from the truck in the loading bay. Tall metal shelves, stacked from floor to ceiling with crates, boxes, and pallets, divided the space into a maze of aisles that were just wide enough for the forklift to manoeuvre. They had just had a delivery from a freighter that had tied up yesterday morning, and the staff were dealing with it: the container would be unloaded, the cargo would be inspected and documented and then sorted and labelled. The inventory would be entered into the warehouse management system, and then each crate would be taken to the right storage location. The crates contained rolls of foam that would be used in one of the family's other legitimate businesses: a company that installed roof insulation across the country, showing customers how to take advantage of generous European Union grants designed to make homes more energy efficient. The Dillons had suckled on that teat for years, and there was no sign that the flow of money was going to stop any time soon. Climate change... Shay *loved* it.

That wasn't all that had been keeping him busy, though. They'd been expecting a shipment from the cartel, and he'd been given a tip that the authorities at the airport had been warned it was coming; Shay had managed to get hold of the middleman at Schiphol just in time to stop it being loaded onto the plane. He was going to have to find another way to get the load into the country; the production line was ready to take the coke and bulk it up, with distribution waiting to get it out onto the street. The delay was annoying. The cartel wouldn't ship the product until it had been paid for—in full —and he'd stretched his finances to the breaking point to get the money in place. He needed to start selling so that he could get out of the red and into the black.

He went outside. The warehouse loomed large on the Dublin Docklands. Their father had bought it years ago, and Shay could remember what it had been like then and the changes that had been wrought since. It had been constructed in the midst of the economic boom that had transformed Ireland after the turn of the millennium, with international corporations rushing to take advantage of the tax breaks the Irish government used to encourage growth. The area, like the country as a whole, had been transformed; new buildings sprang up year after year, and the thicket of cranes on the horizon stood testament to the construction that was still going on. The promised economic miracle had been oversold, though, and his dad had been able to buy the property for a fraction of what it ought to have been worth.

The downturn had been useful; their wealth had been washed through the purchases of warehouses and offices and even whole housing estates, the money parked until the economy recovered, and then withdrawn—laundered and unencumbered—when the time was right. This property, though, had been kept. The family had moved into the import business, and its location—right on the docks—was perfect.

The building was constructed of weathered red brick and corrugated metal and sat at the confluence of the Liffey and the Irish Sea. Shay had always associated it with the very particular smell: the salty breeze mingled with the earthiness of freshly cut wood and the whiff of diesel from passing trucks. It was surrounded by a wrought-iron fence encrusted with peeling green paint, a testament to years of exposure to the coastal elements. A sliding gate, bearing the intertwined *D*s that formed the company logo, guarded the entrance to the compound. The warehouse's exterior was punctuated with rows of narrow windows, mostly obscured by years of grime, allowing only the faintest rays of sunlight to pass inside.

Shay had been planning to attend the hotel for the weigh-in but had had to change his plans after the mess at the airport. He took out the packet of cigarettes from his pocket, tapped one out and lit it. He took a draw as he heard the sound of the main gate drawing back, the scrape of the motor reminding him that Brennan needed to tend to it.

Shay saw the sweep of headlamps as a car drove through and recognised McGrath's BMW as he parked alongside his Porsche. McGrath killed the engine and got out.

Shay took down another lungful of smoke, flicked the cigarette away and went inside to wait for McGrath to reach him.

"Boss," he said.

"I've been sitting on my arse waiting for you all bloody evening," Shay said. "Where've you been?"

McGrath started to reply, then stopped. He was pale, as if all the blood had run down to his feet.

"What is it? You look like you've seen a ghost."

"You haven't heard?"

"Heard what?"

"It's Colm."

Shay rolled his eyes. Colm was the more impetuous of the two, and Shay was always bailing him out of the scrapes he got himself into. "What's he gone and done now?"

"I'm sorry. I'm *so* sorry. He's been shot."

"*What?*"

"There was an attack at the hotel. They had someone inside the building. We're not sure, but we think he was a member of staff. He had a piece, and he was at your brother's table before anyone could do anything to stop him. He shot him, close range... in the head. Rickard, too."

"In the..." He shook his head. "I mean... he... what? Where is he? Where'd they take him?"

"He's gone, Shay. He never stood a chance."

Shay felt the heat in his face. "No." A wave of dizziness swept over him, and, for a moment, he felt as if he was about to collapse. "No, no, no, no, *no!*"

He reached for the nearest thing to hand—one of the tablets they used to access the warehouse management system—and flung it against the wall. The device rang against the metal, spun and then bounced across the floor. Two of the lads were close enough to see it, and, fearing another outburst of Shay's temper, both men disappeared along one of the aisles.

"We had security there," Shay said. "What about them?"

"They fucked up."

"We had a scanner on the door. We had guards. How did they get a gun inside?"

"I don't know, Shay. But if I had to guess, I'd say they hid it somewhere before our lads went in. We think the shooter worked in the kitchen. He wouldn't've been checked."

"What do you mean 'he wouldn't've been checked'? He *should've* been checked. I told you—Billy's been promising to do something like this for weeks. I told you. I fucking *told* you!"

"We've got a name for the man who did it," he said, trying to offer something to deflect Shay's anger away from him. "Mickey Flannagan."

"Where is he?"

"In hospital. He got shot."

"Which hospital?"

"St James."

"Go and check it out."

"I'll go myself."

"Who was responsible for security?"

"Fitz."

"So, this is on him," Shay said, spittle on his breath. "He fucked up. I want to see him. Where the fuck is he?"

"We don't know. We think he might've done a runner."

"Is he involved?"

McGrath shrugged. "He might just be worried about what you'd say."

"Do you *think*? Find him. Find him and bring him here."

McGrath nodded.

"Why are you still here?" Shay said. "Piss off and do what I told you to do."

McGrath bit his tongue. "There's something else. It's Cara."

Shay grabbed McGrath and drove him back against the wall of the building. McGrath was bigger than Shay and could have shaken him off easily enough, but he knew that if he laid a finger on him—if he even *breathed* on him—then Shay would have him cut up into pieces and thrown into the Liffey.

"She was there," McGrath muttered, trying and failing to hide his fear at Shay's outburst. "Colm took her."

"He took her to the weigh-in?"

McGrath didn't look as if he knew what to say, and just nodded.

"Please don't tell me she's been hurt."

"That's the thing, Shay. We don't know where she is."

Shay laid his forearm across McGrath's throat and pressed.

McGrath gasped for breath. "Please, boss. You're... choking... me."

Shay held his arm where it was for a beat, then released the pressure and stepped back.

"What do you mean she's not there? She's nine—where could she have gone?"

McGrath rubbed his throat. "We've checked the hotel from top to bottom. The CCTV has one of the waiters bringing her down. He spoke to one of the police, but something happened, and she ran. Two officers went after her, and they both got their arses handed to them. One of them had his nose broken, and the other was sprayed with CS."

"Who by—the waiter?"

"That's what I heard."

"It must be the Gallaghers. Right? It's Billy. The waiter... he must be in on it with them."

McGrath nodded. "Got to be. I've put the word out on the street. Anyone who gives us anything that'll help us find her gets paid. Anyone who knows and *doesn't* tell us gets a bullet."

"The waiter? Do we know anything about him?"

"His name's Eric Blair. He only started at the hotel a couple of days ago."

Shay took out another cigarette, put it to his lips and lit it. His fingers were trembling, and the flame jumped and jerked. "Find out everything you can about him."

"Yes, boss."

"What about the Gallaghers? Where's Billy now?"

"I don't know."

"Find out. I want him watched. And get the boys together. We need to be ready."

Clondalkin was about ten kilometres southwest of Dublin. Milton looked out of the window at a mixture of residential, industrial and commercial areas. It was run-down, with streets that would charitably be described as 'gritty,' yet there were signs of pride in the community: Irish flags were displayed inside windows, and building works funded by European Union grants were restoring older buildings. The architecture was a mix of old and new, with modern developments cheek by jowl with historic landmarks.

He had just pulled into a car park with the intention of ditching the van when his phone rang.

"Hello?"

It was Maria. "Where are you?"

"Nearly there. You're at the hotel?"

"I'm outside the house."

Milton sucked his teeth. *So much for keeping her out of it.* He would much rather she stayed away to avoid being drawn into the situation herself. He had seen it before: he exerted a malign gravity, and those caught up by it had often found themselves imperilled. Milton paused, wondering whether he should tell her to go back to the hotel, then realised that he was going to need her. He was going to have to do a little digging to find out what had happened at the hotel. He also needed to find out whom to return the girl to, and it would be much easier for him—and safer for her—if he was able to leave her with someone while he was out and about.

"Okay," he said.

"Okay?"

"Okay. That's fine."

"It wasn't up for debate. I want to help."

"Thank you," he said. "We're almost there. I'll see you in a minute."

He ended the call and turned to Cara. "We need to walk the rest of the way. Is that all right?"

The girl stared at Milton. Her eyes were wide and full of fright, but she gave a nod of assent. Milton watched her and knew that he was going to need help in finding out who she was and how to get her back to her family.

He needed to speak to Ziggy.

M ahoney pulled over next to the bar and killed the engine. He pulled down the visor and flicked the switch to turn on the light for the vanity mirror. He squinted at his reflection; it wasn't a pretty picture. His nose was a mess, and the only good thing about it was that it had given him an excuse to get away from the hotel. He had told Lynch that he was going to drive over to the hospital and get it looked at but had no intention of doing that. Instead, he'd plugged his nostrils with toilet paper to staunch the blood and driven here. His nose was crooked, and he was going to need someone to take care of it for him, but it would have to wait. The broken nose and the blood on his shirt were badges of his failure, and he knew that Billy Gallagher did not abide failure.

He got out and looked at the bar. The name—The Confessional—was written in gold across the black façade. It was midnight, and the bar had long since emptied out. He went up to the door, which had a frosted etching of the silhouette of a priest on the glass, took a deep breath, and knocked. He watched through the glass as a barman, who had been stacking chairs on the tables, came over and opened up.

The man clocked his uniform. "No one's called you."

"Is Billy in?"

"Who are you?"

"Just tell him Michael Mahoney's here. He's expecting me."

The man shut and locked the door again and disappeared inside. Mahoney waited, trying to marshal as much conviction as he could. He needed to convince Billy that he could make up for what had happened. He didn't know how likely that was, and that—and the consequences that might follow—made him nervous.

He looked through the glass and saw the barman making his way back to the door. There was the rasp of metal on wood as he unlocked it again and swung it open.

"He's in the lounge at the back," the man said, stepping aside to let Mahoney enter. "Go through."

Mahoney followed the man's point to a separate room at the rear of the pub. He could hear the sound of the television, and as he turned into the room, he saw that a mixed martial arts fight was playing on the big eighty-inch screen that was fixed to the wall. Two bloodied fighters were locked in a clinch, the referee hovering over them both and watching to see whether one would tap out.

Billy was sitting on a sofa with his back to Mahoney. "You know these two?" he said, gesturing to the screen.

"I don't," Mahoney said. "Not really my thing."

"Red trunks is my boy, Charlie. Watch—what do you reckon?"

Mahoney watched the screen as Charlie Gallagher went to the mat with his opponent on top of him. He wrapped his legs around the other man's arm, securing it between his thighs, then gripped his wrist with both hands and locked it tightly in place.

"Look at that," Billy said. "Smooth as silk."

Charlie arched his hips upward, hyperextending the elbow joint. The other man slapped his hand against Charlie's shoulder, and, at the referee's urging, Charlie broke the hold.

Billy nodded with satisfaction. "Wait until the fight. He gets Farley in an arm bar like that and it's all over."

Mahoney didn't really know what to say, so he stood there in an awkward silence as Billy used the remote to switch off the TV. He put his legs down and stood, stretching out his arms and then turning around to face Mahoney. His pale face was marked by deep lines and wrinkles, and his skin was fine and delicate and spotted with age. His hair was grey and thinning, emphasising a receding hairline. His eyes, once intense and determined, were now sunken, but still burned with intelligence and the hint of his mercurial temper.

Billy laid a leathery hand on Mahoney's shoulder. "Drink?"

His hospitality was unexpected and suspicious, but Mahoney knew that he couldn't say no. "Dying for one."

Billy went behind the bar, took two crystal glasses from the shelf and poured out two measures of Jameson's. He held out one of the glasses, and as Mahoney reached to take it, he tossed the drink into his face.

"You think you deserve a drink with me? After what happened?"

Mahoney reached up with a hand to wipe the alcohol from his eyes. "No, Billy. I don't."

Billy turned his back to Mahoney and took a sip. Mahoney could feel the whiskey in his hair and his eyebrows and could smell it and taste it as it rolled down to his lips. He wiped his face again.

"Is Colm Dillon definitely dead?"

Mahoney nodded. "Definitely."

"And Rickard?"

"Dead."

Billy shook his head. "What a mess. You have no idea how fucked up things are going to get."

Mahoney *did* have an idea, but he decided it would be better to keep that to himself. "I'm sorry. Really, Billy—I am. It didn't go down the way it was supposed to. I got the gun where it was supposed to be. I got Flannagan to do it. I'm not sure what else I *could've* done."

Mahoney turned round and saw that Billy's right-hand man, Gerry Kelly, had come inside. He was close, too, and it made Mahoney nervous.

"There'll be war now," Billy said. "They'll want revenge. I was thinking—maybe we should tell them you were acting on your own, trying to give me something you thought I wanted. We could drive you over to the docks tonight and give you to Shay Dillon. What do you think? You think we should do that?"

Mahoney felt Kelly behind him and wasn't sure whether this was just Billy being Billy, or whether he really *would* do something like that.

"Wrap him up in a bow and drop him off," Kelly said.

Billy laughed. "We can't, Gerry. They'd never believe he had the balls unless I was paying him to do it." He paused and turned back to Mahoney. "That reminds me, though— payment. You can whistle for it. You're not getting a cent out of me for this disaster. Not one cent."

"That's fine," Mahoney said. "That's fair."

Billy looked over Mahoney's shoulder. "You hear that, Kelly? He says it's fair."

"Big of him."

"Very big of him." Billy gestured to his face. "What happened?"

"I was attacked."

"By?"

"The man who tackled Flannagan."

"But you're a police officer. Why would he do something like that?"

"I don't know, Billy. We're looking for him now."

"So why are you here?"

"You said you wanted leverage—I know what you can use. Colm Dillon's daughter was there tonight."

"I saw her," Billy said. "I said it was no place for a wee girl—didn't I, Gerry?"

"That you did."

"The man who hit me—the waiter—he took her upstairs to get her out of the way, and then he came back down and spoke to my partner. He said he'd got her, and he wanted to find a way to get her back to her family. My partner told him to bring her to him. I was there when he did. She saw me and panicked."

"Why?"

"She recognised me. I've been trying to think where from, and the only answer I have is that she was in the car when I pulled Dillon over a couple of weeks ago. You remember—you asked me to put the screws on him?"

"I remember."

"I said I thought he was driving erratically, and I wanted to breathalyse him. It got heated. He shouted at me. I threatened to nick him. There was a kid in the back, but I didn't really pay any attention to them. If it *was* her, though... I don't know, maybe she remembered me? Maybe he said something to her? Whatever—it doesn't matter. I said I'd get her back to her mother, she ran, I went after her, the waiter came after me. He broke my nose and sprayed my partner with CS."

"And then?"

"And then he took the girl and disappeared. Someone stole a laundry van that was on delivery at the exact same time. The driver didn't get a look at whoever it was who took it, but it's obvious—he used the van to get away."

"And you're looking for it?"

"We are." He winced at the pain in his nose. "But that's what I mean. You wanted leverage—right? She's it. *She's* your leverage. I was going to bring her to you. As long as you have her, what are the Dillons going to do?"

"Are you stupid?" Kelly said.

"What?"

"You're a police officer. People would've seen you with her, and then she doesn't show up? You don't think they'd ask questions?"

Billy shook his head. "Gerry's right—it would've been a stupid idea. You're lucky you got beaten up. Our friend the waiter did you a favour."

"I would've—"

"You would've made things worse than they already are," Billy cut across him angrily. Mahoney was going to protest, but Billy held up his hand. "But much as it pains me to say so, you might have been right about her value. They won't do anything if we have her. It'll give us time to prepare."

"But he *doesn't* have her," Kelly said.

"No," Mahoney said, "but I'll find her."

"How are you going to do that?"

"Through Blair—the waiter, that's his name. Eric Blair. I'll find him."

"You'd better. You need to find a way to make up for the shitshow at the hotel. I want the girl here tomorrow. If you don't find her, you might as well run and keep running. Understand?"

"Yes, Billy."

Kelly thumped him on the side of the head. "Yes, *Mr. Gallagher.*"

Mahoney clenched his fist, but bit down on his lip before he could say something that would get him shot. "Yes, Mr. Gallagher," he said. "I understand."

51

Lilly looked out of the window of the car as the driver took them deeper into the countryside. They had arrived in Dublin yesterday evening and, as per their instructions, had split into two pairs: Lilly and Number Two were Bravo Team, operating under legends that had them as husband and wife. They had taken a taxi into the city and taken a room at the Westbury on Balfe Street.

An update had been waiting for them. Jimmy Moon's house had been put under surveillance, and, although there had been no actual sight of either Milton or Ziggy Penn, they had found evidence that proved that the latter—at least—was in the city. Jimmy's house bristled with cameras and other security devices, and, since the cameras uploaded their feeds directly to the cloud, it had been a simple enough task for Group Two to gain access to the historical data. The last seven days' footage had been analysed, and the camera positioned above the main gate had recorded the suspicious activity of a man who had passed up and down before it several times. His image had been pulled and compared to the photographs of Penn that were still held on file; a match was confirmed with one hundred per cent confidence.

He was here.

That probably meant that Milton was here, too.

Lilly had wanted to get started, but preparations were still underway, and they were told to burnish their legends as tourists. The day had been spent seeing the sights: they visited Kilmainham Gaol and then the Guinness Store-house, finishing with a pleasant meal at Lennox. They were texted as their desserts were being cleared away, and told to meet a driver outside. The man—most likely a Group Five logistician—explained he would take them to the local arms cache where they would be able to equip themselves for the operation. He hadn't said anything else, and they had listened to an Irish talk radio station as they left the city and headed into the darkness. The DJ was inviting listeners to comment on crime in the city following a shooting earlier that evening that had left three men dead and was reputed to be connected to a feud between local gangsters.

The driver turned off the main road, and they followed a smaller road before exchanging that for a track that was only just wide enough for their car. It was unpaved, and they bounced up and down through the puddles and potholes, able to see no farther than was allowed by the high beams.

"We're here," the driver said.

The headlights showed a small, ivy-covered cottage with a thatched roof that was showing signs of disrepair. The windows had cracked wooden frames and dusty, broken panes of glass. A cobblestone path, now overrun by weeds and moss, led up to the front door. The remnants of what must once have been a charming garden lay in disarray, with overgrown bushes and untended flowerbeds. A dilapidated wooden fence encircled the property.

They heard the sound of another engine and, turning back, saw the lights of another car as it negotiated the narrow track. It came into view and pulled up next to their vehicle. One and Three stepped out, and Lilly and Two got out of their own car and joined them.

"All okay?" Two asked.

"All good," One said. "You been inside yet?"

"We just got here."

The front door was slightly ajar and hanging off one of its hinges. It creaked with the wind and protested more volubly as Two went over and pushed it open. He took out a penlight from his pocket, switched it on and stepped carefully into the cottage. A thick layer of dust blanketed every surface, and cobwebs stretched across the corners, their delicate patterns shining in the glow of the flashlight.

The other three agents and the driver followed him inside. "The front room," he said. "There's a hatch under the rug."

The room featured a stone fireplace, now cold and dark, with charred logs in the hearth. There was a worn, faded armchair and a tattered sofa, both of which had seen better days. An old wooden table, its surface marred by scratches and stains, stood to one side, with two mismatched chairs shoved up underneath it and with two of its legs on a rug that had been discoloured by damp and mould.

Two went to the table and pushed it back so that he could get to the rug. He folded it, pulled it aside, and then shone the beam of his penlight on the hatch revealed beneath. He opened the hatch, and they looked inside. A dark, narrow space lay before them, its contents shrouded in shadows. The light glinted off cold steel—the weapons that had been left there. The cache was meticulously organised, with each item placed in a specific order, reflecting the precision and care of the quartermaster who had assembled it. Rifles, shotguns and handguns lay neatly arranged on a custom-built wooden rack, their barrels gleaming. Ammunition boxes, filled with rounds of various calibres, were stacked nearby. The weapons were well maintained, with their finishes still in good condition, a stark contrast to the disrepair of the cottage above. In addition to the firearms, Lilly saw a collection of knives and other bladed weapons, their edges sharp and free of rust. Lilly had visited Group caches before, but this one was particularly well stocked and maintained.

Two reached down and picked out a rifle, setting it down on the floor and reaching back for a pistol and two boxes of ammunition. Lilly took out a Browning Hi-Power 9mm and, should longer-range work be necessary, the short-barrelled version of the L119A1 rifle. She reached back into the void and fetched out an FS knife of the sort once used by the SAS. She pulled the blade out of the scabbard and ran her finger along the edge; it had been whetted and was sharp. She thought of Milton and how the knife could put an end to all her problems; if only she was able to find him and get close enough to use it.

Two took out a shoulder holster and handed it to her, then found one for himself. He took out an extra couple of boxes of ammunition and put them, plus his own knife, in a kit bag.

"Got everything you need?" he asked her.

"I'm good."

One and Three likewise equipped themselves. Finally, Three removed a vinyl case that, when it was opened, revealed a collection of surveillance devices: miniature cameras, a digital voice recorder and covert microphones, GPS trackers, bug detectors and other gear that Lilly didn't recognise.

"Enough?" Two asked.

Three nodded. "Everything I need."

"All right, then." One lowered the hatch back over the void, unfolded the rug back over it, pulled the table back into position and stood, brushing off the mildew that had adhered to the knees of her trousers. "Penn's in the city somewhere. Let's go and find him."

PART IV

52

Shay drove across the city to his brother's house. Colm, Grainne and Cara had only recently moved in; it was a new build, with the best architects and builders in the city involved in the project. It was a striking building, although a little too bling for Shay's tastes. The exterior had a garish red-brick façade with intricate white accents that made it obvious that this was supposed to be a grand address. The windows were arranged symmetrically to match Colm's instructions that it 'look Georgian.' It had large sashes with white wooden shutters and clean stone lintels. The entrance was through a white door with a brass knocker, with an elaborate fanlight above and two slender, decorative columns on either side.

Shay parked and took a moment to compose himself, and considered what he was going to say to Grainne. He had never been good at empathy, and, although he was fizzing and popping with anger, he knew that he would be expected to offer consolation. She was big on emoting, and the thought of dealing with her in these circumstances filled him with dread.

At least she wasn't Cara's mother. Grainne had only been on the scene for a year after Colm's first wife, Clare, had walked out. Colm had been gutted, then stunned when Clare had had the brass to tell him that she wanted to take Cara with her. Lawyers had been involved, and Colm had been terrified that Clare would use her knowledge of the business to paint him as an unsuitable parent to care for a child. Shay had taken care of all that for him. He had put the screws on the lawyers until they withdrew from the case, and then intimidated the next two firms she turned to until she was left with no other choice but a hopeless old drunk who couldn't litigate his way out of a paper bag.

Even then, badly outmatched by the team that Colm had on his side, she'd still made trouble. She'd contacted seemingly every newspaper, radio and TV station in Ireland in an attempt to tell her story. None of them would touch her, knowing they'd be on the receiving end of an injunction if they were lucky or a late-night knock on the door from men in balaclavas if they were not. There had been one journalist —and Shay used that word advisedly—who had agreed to write a story. He had a popular blog that railed against the Irish underworld and police corruption; he'd written about the Dillons before and hadn't been intimidated by the usual threats. Shay had decided there was no point in wasting time with pleasantries this time and had arranged for the man to be tossed in the back of a van, driven out into the countryside and shot.

He'd gone to Clare afterwards and explained it would be better for her to take the money she'd been offered, forget about the girl and piss off back to Cork. Finally, after everything that had happened, she'd agreed. They hadn't seen her since.

Colm had found Grainne in a club in the city. Shay

hadn't liked her from the off. He'd asked around, and the reports that came back hadn't been positive. She'd been going out with a guy who played corner-back for the Jackeens, and, at the end of the relationship, she'd sold a lurid kiss-and-tell to the papers. Everything Shay was told suggested she was a gold digger, he'd warned Colm, but his brother had angrily told him to mind his own business. Shay let it slide, quite certain that he would be called in to sort out the mess when things inevitably went wrong. It hadn't happened yet, but it was just a matter of time.

He climbed the polished stone steps to the front door and knocked. The lights were on inside, and he saw movement through the glass.

The door opened.

Shay stopped in surprise. "Ma."

Eileen Dillon was in her early seventies. Her hair, now a silvery grey, was styled in a dated perm that framed her face, adding a little formality. Her face was etched with deeply set wrinkles and lines, the most prominent being the creases that radiated from her nose to the corners of her mouth. Her eyes were cruel, buried in deep sockets, and her eyebrows were arched so that she had a naturally disapproving look.

She reached out and drew him to her. Shay breathed in her scent—fresh laundry with her usual lavender perfume over the top of it—and allowed his guard to fall. He held onto her and blinked the tears from his eyes, only letting go when he was sure that they had stopped.

She looked up into his face. "No," she said sternly. "We're not having that. No weeping, Shay. No *weakness*. You show them that and they'll think you're there for the taking, and then they'll take advantage. Everyone needs to see that you're strong, or else maybe they think the time's right to have a go at us. We can't have that—not now. Not *ever*."

He sniffed, used the back of his hand to swipe away the tears, and nodded. "I'm fine, Ma."

Eileen stared into his face, waited, then nodded. "You need a drink."

He followed her into the house. She led the way to the big entertaining space at the back with the vast extension with the glass roof and the bar that Colm had installed. Shay watched as she led the way; his mother's fashion choices leaned towards conservative and traditional, and, as usual, she was wearing a floral dress and a simple pair of black shoes. She was wearing the same pearl necklace that she always wore, the one that Shay's father had bought for her on the birthday before he topped himself.

She took down two crystal tumblers and poured out double measures of whiskey from the decanter on the bar. She handed one glass to Shay and held up the other. Shay dipped his head and touched his glass to hers.

She put the glass to her lips and sipped. "Where have you been?"

"The warehouse. I didn't hear until an hour ago. I came straight over."

"They killed him—they shot him, in front of everyone. Shot him like a dog."

"I know, Ma. They told me. Where's Grainne?"

Eileen sniffed. "Not here, apparently. She's gone on one of her city breaks."

"Colm didn't say. Does she know?"

"Not from me. We can tell her in the morning. We need to deal with what happened. What have you heard?"

"Someone from the hotel had a gun—they shot Colm and Frank Rickard. I've put feelers out."

She eyed him. "It's the Gallaghers, isn't it?"

"We don't know that for sure."

"Yes, we do. It's Billy. He's been smarting ever since you moved into his territory. I said he'd end up doing something like this, didn't I? I said he'd do something like this, and neither you nor your brother paid any attention. And now look."

"Not now, Ma."

"Not now?"

"I didn't hear you complaining about the extra money we've been making. You were happy enough with that, so let's not get into recriminations." She started to protest, but he raised his hand, and, for once, she held her tongue. "You're right—it's probably him. It's not impossible that it's someone else, but I wouldn't put much on it. But we're going to make abso-*fucking*-lutely sure that we're right."

"Before?"

"Before we go to war. So you're going to listen to me, and you're not going to do anything stupid until we've got to the bottom of it—all right? You're going to let me find out what happened, and then you're going to let me deal with it. Tell me you understand."

"I'm not stupid, son. I've been at this for longer than you've been alive."

"So you're always reminding me." He sat down. "There's something else you need to know. Cara was with Colm."

"What? At the hotel? I thought she was with Grainne."

"He took her with him, and now we don't know where she is. I heard one of the waiters got her out of the way after it all went down, but now we don't know where she's gone."

"You listen to me," she cut across him. "She's my grand-daughter. Your niece. What are you doing to find her?"

"The lads are asking around."

"We can't sit on our hands while your knuckle-draggers run around town looking for her."

"What else can we do?"

"Go to the police like normal people."

"No."

"They can do things that we can't."

"We're *not* normal people, Ma."

"We need to get them involved."

"It's *the police*. Do you really think they'd be interested in helping us?"

"Of course they'll help. She's a nine-year-old girl. They *have* to help."

He was about to answer back but took a breath. He knew she was right. He had no love for the police—and knew the feeling was reciprocated—but these were unusual circumstances, and he couldn't just rely upon his own efforts to find Cara.

"All right. Fine. I'll go and see them."

"Now?"

"Ma..."

"Now, son. Sooner the better." She finished her drink and put it down.

"What are you doing?"

She picked up her coat. "I'm coming, too."

53

Milton followed the directions on his phone to Castle View Road. It was a terraced street where rows of houses with similar run-down façades lined either side. It was quiet, with only a few parked cars scattered along the kerb. Most of the vehicles were old and dented, evidence of their owners' financial struggles. The houses were two storeys, with peeling paint and weathered bricks and the occasional boarded-up window. The atmosphere was one of neglect and poverty, a contrast to the more affluent areas of the city through which they had passed.

Maria was outside number fifty. Milton led the way across the road and up the drive.

"Are you okay?" Milton asked her.

"I'm fine."

She looked uncertain, and Milton had to remind himself that she had found herself in a situation that must have been frightening and difficult to understand.

"What about the hotel?"

"Police everywhere."

"No one saw you leave?"

"I don't know—they might have done. Why?"

"Just wanted to make sure that you weren't followed."

"Why would I have been?"

"I know—you're right. I'm being paranoid."

She turned to Cara and smiled. "Hello, lovely. Are you okay?"

The girl gave a little nod of her head, disengaged her hand from Milton's, and went over to be folded in Maria's embrace.

"She's been brave," Milton said.

The girl buried her face in Maria's neck.

Milton looked up and down the street again. "We should get inside."

Maria carefully disentangled herself and, still kneeling down at Cara's height, laid a hand on the girl's cheek. "He's right—you're cold. We'd better get you inside to warm up."

She straightened, took Cara's hand and led the way to the front door. The house had a single-storey extension at the front, and there were two large bags of aggregate sitting next to the front door. It looked as if the fence to the left had been replaced, and there was evidence of work being done to create a flower bed next to it.

Maria crouched down and lifted a loose brick to reveal a key. She used it to open the door and went inside. Milton followed, closing the door behind him. He was hit by the musty smell of damp and neglect. The hallway was narrow, with peeling wallpaper and scuffed linoleum flooring. To his left was the living room, where an old sofa with torn upholstery sat next to a cheap wooden coffee table. He carried on down the hallway and passed a small kitchen, where pots and pans had been stacked haphazardly on the worktop, and an old fridge hummed in the corner. There was a small downstairs toilet and a door that led out onto the garden at the rear. Milton climbed the stairs and checked the first floor: two bedrooms and a bathroom, all empty. He went back to the ground floor and the front of the house.

Maria was in the living room. She had switched on the light, and Milton saw that the walls were hung with faded photographs. A crucifix hung above a small fireplace; if prayers had been made here, it wasn't obvious that they had been answered.

Milton gestured around. "No one lives here?"

"Not at the moment."

"Who owns it?"

"A friend," she said.

"And what does your friend do?"

She glanced away. "He's not really my friend."

"Maria?"

"He brings people into the country."

"Illegally?"

She nodded. "This is where they come when they arrive. They stay until papers have been arranged and they've found somewhere else."

Milton looked at her. "Like you?"

She nodded.

"But he doesn't know you're here?"

"No," she said. "But I knew it'd be empty. I had some things here, and I came back yesterday to get them."

Milton wasn't convinced that staying in the house was wise, but it was late, and they had no other option. He doubted they would need to be here for long. He didn't know anything about the girl yet, but he was confident they would be able to find out everything they needed in the morning. She might be ready to talk after a night's rest, but, even if she wasn't, there would be other ways of identifying her. Milton assumed that she would be reported as missing. Failing that, Milton knew Ziggy would be able to discover what they needed without too much bother.

"Come on," he said. "It's late. We should get some rest."

He climbed the stairs and went into the first bedroom. There was a worn carpet on the floor; the walls were painted a dingy shade of white, and thin curtains hung limply at the window, providing little insulation from the cold or the light from the flickering streetlamp on the pavement below. The room had two single beds, they had been pushed up against the walls, and a small bedside table with a lamp sat between them. The beds had sturdy metal frames and were covered with plain white sheets and blankets. There was no decoration aside from a faded poster of a K-pop band taped to the wall.

"I'll sleep here with her," Maria said, sitting down on the nearest bed. "You have the other room."

Maria smiled at Cara and patted the mattress next to her. The girl looked exhausted, with dark rings beneath her eyes. At Maria's bidding, she sat down on the edge of the bed next to her and allowed her to slip an arm around her shoulders for a brief hug.

Maria disengaged and pointed at the duffle coat the girl was wearing. "Let's get that off."

The girl didn't demur as Maria undid the buttons and removed the coat. Milton reached down and took it, turning it around so that he could go through the pockets for anything that might help him work out her last name. He found a pair of woollen mittens and a half-eaten packet of Haribo, but nothing else.

"I just realised," Maria said. "We haven't told you our names. I'm Maria."

"And I'm John."

With horror, Milton realised he'd slipped up. He hoped Maria might have missed it, but he was not so lucky. She caught it at once, looking up at him with an expression of confusion.

"*John?*"

"I'll explain later."

She turned to the girl and gave her a reassuring smile. "John and I are just going to have a little chat. Why don't you get ready for bed? Can you do that?"

Cara nodded again.

"Good night," Milton said to her as he and Maria stepped out of the room. "We'll see you in the morning."

54

Maria came outside, pointed to the second bedroom and followed him into it.

Her eyes flashed with anger. "*John?*" she hissed. "Who's John?"

"Me. That's my name."

"You said your name was—"

"Eric," he said. "I know."

"Why would you say it's your name when it's not?"

"Because I have things in my past that I'd rather stayed in my past."

She shook her head. "No. That's not good enough. How can I look after her"—she pointed in the direction of the other bedroom—"if you're lying to me about who you are? I've taken a risk to be here with you."

"There are people out there who would like to know where I am, and using a different name makes it harder for them to find me."

That didn't help. "These people are dangerous?"

"Yes."

"Then that makes it worse!"

"They don't know where I am. I'm very careful to make sure it stays that way."

That *was* true, and Milton *had* been careful. He was confident that the trail had run cold and that the Group would have to work very hard to pick it up again, at least until what had happened at the hotel. That had been the antithesis of discretion, and he knew what he had done risked giving them his scent once more. It didn't matter; he would've done the same thing again.

Maria was staring at him. "Is that the only thing you lied to me about?"

"Yes."

"I don't believe you."

"Maria—"

"No. You tell me everything, or I'm going to call a taxi and take her straight to the police."

"You can't do that. I told you—it's not safe."

"And staying with a man who lies about his name *is*?"

"Fine," Milton said, raising both hands. "But please keep your voice down—we don't want to scare her any more than she already is. What do you want to know?"

"Your full name."

He wasn't about to tell her that. "We'll have to leave it at John."

"Who are you hiding from?"

"Some people I used to work for."

"Who? Criminals?"

"No. I'm not a criminal."

"What *are* you, then?"

"I can't say." He tried to think what he *could* say and sighed. "This is the best I can do—I used to work for the government. I did things for them that I wasn't proud of. Not criminal things. I didn't break the law." That was a contentious point, but he was pleased to see that she didn't ask him to elaborate. "That doesn't mean I *liked* what I was being asked to do. I *didn't*—and, eventually, I came to hate it. I left that job, but the people I worked for weren't happy about that and tried to make me stay. I'm not going to do that, so here I am." He spread his arms. "I go from job to job, from city to city, country to country, never staying in the same place long enough for them to get too close to me."

"The government?" She stared at him. "What does that mean? You're a *spy*?"

"No," he said, uncomfortable with the leaps she was making—and that she might make. "I'm not a spy. And that's all you're going to get out of me."

She bit her lip. "I'm here because you asked me to help, and now I don't think I know you at all."

"You hardly knew me before. I was just Eric in the kitchen. That's all I ever said."

"But that's not who you are."

"These days it is—I'm a cook. That's it. I'll move on once we've got Cara back to her family, and I'll be a cook somewhere else."

She shook her head, still unconvinced.

"We all have secrets," Milton said. "I do and so do you." He gestured around them. "You didn't tell me you were here illegally, did you?"

She clenched her jaw; Milton could see the muscles tensing in her face. It was going to be difficult for her to argue: the two of them had both hidden their truths.

"I'm not going to say anything about that," Milton said. "I don't care if you don't have a visa. It doesn't mean anything to me. The only thing I care about at the moment is the little girl in the room next door. We need to get some sleep, and then, tomorrow, I'll find out what we need to know to get her back to her family. All right?"

She exhaled, then nodded. "Okay. But on one condition?"

"What's that?"

"No more secrets. You understand?"

"No more secrets."

No more secrets? He couldn't promise that, but there was no need for her to know anything more than she already did. The truth wouldn't help her; it would frighten her. She was scared enough as it was, and Milton knew that, above all, he needed to shield her from the truth about who he was and what he had done.

55

Mahoney drove back to the hotel with a lot on his mind. He was nervous: complications had arisen, and he was starting to feel as if things were running away from him. And that feeling—when the stakes were as high as this—made him nervous. There was so much for him to do, and none of it was easy. Flannagan was his first concern. He would need to find out where he had been taken and then go and assess how much of a threat he posed. It would be so much more convenient if he *didn't* recover from his injuries; perhaps he would be able to help nudge fate in that direction.

And then there was the issue of the girl.

And the man who had taken her and had seen him leave the gun.

There was still a lot of activity outside the hotel. Crime scene tape sealed off the entrance to the building, and Alfie Fox was guarding the door. There were half a dozen patrol cars and several cars that Mahoney recognised as belonging to detectives left in the car park. He parked his patrol car next to Jackie Munro's Nissan, picked up his hat from the passenger seat and got out.

He went to the door, lifting the tape and sliding beneath it.

Fox saw him. "All right, Michael?"

"No, I'm not. I'm knackered, and there's absolutely no way any of us are going to be able to knock off until God knows when."

"That's the truth. I spoke to the gaffer—it's all hands on deck." He shrugged. "Still—think of the overtime."

"I don't need the overtime; I need a whiskey and my bed."

That, at least, was true: he *didn't* need the money. Gallagher gave him more than enough, but the cash came with a caveat: he paid top dollar and expected top work. He wouldn't stand for it if jobs weren't done properly. Like this one, he thought miserably.

Mahoney went inside, following the corridor to the back of the hotel and the elevator used by staff to navigate the building without disturbing the guests. He stepped in, pressed the button for the fourth floor, and the lift started to climb. He wanted to nose around in Blair's room. He had disappeared, and Mahoney had nothing he could use to find him. There had to be something, and he was due a break.

The lift stopped, the doors opened, and he disembarked. There were doors to the left and right, the spaces between them suggesting that the rooms were modest. Each door bore a name card with the occupant's name. He turned left and passed four rooms—MILEY, KILROY, RAFFERTY, SELES—until he reached a door with a card that read BLAIR.

Mahoney turned the handle. The door was locked. With

a quick glance down the hallway, he pulled a worn-out credit card from his wallet. He slid it into the narrow gap between the door and the frame, feeling the resistance of the latch. He positioned the card perpendicular to the door and applied pressure, simultaneously nudging it with his free hand. There was a brief moment of resistance, the card bent, and then, with a satisfying click, the latch gave way.

The room was small with simple furnishings: a single bed against the wall, dressed in clean linen and with a single pillow; a sturdy wardrobe against the adjacent wall, offering a place for Blair to store his clothing and personal belongings; a bedside table with a lamp, the bulb switched on and casting a warm glow across the room. There was no bathroom; Mahoney assumed that there would be communal facilities.

The bed hadn't been slept in. It had been neatly made, and, as Mahoney looked around, he saw that the same neatness was evident in everything else. The running shoes next to the bed were aligned perfectly, and when he opened the wardrobe, he saw that the small collection of clothes had been ironed and folded so that everything lined up. It was weird, and it reminded him of the suicide of a soldier he'd investigated last year. The man had drowned himself in the Liffey, and Mahoney had gone back to his house to break the news to his wife. He had seen the same neatness and organisation there as in Blair's room now.

Could Blair be ex-military, too?

He put on a pair of nitrile gloves, then knelt down and looked under the bed, reaching beneath to pull out a suitcase. He put the case on the bed, popped the clasps and opened it. It was empty save for three paperback books: *Nineteen Eighty-Four*, *Middlemarch* and *The Catcher in the Rye*. Mahoney picked up *Middlemarch* and flicked through it; a piece of paper fluttered down to settle on the duvet. He picked it up and saw that it was a train ticket, but not one that he recognised: the right-hand corner had the logo of a company he didn't recognise, and HAPPY JOURNEY had been written in the left. The ticket was for a journey a month earlier from New Delhi to Jammu Tawi.

He recognised New Delhi, of course, but not the destination. He took out his phone, Googled it and saw that it was in Kashmir. Mahoney stared at the ticket and wondered what business Blair would have had there. Was he a back-packer, perhaps? He looked too old for that, but who knew? Midlife crisis? He wouldn't be the first to do something like that.

Mahoney snapped a photograph of the ticket and then put it back between the pages of the book. He replaced the volumes in the case, closed it and put it back under the bed. He was about to leave when he noticed that the carpet in the corner of the room had peeled back a little. He knelt down, gripped the edge between his thumb and forefinger and gave it a yank. The carpet came up and, hidden beneath it, he saw a clear plastic folder. He took the folder, opened it and tipped out the contents: three passports, a decent amount of money in both dollars and euros, and a leather pouch that, when he unrolled it, contained a set of lock picks.

He examined the passports one by one: dark blue for the United Kingdom, Bordeaux-red for France and blue for Croatia. He flipped to the photo pages and saw the same photograph of Blair in all three, save that the details were different each time: the British passport had him as Eric Blair, the EU had him as Peter Murphy, and Croatia had him as Miroslav Krleža.

Mahoney stared at the three documents in bemusement.

Who *was* he?

Certainly not who he said he was.

He took photographs of all three passports and put them back in their hiding place beneath the carpet. He got back to his feet and, satisfied that he hadn't missed anything else, left the room and continued down the corridor. He stopped at the communal bathroom and went inside: it was clean and well maintained, with three shower stalls, three sinks, and two toilets. Rows of hooks and small lockers provided space for toiletries and towels. There was nothing to cast any further light on Blair.

He gazed out of the window to the street below.

One thing was obvious: Blair wasn't a cook.

But who *was* he? He removed the gloves, then went back to Blair's room to relock the door.

"Excuse me?"

Mahoney turned. A woman had come out of one of the rooms and was looking at him.

"Hello," he said. "Who are you?"

"Louisa," she said. "I work downstairs on reception. Can I help?"

"I'm looking for the man who lives here."

"Eric?"

"That's right—Mr. Blair. Do you know where he is?"

"No. But he was involved in what happened downstairs, wasn't he?"

"I'm afraid I can't talk about that."

"It's all right—I know he was. Everyone's talking about it. There's something you ought to know about. My friend— Maria—she's gone, too."

"Really?" Mahoney felt his pulse quicken.

"Eric and Maria brought a girl up to Maria's room. I

spoke to Maria—she said the girl had been downstairs when it happened, and they brought her up here because it'd be safer until the police arrived. Eric went down for a bit, then came up here again and took her back downstairs with him."

"And didn't come back?"

"No."

"What about Maria?"

"She left afterwards. I asked her where she was going, but she didn't say."

"Was Maria friendly with Eric?"

"She liked him. He's too old for her, but... anyway, that doesn't matter. I thought you should know."

"How did she look?" he said. "When she left, I mean?"

"Worried."

"And you've no idea where she might've gone?"

"No," she said. "I'm sorry."

Mahoney scratched his cheek. He wondered whether he might have—finally—got a lucky break.

"Which one is her room?"

Louisa pointed along the corridor. Mahoney went to it and tried the handle. It was locked.

"Don't you need something to get inside?"

"Do you mean a search warrant? No. Not when I'm worried about her."

"*Are* you worried?"

"Three men were killed earlier tonight, and Mr. Blair was involved."

"But he was trying to help."

"It looks like that, but we won't be able to say for sure until we've been able to speak to him. The fact that he's not here is concerning. The same can be said for Maria. I need to look in her room for anything that might help us find her."

"Okay," Louisa said. "I've got a key for her room. I'll go and get it."

56

S hay drove them both to the Bridewell Garda Station on Chancery Street in the middle of the city. It was very early in the morning, the roads were quiet, and the big car park at the back of the building was empty.

"I know this sticks in the craw," his mother said as he switched off the engine. "Going to ask the police for help. But we're doing it for Cara."

"And if they start poking around about what happened?"

"Then we tell them the truth—we don't know what happened. And we don't, do we?"

"We have an idea."

"But we'll be keeping that to ourselves."

"Fine."

"No attitude, Shay. We need them on our side—at least until we've got her back again. After that? We find out who did it and make sure they get what's coming to them."

"We *know*, Ma. We know it was Billy."

She stared at him.

"Okay," he said, giving in. "I get it—you're right. I'll be good."

They left the car and walked into the station. The doors were open, and, although the desk was unmanned, an officer appeared as soon as Eileen pressed the button to sound the bell.

"Hello," she said. "How can I help you?"

Shay stepped up to the desk. "My niece has gone missing."

"I'm sorry, sir—what did you say?"

"My niece," he said, his fists clenched. "She's missing, and I need you lot to help me find her."

"Can I have your name, sir?"

It would have been funny if he weren't so desperate. "I'm Shay Dillon. And this is my mother, Eileen."

The woman didn't react. "Take a seat, please, Mr. Dillon. I'll have a detective out to see you straight away."

Dillon led his mother to the waiting area, and they both sat down. This whole thing was surreal: coming into the station and asking for the Garda's help. He hadn't even had a chance to think about what had happened to his brother, but, as he lowered himself to the plastic seat and sat, he felt a jolt of anger so intense that it blurred his vision.

He *was* sure it was Billy Gallagher. No one else would have the bottle to do something so reckless—so *stupid*—especially given the certainty that the retaliation would be brutal. He knew Billy held them responsible for what had happened to his son, as if they were answerable for the lack of control that had him put too much of their dope into his arm. It was true that Eileen had warned the boys about selling their product on Gallagher's side of the city, but they had ignored her. Shay had no respect for the old bastard, and he wasn't the sort of fella to let an opportunity to make money pass him by because of the fear of causing offence. Shay liked to say he had a Darwinian view of business: it was the survival of the fittest, and although Billy Gallagher might once have had something about him that deserved respect, he didn't have it anymore and didn't deserve his place at the table.

Eileen opened her bag and took out the book of Sudoku that she always had with her. She opened it to the puzzle she was working on and took out a pencil.

"How can you do that *now*?"

"Helps keep my mind off it," she said.

He looked at the grid filled with her spidery script, snorted his disdain and took out his phone. He was hoping that there might have been an update from McGrath, but he had no messages and no calls. He had just started typing a message to send to him when he glanced up and saw a detective making her way across to them.

"Ma," he said, nudging her.

The woman sported shoulder-length dark brown hair pulled back into a simple ponytail. She was dressed in practical clothes—a button-down shirt, black trousers, and a jacket—and she wore hardly any make-up. Her tall frame and athletic build gave her a commanding presence.

"Hello. I'm Detective Superintendent Meaney. I understand you're here because of your niece."

"That's right."

"My granddaughter," Eileen said.

"Of course. I know who you are—you're Eileen Dillon." She turned. "And you're Shay Dillon."

Shay wasn't remotely surprised; their notoriety went before them.

Meaney stepped to the side and gestured to the door at the other end of the room. "Do you think you could come into the back with me? We'll take a statement from you, and then we'll see about finding her."

57

L ouisa gave Mahoney a key and waited as he unlocked the door to Maria's room.

"Thank you."

She paused until she realised what he was saying. "Yes, of course. I'll be in my room. Number six. Knock on the door when you're finished so I can get the key again."

"Will do. Thanks again."

She lingered for a moment more before going to her room. Mahoney opened the door and went inside: it was similar to Blair's room, although, where his was ascetic, Maria had gone to the effort of making hers look homely: a floral duvet cover, a vase of flowers, framed photos on the wall. He reached into his pocket for the nitrile gloves and put them back on. He went to the bedside table and picked through the things left there: a charger for a mobile phone, a Kindle, a glass of water, lip balm and hand cream, and a notebook and pen. Mahoney picked up the notebook and flipped through the pages; it looked as if she was using it as a journal, but it was written in a language—Spanish or Portuguese, he thought—he didn't understand. He flicked through to the back and looked down as a piece of paper slipped out and fluttered to the floor. He picked it up, turned it over and saw that it was a receipt from Harmony, a dry-cleaning business at the Mill Shopping Centre in Clondalkin. There was little in the way of detail—Maria's name, the date the items were dropped off, and, on the back, the store's terms and conditions—but it was a start. Mahoney used his phone's camera to take a photograph of it, then put it back into the notebook and replaced it on the bedside table.

He looked through the wardrobe but found nothing else of use. He left the room, locked the door and went down the corridor to Louisa's room.

"Did you find anything?"

"How long has she lived at the hotel?"

"Not long. Two or three weeks."

"Do you know where she was before that?"

"We never talked about it."

"Clondalkin?"

She shrugged. "She never said. Why?"

"Never mind. If you can think of anything or if she gets in touch, please give me a ring." He reached into his pocket and took out a card with his name and telephone number. He gave it to her. "This is me. You can call me day or night."

She took the card. "I will," she said.

Mahoney went to the stairs and descended to the next landing down. He waited there, turned up the volume on his radio and pressed the push-to-talk button.

"Dispatch, this is Sergeant Mahoney, badge number 14432. Over."

"Dispatch here, go ahead, Sergeant Mahoney. How can I help? Over."

"Dispatch, I'm investigating the report of a missing

person. Can you provide me with any available information on a Maria Quitéria de Jesus? Over."

"Copy that, Sergeant Mahoney. Let me check. Stand by. Over."

A window looked out onto the Dublin skyline. Mahoney gazed into the darkness and wondered where Blair and the woman had gone with the girl. He needed something to offer Billy, and if he couldn't find her, he wasn't sure what he would do.

The radio squelched. "Sergeant Mahoney, this is Dispatch. I've got something for you. Maria Quitéria de Jesus is part of an investigation by the National Immigration Bureau. She's suspected of being in Ireland illegally."

"Any previous addresses?"

"No, afraid not."

"Anything that might give me an idea where she is?"

"Nothing obvious. You'd have to speak to the bureau."

He rapped his knuckles against the wall in frustration. "Thank you."

"Anything else?"

"That's all."

He turned the dial to quieten the radio and thought for a moment about what he could do. He could speak to the bureau, but, if he did that, he'd have to share the news that the woman was missing along with Blair. It would be inevitable, eventually, but he wanted to keep it to himself for as long as he could. Mahoney had been coppering for long enough to know she was the best lead he had, and the moment he passed the information along, he would lose his advantage.

The more he thought about it, the surer he was: find her, find Blair, find the girl.

Where had they gone?

58

Milton had been much too on edge for sleep and hadn't even bothered to undress. He got up off the bed and, treading carefully across the noisy boards, crept up to the door to the other bedroom. It was ajar, and he pushed it open a little more so that he could look inside: Maria was in the bed nearest to the door, and Cara was in the one beneath the window. Both were asleep, their breathing deep and even.

The second bedroom was similar to the one that Maria and the girl had taken, save that it had a double bed. The mattress was thin and worn, with lumps and bumps suggesting its age, and the pillows were filled with synthetic stuffing and covered with plain pillowcases. Milton went to the window, pulled back the curtain and looked down at the tiny backyard and the alley behind the house.

Everything was quiet.

He took out his phone and called Ziggy.

"It's late," he complained.

"And I knew you'd be up."

"The price of Bitcoin is about to fall. I want to be ready to load up."

"How do you know that?"

"Best not to ask," he said. "Are you okay?"

Milton watched the lights of a jet as it crossed the night sky. "I'm fine. I've found somewhere to lie low while I work out what happened at the hotel. That's why I'm calling—have you got anything yet?"

"Not much. Still looking."

Milton saw a light flick on in one of the houses on the other side of the alley. "What are the police saying?"

"It's complete chaos—they're running around like headless chickens at the moment. They're saying another man was killed—someone from the kitchens?"

"He was a kid," Milton said. "A student, worked there to pay his way through college. The killer cut his throat. His name was Padraig."

"Padraig Farrell," Ziggy said.

Milton clenched his fist. "I can't let that stand, but I need something to go on, Ziggy. I can't do anything if I'm in the dark."

"There's a police briefing later this morning," he said. "I might be able to get something after that's been written up."

A figure was silhouetted in the window. "What about the girl I told you about? I think one of the victims might have been her father."

"Is she with you?"

"Yes, and I can't get her to speak. I don't know her full name, where she lives, how to contact her family—nothing. If it *is* her dad, she saw him shot dead in front of her."

"Shouldn't you take her to the police?"

"Tried that. I was going to hand her over to an officer, but she recognised him, freaked out and ran. I tried to get in between the two of them, and he got heavy. I think I might've broken his nose. His partner, too—he got a face full of tear gas. I don't know how she's relevant, but the police doesn't feel like the best option for her until I can find someone who's definitely on the level."

"You got *anything* for her?"

"Just her first name—I think it's Cara."

"I'll search on it and see what I can find."

"And the policeman, too. Anything you've got on him. His surname's Mahoney, but that's all I have. I didn't get his badge number."

"Mahoney," Ziggy repeated. "All right. This is all ASAP?"

"What do you think?"

"I'll call you back in an hour or two. Will you be awake?"

"I won't be able to sleep."

"Leave your phone on."

59

Meaney took Shay and his mother to a stark and utilitarian interview room designed to be as oppressive as it was functional. The walls were painted a drab institutional green, and the fluorescent lights overhead cast an unflattering, almost sickly pallor over everything, picking out the cracks in the paint and the faded water stains across the ceiling. There was a single small window in one wall, high up and barred, allowing the light from a streetlamp outside to filter through the grime-streaked glass. The air seemed to hang heavy with the weight of a thousand confessions, but it didn't bother Shay. He had seen more than his fair share of rooms like this over the years, but, thanks to thorough planning, the best legal advice that money could buy, and—he wasn't afraid to admit it—a little luck, his experience of the Irish criminal justice system had never gone beyond the occasional unfriendly chat.

The table was scarred and pitted from years of use. There were four metal chairs, cold and uninviting, and a man was waiting in one of them.

Meaney indicated him. "This is Detective Inspector Tarrant."

Tarrant didn't get up, and Shay just glared at him.

"Take a seat," Meaney said.

Shay pulled out a chair for his mother and then took the one next to her. A digital voice recorder sat on the table. The walls were bare save for a faded poster outlining the rights of the accused, its corners curling with age, the ink blurred and smudged.

"First of all," Meaney said to them both, "I know you're here because of your niece, but we know what happened at the hotel tonight, and we're very sorry for your loss."

"Thank you," Eileen said.

"I should explain before we get started—I'm in charge of the investigation into the murders, and DI Tarrant is assisting me. Aside from Colm, two other men lost their lives, and, as you can imagine, we're treating this very seriously."

Shay nodded. "Good."

"What can you tell us about what happened?"

"I don't know," Shay said. "I wasn't there."

"Neither was I," his mother added.

"But you must have spoken to someone about it?"

Shay took a breath. "One of the men who worked for me told me what had happened, but he wasn't there either."

"Go on," she prodded. "What did he say?"

"He said a man shot my brother and another man we were working with."

"That's it?"

"He said the man who did it is Mickey Flannagan. Is that right?"

"We think so," she said. "What do you know about him?"

"Nothing," Shay said. "I've never even heard of him before. What can you tell us?"

"He worked at the hotel. Beyond that, I'm afraid we can't tell you anything at the moment."

"Can't or won't?"

"The investigation is proceeding," Meaney said. "We'll let you have our findings when the time is right."

Tarrant tapped his pen against an empty page in his notebook. "So you definitely weren't there."

"I just told you that. I went straight to Colm's house when I heard. My mother was there, and then we came here. I'll find out more later, but, given that my niece is missing, I thought I should speak to you before I did anything else."

"Quite," Meaney said.

Tarrant tapped his notebook again. "You must have an idea about who was behind this."

"We might as well stop beating around the bush," Eileen said. "You know who we are, and you know that there are plenty of people in Dublin who would like to hurt us."

Meaney nodded. "Let's be completely open, then. Who do you think did it?"

"Billy Gallagher," Eileen said. "Who else?"

"What about the O'Reillys?" Tarrant suggested, referring to one of Dublin's other well-known crime families.

"Or the Cavanaghs?" Meaney added, referencing another. "Or the Albanians?"

"Maybe," Eileen conceded. "But it wouldn't be where I'd put my money."

"It's Gallagher," Shay insisted. "That's who you want to be bringing in here and questioning."

"We'll bear that in mind," Meaney said.

"One more thing," Tarrant said, "before we move on to

your niece—we've been looking for you all night. If you weren't at the hotel, where were you?"

"Working. I had business."

"Can I ask where that was?"

Shay felt his anger kindling. "At my warehouse on the docks."

"There'll be people there who'll back you up?"

"Of course—all the men who work there. Why are you asking me that?"

"Just because it's strange," Tarrant said. "You had a big event, the whole hotel was booked out, yet you weren't there. Can you see why we're finding that hard to follow?"

Shay leaned forward, his elbows on the table. "Listen," he said, eyeing the man. "My brother was killed, and my niece is missing. Some bastard took her from the hotel. You either help me to find her, or I'm going to piss off out of here right now and find her myself."

Eileen reached out, took his shoulder and gently pulled him back into his chair. "My son is upset," she said. "We both are. Losing my boy would be bad enough, but now we're beside ourselves with worry about Cara."

Shay put his hands in his lap to hide his bunched fists from them. He felt claustrophobic.

Meaney put her hands on the table. "You have my word that we'll do everything we can to find her. We'll have questions for you about what happened, and why, but they can wait. I agree—Cara's the priority now."

The red mist that had descended across Shay's vision lifted a little. "Good."

"So," she said. "Let's start there."

She opened the folder, took out a piece of paper and laid it on the table in front of Shay. It was an image of a man:

average height, average build, middle-aged, dark hair, blue eyes.

"Who's that?" he said.

"You haven't seen him before?"

"I wouldn't need to ask who he was if I had, would I?"

She gave a thin smile. "His name's Eric Blair. He works in the hotel kitchen as a cook. He started last week."

"He was working as a waiter during the fight," Tarrant said, "and CCTV shows him getting involved after your brother was shot. He tackled Flannagan to the ground. There was a struggle, and Flannagan was shot."

Shay remembered what McGrath had told him. "What does he have to do with Cara?"

"We can't be sure, but it looks like Mr. Blair got her out of the room, possibly to keep her safe. He came down again later to speak with one of our officers. The officer says that Blair agreed to go and get the girl so that she could be handed over, but then there was some sort of altercation. From what we've been told by the officer and his partner, Cara panicked and tried to run away. The officers and Blair chased her, and then—and we don't know why this is— Blair attacked them both."

"Have you spoken to them?"

"We have, and they have no idea."

Eileen frowned. "Where is he now?"

"We think he left the hotel with Cara."

"You've searched it to be sure?"

"From top to bottom," Tarrant said. "She wasn't there, and another member of staff can't be accounted for either— Maria Quitéria de Jesus."

"Quitéria de Jesus is a Brazilian immigrant," Meaney said. "She works in the kitchen, too."

"And you think it's them?" Eileen said. "They took her?"

"It seems likely. A laundry van was stolen just after the officers were attacked. The driver didn't see who took it, but it seems reasonable to suggest that Blair or Quitéria de Jesus used it to get away. Of course, the whole thing *might* be innocent. It might be that they wanted to get Cara somewhere as far away as possible, but that would still be suspicious. And we don't know why Blair attacked the two officers."

"Who were they? The officers, I mean."

"I can't tell you. We're still investigating that."

"And Flannagan?"

"He's in hospital."

"He must've had help, though. He couldn't have done this by himself."

"Why do you say that?" Meaney asked.

"Because it wouldn't have been possible. We had security there."

Meaney shrugged. "But it's hard to see how Blair could've been involved in what happened. He was the one who stopped Flannagan."

Shay closed his eyes. He liked to be in control, and, right now, he most certainly was not. He'd run rings around the police for years and had seen how hopeless they were. That he needed them to be better now was an irony that wasn't lost on him.

"Can we help you with anything else?" Eileen asked them.

"No," Meaney said. "We have all we need from you for now. Our priority is finding Cara. As soon as we have anything, we'll be in touch."

Shay took the printout of Blair's photograph and, before either officer could object, folded it once and then twice and slipped it into the inside pocket of his jacket.

"One more thing," Eileen said. "Where's my son's body?"

"City morgue."

"I want to see him."

"We were going to suggest doing that in the morning. We'll need you to identify him."

Eileen stood. "No—not in the morning. Now. I want to see him *now*."

60

Mahoney took one of the few empty seats around the conference table and looked around. The room was large, with white walls and fluorescent overhead lighting. A whiteboard was mounted on one of the walls, with photographs of the Southside Hotel's events space stuck to it. A corkboard held additional information: a map of the area and a suggested timeline. A large rectangular table dominated the centre of the room, and almost all of the office chairs around it had been taken; other officers leaned against the walls. The full complement of detectives and senior uniform was in attendance, all waiting to be briefed by Detective Superintendent Meaney.

They all knew that the story would gain national attention as soon as the new day began. An outside broadcast truck had already set up, the reporters getting ready to discuss the story on the morning news, and there would be others. The investigation would be put under the microscope, and the attention was not something that Mahoney relished.

Meaney and Detective Inspector Tarrant came inside and took their seats at the head of the table.

"All right," Meaney said. "Pipe down. Lots to get through. We need to get cracking."

The chatter quietened.

"I'd apologise to those who've been hauled out of bed, but since the job is the job and this is going to be a bloody important enquiry, I'm not going to bother. We're all hands on deck until we get to the bottom of what happened yesterday evening. We've got three dead victims, and you know as well as I do that the press is going to be over this like flies on shit."

Garvey raised his hand. "What about the shooter?"

"Mickey Flannagan," Meaney said. "He'll be familiar to some of you."

"Dead or alive?"

"Alive," Meaney said, "but in intensive care. We've put Eoin Lynch outside the room to keep an eye on him. He called ten minutes ago—the doctor has just been to see him, and he says it looks like he's over the worst."

"He's going to make it?" Mahoney asked.

"Seventy-thirty, he said."

"They give you any idea when he might be fit to be questioned?"

"No," she said. "We'll play it by ear."

They moved on to the rest of the briefing, with Meaney going through the timeline of what had happened and suggesting possible lines of enquiry. The officers listened attentively, taking notes in their notepads or on their tablets. Tarrant took over, identifying the three victims and passing on as much of their backgrounds as would be useful. Mahoney worked hard to appear engaged, worried that his creeping fear would be obvious to anyone who looked at him.

Flannagan was going to make it?

Surely, they'd find out what Mahoney had done?

Tarrant handed back to Meaney.

"Getting to the bottom of what happened at the hotel is a priority, but there's something else. We had a visit from Shay Dillon this morning. His niece, Cara, was at the hotel, and now she's missing. We've gone over the CCTV from the event, and she was on the same table as her father. Flannagan shot Rickard and Dillon but was stopped from escaping by this man—here."

Tarrant tapped his laptop keyboard and gestured up at the screen and the still image from the hotel's CCTV. Mahoney looked up with the others and saw the man who had attacked him in the hotel.

"His name is Eric Blair," Meaney said. "He arrived in the country two weeks ago under a UK passport. We've asked immigration to run a check on it, and the early indication I've been given is that there's a good chance it's fake." She looked down at her notes. "He started work at the hotel this week and had a room in the staff quarters. He normally worked as a cook, but they were short of waiters for the event, and he was asked to go and work on the floor. He left the room with Cara after the shooting and took her out of the way. He came back down to the ballroom once we had it under control and spoke to Lynch and then Michael." She gestured to Mahoney. "Michael?"

Mahoney nodded. "He told Eoin that he was looking after a girl who'd been at the table and that he wanted to make sure she was safe. Eoin told him to bring her down, and he did. I spoke to the girl, but something spooked her, and she ran."

"Why?"

"I don't know."

Meaney pursed her lips. "Scared of the police on account of what her dad might've told her?"

"That's what I thought. I went after her, grabbed her to try to get her to calm down, and she panicked. The next thing I know, it all goes to shit. Blair pulls me away and butts me—hence my nose." There were sympathetic winces as Mahoney turned his face so they could all see. "Lynch tried to subdue him, but Blair took my CS and sprayed him in the face. He took the girl and vanished."

"And then?"

"A van delivering laundry was stolen," Tarrant said. "We can't say for sure, but the working theory is that he took it."

"Why?" Mahoney said. "He gets involved, asks for police help, attacks the police and then runs? None of it makes a jot of sense."

"I agree," Meaney said. "It doesn't."

Tarrant looked over at Mahoney. "Anything else, Michael?"

Mahoney shook his head and put his notebook away. There was plenty he *could* have said: he could have told them about the fake passports that he had found in Blair's room, but he decided to keep that to himself, at least for now. He could have told them about Maria Quitéria de Jesus but kept that quiet for the same reason. He knew he'd have to report it eventually, but not yet. He wanted to see what he could find out before anyone else could get to her.

"All right," Meaney said, standing. "Get out there and find out what happened. Put out feelers, go see your CIs, see what people are saying, make it obvious that we'll go in hard on anyone who knows what happened and isn't coming forward to tell us." She clapped her hands. "Dismissed."

61

Milton closed the bedroom door and made his way down the stairs. A collection of flyers and circulars had gathered beneath the letterbox, and he picked one up and, using a pen he found in the cutlery drawer, wrote a note to Maria explaining that he had had to go out and that he would be back as soon as he could. He didn't expect that he would be more than an hour or two, but the last thing he wanted was for either Maria or the girl to think he'd abandoned them in the night.

He went outside, checked his phone and found the nearest car park. He knew it would be unsafe to use the laundry van again; he had to assume the police would be looking for it, and it was distinctive. He would leave it where he had dumped it and find an alternative. The car park was a ten-minute walk to the west and served a shopping centre. It was large, and, although it was almost entirely empty at this time of day, there were still half a dozen cars that had been left. He ignored the more modern vehicles and crossed the space to an old BMW coupe that had been parked beneath the boughs of a sickly-looking larch. He forced the door and, working with deft fingers, hotwired the engine. He put the car into reverse, pulled out and, after inputting the address that Ziggy had given him, started the thirty-minute drive to the east.

ZIGGY HAD SENT a message suggesting that they meet in KC Peaches on St Stephen's Green. Milton drove into the city, taking the moment to consider how the events of the last few hours had changed his plans. He wasn't prepared to abandon Cara, but he felt as if he had already outstayed his welcome here and that it would be a good idea if he looked at ways to exfiltrate as quickly as possible. He had only intended to be here for as long as it took him to find out whatever he could about Lilly Moon; he would get whatever he could from her ex-husband and then disappear to plot his next move. That felt even more important now. He knew his presence at the hotel during the shooting would have made it more likely he would be compromised. He wasn't concerned about the Garda, but more that any footage of the attack was now likely to be on a police server and that the analysts from Group Three might stumble across it. They had found him before, soon after he had fled London for Ciudad Juárez. He needed to stay ahead of them until he could get to Control so she could corroborate his version of the betrayal in Russia.

Milton parked the car and got out, walking the rest of the way to the café. It was open twenty-four hours a day and quiet given the early hour. He went inside. The seating area was divided into two sections; the first was located at the front of the café and featured a large bay window; the second section was located towards the back and was more private. Ziggy was waiting at a table at the back. His laptop was out, he had his headphones on, and he was lost in whatever it was that was on the screen.

Milton came over and plucked the headphones from his head. "Morning."

Ziggy frowned at him. "Don't do that, you dick. You could've been anyone."

"Exactly. A little advice: want to make sure no one can come up behind you without you noticing? Choose a table up against the wall. Facing the wall makes you look like an amateur."

Ziggy looked as if he was going to protest but thought better of it. Milton indicated the booth over to the right, and Ziggy picked up his computer and joined him there. The bench seats were upholstered in soft leather, and the booth was arranged in a way to allow for privacy.

Milton pointed to the laptop. "What have you got?"

"Quite a lot." Ziggy turned the laptop, and Milton saw that he had three open windows. "I got into the Garda's server. It's still pretty fuzzy, but it looks like what happened at the hotel involved two criminal organisations going after each other. How much do you know so far?"

"Nothing."

"I'll give you the bird's-eye view, then. On the one hand, you've got Billy Gallagher—an old-school villain who's been active in the city for decades, interested in extortion, money laundering, illegal gambling, loan sharking. All the *old-fash-ioned* vices. And then you have the Dillons—more recent, different way of looking at things, players in the drugs business, importing product and sending it into the UK. The two families have been jostling for position for months. It's all macho bullshit. Gallagher has this idea that there's a code of practice—honour among thieves, blah, blah, all that—and the Dillons are brazen and in-your-face. I also found a report that suggested that Billy had a son who OD'd and that he says the drugs came from a shipment the Dillons brought in."

"So there's personal animus."

He nodded. "Looks that way. Could be the motive, but we're speculating. The police haven't taken a view yet."

"Who are the dead men?"

"The first is Frank Rickard. American, works as a fight promoter, over here to see the MMA fight tomorrow. The second man is much more interesting. Colm Dillon. He and his brother are in charge of the Dillon family."

"And Flannagan?"

"Mickey Flannagan. Petty criminal, been in and out of prison four times over the last half a dozen years—two charges for dealing and one for assault, plus multiple cautions for possession. Bad behaviour runs in the family— his son was charged with assault last year, and his trial is coming up. They've got no idea on motive, though."

"Money," Milton said. "He was picked because he's not afraid of violence and because he would've been disposable if anything went wrong."

"One thing they've struggled with is how he got the gun through the security."

"I know *exactly* how they did that. It was hidden in the hotel bathroom the night before."

"How can you be sure?"

"I was in the bathroom when it was left."

Ziggy stared at him for a beat. "Who did that?"

"We'll get to that," Milton said. "Let's assume motive comes out of a struggle between the Dillons and Gallagher. I think the fight on Saturday might have crystallised it. The main event is Charlie Gallagher—Billy Gallagher's son—against Danny Farley. Farley is the Dillons' man."

"The Dillons paid for Farley's training in return for half of his earnings."

"That might be relevant. How do you know that?"

"I follow MMA. Farley could be the next Conor McGregor. If he is..." He shrugged. "They'd all make millions."

"That won't sit well with Gallagher. What about the girl?"

Ziggy moused over to the second window and maximised it. A picture of Cara filled the screen. "Cara Dillon."

"Colm's daughter?"

He nodded. "Nine years old."

"Where does she live?"

"I'm still looking. The Dillons own property all over the city, so it's not easy to be sure. They're careful with data security, too. I haven't been able to get anything on them beyond what I've already told you."

"The police don't have an address for Colm?"

"They do," Ziggy said, "but I had a look—it's empty. Looks like he moved. I'll get it eventually, but I'll need a little longer."

Milton winced. "I need something now. I can't be in the city after what happened, but I can't leave until I've got her back to her family."

"There is one address that might be worth a visit. Danny Farley is being trained by a man called Paddy Coffey, and Coffey has a gym in Corduff—on the outskirts of the city, northeast from here. Try there. Maybe Coffey knows."

"Send me the address."

Ziggy sent it. Milton tapped the screen, his map popped

up, and he plotted a route: ten kilometres to the west, near to Blanchardstown.

"What about Mahoney?"

Ziggy nodded. "I found out a lot about him. He's *very* interesting."

He clicked the third window and maximised an extract from a personnel file. It was marked 'private and confidential' in one corner and bore the harp of the Garda in the other. There was a photograph of Mahoney and then a list of his personal details: address and length of service, with links to his annual appraisals.

"He's been a policeman for fifteen years. Very good appraisals for the first three years, but things start to go downhill after that. He made it to detective inspector but was demoted after a siege he was involved with went south and he took the blame. It all came to a head this year. Turns out he's being looked at by the ombudsman."

"For what?"

"They've opened an investigation into allegations that he's misused his authority to cancel minor offences in exchange for payment. There've been other allegations in the past, too: intimidation of witnesses, bribes, stolen evidence, falsified reports. It's easier to say what he *isn't* accused of."

"Violence?"

"Nothing in the file."

"And he's still a policeman?"

"Nothing's been proven. You think he's involved with the murder?"

"He is," Milton said. "He's the one who left the gun for Flannagan. I saw him in the bathroom the night before, and then the kid from the hotel was stabbed in the same bathroom before the shooting. Mahoney left the gun; Flannagan took it and killed the kid after he saw him with it. I'd bet you anything you like that's what happened. Mahoney went after Cara, too. Why would he do that?"

"Maybe she was the whole point all along."

"Maybe," Milton said, "but I don't think so. I think the hit went wrong. Maybe Dillon *wasn't* the target—maybe it was the other guy, and Dillon got involved."

"And the girl?"

"Insurance. Maybe Mahoney thinks having her keeps the Dillons off his case while he works out how to get away. Or maybe not—maybe it's something else."

"Or he was going to take her to the Gallaghers."

"You seen anything specific that might link him to them?"

"No, but I wasn't looking. I can go back in and dig around."

"Please," Milton said. He gestured to the laptop. "This is good stuff. Thank you."

Ziggy smiled with satisfaction. "I'll get an address for Cara. I'll just need a little longer."

"And I'll visit Coffey and see if that gets me anywhere."

"And then? You'll take her back?"

"Of course."

"You could just let the police do their job."

"Can't. Mahoney's crooked—what if he gets involved? I need to sort it out myself."

He stood.

Ziggy held up a hand "One more thing. You wanted to know about Control and Otto Sommer. It's about as difficult as you'd expect to dig much up on him, but I think I might've found something that could be useful."

Milton sat back down. "Go on."

"The FSB has an encrypted messaging system for use by

their officers. Group Three have been monitoring it for years, and I used their exploit to get in. There's chatter that a high-value intelligence asset was secured and transported to a facility run by Unit 29155 in Siberia."

"Control?"

"There's nothing *specific* that'd suggest that."

"So why are you telling me?"

"Because I found a waybill for a six-month supply of insulin being sent from the Unit's medical facility in Krasnodar to Salekhard."

"Where?"

"Up in the Arctic Circle. There's nothing there—just fish canning, sawmills and a base for the gas fields."

"And that's relevant how?"

"Control's diabetic."

Milton paused. Was it possible that was where she was? He was about as sure as he could be that they wouldn't have killed Control, she was an asset of the most exceptional value, and Sommer would stow her somewhere safe while he bled as much intelligence out of her as he could before she broke.

"Do you have a specific location?"

"No, and I doubt I'll be able to get one. But I *did* find someone who might be able to help. Have you heard of Nikita Yevtushenko?"

"Should I?"

"Russian operative. Defected twenty years ago."

"Before my time."

"It was kept quiet—the suggestion is that he came out with a lot of very valuable intelligence. His records have been buried, but the implication I've been able to draw from the ones I've found is that he had a crisis of conscience about the things that he'd done before he defected. He had a breakdown and killed a delivery driver in Hastings when he thought he was an FSB agent come to kill him. The government put a D-notice on it to keep it out of the papers and tried to bring him back into the fold, but he disappeared. His clothes were found on the beach, and the assumption was that he'd walked out to sea and drowned himself, but then he turned up again last year."

"Where?"

"Eastern Ukraine. Fighting *against* the Russians."

"And how is he relevant to Control?"

"Yevtushenko was one of Sommer's killers. Might have been his *best* killer. He did ten years in the Unit before he came over. It's almost impossible to find anyone you could talk to about the Unit, but if anyone can tell you about Sommer and where he might have taken Control, it'd be him."

62

Mahoney went to his desk after the briefing had concluded. He sat down, booted up his computer and navigated to the PULSE system the Garda used to access information on people of interest. It allowed officers to access and share information on criminal records, incidents, investigations, and intelligence, and —he hoped—might give him something to go on in his attempt to find Blair before anyone else.

He didn't expect anything on Blair himself but checked anyway, no results of relevance were returned, and he closed the query and opened another to start again. He typed out Maria Quitéria de Jesus's name and hit return.

The system took a moment to work through its databases, but, when it reported, it returned a file note from the Garda National Immigration Bureau. Mahoney had expected it: he opened it, leaned forward in his chair and read.

The file was a summation of an ongoing investigation into the Southside Hotel. They had been given a tip that the business was employing illegal immigrants, and had opened a joint investigation with the Irish Naturalisation and Immigration Service. Five employees had never applied for or been given a visa, including Quitéria de Jesus. A South American crime syndicate was reputed to be behind the scheme; they flew the immigrants into Dublin on commercial planes, told them not to go through immigration and then smuggled them out in catering trucks. No moves had been made against the individual immigrants while the investigation concentrated on the criminals behind the scheme. The police had identified several properties throughout Dublin that were used to house the immigrants, who were provided with forged papers, jobs and permanent places to live.

Three houses were in Clondalkin.

Mahoney remembered the dry-cleaning receipt that he had found in her room. He found the photograph he had taken of it and enlarged it so that he could read the address: the Mill Shopping Centre in Clondalkin.

He opened Google Maps on the computer, entered the address of the dry cleaner's and then, one by one, added the addresses of the safe houses. All three were close. He stared at the screen and bit down on his lip. It was a long shot. He had no evidence that the woman had been at any of the addresses—the dry cleaner's could be a coincidence—and even less that she would have returned.

But his gut told him he was onto something.

And he had nothing else.

He wanted to drive over to Clondalkin now, but it would have to wait. There was something else—something much more important—that needed to be done first.

63

S t James's Hospital was on James Street. Mahoney parked his patrol car in the car park and walked over to the entrance. The receptionist at the desk looked up at him, her gaze lingering on his uniform.

"Can I help you?"

"I'm looking for Mickey Flannagan. He would've been brought in two or three hours ago. Gunshot wound."

She tapped on her keyboard and examined the results that were brought back on her screen. "He's in the ICU," she said. "Third floor. Lifts are over there."

"Thank you."

Mahoney followed her instructions, went to the elevator lobby and pressed the button to summon one of the cars. He hated hospitals. The smell of disinfectant was everywhere, reminding him of sickness and death. It reminded him of his mother. She had been in Mercy Hospital in Cork for weeks, hanging on as her cancer finally consumed her. Her death had broken him. It was the reason he had gone off the rails, and his months of dissolute living had led him to Gallagher and everything else that had followed after that.

Mahoney rode the lift to the third floor. The doors parted, and he stepped outside. The ICU was a stark and sterile place, with walls painted white and bright fluorescent lights throwing out a harsh glare. The air was cool and dry, with the smell of antiseptic and cleaning agents. The unit was divided into individual bays separated by plastic curtains. Patients lay supine in their beds, some were on ventilators, and all were connected to IV lines to deliver their medicine.

A station stood between him and the bays, and, as he approached, one of the nurses came over. "Evening, Officer. Who are you after?"

"Mickey Flannagan."

"Do you have identification?"

"Course." He took out his warrant card and waited as she examined it.

"Down the corridor, on the right," the woman said. "He has a room to himself. Another officer is outside."

Mahoney made his way along the corridor, turned left at the end and saw a row of doors on either side. As he passed, he saw that each room contained an intensive care bed; these suites were reserved, he guessed, for those who needed isolation from everyone else.

Lynch was guarding the door at the end of the corridor.

Mahoney walked up to him. "They said you'd be here."

"They sent me to keep an eye on him."

"They think he's in danger?"

"He shot Colm Dillon, Michael. That's a life-shortening decision."

Mahoney put his face to the glass in the door and looked between the slats of the blind. The room was awash in a pale light. Flannagan was unconscious in bed, tethered to a network of tubes, wires, and monitors. There was a ventilator to one side—unused—and an intravenous infusion pump with clear plastic tubing that snaked to Flannagan's arm. A digital monitor behind the bed showed his heart rate, blood pressure, and oxygen saturation. A crash cart, stocked with emergency medications and equipment, had been left against the far wall.

Mahoney turned back to Lynch. "How's your face?"

He gestured up with his hand. "The CS? I'm fine."

"Your eyes are still red."

"Dunked my head in the sink and got rid of most of it. Honestly—I'm fine." He pointed. "What about your nose?"

"Been better. What does it look like?"

"Like you've gone ten rounds with Tyson Fury. I thought you were going to get it seen to."

"That's why I'm here," Mahoney said.

"In the ICU? Don't be a drama queen. You want A&E."

"I thought I'd come up and see how you were first. And how he is. How long have you been here?"

"Couple of hours."

"Doctors been around?"

Lynch nodded.

"And?"

"They say he lost a lot of blood, but they think they got to him in time."

"So he'll make it?"

"That's what they said."

"That's something."

"DS Meaney's dying to speak to him."

"I bet she is."

Lynch gestured to the window. "Reckon he'll spill?"

"He'll want a deal. Depends on what he gets offered in return."

Mahoney looked into the room again. He knew he

couldn't leave Flannagan to recover; the risk that he might wake up and decide it was better to cut a deal in exchange for testifying was much too great. Mahoney didn't know how much Flannagan knew about Gallagher's involvement, but, if he *did* know, offering to grass Gallagher up would be like signing his own death sentence. But Flannagan wouldn't see *Mahoney* in quite the same way; offering up the bent copper responsible for a hit leading to three deaths would be very valuable indeed and much less dangerous.

"Want me to cover for you for ten minutes?" Mahoney offered. "Stretch your legs?"

"You sure?" Lynch said. "I could do with a piss."

"Go for it."

He got up. "Cheers. I'll get a brew, too. There's a vending machine in the lobby. Want anything?"

"I'd kill for a coffee."

"Right you are. I'll go have a piss and a fag, and I'll bring you one back up." He set off and then stopped and turned back. "There's one good thing about all of this."

"What's that?"

"Overtime on tap. The missus has been bugging me for weeks about going away somewhere hot. Maybe now I'll be able to afford it." He took out his fags. "Black and no sugar?"

"Perfect. Take your time—I'm in no rush."

64

The mattress moved as the girl turned over, and, as Maria lay still, she heard the soft snuffling sound of her crying.

Maria reached out a hand and laid it on Cara's shoulder. "It's all right," she whispered. "Try to sleep. We'll get you home in the morning."

At least Cara had managed *some* sleep. Maria hadn't had much at all. It had taken a while to relax, but even then, her thoughts had been a riot: horror at what she had witnessed in the hotel, confusion about Eric—*John*, she corrected herself—and worry about what all of it might mean for her future.

It wasn't as if Maria had no experience of violence. She had grown up in the *favelas* of Rio, and her childhood had been a harrowing tapestry of violence and survival. She could remember, from the earliest age, being exposed to the raw, brutal reality of life on the fringes. Her days had been punctuated by the crackle of gunfire and the chaos of drug wars fought in narrow, winding alleys. It wasn't uncommon for her path to school to be blocked by the aftermath of territorial clashes, the ground stained with evidence of the previous night's struggle. Homes like hers were routinely searched by the police, and the ramshackle walls offered no respite from the cacophony outside. Her innocence had been prematurely eroded by the things she had seen, it had moulded her into a hardened survivor, but the cost of that early maturity had been high.

Maria thought of Cara and wondered how much she had seen. John had recounted what had happened, and said that the girl had been close by when the gunman had opened fire. Maria, too, had seen a man shoot another man, and had seen dead bodies. And if the man was, as John suggested, her father... it really didn't bear thinking about.

She found her thoughts drifting to what she'd done, and the consequences of agreeing to help John with the girl. She wasn't naïve about how the world worked, and knew that she wouldn't have control over events from now on. It was frightening to realise: she didn't know anything about the girl, not really, nor her family nor the reason for the murders in the hotel. She recognised the killer from the kitchen, but the motive for what had happened was opaque. And despite all that, and knowing she knew nothing, she had still agreed to help. It had been automatic. One moment from her childhood had been seared into her memory: she'd been just a little younger than Cara when her father, a man of humble means, was gunned down in front of her. A corrupt policeman had arrived at their house, an argument had followed, and then there had been a single gunshot. Her father fell, and his life had bled out on the dirty floor. She'd resolved to leave Rio then, and although it had taken her years, she had done it. She still had nightmares about what she had seen, and didn't doubt that Cara would be the same. They needed to get her back to her family as quickly as they could.

She looked over to the window, dawn had broken, and brightness was gathering in the gap between the curtains. A car passed on the road beneath the window, and somewhere close by, swifts began their high-pitched screeching as they prepared to feed. Maria checked her watch: it was nearly six. Cara had drifted off again, her breathing deep and even. Maria exhaled and closed her eyes, hopeful that her thoughts might quieten so she might be able to steal an hour's sleep before the start of the day.

65

Mahoney opened the door and crossed the room to Flannagan's bed. His heart was pounding, not because of what he was about to do, but because of what would happen were he to be seen. He had killed before, but not like this. It felt reckless and dangerous, but there was nothing else for it. This would be his only opportunity to make sure Flannagan didn't bring him down. He went back to the door and glanced out into the corridor, left and right, but there was no one there.

He stepped back inside and crossed the room to the crash cart. It was full of equipment: a defibrillator, IV supplies, catheters and masks, tubes and an oxygen tank. He opened a drawer and found what he was looking for: a syringe. He tore the plastic packaging away and then pulled back on the plunger so that the barrel filled with air. He removed the cap.

Flannagan looked fragile. His complexion was pale; not surprising given the blood he must have lost. The room's stark lighting picked out the shadows beneath his closed eyes. The gunshot wound to his chest had been dressed, but the white sheets were speckled with red. His breaths were shallow and laboured, and, for a moment, Mahoney felt a tiny flicker of doubt.

It didn't last.

He found the IV line delivering medication and carefully inserted the syringe into the tubing, ensuring it was secure. He pressed the plunger, injecting an air bubble into the line. He withdrew the syringe, put the cap back on the needle and put it in his pocket.

He went outside, shut the door and took his seat again.

He looked at his watch. He had no idea how long it would take. Thirty minutes or an hour—sometime after he had left—would be best.

It didn't take as long as that.

The alarms in Flannagan's room screeched.

A nurse hurried into the corridor, yanked the door open and went to the bed.

Mahoney stood and went to the door. "What's happening?"

"Stay in the corridor, please."

"I need to know what's happening."

"His blood pressure just fell off a cliff, and he's short of breath. Now—please—*out*."

A doctor and then another nurse arrived.

Lynch turned the corner, a Styrofoam cup in each hand. "What happened?"

Mahoney spread his arms helplessly. "I don't know. The alarms went off. The nurse said his blood pressure dropped."

"What? Just like that? They said he was stable."

"I have no idea—I'm just telling you what she told me."

Another doctor arrived.

Lynch stopped him at the door. "Excuse me. What's wrong with him?"

"I just got here, sir. Please—let us work. I'll come and speak to you once we've stabilised him."

The doctor went to join the others at the side of the bed.

Lynch put the coffees down on the chair and took out his phone. "I need to call Meaney."

Mahoney reached down for his coffee. He sipped it, looking over the lid at the chaotic activity in the room across the corridor. The crash cart had been wheeled closer to the bed, and the defibrillator was being prepared. The alarms were still sounding, and the distance between the spikes of the heart rate monitor was lengthening. Mahoney didn't care. Flannagan was a scumbag who had served his purpose. He had cancer, too, and going out like this—probably not even aware of what was happening to him—would be better than being eaten alive by his tumours, like Mahoney's mother had.

When you put it like that? I'm doing him a favour.

Mahoney heard the high-pitched whine as the defibrillator powered up, then the sudden crackle of the electricity as it was discharged. He thought of Gallagher: he was going to be well pleased.

66

Clondalkin was on the western side of the city, and Mahoney followed the R810 through Inchicore and then south towards Ballymount before turning off. The first property that had been identified in the immigration investigation was on Deansrath Road. He drove by it slowly enough to see that it was in a state of disrepair. The once-white paint on its exterior had long since faded and peeled away, revealing the weathered wooden boards beneath. The front garden, left untended for years, was overgrown with weeds and tall grass. The windows were grimy and cracked; some panes were shattered, leaving jagged shards of glass clinging to the frames. A tattered curtain hung limply behind one of the intact windows. The roof had missing and broken tiles and a sagging gutter that dripped water onto the wall below.

Mahoney turned around at the end of the road and drove back again. He parked the car and got out. There were no lights on in the house, but that was to be expected given the hour. It didn't look as if it was occupied, but he needed to be sure.

He opened the rusted black iron gate and made his way along the garden path. The blue paint of the front door was chipped and scratched. There was a glass panel above the handle, and Mahoney peered through it; the hall beyond was too dark to make anything out. He took out his penlight, switched it on and shone the beam inside. He could see a collection of envelopes scattered beneath the letterbox and cardboard boxes stacked along one side of the hall.

He ventured around to the back of the house, and the state of decay became even more evident. A rickety garden shed leaned precariously to one side, its wooden planks rotting and covered in moss. An old, rusted bicycle lay abandoned in the grass, the tyres flat and the chain entangled. The slabs of a patio were barely visible through the overgrowth, and the remnants of outdoor furniture, rusted and twisted, lay scattered about. The back door of the house, much like the front, was weathered and peeling, hanging askew on rusted hinges.

He pushed the door open and stepped inside, placing his feet carefully on a small doorstep that was covered with a slick carpet of moss. The house was unoccupied; all the rooms were empty, and the only evidence that anyone had been here recently was a newspaper from two weeks ago that he found in the main bedroom upstairs.

He clenched his fist and rapped it against the kitchen counter in frustration, then took out his phone and scrolled down for the next address. It was on James Connolly Park, a mile to the west from where he was now. He could be there in ten minutes.

67

Milton drove out to Corduff and followed his phone's directions to the gym. He turned off the road onto a large car park that served a church on one side and a small arcade of shops on the other. The church was an ugly concrete block with a slender cross and a placard that announced it as St Patrick's, Corduff, with the times for each mass alongside. The arcade was down-at-heel, with a discount store, a hair salon and two takeaways. The smartest building was Leonard's Bar and Lounge, complete with a fresh red paint job and new roller doors that sealed the entrance. A Guinness truck had pulled up next to a side entrance, and the driver and a helper were rolling barrels down a ramp at the back. Milton drove slowly by the truck and saw the gym nestled between the bar and the discount store. He parked outside the hair salon, choosing a space that would allow him a clear line of sight to the gym without making it obvious that he was watching.

He reached forward, switched on the radio and tuned in to RTÉ's 2FM. The time on the dash showed half past six, and the DJ handed over to the newsroom.

"Three men were killed, and at least one other sustained severe injuries, when shots were fired at a mixed martial arts weigh-in yesterday evening. The event took place at the Southside Hotel in North Dublin, which was filled with fight enthusiasts. The intended victims of the assault were believed to be prominent members of a Dublin criminal organisation. One of the deceased individuals was known to the Gardaí as being involved in organised crime."

Milton turned down the radio and drummed his fingers against the wheel. It was obvious that the story was going to get heavy coverage, but it wasn't something that filled him with enthusiasm. The bigger it got, the more attention it would receive. He gripped the wheel a little more tightly and acknowledged, again, what he had already decided: he would stay in the city for as long as it took to get the girl back to her family, and then, and only then, would he leave. He would just have to be careful.

The news report ended, and the DJ started the next half hour with a Miley Cyrus song. Milton reached forward to turn it up a little when he noticed movement from the road. He turned and saw two men: one of them was on a bicycle, and the other, dressed in shorts and a singlet, was running. The man on the bike turned into the car park and free-wheeled to a stop just ahead of the dray. The second man followed, slowing to a walk and then stopping at the corner of the building. He bent double and caught his breath.

Milton watched them both. The older man had a rugged face, with deep lines and wrinkles around his eyes and mouth, a prominent nose and a defined jawline. He wore a beanie on his head, and, as he took it off and used it to wipe the sweat from his face, Milton saw he had short grey hair. He looked fit and healthy, although not overly muscular or bulky. He was of medium build with broad shoulders.

The younger man was of average height and weight, with a lean and toned body. His muscles were well defined, and he had a broad chest and shoulders and a narrow waist. His legs looked powerful, with defined quads and calf muscles. He straightened up so that Milton could see his face: he had a chiselled jawline and high cheekbones, with a sharp, defined nose. He had light blue eyes and a beard kept short and well groomed. Milton recognised him from the weigh-in: Danny Farley.

The two men shared a conversation and then made their way into the arcade. The older man took out a key, unlocked the door to the gym and led the way inside. Farley followed. Milton waited for a moment. He knew that Ziggy would find another way to get to the Dillons, but there was no way of knowing how long that might take. Milton guessed that the older man was Paddy Coffey, and, if he was right about that, then there was a good chance that he might be able to get the information he needed right now.

He got out of the car. The two deliverymen got back into the truck, and it rumbled away. Milton stepped over the raised kerb and followed the two men to the gym.

68

Dawn was breaking when Mahoney arrived at the apartment block. He parked down the street from the block and looked back at it; the building's exterior was worn and faded, its once-bright paint now chipped and peeling, revealing the concrete and brick structure beneath. The block was three storeys tall, with narrow balconies running along each level. The balconies were cluttered: clotheslines laden with laundry, bicycles, abandoned white goods, satellite dishes and potted plants. The railings lining the balconies were corroded and in need of repair or replacement.

Mahoney got out of the car. The address he had been given was on the third floor; he found the stairs and climbed. Graffiti covered the walls of the stairwell, a chaotic mix of tags, crude drawings, and scrawled messages. The steps were smeared with dog shit and littered with evidence of drug use: discarded needles, burnt spoons, and empty vials that had been crushed underfoot.

He reached the door, knelt down and peered through

the letterbox. It was dark inside, and he couldn't see anything.

He knocked.

The sound echoed down the balcony. He stepped back, and, after a few moments, he heard the sound of movement from within. The door creaked open to reveal a dishevelled and sleepy-looking man who had clearly just been roused from sleep. He was of average height, with a lean but sturdy build that suggested a life of hard work. His short black hair was peppered with flecks of grey, the first signs of age creeping in. His eyes squinted against the morning light; they went wide as he saw Mahoney's uniform.

"What is it?"

"I want a word."

"But I've done nothing wrong."

He had an accent that Mahoney couldn't place. "What's your name?"

"Luis."

"When did you get to Dublin, Luis?"

The man started to speak, then—perhaps realising his predicament—held his tongue.

"You shouldn't be here, should you? I bet if I was to run your details, we'd find that you don't have a visa. Am I right?"

The colour ran from the man's face.

"It might be your lucky day. I'm not actually here for you. I'm looking for someone else."

"Who?" the man said. "I help if I can."

"Who's inside?"

"My wife."

"Who else?"

"Another man—he came over at the same time as we did."

"Is that it?"

He nodded.

"No one else?"

"No one."

"You won't mind me having a look, then, will you?"

Mahoney stepped forward, putting his hand on the man's shoulder and moving him out of the way. The flat was tiny, with a kitchen and sitting room and two bedrooms. Mahoney worked through the rooms one by one; a woman was in the first bedroom, her eyes wide with fright, and a man was in the second, still asleep.

Luis stood in the hall, his hands fluttering in front of his chest, and watched as Mahoney went from room to room.

"How long have you been here?"

The man bit his lip.

"You can either answer the question now, or I can take you back to the station, and you can answer it there. The first'd be better, but it's up to you."

"Two weeks."

"Who was here before you?"

"Don't know."

"I don't believe you."

"It was empty when we arrived. I don't know who was here—I swear."

"Who brought you here?"

"A man. Don't know his name."

"He worked for the people who got you through the airport?"

He nodded.

"How do you get in contact with him?"

"I don't. He said he would come back when he had our papers."

Mahoney stepped close to the man and backed him up against the wall.

"Are you telling me the truth, Luis?"

"I am," he said. "I swear."

Mahoney paused in the hallway, looking around one final time in the event that there was something that he might have missed, before ignoring the man and stepping back out onto the balcony. He waited there, looking out onto the construction site on the other side of the road and the brightening sky beyond it.

He was about to start down the stairs when his phone rang. He reached into his pocket, took it out and saw that it was Billy. He looked at the screen for three rings and then four, wondering whether there was any way he could let it ring to voicemail without landing himself in more trouble than he was already in. There was not: Gallagher was not the sort of man you could ignore.

"Hello, Billy."

Gallagher spared him any attempt at small talk. "Well?"

"Nothing yet."

"Nothing?"

"A couple of leads."

"On the man?"

"No," he said. "Not him. I think he's with one of the women from the hotel. Looks like she's here illegally—she's being looked at by immigration. The gang that smuggled her in have safe houses in the city. I'm working my way through them."

"And the girl might be with her?"

"It's possible. If she is, I'll find her."

"I need her, Mahoney. I need the leverage."

"I know you do. You made that clear."

"I hate repeating myself, but I can't help feeling you

don't know how disappointed I am about the way this went down. You promised me it'd get done, and the way I see it now, fucking it up the way it's been fucked up just makes things worse. The Dillons are going to make a move now. We need the girl."

Mahoney closed his eyes. "I know, Billy. And I'm doing everything I can to find her."

"Call me when you have her."

The line went dead. Mahoney put the phone in his pocket and turned to look at the windows of the apartment. The man was watching him, and seeing that he was observed, he pulled away and jerked the curtains closed.

Mahoney had one more address to check.

She *had* to be there.

He didn't know what he was going to do if she wasn't.

The gym was a gritty space, lit by a few weak bulbs hanging from the ceiling. It had a smell that Milton remembered from the time he had spent in similar places: heady with sweat and the scent of leather and canvas. The ceiling was high, and curtained windows let in a small amount of natural light through grimy panes. The middle of the room was commanded by a ring. The ropes had a little slack, and the canvas was worn and in need of changing. Folding chairs surrounded the ring. The equipment scattered around the periphery of the room was similarly well worn and well used: heavy bags and speed bags hung from the walls, their leather skins bruised and battered. Fading posters clung to the walls: Barry McGuigan and Tyson Fury, and, from longer back, Jimmy McLarnin and Jack Dempsey. Time had weathered the paint and plaster, but, despite it all, the place wore its scars with pride. This was spit and sawdust, as boxing was supposed to be, shorn of the glitz and glamour that neutered fights nowadays, making it cheap and tawdry and disposable.

Milton looked around with nostalgic longing, remembering the hours he had spent training for the bouts he'd had in the military. It had been a simpler time then, and he would have given a lot to have been able to go back to it.

Free weights were stacked on racks, yoga mats were rolled up and propped against the walls, and an old TV was tuned to a channel showing the video for Metallica's 'Enter Sandman.' Milton heard the slap of a skipping rope and followed it around the ring to a separate space on the other side of the room. Farley was shirtless and working hard, the skipping rope slapping against the floorboards with metronomic regularity.

The older man was watching, and he looked up with a frown as Milton turned the corner.

"We're not open."

"I'm not here to train."

"What do you want, then?"

"I'm looking for Paddy Coffey."

Farley stopped skipping and turned. He was even more impressive up close. His muscles—his shoulders, his pecs, his abs, his quads—were all very clearly defined, and his upper arms bulged with power.

"Are you now?" the older man said. "And who might you be?"

"My name's Eric. You're Paddy?"

"Aye."

Milton turned to the younger man. "You're Danny Farley."

Farley stepped a little closer. "That's right."

Milton could smell the sweat on him. Farley was trying to intimidate him, but Milton held his eye until the younger man backed down and looked over to Coffey.

Milton looked to him, too. "You knew Colm Dillon?"

"Why'd you think that?"

"It'd be helpful if we could get past the nonsense. I'm not police. I've got no interest in what happened other than the fact that I'd like to return his daughter to her family."

That caught Coffey's attention. "What'd you say?"

"It's about what happened at the Southside yesterday."

"I was there. And you?"

"I work in the hotel. I disarmed the man with the gun, and then I took Cara Dillon out of harm's way."

"And you have her now?"

"Yes."

"So maybe you ought to take her to the police?"

"I tried to do that," Milton said. "I took her to one of the officers, and she ran away from him. She was terrified. He tried to grab her and... well, it went badly."

"Meaning?"

"Meaning there was a fight. I put him down—him and another officer."

Farley laughed. "Serious? *You* did?"

"Is that funny?"

"How *old* are you, mate?"

There would have been a time, before Milton found the Rooms, that he would have invited Farley into the ring so that he could show him just *how* serious he was, but those days were gone.

Coffey chuckled. "You serious?"

"I am."

"So you can't take her in because you're worried you'll get nicked. Right?"

"More than that. I think the officer was involved in what happened. It'd be better all around if I get her straight back to her family rather than take any chances with police officers I don't know and can't vouch for."

Farley frowned. "What'd you say you do at the hotel, old man?"

"I'm a cook."

"A cook who disarmed a man with a gun and then got into a scrap with a police officer—you expect us to believe that?"

Milton turned to face him. "I don't really give a shit *what* you believe," he said, taking a step so that he was within arm's reach of him. "I came here because I need to find a way to get in touch with the Dillons so I can get their girl back to them again. The two of you can either help me do that, or you can keep trying to call my bluff, but, if you do that, I'm going to go away and see if I can find another way to do what I need to do. But that'll probably take me longer, and, when I *do* find Shay Dillon—and I will, eventually—I'll be sure to tell him that the delay in getting her back safe and sound was because of you. How's that sound?"

"Easy," Coffey said. "There's no need for any of that."

Farley was staring at Milton. He jerked his head, trying to get Milton to flinch, but it didn't work.

"Danny," Coffey said, "are you fucking kidding me? You're fighting tonight. You really want to get in a scrap now?"

Milton kept his eyes on him but said nothing. Farley was at least twenty-five years younger, but Milton was taller and heavier. He doubted he would have been able to go toe-to-toe with him, but that wouldn't have stopped him from trying. And Milton had never had any compunction about fighting dirty.

"*Danny.*"

Farley manufactured a chuckle and a sneer, then turned his back and started with the rope again.

Milton cocked an eyebrow at Coffey. "Can you help me, then?"

"I'll give him a call," he said.

70

Milton went and waited next to the ring while Coffey called Dillon. He looked at the posters on the wall opposite the Irish fighters: Ali and Foreman in the Rumble in the Jungle, Hagler and Hearns in the Battle of the Bay, Ali and Frazier in the Thrilla in Manila.

Milton went over to the heavy bag hanging in the corner. A pair of gloves and a roll of tape had been left on the windowsill next to it. He wrapped his hands in the tape and slipped on the gloves. He hit the bag with a right and then a right-left-right combination. He drove his fist into it, giving it extra power from his shoulder, the sound echoing through the gym like a gunshot. He fired out a right and a left and another right, hooks and then a cross, pounding the bag. Each hit landed with a satisfying thud, a rattle of the chain and puffs of dust. He moved around the bag with a fluidity that belied his age, his footwork coming back to him. He'd worked out with heavy bags for hours, and, though it was years ago and another life, it all came back to him. He started to sweat but didn't mind; he felt the buzz of the adrenaline in his veins and the thud of his heart in his chest.

"Not bad."

Milton uncorked a big right-hand hook, drilling the bag at rib level and sending it up and back down again. He caught it and looked back to where Coffey was watching him.

"Sorry. Got carried away."

"Ever done MMA?"

"More of a boxer."

"When's the last time?"

He shook his head in bemusement. "Twenty years ago. Might be more."

"You're rusty. Telegraphing your punches. Work on being more efficient with your movements."

"You think?"

"Watch your jab," Coffey said, stepping closer to the bag. "You're winding up before you throw it. You'll give the other guy too much time to react. Shorten your motion and snap the punch off quickly. Like this."

He stepped up and fired a jab into the bag, then another. The blow was much less powerful, but more efficient, snappier, with less wasted motion.

Milton took off the gloves and unwound the tape, bloodied from where he had chafed the knuckles of his right hand.

"I spoke to Shay," Coffey said. "He'll see you."

"When?"

"As soon as possible. Give me your number—he says he'll give you a call."

71

Mahoney wasn't happy. He'd been driving around the city all morning, and he had nothing to show for it. He was tired, he was hungry, and he needed a piss. He would have liked nothing better than to turn around and head home, but he couldn't do that until he had found the girl. He had the last address to check, and given that it was the only lead he had left, he couldn't ignore it.

He went back to the station and clocked off, changed out of his gear and then went over to his Volvo. He put the car into gear and pulled out just as Eoin Lynch arrived; he raised a hand in greeting, wondering what, if anything, had happened with Flannagan. He couldn't avoid the fact that Flannagan had been fine before he had arrived and dead soon after. He'd say it was a coincidence, but he knew they'd have to look into it. How likely was it that they would find out what had happened and then attribute it to him?

He didn't know. But he couldn't dwell on it; too much to do for that.

He drove back to Clondalkin and navigated the streets to

Castle View Road, taking out his phone and waking the screen so that he could see the third and final address. He muttered a curse; he'd just driven past it. He pulled over and parked the car fifty yards down the road beneath the shelter of a tree heavy with pink blossom. Mahoney didn't know whether the girl had been brought here or not, but the man who had removed her from the hotel was clearly capable; Mahoney's nose was testament to that. And if Blair was indeed here, it was reasonable to assume that he would be cautious enough to notice a car with a man inside it parked outside. It made sense to be careful, and this spot was far enough away from the property so as not to be obvious.

He reached for the ignition and killed the engine, then glanced up in the mirror and saw movement. He adjusted the mirror, then abandoned that to swivel around in the seat and look back through the rear window. A car was reversing onto the drive. A red BMW, old and battered. The car stopped, the door opened, and a man stepped out.

It was him.

Blair.

Mahoney reached across the cabin to the glove compartment, opened it and took out his pistol.

The man walked up the drive and went into the house.

Mahoney breathed out, then took out his phone.

"You'd better have good news," Gallagher said.

"How long would it take you to get a couple of your lads to Clondalkin?"

"I don't know—an hour? Why?"

"Can you get them here any quicker? I think I know where they've taken the girl."

72

Milton put the plastic bag of groceries on the kitchen counter. He had stopped at a convenience store on his way back and picked up a few supplies: a jar of coffee, a loaf of bread, packs of butter and cheese, and, on a whim as he waited at the counter to pay, three bars of chocolate. He didn't know what Cara would like to eat but felt confident the chocolate would go down well. He could go back to get anything else they needed later, although he was reasonably optimistic that wouldn't be necessary. The meeting with Coffey had gone as well as could be expected, and he was hopeful that he would be able to return the girl to her family before the end of the day. And once that was done, he'd be gone.

He paused at the foot of the stairs and listened, it was still early, and he had expected Maria and Cara to be asleep, but he could hear the creak of footsteps across the old floorboards above him.

He went back into the kitchen. It was small and basic, with just enough room for a table and chairs. The walls were painted a faded yellow, and the linoleum flooring was worn and stained in places. The cabinets were made of plywood and had seen better days, with chipped edges and faded paint. The countertops were made from a basic white laminate; there were a few small appliances, including an old electric kettle and a toaster. Milton filled the kettle and set it to boil and was taking out the groceries when he heard someone coming down the stairs.

"Morning."

Maria stood in the doorway, reaching up a hand to push her hair out of her face.

"Good morning," Milton said. "Are you okay?"

"Tired."

"Where's Cara?"

"Asleep. She didn't have a very good night. She woke up crying."

"Did you get any sleep?"

"Some."

He pointed to the jar of instant coffee. "Want one?"

"Yes, please."

"How do you take it?"

"Black."

Milton opened the jar and pierced the seal with a spoon.

She went over and sat at the table. "I saw your note."

"I didn't want you to think I'd left you and wouldn't be coming back."

"I didn't think you'd do that."

"That's kind, but you don't really know me."

Milton opened the cupboard and took out two mugs. Maria looked tired, with dark crescents beneath her eyes. He had been concentrating on how Cara had been coping with the ordeal, but now he could see that Maria had been affected, too. Her struggles weren't surprising; she had been in the room during the attack, and, although she hadn't spoken about it, she'd seen the shooting and the bodies on the floor. Milton was used to the consequences of violence —he was inured to it—and it was sometimes easy to forget not everyone shared his familiarity.

"Where did you go?" she asked him.

Milton scooped coffee into the mugs. "I spoke to a friend who was able to get me a little extra information on what happened. The shooting was connected to two criminal gangs—the Gallaghers and the Dillons."

"How does that help us?"

"Because Cara is a Dillon. It *was* her father who was killed."

She put a hand to her mouth. "Poor girl."

"Has she spoken?"

"Not a word. We need to get her back to her family."

"That's what I've been trying to do. My friend gave me an address to try—someone who knows the Dillons. I went out to see him an hour ago, and he said that he'd have them call me. I'll set up a meeting."

"Taking Cara?"

Milton had already given thought to that. "Not to start with. I want to make sure that she's going back to the right people."

The kettle boiled. Milton filled the mugs with water and handed one of them to Maria. He pulled out the other chair at the table and sat down. His phone buzzed in his pocket. He took it out and saw a number he didn't recognise on the screen.

"Speak of the devil." He answered the call. "Hello?"

"Is this Mr. Blair?"

"Mr. Dillon?"

"Aye. Paddy Coffey called me earlier. He said you have my niece."

"I do."

"And?"

"She's fine. Frightened, but that's hardly a surprise, given what happened to her yesterday."

"Where is she?"

"With me."

"Where?"

"Could we meet?"

"And you'll bring her?"

"I'd like to speak to you first—with her mother, if that's not too inconvenient."

He frowned. "What? Why?"

"I don't know you, Mr. Dillon, and I want to make sure I'm handing her over to the right person. Put yourself in my shoes—you'd do the same if you were me."

"Do you know who I am?"

"I do, and I'm not doing this because I want to upset you. I'm doing it because I want to be sure I'm doing right by Cara. It'll just delay things by an hour or two. Let's meet, with her mother, and, provided everything is as it should be, I'll go back and get her."

"Her mother's not around anymore."

"Meaning?"

"She's dead. Died last year. I'm her uncle. You deal with me."

"We still need to meet. I don't know you, and I want to make sure you are who you say you are."

Milton could hear the tightness in his voice. "Whatever. Where are you?"

"Clondalkin."

"Where do you want to meet?"

"There's a shopping centre."

"I know it—the Mill."

"I'll be in the McDonald's."

"I'll be there in half an hour. Make sure you're waiting."

73

Mahoney kept his eyes on the house. He wondered whether he ought to go in and get the girl himself. He had his gun, and, however able Blair might be, it wouldn't make much difference with a pistol pointed at him. Popping him would make things a lot easier, too. It'd remove the threat that he could testify about him being in the hotel bathroom.

Still, Mahoney decided to wait. Impetuousness might get him in trouble, and Gallagher was sending his men; it made more sense to be patient. They could take care of Blair, and, if they messed up, Gallagher would blame them and not him.

The front door opened. Mahoney turned so that he could look through the window and saw Blair step outside. He paused on the doorstep, scanning the street before getting into the BMW and pulling out. Mahoney found that he was holding his breath. He knew he had to remain inconspicuous; if Blair saw him now, it would mess everything up.

Blair turned left and continued down the road, disappearing behind the trees.

Mahoney took out his phone and called Gallagher.

"It's me. Where are your guys?"

"They'll be with you in ten minutes."

"Blair just left the house."

"With the girl?"

"Alone."

"Are you sure she's inside?"

"No," he said. "I'm not sure. But where else could she be?"

"Returned to the Dillons?"

Mahoney winced. It was possible. "I don't know, Billy. I found her, like I said I would, and I still think she's inside." He felt a knot of tension in his gut. "Tell your lads to hurry. They need to be here *now*."

74

The Mill was close enough for Milton to be able to get to it quickly and yet far enough away that it would be impossible for Dillon to find the house if the meeting didn't go the way Milton hoped it would. He arrived just before eight. The businesses in the precinct were arranged around a large car park; there was a department store, a taxi firm, a store selling DVDs, and, opposite those, a McDonald's drive-thru. Milton parked, walked over to the restaurant and went inside. There were half a dozen customers waiting for their food to be prepared and another half dozen struggling with the screens where they could place their orders. None of the booths were occupied, and Milton took one at the back of the restaurant that offered him a generous view of the interior and, through the windows, the cars outside.

Dillon had said that he would be there at eight, but there was no one who looked like it might be him when Milton looked at his watch at ten past. He realised that he didn't have any idea what Dillon looked like, and that he hadn't—deliberately—given Dillon a description of his own appearance. Milton took out his phone and was about to dial the number that Dillon had used to call him when he saw a flashy Mercedes G-Class SUV drive slowly into the car park. It was painted in black, and its muscular frame loomed over the other cars. The sunlight, filtered through a patchy sky, danced across the glossy black paintwork and chrome accents. The windows were tinted, hiding the occupants from view; Milton watched as the car pulled over and parked across two empty bays.

Two men got out, came into the restaurant and stopped.

Milton raised his hand, and they came to his booth.

"Mr. Dillon?"

He was handsome, with striking features: a strong jawline, high cheekbones, and piercing blue eyes. He had a lean and athletic build, with broad shoulders and a toned physique that suggested strength. He had a natural ease and confidence.

"Aye. Blair?"

Milton nodded, then gestured up to the second man. "Who's he?"

"He works with me. You don't need to worry about him."

The second man was lean and tall, perhaps six feet three. His face was angular, with a sharp nose. He had a broad forehead, thick, bushy eyebrows and blue-grey eyes. His hair was light brown and worn in a tousled style. He looked unpleasant.

Dillon sat down. "You've got some balls."

"Why'd you say that?"

"Do you know who I am?"

"I have an idea."

"And you still thought it was a good idea to hold onto my niece?"

"I'm not holding onto her."

"So where is she?"

"I told you—I need to be sure that I'm handing her over to the right people."

He stared at Milton. "And *I* told *you*—I'm her uncle." Dillon held his eye, shook his head and waved a hand. "Go on, then. Tell me what happened."

"I took her out of the hotel last night. I tried to take her to the police, but she panicked and ran. One of the officers —the one I asked to help—chased after her and... well, it didn't go well. He grabbed her, and I got involved."

"Meaning?"

"I knocked him out and sprayed his partner with CS. I decided that until I knew what was going on, it'd be safer for her if I took her away. I'm sorry it's taken me so long, but I didn't know what to do with her. She's not talking."

"She doesn't," Dillon said. "She's on the spectrum. She's in her own world most of the time, and stress just makes it worse."

"She was close by when your brother was shot."

Dillon stared hard at him. "You saw it all?"

"I was right there."

"Go on."

Milton kept his eye on Dillon. "It was professional. Well planned. And I don't know for sure, but I think the detective who frightened Cara was involved. I'm not going to make a judgement on any of it, but I wasn't about to leave a girl her age to fend for herself."

"You're not going to make a judgement? What does that mean?"

"I know what you do," Milton said. "I know your business. I don't approve of it, but it's not relevant to getting Cara home."

"You don't 'approve'?"

"I don't."

Dillon turned to the second man. "You hear that? He doesn't approve."

The two of them shared looks of incomprehension, as if the idea of Milton—a mere cook from the hotel—showing no fear of men like them was the height of preposterousness.

Milton had no time for it. "You said her mother's dead."

"That's right."

"Who's going to be looking after her, then?"

"My mother—her grandmother. Cara loves her."

"Why didn't you bring her?"

"Who?"

"Your mother."

"*Jesus*, mate. Who do you think you are? You don't tell me what to do."

"Fine," Milton said. He stood.

"Where are you—"

"You've got my number." Milton spoke over him. "Call me when she's here."

"Don't be a tool," Dillon said. "My mother's grieving. Her son died last night. She had to go and identify his body in the morgue this morning, and there's no way I'm bringing her out to meet you so you can decide whether she's fit to look after my niece. I told her I was coming out here to see you, and I promised her I'd be bringing Cara back again."

Milton could see they would get nowhere unless he relented a little. "Show me something with the two of you together."

Dillon stared at Milton, over at the second man, back to Milton, then snorted—with exasperation, perhaps, or amusement—and took out his phone. He swiped across the screen and then laid it on the table and turned it around so that Milton could look down at it. He had found a photograph of four people: himself, Colm Dillon, an older woman and Cara.

"That was taken at Disneyland last year. You've got me, my brother, my mam and Cara." He spread his hands. "Satisfied?"

It wasn't perfect, but Milton doubted he would be able to manage anything that was. He didn't have the luxury of time to be as thorough as he would have liked, either. He was going to have to compromise.

"All right," Milton said. "Thank you."

"You'll take me to her?"

"No. I'll bring her here."

Dillon looked as if he was ready to argue, but, once again, he hid his annoyance behind a snort of indignation. "Like I said, mate—you've got some balls on you."

"Wait for me. I won't be long."

Dillon nodded, then looked over at the second man. "You hungry, Barry?"

"I could eat."

"I could go for an Egg McMuffin. You want to go get that for me?"

"Sure."

"Coffee, too. And hash browns."

The second man—Barry—went over to one of the vacant digital ordering stations.

Dillon looked back at Milton. "What are you waiting for? Off you go. Go get her."

75

The BMW arrived ten minutes after Blair's departure. Mahoney had been persuading himself that he should go in and get the girl himself and had almost made the decision to do that when the car pulled up behind him. He could see two men in the front and waited as the driver got out and walked forward. The man opened Mahoney's passenger door and lowered himself inside.

"You took your time," Mahoney complained.

"Which house?"

Mahoney gestured back up the street. "The one with the skip outside."

"Who's inside?"

"I don't know."

"The girl?"

"I can't say for sure. It's not like I've been in to have a look."

"So it's possible *no one* is inside?"

He tried not to get flustered. "Is it possible? Yes. But that house is connected to the woman who's with Blair. She's not at the hotel. The girl's not at the hotel. They're probably in there."

"Lots of probablies."

He spread his hands helplessly. "What else do you want me to say?"

"When did Blair leave?"

"Ten minutes ago."

The man pursed his lips. "Fine. We'll go and have a look. Keep an eye out for him. We won't be long."

76

Maria knew that Cara would be frightened if she awoke and there was no one there, so, when she heard the sound of movement from the bedroom, she hurried up the stairs. The girl had got out of bed and was standing by the window, looking down into the street below.

"Good morning," Maria said, putting as much warmth into her voice as she could. "Are you all right?"

The girl didn't respond. That wasn't surprising—she hadn't said a word since she had known her—but she didn't even turn to acknowledge her.

"How are you feeling?" Maria asked her. "You must be tired. You didn't have the best night's sleep, did you?"

Cara remained silent, but she turned her head to look back at Maria and then pointed out of the window to the street below. Maria crossed the room to join her and saw two men standing next to the skip in the driveway.

"Don't worry," Maria said. "It's nothing. No one knows we're here." She put her hand on the girl's shoulder and drew her away. "You must be hungry. John's out now, but he's been to the shop to get breakfast for us. What would you like? I could make you some toast. Do you like toast?"

There was a knock on the door.

The blood ran from Cara's face.

Maria tried to hide her own fear.

"We won't answer it," she said.

Cara shuffled closer to Maria.

The knock was repeated.

"It'll be fine. You don't need to worry. John will be back again soon, and then we'll make sure you can get home to your mum. This will all be over before you know it."

There was a third knock, and a moment later, they heard someone try the door.

Maria glanced around the room, looking for something that might help: the bed was too large to easily move across the small room, but there was a rickety wooden chair next to the old sealed-up fireplace.

There was the sound of a heavy impact and then a second thump as the door crashed against the wall.

"Police!"

Maria shut the bedroom door.

"Police!" came the shout again.

Cara huddled in the corner, arms wrapped around her knees and tears streaming down her face.

"Shh," Maria whispered. "Everything's going to be fine."

She took the chair and wedged it under the doorknob, then slid down next to it so that she could add her own weight.

The sound of heavy footsteps echoed from the downstairs hallway.

She looked over at Cara and put her finger to her lips. The girl nodded, her lower lip quivering as she tried to hold back a sob.

The footsteps came up the stairs.

A floorboard creaked outside.

The handle turned.

"Police. Come out, please."

Someone tried to open the door. The chair held. There was a heavy thump. Maria flinched but remained rooted in place. She braced her back against the door and put her hand into her pocket for her phone.

"Police," the voice said again. "Open up now."

Maria woke the screen, but, panicking, made an error when she tried to enter her passcode. She tried again, managed it, looked for her recently dialled numbers.

There was a thump from the other side of the door. It opened an inch, but Maria pushed back and held it there.

"Leave us alone!"

There was another thump and a grunt of effort, the door opened a little more, and Maria started to slide across the floorboard. She pushed back and managed to close it an inch. She knew that she wouldn't be able to hold the door and call John. She used her foot to slide the phone across the room.

"Call John," she said to Cara. "He's the last number."

The girl just looked at her. She pulled her knees up tight to her chest and started to rock from side to side.

Two more blows and then a third; the door shuddered.

The man swore colourfully.

"On three," a second voice said.

"Call John."

"*One.*"

"Cara," Maria said, "everything's going to be fine."

"*Two.*"

"I'm not going to leave you."

"*Three!*"

jumped into the BMW. He pulled out and smoked the tyres, looking left and right for any sign of the two vehicles.

Nothing.

He followed Castle View and saw two joggers turning into Bushelloaf Park and then rows of houses with well-kept gardens and people emerging to start their days.

Nothing.

He looked at the satnav and saw that he was approaching the ring road: he could turn left and go clockwise or turn south and go counterclockwise. He had no way of knowing where the two cars might be going. They could very easily have turned off, in which case he would have lost them minutes ago. But something told him that was unlikely. If they were travelling farther, then surely it made sense that they would use the ring road rather than struggling through the city itself. Assuming he was correct, there was one question he was going to need to get right: would they head north or south?

He passed the Ibis hotel and had to make a decision. With no options other than to hope for dumb luck, Milton peeled off to the left and went northbound.

The two-lane slip road merged into the four-lane M50. It was quiet, and Milton had no difficulty drifting over to the fast lane. He pressed down on the accelerator, bringing the car up to a hundred and then a hundred and ten miles an hour. He raced by the slower-moving traffic, edging back into the middle lanes so he could overtake two cars that were staying at the speed limit and then turning back into the fast lane once he had gone by them.

He saw the Volvo first and then, two cars ahead of it, the BMW. They were in the middle lane, following the speed limit.

Milton stepped off the gas a little, slowed a touch, but still wound them in.

80

The two cars turned off the M50 by way of the large interchange at Castleknock and then continued west on the N3. It was another major road, with three lanes on each side of the raised central reservation. Milton looked at his phone's map in the hope that he might be able to guess where they were going, but it was impossible. Their destination was probably not to the immediate north of the city—they would have stayed on the M50 if they were heading there—but the N3 became the M3 and could have brought them to Navan or Kells or Virginia or anywhere in the north of the country. He couldn't anticipate where they were going to go, so he had no choice but to continue to follow them and hope that he wasn't seen.

His phone buzzed. He glanced at the screen, saw it was Ziggy and pressed to answer.

"There's been a development," Ziggy said. "Where are you?"

"Trying to sort out the mess I've found myself in. What development?"

"Lilly Moon's husband and daughter have come back.

They got the Eurostar this morning. I'm watching the cameras at the house now. They arrived fifteen minutes ago."

"They weren't due back."

"He's changed his plans. It looks like he got a call last night from someone in Dublin. I'll try to find out who."

"Keep me posted."

"I was going to suggest something else. I've got a tracker in my bag. It'd be helpful to have it on his car."

The Volvo ahead started to slow.

"Milton?"

"Can you do it safely? Without being seen?"

"The car's behind the gates at the moment."

"Then don't."

"But if he goes out somewhere? I could do it then—it wouldn't be the first time."

The Volvo's indicators flicked on, suggesting it was about to turn off. The BMW continued ahead with no suggestion that it was going to do the same. Milton hesitated; he wasn't close enough to either car to know which one contained Maria and Cara. He would've guessed it was the BMW, but it could only ever be that—a guess—and choosing incorrectly could have serious consequences.

"Milton?" Ziggy pressed. "Are you there?"

Milton was distracted. "Fine. But be careful."

"Will do."

The driver of the Volvo hit the brakes, and the car suddenly lost all of its speed. Milton found himself alongside it before he could react. He looked over and briefly locked eyes with Mahoney. He was irritated with himself for being made, but, before he could think about how best to react, he saw Mahoney bring a handgun up and aim it at him through the open window.

The gun fired.

Milton ducked. The bullet punched a hole through the window on the left, streaked across the cabin and punched out through the window on the right.

Milton stayed low and stomped on the brake.

Mahoney braked and matched him.

The gun fired again; the round thudded into the door panel. The steel rang out, and the slug sliced right through, lodging into the dashboard.

Milton yanked the wheel and turned into Mahoney. The two cars touched, the impact juddering through the chassis; then they parted.

Mahoney fired for a third time.

Milton heard a bang, and, a moment later, felt the jerk as the car lurched down over a burst tyre. Sparks flew by the window as the rim scraped against the asphalt, and Milton lost control. The BMW swerved to the left, crashing into the Volvo again. Milton looked ahead, saw the green-and-white bollard that marked the point where the slip road met the main carriageway, and thought he was going to strike it. He didn't—he missed it by inches—but now the two cars were barrelling down a road that was only just wide enough for the two of them to fit side by side. A set of traffic lights governed the junction ahead, and a queue of traffic had formed behind them. Milton tried to take evasive action, but there was nowhere to go. He slammed into the back of a white van, the air bag detonating in time for him to be enveloped by it. The queue wasn't as long to Milton's left, and Mahoney's car disappeared before it, too, struck a waiting car.

81

Milton assessed himself quickly: the seatbelt had yanked hard across his shoulder and chest, and the rest of the impact had been absorbed by the airbag; he knew that he'd be bruised, but that aside, he was unhurt. He needed to move, though; Mahoney had a gun, and Milton didn't know where he was. He pushed the airbag away, opened the door and slithered down to the ground.

He had crashed into the back of the van at a decent speed, enough to crumple the bonnet of the BMW back onto itself. The windscreen had shattered, and the powder from the airbag was slowly drifting out of the newly opened aperture. The van had been shoved forward, the tyres laying double black tracks, and its doors had buckled inwards. There was no sign of Mahoney; his car had continued a little farther down the road before crashing into the tail end of the queue in the left-hand lane.

Milton stayed low, edging to the front of the car and then continuing between the van and the temporary fence that had been erected so that the run-off to the right could be given a layer of fresh gravel. Milton reached the front of the van and glanced back into the cab; the driver had a hand pressed to his forehead while blood ran out of his nose. He must have head butted the wheel.

Milton looked over the steeply sloped bonnet and saw the Volvo. It had crashed into the back of a silver Hyundai, catching it on the rear end so that the Hyundai had turned through forty-five degrees.

The Volvo's door was open, and the cabin was empty. Milton looked past the stricken car: the side of the road was overgrown with weeds and a large bramble bush, and, behind that, a metal fence marked the boundary with the car park of a second-hand car dealership and the forecourt of a petrol station. He scurried across the gap between the van and a Honda Jazz ahead of it, and then slid into the cover provided by the filthy trailer of a truck waiting for the light to turn green. He looked around it and, just in time, saw movement; Mahoney had been standing behind the Mercedes saloon at the front of the queue in the left-hand lane. The light changed from red to green, the car started to move, and Mahoney—his cover gone—aimed and fired.

He shot without aiming, and the bullet clanged against the side of the trailer.

Milton tried to recall how many shots had been fired. Four? Five? Mahoney probably had the same again, and Milton was unarmed. He was going to have to proceed with care.

"It's finished," he yelled out. "Give up."

There was no answer, and, instead, Milton heard the rumble from the truck's engine as the trailer started to roll forward. He swore, knowing that he was about to be exposed; he hopped onto the platform at the rear of the trailer and hung on, looking at the two lines of cars, as the driver turned right.

Milton saw Mahoney. He was beside the silver Hyundai that he hit and had forced the woman driving it to get out. Now he got in and smoked the tyres as he raced ahead, running the light as it went to red and swerving through oncoming traffic as he sped into the industrial estate beyond the junction.

Milton slammed his fist against the rear of the truck and hopped down.

Was this a sign? Should he leave now, get out of the city and keep going and forget about Maria and Cara and everything that had happened to him over the last two days? The Group were coming—perhaps they were already here—and the longer he stayed, the more likely it was that they would find him and bring him in.

But then he remembered the girl.

He remembered how small she had looked curled up in her bed last night, how frightened she had been at the hotel, and knew he was committed. He was involved now, for better or worse, and that was that.

He jogged across the junction, clambered over the fence and found a way into the car park where the dealership's vehicles were stored. He needed a fresh set of wheels, and quickly, so he could put some distance between himself and what had happened here before the police arrived. He thought of Shay Dillon, who was expecting him to return with Cara, and knew that he had some explaining to do.

82

Milton boosted a second-hand Hyundai from the garage. There was a CCTV camera high up on a concrete post that would catch his likeness, but he was beyond worrying about things like that: he'd already been recorded at the hotel and who knew where else, and, if the Group were looking for him, one more instance of sloppy tradecraft wouldn't make any difference. He needed to be on the move more than he needed to stay hidden.

He called Dillon as he drove back, apologised for the delay and said they needed to meet again. Dillon didn't take it well—muttering curses and threatening all manner of unpleasant fates if he decided Milton was messing him around—but eventually gave him the address of a warehouse on the docks and told Milton to meet him there.

~

THE WAREHOUSE, nestled on the docks, was made of weathered red brick and corrugated metal. Milton got out of the car and immediately smelled salt, the earthiness of freshly cut timber and the lingering stink of diesel. The building was surrounded by a sturdy wrought-iron fence with a sliding gate adorned with interwoven *D*s. There was an intercom set into one of the pillars, and he pressed the button to speak.

"Who is it?"

"Eric Blair. I'm here to see—"

The gates started to scrape back on their runners before Milton could finish speaking. He drove in and parked the Hyundai next to Dillon's G-Class and got out. Dillon's muscle, Barry, was waiting for him at the door.

"This way."

Milton followed him inside. The warehouse was busy, with a forklift sliding a pallet of cardboard boxes onto a shelf and half a dozen men and women in bright overalls making their way up and down the aisles. Barry took Milton to an office that had been built in the corner of the space, flimsy-looking walls reaching halfway to the roof of the main structure. Dillon was sitting at the single desk, staring at something on his phone.

"Boss," Barry said.

Dillon looked up and eyed Milton. "Are you messing me around?"

"No," Milton said.

"You must be."

"I'm not."

"So where's my niece?"

"Someone found out where she was."

"*What?*"

"The door had been kicked in. There was blood on the floor. They took her—her and the friend I'd left there to look after her."

"What do you mean?" Dillon said, anger flickering across his face. "Who? *Who* took her?"

"Two cars pulled away as I arrived. A Volvo and a BMW. I didn't get their plates, but I know one of the drivers—a man called Mahoney. He's a police officer. He was the man who frightened Cara in the hotel."

"Mahoney," Dillon said, looking up at Barry. "Do we know him?"

"Name doesn't ring a bell. I'll ask around."

"Wait until afterwards," Dillon said. "Stay and listen to this." He turned back to Milton. "Go on."

"I think Mahoney was involved at the hotel. I think he left the gun that Flannagan used."

"How do you know that?"

"I saw him in the bathroom where the young lad from the hotel was killed. I think Mahoney left the gun, the lad saw Flannagan getting it, and Flannagan killed him."

"Why didn't you tell me that earlier?"

"Because I would've rather had the police deal with it."

"And now? Where's Mahoney now?"

"I chased them around the ring road, but Mahoney had a gun. We crashed, but he got away."

"And the other car—the one with Cara?"

"It kept going."

"You fucked up, then—that's what you're saying?"

"No, I didn't. I didn't tell anyone where she was. I didn't tell you."

"So?"

"I don't know what happened. But I'm going to find her."

Dillon turned to Barry again. "You hear that? He lost her, and now he's going to find her."

Milton felt his own temper flaring but kept it under control. "I didn't have to come back. I could've driven out of

the city and forgotten about you and her and all of it, but I
didn't. I'm here. And I meant what I said—I'll find her, and
I'll get her back."

"You talk the talk, don't you? But you can't back it up."

Milton eyeballed him. "Try me."

Dillon held his gaze for longer than Milton had
expected; Milton didn't look away, and, eventually, Dillon
baulked.

"Who's this friend?" Dillon asked.

"Someone from the hotel."

Dillon shrugged. "So maybe it was her."

Milton shook his head. "No."

"Name?"

"No," Milton repeated. "You don't need to know that."

"But *you* didn't say anything about where Cara was—
right? So that just leaves her. Tell me her name."

"You can ask as many times as you want, but it won't
make any difference—I'm not telling you. She's caught up in
this, too, just like me. Whoever has your niece—and I'm
guessing it's the Gallaghers—took her as well."

"Maybe that's what she wants you to think. Maybe she's
been paid off, and she's on the way to the airport."

Milton held Dillon's eye again. "No."

Dillon's lips were tight and bloodless, and Milton could
see the potential for an explosion of anger. He didn't care.
Milton wasn't afraid of him—he wasn't afraid of anyone—
and what he said or didn't say would have no effect on what
Milton was going to do next. But it would be useful to have
his cooperation; it was the only thing that was stopping
Milton from walking. He might have been able to find
Gallagher through Ziggy, but Dillon could short-circuit all
of that. Timing was an issue. Milton was concerned that
whoever had Cara and Maria might see Maria as a liability,

and, if he was right, the clock was ticking for him to get her back.

"Let's say I *don't* have you chopped into little pieces for this mess," Dillon said. "What are you going to do?"

"Do *you* think this is Gallagher?"

"You said you know what I do for a living, so you'll know I have lots of enemies. But if you asked me to pick one, it'd be him. We're rivals, in lots of ways. The fight, for example. You know about that?"

Milton nodded.

"See," Dillon said, "I'm not sure Colm was the target at the hotel. The other man who died was Frank Rickard—he's an agent and promoter in the States. He'd just agreed to represent my fighter. Gallagher wanted him to represent his boy, and Frank turned him down, and I don't think he would've been polite about it. I doubt that went down well, and Billy's the type who'll bear a grudge."

"That can't be reason enough to do what he's done, surely? Does it have anything to do with the money from tomorrow's fight?"

"Not that, no—the purse isn't anything special. But the *potential*? That's something else. Whoever wins gets a title shot next year. That'll be in Vegas, and the contracts will be worth millions—two or three million, with the same again for the winner's first defence. I don't know this for sure, but, if you asked me to guess, I'd say Billy was throwing his toys out of the pram because of that. My brother wouldn't have sat quietly and let someone come into our event and do what he did. I think Colm tried to be a hero, and I think he got shot because of it."

"And Cara?"

"Billy knows there'll be payback for Colm's murder. I don't think he meant it to happen, and now he's panicking.

Maybe he thinks having Cara stops us doing that. He wants to give me a reason *not* to go after him after what they did to Colm. I know how he thinks. He'll propose a sit-down so that we can hash out terms."

"And then he'll give her back?"

"Maybe."

"But as soon as you have her back..."

"Right," Dillon said. "All bets are off. But what else is he going to do?"

Milton let that sink in. Dillon's suggestion for Gallagher's motivation was sound, but it didn't make a huge amount of difference to what Milton had already decided. In some ways, it cemented it: Cara had value, and it made no sense for Gallagher to hurt her. Maria, on the other hand, had no value. Maybe she could identify the men who had taken her. Maybe they hadn't blindfolded her, and she knew where they were. In that light, there was a good chance Gallagher would decide he couldn't let her walk and that it was safer to do away with her. The more Milton thought about it, the more he was concerned. She was in serious danger; he had to find her, and fast.

He placed his hands on the table and stared at Dillon. "This is what I'm going to do. I'm going to find them—Cara *and* my friend—and I'm going to get them back."

Dillon sighed impatiently and shook his head. "Come on. Like I say, you've got balls, but you're off with the fairies if you think you can help. You work in the kitchen, pal. What are *you* going to do?"

Milton didn't take his eyes off him. "I didn't always do that. I was a soldier for years, and then I worked as a free-lancer. I got out of that because I didn't want to do it anymore."

"Freelancing as what?"

"Use your imagination. I travel now, and I mind my own business unless I see something that I don't think is right. And then, when I do—like now—sometimes I get involved. I don't approve of you or Gallagher or what you do, but—at least for the moment—I haven't seen anything that gives me a reason to stick my nose in. But Cara? That's different. And a kid I know was killed at the hotel. *That's* different. My friend being taken. *That's* different. Any one of those things would be enough for me to take an interest. All three of them?" He shrugged. "I'm in now—all the way in—and it won't make a blind bit of difference whether you're on board with that or not. I'm going after them. Your choice is easy: do you want to help me or not?"

Dillon narrowed his eyes for a moment, considering, then nodded almost imperceptibly. "What do you need?"

"A weapon."

Dillon looked over at Barry, a faint smile playing at the corner of his lips. "Okay. And?"

"Find out what you can about Mahoney."

"Trust me—that's the *first* thing I'm going to do. What else do you need?"

"Gallagher," Milton said. "Where can I find him?"

83

Mahoney drove the stolen car back to Castleknock.

He had been filled with a mixture of emotions as he headed back home. There was anger at the second intervention of the man from the hotel, and frustration that they hadn't been able to get away from the house before he'd returned. He also felt relief, a weight off his shoulders now that he had decided to do the thing he should have done weeks ago: he was going to pack up his things and leave. There was too much heat on him now, and too many connections to tie him to the shooting at the hotel. It would have been naïve to think that the investigation wouldn't eventually alight upon his involvement—the pistol and what Blair had seen, the death of Flannagan, his first attempt to get Cara Dillon—and that all ignored what the girl and Blair's friend would say whenever they were released. Both would know he was involved in what had happened, but he doubted their testimony would be necessary; he would have been found out long before then.

No. He knew it now: he *had* to run. He had no choice.

There was a peacefulness in that decision, but a certain urgency as well, now that he'd decided to act. He had his bolthole in Panama, and he had his money; he just had to get out of the country before they put out a Garda Alert to stop him.

His apartment block—Cherry Lodge—was next to the junction between College Road and Carpenterstown Road and close to the wide-open space of Phoenix Park. The apartment had cost him more than half a million euros when he bought it two years earlier, a stretch on his budget that looked unwise in the cold light of day. The slump in the market after he had purchased at the peak and his rising mortgage repayments had left him in negative equity, and it had been the bank's increasingly intemperate letters that had contributed to the sense of financial unease that Billy Gallagher had exploited so adroitly.

He turned off the road and drifted to a stop. The development was ahead of him: a series of large buildings arranged around a crescent of grass and divided into apartments. The buildings were made of light grey concrete and had been designed with an asymmetrical distribution of balconies, one for each apartment, to break up their otherwise bland regularity. A large glass awning formed the entrance, while the imposing door beneath it provided a contrast to the glass and concrete that dominated the rest of the façade. The street was quiet, an Amazon delivery driver was arranging packages in the back of his van, and a woman walked her dog on the grass.

Mahoney dabbed the accelerator to continue and then stamped on the brake.

There were half a dozen cars parked on the left and right of the road. None of them was particularly noteworthy, save for the grey Hyundai that had been shoved right up against the hedge that demarked the narrow sliver of garden between Mahoney's block and the road. The car was occupied: two men, one in the driver's seat and the other next to him. Mahoney put his car into reverse and backed up until he was able to park behind a large Range Rover. He left the engine running and watched, hoping that he was wrong and the men would drive away.

They didn't.

Mahoney leaned forward and rested his forehead against the top of the wheel. He squeezed his eyes shut, raised his head and banged it against the wheel. He couldn't leave without getting his stuff from his apartment, but he couldn't ignore the men in the car. It was most likely they were there on Billy's orders, but it didn't have to be him; maybe the Dillons had discovered his involvement and the men were there on their behalf.

It didn't matter. They were waiting outside his apartment, and given all the context, that couldn't be a coincidence.

He took out his phone and dialled Lynch.

"What's up?" Lynch said.

"I need your help."

"About?"

"Can we meet? I'd rather talk face to face."

"Ominous."

"It's sensitive. Please?"

"Sure. I was just heading to the station to clock off."

"Not there. Can you meet me at the tea rooms in Phoenix Park?"

"It's a bit out of the way."

"Please."

"Okay," he said. "Fine. I can be there in an hour."

"Thanks," Mahoney said. "I owe you."

84

Dillon said that he would find a weapon and would call Milton so that he could collect it. Milton went outside to his car, took out his phone and saw that he had missed a call from Ziggy. He texted him back and suggested they meet; Ziggy said that he was still in the coffee shop on St Stephen's Green.

Ziggy was in the same booth as before, his laptop set up on the table, surrounded by three china mugs marked with the coffee shop's logo.

Milton sat down opposite him again. "Have you moved *at all*?"

"I've been busy. I get distracted when I get my teeth into something. I lose track of time."

"They don't mind you being here?"

"Not as long as I keep buying coffees."

Milton pointed to the empties. "You want another?"

Ziggy held up his hands. "Pass. I'm pretty wired."

Milton went and got himself one and, because he doubted Ziggy had had anything to eat, bought him a poppyseed muffin and a banana.

"Didn't know you cared," Ziggy said as Milton deposited the food on the table.

"It's for my own benefit. You're even more of a diva when you're hungry."

"True." He broke the muffin into quarters and stuffed one into his mouth. "I'm glad you're here," he said, crumbs tumbling from between his lips. "I've been digging into the Dillons, and I've found out more about the girl. She's had a rough start in life."

"I know," Milton said. "Her mum died."

Milton could hear his confusion. "Who told you that?"

"Shay Dillon—why?"

"She didn't die. She lives in Cork."

Milton frowned. "Really?"

"Her name's Clare. She and Colm Dillon got divorced last year. I found the court papers, and from what I can tell, it was *brutal*. The two of them were fighting over custody of the girl, and it got nasty. She had a firm of lawyers on her side, but they dropped her in the middle of preparing for the hearing. She couldn't get anyone else to step in, so she had to do it herself. She made all sorts of allegations at the hearing, but the judge didn't go for any of them and awarded custody to Colm. But that's where it starts to get interesting. She contacted an investigative journalist—a guy called Peter Duffy—and told him everything: what it was like being married into the family, that she had evidence against the brothers that would put them both away, and how the whole custody battle had been rigged against her. She said that she'd complained to the Judicial Conduct Committee that the judge had been bribed, but she didn't have any evidence, and they turned down her complaint. She said she went to the papers, but none of them would risk running her story."

"This is all online?"

"It was—for about a day. There was a story on Duffy's blog, but it was taken down. I found a cached version."

"Send it to me."

"I will—it's a good read."

"Why was it taken down? Because the Dillons sued him?"

"No," Ziggy said. "At least I couldn't find any evidence of that. It looks like Duffy took it down himself."

"When?"

"Last year. And you want to know the weirdest thing? He used to be prolific. *Seriously* prolific: a post every day, sometimes multiple times each day, and then he just stopped. I got into the CMS of his blog and pulled the user log—it wasn't just that Duffy never wrote anything else: his last activity was to unpublish that entry, and then there's been nothing. He never even logged in again. That'd be strange enough, but I can't find any sign of him on the internet at all. No social media activity. No outbound email. And then I found this."

He tapped the screen and turned it towards Milton. It was the missing persons page on the Garda's website: a series of photographs of men and women with their names beneath and the date they'd gone missing. A picture in the middle of the page was of a middle-aged man with receding dark hair and a melancholic cast to his face; the name underneath read Peter Duffy, and he was listed as missing eleven months ago.

"You can guess what I'm thinking," Ziggy said.

Milton exhaled wearily. He had harboured doubts about

returning Cara to Shay Dillon, but now he knew he couldn't possibly do that.

"The mother," he said. "Can you find an address?"

"Done that already. She lives just outside Cork, goes under her maiden name—Clare Dolan—and works as a primary school teacher. I've got her email and phone number, too."

"Send it over."

"I will."

"I'm going to need something else from you. Do you have a listening device? Something small?"

"Of course."

Ziggy opened his bag and took out a clamshell case. He unzipped it and opened it, revealing a collection of devices and gadgets. Milton knew what some of them did, but others were esoteric and outside of his experience. Ziggy took out a small black oblong, around the same size as a credit card and perhaps a centimetre deep.

"This is about the best on the market," he said. "It's GSM and works over 4G. You switch it on here"—he pointed to a button on the side—"and then leave it wherever you want. It has microphone amplification and noise dampening to reduce static interference. It's got a tracker in it, too."

"And you can monitor it remotely?"

"I can set it up to record to the cloud. Easy."

"Perfect."

Milton put out his hand, and Ziggy dropped the bug into his palm.

Ziggy closed the case and zipped it up. "Can I talk to you about Jimmy Moon?"

"Where is he?"

"Still at home, but not for long. He's playing golf with a

friend this afternoon. It'll be the perfect time to put the tracker on his car."

"Be careful."

"Worried about me?"

"Worried you'll do something stupid and get us both in trouble."

"Please," Ziggy protested. "This is the best chance we'll get. He leaves his car in the car park and disappears on the course for hours—I'll be done in thirty seconds."

"Do it and then get clear. Don't mess around."

"As if I would."

"I need you to concentrate on Dillon. I'll place the bug— monitor it for me."

"Understood," he said. "You need anything else?"

"Anything you can find on the Gallaghers. Addresses, phone numbers—anything."

Milton's phone buzzed with a message. He tapped the screen and read:

>> *Meet at Wilson Freight, Pigeon House Road. ASAP.*

Ziggy craned his neck to look at it. "Is that from Dillon?"

Milton nodded. "I'd better go."

"One more thing. I've been trying to get a solid lead on Yevtushenko."

"And?"

"And he's difficult to find," Ziggy said. He reached into his pocket and took out a thumb drive. "This is everything I've managed to get so far. It's not a huge amount, but it'll give you a few leads to go on. I'll keep looking."

Milton pocketed the drive and held Ziggy's eye. "Thanks. You've outdone yourself this time."

Ziggy smiled with satisfaction. "Glad to help. I'll look into the Gallaghers and call you when I have something."

Paddy Coffey watched as Danny Farley moved on to the speed bag. It had been a light session, the fight was tonight, and the last thing he wanted was for the kid to tweak something before he stepped into the octagon. He wanted him to work up a light sweat, enough to get his heart pumping, and then he was going to insist that he take it easy for the rest of the day.

Farley's hands were a blur as he threw a flurry of quick, precise punches that hit the bag with a rapid-fire rhythm. His focus was intense and his movements almost mechanical as he built up his hand speed. Sweat beaded on his forehead as he increased the intensity, the sound of the bag striking the wooden board filling the gym. His movements were precise and fluid, each punch landing with a satisfying thud.

Coffey's cut man, Seamus Cahill, was watching from across the room, and the two men shared a knowing look. They both knew that Farley favoured the speed bag because it was easy for him, and it made him look good. Coffey had tried to get the kid to put the double-end bag into his routine, but Farley had said no. It was more challenging—the bag was attached to the floor and ceiling with elastic cords that meant it moved unpredictably—but, because it was harder, Farley had refused. They'd argued about it, and, eventually, Farley had threatened to complain to Dillon. The whole episode was emblematic of the kid: he liked anything that allowed him to show off and avoided the equipment that pushed him out of his comfort zone.

Farley's breathing became heavier until he hammered the bag with a final jab and stepped back.

"There," he said, taking off his gloves and dropping them on the floor. "Done."

Coffey reached up to stop the ball. "I want to talk to you about tonight."

"Not now. I'm seeing Morag. I said I'd pick her up an hour ago."

"Today?"

He shrugged. "Yeah. So what?"

"So what? Are you serious? You don't need any distractions."

"Relax. It's fine."

Coffey frowned. The hours before a fight were important, and Farley was being flippant about it. Cahill was watching from the other side of the room, hiding his interest as he put together the gear in his bag.

Coffey pointed to the apron. "Sit down."

Farley pointed to the door. "I'm late."

"*Sit.*"

Farley muttered something under his breath and sat on the edge of the apron. "What?"

"You're not taking this seriously."

"I am."

"No," Coffey said. "You're *not*. You can't go to sleep on Gallagher."

"Come on, Paddy. We both know he's out of his league."

"It just takes—"

"I know, I know," he cut over him. "You've told me enough times: 'One lucky punch.'"

"You don't agree?"

"Sure I do, but it'll be tough for him to throw a punch when he's flat out on his back. You know it—he doesn't deserve to be in the same ring as me." He looked over at Cahill. "Right, Seamus?"

"I don't know, Danny."

"Well, I do. I'm going to make sure everyone knows that tonight, and then I'm going to go to Vegas to do the same to whatever bum they put in front of me there."

Coffey rolled his eyes. "Seriously? You think Pedro Rodriguez is a bum?"

"None of them are fit to lace my boots."

"Duane McCallister? Ronnie Thompson? Are they bums?"

"Same." He slid off the apron.

"Where are you going?"

"I said—I'm going to see Morag."

Coffey could see that Farley wasn't going to listen to him and that the best he could hope for was to limit any possible damage. "Be careful what you eat. Nothing goes in your mouth that's hard to digest. And get to the arena by five. I've got Laura booked to give you a massage. We need you loose and relaxed."

"Fine," he said. "Whatever. You need to chill out. Getting my end away is what I do to relax."

He grabbed his bag and made for the exit.

Coffey went to the speed bag, stooped down and picked up the gloves that Farley had left there.

Cahill joined him. "Arrogant little prick. He treats us like we're the shit he brought in on his shoe."

"What am I supposed to do?"

"I wouldn't stand for it. You either speak to me with respect, or you don't speak to me at all."

"Easy to say. Not easy to keep him in line when he's Dillon's boy. He knows my hands are tied."

Coffey picked up Farley's discarded towel and tossed it in the wicker basket.

"Are you okay?" Cahill said.

"How'd you mean?"

"After the hotel."

Coffey sighed again. "I wasn't anywhere near it."

"You saw it, though. Right?"

"I saw it." He leaned back against the apron. "It's not the first time I've seen someone get shot."

"I know."

"That's not what's on my mind. It's this." He swept his arm around the gym. "Farley's a little prick with an attitude, but I've worked with fighters like him before—it gets knocked out of them pretty fast when they come up against someone they can't bully, and then you can really get down to work and make them better."

"It's Dillon, then?"

Coffey inclined his head. "You know what he's like—how much money we stand to make because we're associated with him, how Danny's going to win the belt, and how much money that'll bring in. It all sounds good, but it's not. He and his brother came in here before the weigh-in, and he had the gall to tell me that he's not happy with the deal we negotiated and how he wants to change the terms, and it all got me to thinking—is the juice worth the squeeze?"

"You said it yourself—Farley's good."

"Aye. He's got the potential to be up there. And he's right —Gallagher's got no chance. He'll stand back and trade, and he can't beat Farley that way. Danny's got too much power. But he goes over to the States, and they'll put him in with submission specialists and he's toast. He's got no ground game, and he won't let me train him to get one. You get someone with decent jiu-jitsu and a solid chin—they'll get in close and get him on the mat and he'll tap. I had one of his sparring partners put him in an arm bar last week, and he squealed like a pig when the pressure went on."

"Does Dillon know this?"

"I told him, but he didn't listen. 'How are they going to get in close when he strikes the way he does?' Or he'll say I'm being negative, and I need to be optimistic or it'll 'infect' Farley. Blah, blah, blah. He thinks he understands how it works, but he doesn't. No clue. What happened at the hotel was the final straw. I'm no shrinking violet—you know I'm not—but I'm getting too old for shit like that."

Cahill sat down next to him. "So what are you going to do?"

Coffey leaned back, feeling the give of the ropes against his shoulders. He'd been thinking about that since the shooting, and now he'd come to a decision. It wasn't something that he had decided lightly, but he was long enough in the tooth to know how to read a situation and, specifically, when to twist and when to stick.

This felt like the time to make a move.

"I'm going to teach them some respect."

86

M ilton followed Dillon's directions to the entrance to one of the freight terminals; dozens of containers were stacked one on top of the other in long lines behind a tall metal fence. Milton pulled up and parked; Dillon's car arrived five minutes later. Milton went over to it and got into the back before Dillon could get out. Dillon's muscle—Barry—was driving.

"Here," Dillon said, handing Milton a jiffy bag.

Milton opened it and took out a Glock 9mm. He examined it and saw that the serial number had been filed away.

"Dump it when you're done."

Milton didn't intend to use the gun but knew there was a good chance he would need to at least wave it around.

"Thanks."

Dillon put a hand on his shoulder. "Don't mess up again."

Milton used the moment's distraction to drop Ziggy's device into the pocket of Dillon's jacket.

"I won't."

He pulled the handle, opened the door and stepped out.

The car drove away before Milton was halfway back to his own vehicle.

He called Ziggy.

"All good?"

"Broadcasting loud and clear. Want to have a listen?"

There was a moment of silence before Milton heard the sound of Dillon's voice again.

"What do you think?"

"He's got something about him."

"Why would he get involved?"

"Maybe it's the woman? Him and her?"

"Maybe."

"How long do you want to wait?"

"Until tonight," Dillon said. "We're not ready yet, are we? It'll take time to get the lads together, get them tooled up. No harm in letting him have a go first, is there?"

"Probably not."

"If he gets nowhere? Doesn't matter. We hit back when the fight's on, when Billy's not expecting it."

The conversation petered out, and the radio was switched on.

"Hear all that?" Ziggy said.

"Loud and clear. You're recording?"

"Yes."

Milton reached his car and got inside. "How long do you think the battery will last?"

"Couple of days. That enough?"

"Should be fine—especially if I'm able to shake things up."

"I might be able to help with that. I found Billy Gallagher's place. Cameras everywhere, easy enough to spoof, so I had a quick look around. I counted half a dozen men. They all looked nervous."

"I'm not surprised. What about the girl?"

"Didn't see anything. That doesn't mean that she's not there."

"He'll have her somewhere else."

"Charlie Gallagher isn't there, either. I got into his trainer's phone. His schedule is listed in the calendar. He's doing a light workout this afternoon."

"Where?"

"A gym in Ballsbridge. I'll ping you the details. What are you going to do?"

"Gallagher has leverage," he said. "I need some of my own."

87

Number Three put the van in gear and prepared to pull away from the kerb.

"Two to Group," Number Two said over the radio. "Proceeding south, just about to reach the junction with Military Road. Over."

"Two, this is Six." Lilly said into her throat mic. "We're south of your position at Commons Road. Ready for handover. Over."

"Acknowledged, Six. Turning off now. Out."

Three pushed down on the accelerator, and they moved away, indicating left and waiting at the junction for Jimmy's car. Lilly was in the back, but she had a good view through the windscreen and saw the big, ostentatious Mercedes as it went by. There was nothing else heading south on Shanganagh Road, and Three was able to take up position directly behind. He reduced their speed a little so that Jimmy could pull away, but not so much that there was any prospect that they might miss him.

The quartermaster had found a panel van marked with the livery of Vodafone Ireland that they could use. They had three vehicles in total, and, with them all on the move whenever Jimmy moved, they were able to conduct rolling surveillance. Number One had been waiting at the end of Saint George's Avenue, and, when she was alerted that Jimmy looked as if he was about to set off, she'd been in place to begin the tail. She followed for the first ten minutes as Jimmy drove south out of Killiney. They reached Shankill, and One peeled off so that Number Two could take over. Their caution wasn't because they were worried that Jimmy would see them; it was because they knew that *Milton* would, and all their efforts in tracking him to the city would be for nothing if he suspected they were here, too.

All of Jimmy's devices had been tapped, and Lilly had been able to listen to his voice as he called his friend late last night and arranged a game of golf at Dun Laoghaire Golf Club in Enniskerry. It had been a weird and strangely uncomfortable experience for her; their last conversations had been unpleasant before they both agreed that it would be better to communicate through lawyers from now on. But hearing him earlier had reminded her of what he had sounded like before their marriage had imploded: jocular and relaxed, with warmth and ease and a lightness in his tone. He had laughed at an off-colour joke, made a playful comment about his playing partner's slice and then offered to double the wager that was evidently usual when the two of them teed off together.

Lilly felt awkward to be eavesdropping, but she would have been lying if she said that she didn't enjoy the feeling of power it gave her. She had been on the back foot during the custody proceedings on account of Jimmy's seemingly limitless budget, and, before that, he had always taken the lead in their marriage. He had described himself as 'old-fashioned'; she saw through that now and would have chosen 'chauvinist.' But he had no idea what she did for her work, and to have him involved in the middle of it like this, even unwittingly, gave her a sense of superiority that was novel.

It did mean that she needed to stay out of sight, however, and that had relegated her by necessity to a role in charge of the Group's signals; she was tasked with watching the surveillance footage and monitoring the calls Jimmy made and received. She couldn't ride in the front of the van, either; she had to stay here, hidden in the back.

"He's turning off," Three said.

Lilly looked up; Jimmy was indicating that he was going to turn right. She checked the map; the real-time traffic information suggested there was a delay up ahead, and she guessed that Jimmy's satnav had picked an alternative route.

"Group, this is Six," Lilly said. "Target is turning onto the R116, heading west in the direction of Kilternan. Best guess is that he'll turn south there and approach the club through Scalp and Countybrook. Over."

"This is One—Roger that. Stay on him. I'll get ahead of you and pick him up at Puck's Castle Lane. Out."

Lilly acknowledged the message, and the channel fell silent. She found her thoughts going back to Lola. Jimmy had left her at home with a nanny. They'd watched the woman arrive thirty minutes before he had set off, and Lilly had watched the footage jealously. She was young and pretty, and the thought of her—a stranger, at least as far as she was concerned—looking after her daughter when Lilly should have been with her was a difficult one for her to accept.

Three glanced back at Lilly. "You think he'll turn up?"

"Milton? I don't know."

"What's he like?"

"What you'd expect."

"You're the only one with direct experience."

"There's nothing about him that stands out. He's like us."

"Just older."

"Don't underestimate him."

"I'm not," Three replied. "I read the report. He gave you the run-around."

Lilly left that unanswered. It was true—he *had* done that—and her failure to take care of him when she had the chance was a source of continuing annoyance and regret. She was confident that her deception had gone unnoticed, and that she had now manoeuvred herself into a position where she could offer Sommer a supply of excellent intelligence. She had to make sure nothing changed to threaten that, because it was the fulcrum upon which everything else turned. Sommer had promised her the money to fight Jimmy for custody of her daughter; without him, she had no chance. Milton could bring everything crashing down around her, and Lilly was not going to allow that to happen.

She needed to find him, and *this*—following her ex-husband on his way to golf—was her best chance of doing that.

The Phoenix Park Tea Rooms were housed in a Victorian building painted in pastel hues with curved bay windows and decorative fretwork. A string of colourful bunting fluttered in the gentle breeze; the canopies of mature trees rustled overhead. Lynch, still dressed in his uniform, was sat on one of the benches inside the railings.

"Sorry I'm late," Mahoney said.

Lynch looked up at him, using his hand to shield his eyes from the sun. "Jesus. What's happened? You look awful."

"I'm in trouble, Eoin. Big trouble."

"What is it?"

He sat down on the opposite side of the bench. "I've been weak," he said in a quiet voice. "I've been weak, and it's landed me in a spot I don't think I can get out of."

"Relax," he said. "Whatever it is, it can't be as bad as all that."

Mahoney chuckled bitterly. "It's worse." He sighed,

composing himself, then lowered his voice again. "I've been working for Billy Gallagher for the last six months."

Lynch's mouth fell open. "What?"

"I had money trouble. My mam had just died, and I wasn't thinking straight. The bank kept telling me I was behind on the mortgage, and they were going to take the apartment back. I had gambling debts from when I tried to get ahead enough to pay some of the mortgage off, and I had trouble at work. I went to Billy for a loan and... I know. You don't have to say. I fucked up. I was stupid."

"Billy Gallagher," he muttered. "Shit. Billy Gallagher."

"You know what he's like—once he's got his claws in, he never lets go."

"Why didn't you come and talk to me about it?"

"You would've paid my mortgage for me?"

"No," he said. "Course not. But I might have been able to stop you doing something stupid."

"I know. I'm a fool, but I didn't know what else to do."

"What do you do for him?"

"Mostly information, at least to start."

"Like what?"

"Like when the lads in vice are looking into one of his brothels. I tell him they're planning a raid, and he's able to clear it out before they hit it."

"And?"

"And I find people for him. Someone owes him money and does a runner—I track them down. Or one of the dealers working for the Dillons starts selling in Billy's neck of the woods—I happen to let slip I know which house they're operating from. That kind of thing."

"'That kind of thing'? You know what he's like—he's liable to get people like that beaten up, and that's if they're lucky."

"I know," Mahoney muttered. "You don't have to remind—"

Lynch cut over him. "Were you involved with what happened at the hotel?"

"No," Mahoney lied.

"And what about what happened at the hospital?"

"Meaning?"

"Don't treat me like a clown. I was there. What happened to Flannagan—was that you?"

"No," he said. "That was nothing to do with me. I've done some shit for him, but I'd never do *that*."

"Really?"

"I swear."

Lynch shook his head. "I mean, it just seems *strange*. Billy pays Flannagan to shoot up Dillon, it goes wrong and Flannagan gets nicked, then he ends up dead even though the doctors said he was out of the woods. And he dies *minutes* after you turn up to take over from me. Look at it from my point of view, Michael—it looks dodgy as fuck."

"Think about what you're saying," Mahoney said. "That'd be murder. I'll admit I've always been a little bit hooky, but not that. I'd never do *that*."

"So what's happened now?"

"Billy wanted me to get Cara Dillon. It's leverage—he thinks the Dillons are going to come after him after what happened, and he wants something to make them stop and think. He swore she wouldn't be hurt. I was going to take her to him, but she recognised me from nicking her dad. You saw what happened next. We got beaten up, and now she's gone."

"That's why you're running?"

He nodded. "Billy's blaming me for everything. I haven't got a choice—I've got to run."

"Where?"

"You don't need to know that. It's not that I don't trust you, but it's better you don't know."

"So why tell me?"

"Because I need you to do me a favour." He breathed in and out again and hoped that Lynch wouldn't notice that his fingers were trembling. "I need my passport. It's at home, and I need someone to go and get it for me."

"Why can't you go?"

"Because I think Billy's decided to top me."

"What? Seriously? Come on."

"I'm not fucking around," he snapped. "I went back myself an hour ago, and he's got one of his gorillas outside waiting for me."

Lynch leaned back in the seat and bit down on his lip.

"Please," Mahoney said. "I'm begging you. I wouldn't ask, but I can't do it myself, and there's no one else I trust."

"Let me think about it."

"I can't," he said. "I know it's not fair to bump you into doing something like this, but the longer I'm still here, the more likely it is that Billy finds me."

Lynch drummed his fingers on the back of the bench, turned to look across the grass and sighed.

"Please, Eoin. *Please.*"

"All right," he said. "I'll do it."

"Thank you. *Thank* you."

"You got a key?"

He reached into his pocket and took out a keycard. He handed it to Lynch.

"Where's your passport?"

"There's a box in the wardrobe, pushed right to the back. I think it's beneath a pile of shoes. It's in there. There's a holdall there, too. Could you bring that?"

"Sure," Lynch said, getting to his feet. "I've got to go and get my stuff from the nick. I'll go after that. I'll call you when I've got it."

"Thanks," Mahoney said. "You're a lifesaver."

89

Maria's head felt as if it had been split right down the middle. She vaguely remembered being driven away from the house, but most of the journey and what followed had been occluded by a fog through which it was only occasionally possible to see. It had lifted an hour or two ago, although it had taken her a while to realise that the darkness around her was because she had been put into a windowless room. She had stared into it until she had been able to divine gradations in the dark: a pitiful light filtered in beneath what she assumed was the door, and she guessed the dim streaks she could see overhead were thanks to gaps in the roof. Beyond that, though, there was nothing.

She had called Cara's name, but there had been no response, and, as she strained her ears, she'd been unable to hear anything to suggest there was anyone else in the room with her.

She tried to remember what had happened from the fragments of memory that she had been able to hold onto through the throbbing in her head. She remembered waking up with her face pressed against the glass of a car window. She remembered protesting as she was dragged out of the car, then being shoved and stumbling into darkness. There had been a man, too, an older man who had looked at her questioningly before grunting something she couldn't remember to the men who had attacked her.

She took a breath to ready herself and then tried to get to her feet. Her hands were free, and she was able to brace herself on all fours before tilting back onto her haunches. Her legs held for a moment before her balance deserted her, and she toppled over, her back up against the wall.

She reached up and prodded the side of her head where the man had struck her; the pain flared, and she wondered whether she might have been concussed.

She gingerly returned to hands and knees and tried to stand again. She managed it this time, finding a ledge above her head that gave her something to hold onto while she gathered what was left of her equilibrium. She took a step and then another, her hand pressed against the wall so she could position herself in the darkness. She made her way to the line of light at floor level and confirmed that she was right; it was a door. She found a handle and tried it. Locked. A wave of despair crashed over her. She swallowed hard, steeled herself, and began feeling around the edges of the door, her fingers tracing over rough, splintered wood and cold metal. A keyhole. She crouched down and tried to peer through it, but saw only the faintest suggestion of light; it looked as if the key might be in the lock on the other side of the door. She began a methodical search of the room, her fingers skimmed over damp concrete and caught on the rough brick of the wall, but there was nothing that even hinted at a way out.

"Help!"

It was barely more than a whisper, a ghost of sound echoing off the concrete. It sounded pitiful and fraught with despair, and then she realised: it was her voice.

"Help!" She drew in a breath and called again, louder this time. *"Help!"*

She heard footsteps from somewhere on the other side of the door.

"Shut up," a man called, his voice muffled by the door. "Be quiet and behave, and maybe we'll let you out."

She slumped back against the wall and slid down it, drawing her knees up to her chest and hugging them tightly. She tried to recall if anyone had seen them being taken out of the house, if anyone might have called the police, but she'd been too dazed and couldn't remember. That left her with John, but he hadn't been there when the two men had broken into the house. There wasn't anyone else, though, and, if not him, who else was going to find her?

90

They had been watching Jimmy's car for an hour, and still there was no sign of either Ziggy Penn or Milton. The Dun Laoghaire club at Enniskerry was impressive, with a smart new clubhouse overlooking the course on one side and the parking area on the other. Number Three had parked the van away from the car, but close enough that surveillance was easy. One had parked in the next bay across. She had rented a set of clubs from the pro shop and was now arranging them in the bag that had come with them. Two had found a place to wait at the entrance to the club where he would be able to give notice if either target was to arrive. So far, comms had been silent; Lilly hadn't expected that today would yield results, but she had hoped that it might. She was starting to wonder when they would make progress, their lack of success had encouraged doubt among them all, and she was concerned that Milton might have made them and disappeared once more.

Jimmy had parked his car near to the entrance to the pro shop where his partner had been waiting; the two of them had assembled their trolleys and disappeared to the first tee.

Lilly didn't know how long a game of golf usually lasted but guessed that it would take at least a couple of hours.

Her earpiece buzzed. "Two to Group. A grey Nissan Qashqai has just turned off Ballyman Road and is proceeding north to your location. I didn't get a good enough view for a positive identification, but it was a single man who at least bears a resemblance to Penn. Out."

Lilly turned to the screen that displayed the feed from the cameras that had been fitted to the van. She selected the rearward-facing camera that covered the entrance to the car park and waited for the car to appear. The Qashqai crested the hill and turned onto the car park, going past the van and continuing slowly in the direction of Jimmy's Mercedes.

Three turned back so that she could see the screen. "Did you get a look?"

"It's not Milton," she said.

"Penn?"

"Stand by."

Lilly scrubbed back through the footage, isolated the best still and zoomed in: the sun reflected off the windscreen a little too much, so she jogged it forward frame by frame until she had an image that was good enough to compare to the photograph that had been pulled from the Group's records. Lilly looked at the two images side by side and was convinced even before the algorithm confirmed that they were the same person.

"Six to Group," she said into her microphone. "We have a confirmed match. That's Ziggy Penn. Over."

She switched cameras so that she was able to watch as Penn parked his car three bays over from Jimmy's car. He waited inside for a moment, and Lilly took the opportunity to zoom in on him. The picture was clear enough to show him looking all around to check, she guessed, that Jimmy wasn't in the vicinity.

"One to Group. Hold positions. Over."

The door opened, and Penn emerged. He ambled across the bays that separated the Qashqai from the Mercedes, then went around the other side so that he was temporarily out of view of the camera. He stopped, then dropped into a crouch. Lilly couldn't see Penn but wasn't concerned; One had stayed by the pro shop and ought still to have line of sight without revealing herself to him. Penn popped up again and strolled back to his car.

"One to Group. Looks like he's attached a tracker. Over."

"Two to One. Confirm orders. Over."

"One to Group. We do not intercept now. Say again—do not intercept. We observe and follow. Milton will go to Penn and we'll be there. Over."

Lilly watched on the screen as Penn got back into the Nissan and pulled out. One came back over the channel and instructed Two to be ready to begin surveillance. They would need to be especially careful from now on; Jimmy wouldn't have expected to be followed, but Penn had been in the field before and ought to have remembered how important it was to retain an awareness of your surroundings when on operations. She had read his report and had been encouraged that his assessment suggested a man with more faith in his ability than actual aptitude. With the potential prize so high, however, she—and none of the others—was prepared to gamble that his unfounded faith would keep him from making them.

"Here we go," Three said.

Penn drove by and disappeared over the hill. Three started the engine and reversed out; One made her way to her car and did the same.

"Two to Group. I have eyes on the target and will begin pursuit. Over."

Lilly found that her palms were damp with sweat. She wiped them dry on her trousers and took a breath to try to calm her pulse.

She could sense it: they were *close*.

It was the second boxing gym Milton had visited in as many days. This one—the venue for Charlie Gallagher's training—was much more modern, housed in a brand-new building with white-painted walls that glowed in the bright afternoon sun. It looked as if it had been built recently, with the flower beds in the car park still empty save for enterprising weeds that were growing up through the dry earth. There were a handful of cars slotted into the large space, and the two double doors that were the way into the building had been left open. Milton parked in the disabled bay nearest to the building, left the engine running and went around to the rear of the car. He opened the boot, removing the empty jerrycan that was taking up most of the space, and then reached behind him to confirm that the pistol was still shoved into the waistband of his jeans. He went around the passenger seat and collected the programme for the bout and the pen he had picked up from a newsagent on his way here.

He had just started toward the doors when two men came out. One was older than the other, with weather-beaten skin from being out in the sun. The other, younger man bulged with muscle that pressed against the sleeves of his white T-shirt.

Milton didn't know the older man, but he recognised the second.

"Charlie," he said, beaming at him.

Charlie Gallagher stopped and turned. "Who are you?"

"Big fan. Good luck tonight."

He looked nonplussed. "Thanks," he said uncertainly.

He held out the programme. "Do you think you could sign this for me?"

"Charlie's busy," the older man said. "No time for that now."

"It'd take five seconds," Milton said. "It's for my boy. He's a big fan, too."

Charlie made a gesture that suggested weary acceptance, but Milton could see that he wasn't used to being asked and was pleased. He held out the programme and then the pen.

Charlie took them. "What do you want me to write?"

Milton reached around. "To Sean. From Charlie. Something like that."

"How are you spelling that? S-E-A-N or S-H-A-U—"

Milton pulled the pistol and aimed it at him.

"What the fuck?"

"Nice and easy," Milton said, the avuncularity gone from his voice and replaced with a steely edge.

"Put it down, pal," the older man said. "That's Billy Gallagher's lad."

"I know who it is," Milton said. He jerked his head in the direction of the waiting car and the open boot. "In you get."

"Fuck that!"

"Don't make me ask twice."

"I'm not getting in that—"

Milton quickly switched aim, tracking around to the left and then aiming down. He pulled the trigger and shot the older man in the fleshy part of his left thigh, far enough away from his knee to not cause serious damage but still excruciatingly painful. His leg buckled, and he toppled over, falling into Gallagher just as Milton aimed at the younger man for a second time.

"In the boot now or the next one's for you."

"Were you listening to what he said?"

"I was," Milton replied.

"Do you know who I *am*?"

"I do."

"I'll fuck you up."

"No, you won't." Milton tightened his finger on the trigger again. "In."

Gallagher lifted one leg, straddled the lip of the boot and then brought up the other and lowered himself inside. Milton knew he probably had a phone on him but didn't care. He *wanted* him to call his dad. He wanted Billy to know what had happened—especially that Milton was ruthless enough to put a bullet into the older man's leg—and he wanted him to think that the same fate might befall his son if he didn't do exactly what he told him to do.

the file he wanted and tapped play; Mahoney's confession played out, explaining that he had been on Billy Gallagher's payroll and that he had done work for him that would get him ten years—minimum—for corruption. Lynch couldn't believe it; although he knew his erstwhile partner had no problem with dipping his fingers in the till from time to time, it was a stretch to go from there to working for one of the city's most dangerous criminals and murdering someone on his behalf. He stared at the voice recorder, the timer ticking up as Mahoney's confession played, and wondered if he had been naïve.

He shook his head. *No.* It was one thing to know Mahoney played fast and loose with the rules and another thing altogether to know what he knew now. The investigator—Collins—hadn't mentioned any connection between Mahoney and Gallagher when Lynch had gone into the ombudsman's office to see her, although he supposed that might have been something she chose not to share. It was impossible to say.

He took out the business card that Collins had given him. She had told him to call if he had anything useful. He ran his finger up and down the rough edge of the card and wondered what would happen if he called the number on it. He wasn't as white as driven snow himself and had turned his eye to the odd indiscretion in exchange for a favour owed or a banknote pressed into his palm. It wasn't something he did often, but it had been enough to give him a sleepless night after his interview.

Would telling Collins about Mahoney's confession be to his credit, or would it bring down an investigation that might sweep him up in it as it brought Mahoney down?

He put the pistol back in the box, replaced the box in the

drawer and closed it. He went back down the hall, picked up Mahoney's passport and slipped it into his pocket with his phone, grabbed the holdall, then let himself out of the apartment and wondered what he should do.

93

Milton drove south out of Sandymount in Monkstown. He found a quiet spot where he wouldn't be observed, parked up and went around to the back of the car. He held the pistol in his right hand and aimed down as he opened the lid of the boot with his left; Charlie Gallagher blinked up at him, using his hand to shade his eyes from the sudden sunlight.

"This doesn't have to end with you getting hurt," Milton said. "Your father has a friend of mine and a young girl. I'm going to swap you for them. If he's sensible and plays straight with me, you'll get to walk in time to get to the venue for the fight."

"The fight? Are you mad? I can't fight after *this*."

"It's not the *best* preparation, but you never really stood a chance anyway. At least you can turn up and still get your cut of the purse."

"Fuck you," he spat.

"Whatever," Milton said. "I expect you already called your dad. Call him again."

Charlie looked ready to argue, but Milton reached down

so the pistol was inches from his head. Charlie reached into his pocket, fumbled out his phone and dialled a number.

"Put it on speaker," Milton said.

Charlie did as he was told. The call rang twice before it was answered. "Where are you?"

"Mr. Gallagher? My name is Blair. I'm with your son."

"You fucking idiot—you don't know what you've done. I'm—"

"We don't have time for all of that," Milton cut across him. "I didn't want to get involved, but you didn't give me a choice. The woman and the girl have no part to play in all of this, and you need to let them go. Do that, and I'll let you have Charlie. You'll still be able to get him to the arena in time for the fight."

"Where?"

"There's a multi-storey car park on Jervis Street. You know it?"

"Of course I know it."

"Fourth floor."

"When?"

"Two hours."

"On your own?"

"Just me."

"No police?"

"Come on, Billy. I've got your boy in the boot of my car, and I shot the man he was with in the leg. I'm sure Charlie told you that already. My point is—given that—I'm hardly going to want the police involved, am I?"

"And it's as simple as that—the woman and the girl for Charlie?"

"As simple as that. It's a public place with cameras. Funny business will get everyone into trouble. And the feud between you and the Dillons has nothing to do with me. We do this—the woman and the girl for your boy—and I'm gone. You'll never see me again. I don't care what happens after that."

There was a pause, and Milton wondered whether Gallagher was going to agree to the proposal.

Charlie looked concerned, as if he was harbouring the same doubts. "Dad?"

His father muttered a curse. "Jervis Street in two hours."

The call ended. Milton reached down, took the phone and pocketed it. "Not long now," he said, and, before Charlie could complain, he closed the lid of the boot on him once more.

94

Garton and Briars—two of Shay's best men—stood outside the door to the dressing room. Shay approached, waited for them to recognise him and, when they did, indicated that he wanted to go inside. Garton rapped his knuckles against the door and, after waiting a beat, opened it and stepped aside.

Shay went in. The dressing room was busy. Danny Farley was warming up with a rope in the corner, Coffey watching him with a sceptical eye. The cut man was tending to his equipment, someone from the local promoter's office was playing with her phone, and half a dozen of Farley's mates and a couple of women hung about watching. The air was heavy and humid, with an electrical charge that buzzed and fizzed and popped. The dimly lit space was noisy: the rhythmic slap of the jump rope as Farley worked up a light sweat, the buzz of tense conversation from the crew and the entourage, the thud of bass from a rap song rumbling out of a large Bluetooth speaker. It was pungent, too, with the smell of liniment—a blend of menthol and herbs—mingling with the tang of perspiration.

Coffey held up a hand to stop Farley. "That'll do. Go take a seat."

Farley dropped the rope and went over to sit down. Coffey took out a roll of tape and wrapped it around Farley's hands, layering it with an expertise that Shay knew would have come from years of experience.

Farley's muscles rippled beneath the sheen of sweat, glistening like polished steel, and Shay felt a fresh burst of confidence. Charlie Gallagher was a nasty lad, but he wasn't built like Farley, and he didn't have the same killer instinct. He was a decent fella to have if you were going to brawl on the street, but in an environment like this... no way. Farley would go through him like a hot knife through butter. It was difficult not to anticipate what might come next; the idea of taking Farley to fight in Vegas was intoxicating. That thought was quickly superseded by regret that Shay would be going on that journey alone. He didn't mind admitting it: Colm was responsible for all of this. He had been the one who had seen Farley's potential, Colm had pushed Shay to pay for him to be trained by Coffey, and Colm had worked to build the relationship with Rickard.

Shay went over to stand next to Farley. "You all right, son?"

"Feel good."

Coffey reached over for a pair of lightweight gloves and helped Farley put them on.

"Ready?"

"Ready." Farley slapped the gloves together. "First-round KO—you watch."

"Easy," Coffey said. "Don't get cocky."

Farley stood up and fired out a left-right-left combination. "Come on, Paddy. We both know he's out of his depth."

Farley continued with another combination, his precise

punches accompanied by the rhythmic shuffling of his feet on the cold, tiled floor. Each punch, each duck, and each kick was executed crisply, a display that demonstrated how his natural talent had been honed by Coffey's tutelage. The sound of his fists slicing through the air combined with his measured breathing, a steady cadence that melted into the beat of the music.

Shay gestured that Coffey should follow him to the other side of the room where Farley wouldn't hear them. "What do we think?"

"We think he's a cocky bastard," Coffey said.

"Yes—and?"

"I don't want to tell him because it'll just make his head even bigger, but I just don't see any way he loses tonight."

"How confident are you?"

"Very."

Coffey went over to a bucket filled with ice and took out a bottle of Lucozade. He tossed it over to Farley and told him to drink it.

"Electrolytes?" Shay said.

"Aye. Need to keep him topped up."

Farley popped the lid from the bottle and took a swig.

"All of it," Coffey admonished.

"Come on, Paddy. Any more and I'll go and piss myself."

"You'll sweat it out. Go on. Finish it."

Farley muttered something under his breath but did as he was told.

Shay went over to Farley and held his hand against the younger man's cheek. "Go on, son. Kick the shit out of him."

"I will, Mr. Dillon."

"Do it for my brother. He saw the potential in you. He's the reason you're here. You'd still be working doors in Temple Bar if it weren't for him."

"I know that. I'm grateful—to him and to you. I won't let you down."

Shay patted his cheek. "I know you won't, son. Now—go kick his fat arse."

Farley tossed the empty bottle aside and went over to the speedball that had been fitted to the wall. Shay was about to leave when the woman from the promoter's office put down her phone and frowned.

"Got a problem," she said.

Coffey looked up. "Go on."

"Charlie Gallagher hasn't turned up."

95

Milton had asked Ziggy to find a suitable venue for the exchange, and he had suggested the multi-storey car park on Jervis Street. The facility was open twenty-four hours a day, and after stopping the car at the machine to request a ticket, he drove up the ramps to the fourth floor. Everything was lit in the harsh, cold glow of the fluorescent lights overhead. The muted grey of the concrete floor was marked by the white lines that delineated each bay. The smell of exhaust hung heavily in the air, and patches of oil reflected dull rainbow swirls. Towards the far end, a dimly lit stairwell led to the floors above and below.

Milton drove to the quieter side of the floor and parked, leaving the engine running and making sure that he was covered by as many of the CCTV cameras as possible. He took out his phone and the pistol and was about to check for messages when he heard the sound of an approaching engine and swung around in his seat to see a Rolls-Royce Ghost climbing the ramp. The car was enormous, and it was

"Get in the back," he said with as much calm as he could muster.

He waited until they were inside and the doors were closed, and then let go of Charlie's shoulder and gave him a little shove to send him on his way. He manoeuvred around the car until he was next to the driver's door. He got in, closed it after him, and found first gear. He pulled away, half expecting Gallagher to do something rash but hopeful that he'd remember the cameras and think better of it. Their eyes locked for one final time as Milton turned the wheel, but Gallagher made no move to impede him.

He turned the wheel again and descended the ramp to the ground floor.

"John..." Maria started; she stopped, as if unsure what to say.

"I'm sorry," he said. "I messed up. But everything's fixed now. Everything's going to be fine."

"Where are we going?"

"We're going to take Cara to her mother."

96

S hay left the dressing room and followed the corridor through the bowels of the stadium to the exit. He needed some peace and quiet to work out what had happened, and he knew he wouldn't get that with every-thing that was happening in the venue. He checked his watch, the fight was supposed to start in forty-five minutes, and Gallagher wasn't here. He thought of Blair and what he had said about Cara and wondered: could this be something to do with him? Shay fancied himself a decent judge of character, and there was certainly something about Blair that gave him pause. He ought to have been terrified to have found himself involved with players he must have known were dangerous, yet there was no sign of that. Shay had threatened him, and he had been unmoved. Blair had taken the gun as if it had been nothing, and Shay had watched him examine it and knew that it wasn't his first time. There was more to him than met the eye, but an impressive demeanour was one thing; going toe-to-toe with someone like Billy Gallagher was something else entirely.

He pushed the door and went outside just as a Rolls-Royce Ghost pulled into the private parking area. The vanity numberplate—BɪLLY—was superfluous; he recognised the car without it. The rear doors opened, and two men got out: Billy Gallagher on the near side of the car and Charlie Gallagher on the other.

There was plenty of distance between them, but Shay could feel the hatred as Billy stared at him.

"Big mistake," Billy called out across the open space.

Shay frowned, unsure what to say.

Billy leered at him. "What's up? Cat got your tongue?"

"You're late," Shay managed.

Billy snarled at him. "Charlie's going to take care of your boy, and then I'm going to take care of you."

The two of them went through the door and disappeared inside.

Shay's phone rang with a number he didn't recognise.

"Who's this?"

"Eric Blair. I've got your niece. She's fine."

"What did you do?"

"I made Gallagher an offer he couldn't refuse."

"Did it involve his son?"

"Why would you say that?"

"Because he only just turned up for the fight. You shouldn't have done that. What if he wasn't here in time? The fight might have been called off. You know how much is riding on this?"

There was a pause. "You know your niece is more important—right?"

Shay bit down on his lip. "What kind of question is that? Of course she is."

"So all's well that ends well. Good luck to your man. I've seen both of them up close. I don't think he'll need it."

"I want to see you."

"Not going to happen. I'm leaving. I do have one question, though, before I go—what'll happen to Mahoney?"

"We'll deal with him."

"And the Gallaghers?"

"Them, too."

"What does that mean?"

"Billy killed my brother. What do you think's going to happen? He's a dead man."

"That's what I thought."

"I'm telling you—I want to see you."

"And I told you—no."

"Wait. I..."

The line was dead. Two stewards from the stadium came outside and lit up cigarettes. Shay stared at them in irritation, but they didn't react. They were close enough to hear whatever he said, so he opened the door to his car and got inside. He stared at his phone for a moment while he made up his mind what to do next.

He called his mother.

"Shay?"

"How many of the lads are there with you?"

"Half a dozen."

"Are they ready?"

"They've been ready all afternoon."

"Tell them to go and get it done. We hit 'em now—*right* now."

Shay knew it was the right thing to do; it couldn't wait a moment longer. His brother had been killed by a two-bit gangster, but it was Billy who'd pulled the trigger.

And he was going to pay for it tonight.

Farley was going to embarrass his boy, and then, while he was still reeling from that, he'd find out that was just the beginning of what Shay had planned. He was going to get done over good and proper and no mistake.

97

Mahoney parked outside the church in Saint Margaret's, a tiny village to the west of the airport. It was late in the evening, and the road was quiet, with just the occasional car making its way along the main road. Mahoney got out of the car and watched as an airliner took off, gaining altitude quickly until it was five or six hundred feet up when it passed overhead. The roar of the engines was deafening, and, even in the twilight, Mahoney could make out the Aer Lingus livery on the tail. The plane turned to the north and continued to climb, the navigation lights on the wingtips and tail winking red, green and white.

Mahoney had been busy since meeting Lynch earlier. While Lynch was getting Mahoney's things from his apartment, he had gone into the city to buy the other items he would need for his trip. He didn't know how long he would be away, but didn't expect that he would be able to return for months and possibly even years. He needed to make sure he had everything he would need now, before he got on the plane. He bought two large suitcases and proceeded to wake himself up. It didn't work. The noise of the crowd, usually so invigorating, was distant and muffled. The cheers and jeers were no better than a cacophony, a distant echo that wasn't enough to penetrate the fog that had sunk over him. Doubt washed over him, eroding his resolve.

Gallagher entered the cage, reached up and flicked back his hood to reveal his shock of red hair. He came right up to Farley and stared into his face. "I'm going to put you down," he said, the words muffled by his mouthguard.

The referee got between them, ushering them to their corners.

Coffey was waiting for him. "What's up?"

"Feel weird."

"Weird? How?"

"Like my head is full of sawdust."

"It's nerves. It's normal." Coffey undid the robe and helped him to take it off. "You'll be fine once you get going. Remember what we said—don't get stuck in a brawl with him. Pick him off from range. Jab and move, jab and move, jab and move. Piss him off, work an opening, use your feet. Got it?"

"Got it," he said, the words feeling like sand in his mouth.

"Gentlemen."

Farley turned; the referee was in the middle of the cage, gesturing that the two fighters should join him.

Farley turned back to Coffey. "I don't feel good, Paddy."

Coffey patted him on the cheek. "You'll be fine, son. Go on. Go and do what you were born to do."

Farley blinked again, slapped himself with his right hand and then his left, rolled his shoulders and went to the middle of the cage. Gallagher was there already, sweat-soaked muscles shining in the light.

101

S hay watched with growing horror as it became increasingly evident that Farley was losing. He had thrown a handful of punches, but none of them had landed with any authority, and now Gallagher was ignoring them. Farley was retreating around the cage, sheltering behind his guard, his forearms raised to protect his head while leaving his torso exposed. Gallagher was pummelling him at range, mostly with kicks: sidekicks, low kicks to the thigh and calf and then, as Shay winced, a spinning back kick that saw Gallagher rotate his body to deliver a strike into the ribs with the heel of his foot. Farley staggered to his left and teetered, his fall only arrested by the cage.

"What's he *doing*?"

He looked to the corner where Coffey was barking out instructions, but his exhortations to fight back made no difference. Farley stayed on the defensive, shuffling away as Gallagher tagged him with another two-handed combination.

Shay checked his watch: there was still a minute to go before the end of the first round.

FARLEY TOOK a right fist to his cheek and spat out his mouthguard. He took another, and then another, and tasted blood—hot and coppery—in his mouth. The lights dimmed a little, and the noise of the crowd faded until all he could hear was a confusing drone, his ragged breathing and, somewhere behind him, someone—Coffey?—desperately shouting at him. His field of vision seemed to contract, thoughts slipped through his mind like sand, and he felt a heaviness in his limbs that hadn't been there before.

CHARLIE GALLAGHER GRUNTED with the effort as he put everything he had into another combination: a right, a left and then a side kick that, as Farley turned into it, landed flush in his gut. His arms and shoulders burned with the effort of the barrage he had unleashed, but the adrenaline pushed him harder and harder; that, and a sense of almost stupefied wonder that he was dominating the fight so completely. Farley had been on the back foot from the bell and hadn't even laid a glove on him. It didn't make any sense, but Gallagher was not one to look a gift horse in the mouth. He hadn't expected to win, but now, with his opponent barely able to stay on his feet, it felt within touching distance.

He took a breath and glanced left, seeing his father and Gerry Kelly on their feet. The two old men had their arms raised. Their faces were contorted with bloodlust, and their mouths were open wide as they bellowed out encouragement that was lost in the racket from the crowd.

Charlie saw the referee out of the corner of his eye and

was momentarily fearful that he was about to step in and stop the fight. He didn't want that. It was going to end on *his* terms, when *he* wanted it to end. He would punctuate his victory with a moment that would be remembered, something that would make the promoters and executives sit up and take notice. A stoppage wouldn't cut it; he needed to leave Farley flat on his back. He needed an exclamation point.

He closed in, tattooing the ribs once again and then drawing back his right hand. He planted his feet and rotated his hips and torso, power welling up from his lower body. It surged upward through his core and into his arm, his bicep as taut as a tightly wound spring. He unwound it, propelling his fist upward and out, aiming at the point of Farley's chin. It connected, and he felt the reverberation all the way up his arm to the elbow; Farley's eyes rolled up as he toppled back, unconscious before he hit the mat, his head bouncing off the canvas before he lay still.

There was a moment of stunned silence, and then the arena erupted in cheers.

102

S hay rushed to the dressing room. Garton and Briars were still there, but he waved them out of the way and opened the door without knocking. Danny Farley was sitting on the cheap sofa at the side of the room, the back of his head resting against the wall. He still looked dazed, his eyes blinking and a faraway look in his eyes. His entourage, so boisterous before the fight, had deserted him. Rats leaving a sinking ship, Shay thought, thinking about all the money they had sunk into Farley's career and how all of it—every last cent—might as well have been flushed down the shitter.

Shay looked around the room for Coffey, but he wasn't there. And it wasn't just him who was notable by his absence; none of the cornermen—the cut man, the medic—were here, either.

Shay went back to the door and flung it open. Garton turned first, and Shay stabbed a finger in his direction. "Where's Coffey?"

"I don't know, boss."

"And the other one—Cahill—where's he?"

"I'm sorry, boss. They didn't come back, neither of them."

Shay closed his eyes and tried to work out what had happened. There was one answer, but it was so implausible —so recklessly dangerous—that it was hard to give it credit.

Briars shrugged. "Coffey said he was going to see you."

"When was this?"

"Just after the fight. He told us to get him"—he gestured into the room to the stupefied Farley—"back here and that he'd be down once he'd spoken to you. Are you saying he didn't—"

"Yes," Shay snapped. "That's *exactly* what I'm saying. He didn't." He felt the heat in his cheeks. "Where's the doctor? They must have one here, right? From the venue or the promotion or *something*? You need to go get him."

"Why?" Briars said.

"Because we need to test Farley's blood, you eejit. Coffey fucked us. Can't you see what he did? He *fucked* us."

"I don't get it. How?"

Shay took a breath. "You saw what Farley was like, right? It was as if he was half asleep right from the start."

"Yeah," Garton said.

"Coffey *doped* him. He dosed him with something before he went out there to make sure he lost. Look how much money he would've made. The odds on Gallagher were *mad* —thirty to one. Think how much money he could've made if he put down even *ten* grand." The numbers danced through his mind, the sheer scale of them difficult to grasp. "Ten gets him three hundred grand. Forty grand and he clears a *million*."

"What do you want us to do?" Briars said.

"I told you—go and get a doctor." Shay reached up and massaged his temple and then pointed to Garton. "Coffey

"That's it? Nothing else?"

"I don't remember anything else."

He swivelled so that he could look back at Cahill. "What do you think?"

"I think you judged it well. Just enough but not too much. I mean, they'll know when they test him, but it won't matter by then—not if we're quick."

Coffey turned back to the front. "You packed the cases?"

"Of course," Brenda said.

"Tickets and passports?"

"Relax. Everything's done."

"Good." He breathed out. "Good."

He looked up into the rear-view mirror and saw that Cahill had taken out his phone. "Anything?"

"Hold on," Cahill said. "Give me a minute. Bad reception."

Coffey knew they'd take Farley's blood, and, when they tested it, the ketamine would be discovered. It had been difficult to judge the right amount: too much and it'd be obvious that something was wrong, and the fight would be stopped; too little and Farley might beat Gallagher in spite of it. He had bought a bottle from a friend of a friend who worked for a vet in the east of the city. The link between him and the supply would be too tenuous to unravel, but he had still paid well above the odds for the bottle as an acknowledgement that his friend was taking a risk.

Coffey was taking a *much* bigger risk, but he made sure that the pay-out was worth it. He had watched the odds as they lengthened again and again, the bookies delivering their verdict that there was no way Charlie Gallagher would be able to beat Farley. Shay Dillon had laid out thousands on Farley, and that had helped, too, as the bookies offered better odds in an attempt to cover their positions. The irony that Dillon had unwittingly contributed to Coffey's payday was not lost on him.

"Well?"

"I'm in," Cahill said. Coffey looked up in the mirror again and saw that his friend was beaming. "The first one's paid out already. Twenty grand."

"Check the others."

They'd spread their money around as many online bookies as they could find. They could have gone to any number of shops in the city, but it had felt risky. Dillon had contacts everywhere, however, and Coffey knew that he was shrewd; it wouldn't take long for him to realise what had happened, what Coffey had done and where he might go to cash in on his betrayal. It had taken longer to lay the money down this way, but it was safer. Not all of the bookies would pay out, but they had counted on most honouring the bets.

"Another fifty," Cahill said.

Coffey clenched his fist and rapped it against his thigh. "We did it. We *did* it."

Brenda turned onto the M50 and picked up speed. Cork was three hours away. They'd be on the ground and safe before anyone even knew they were gone.

104

Mahoney looked at his watch, Lynch had said that he would be there in thirty minutes, but nearly fifty had passed, and there was still no sign of him. Mahoney had been sitting on the wall that divided the churchyard from the path, looking east in the direction of the airport's runway and watching the jets lift off and fly away. Every one of them was a potential escape to a place beyond the reach of Billy Gallagher, somewhere he would be able to put the confusion and fear of the last few days behind him and start again. His flight was due to take off in two hours, and he knew if he waited much longer, then he would need to rebook his trip. That was fine. He'd go to Paris or Amsterdam or Berlin, whatever was available, and then book another flight from there.

He just wanted to leave; he wanted to be *anywhere* but here.

He heard the whine of another jet, and just as it climbed above the line of trees that marked the boundary of the airport, he saw headlights from an approaching car. He slid off the wall and shielded his eyes against the glare as he looked to see if the car was slowing; it was. The indicator flicked on, and the car turned off and parked in front of the church.

Mahoney found he was nervous. Lynch was a friend, but it would have been a stretch to say that he was a *good* friend. Mahoney didn't really have anyone who would fit that description. He would have preferred to have managed his exit without needing to call on anyone to help, but Billy had made that impossible. He trusted Lynch about as much as he trusted anyone, and that would have to do.

The door opened, and Lynch stepped out.

"Hey."

Mahoney glanced into the car and saw that it was empty. "Did you get it?"

"I did."

Mahoney saw something in Lynch's eyes that made him pause. "You okay?"

"Fine," Lynch said, his voice reedy and uncertain.

Mahoney felt a knob of ice in the pit of his stomach. He put out his hand. "Come on, then. I need to get going."

Lynch didn't reach into his pocket or do anything else that might have suggested that he was ready to hand over the passport.

Mahoney heard the sound of another engine and looked to his right as a second pair of headlights appeared. A white police van came into view from behind the overgrown hedge on the corner.

He turned back to Lynch. "You *didn't*."

The van slowed and came to a stop. The rear door slid open, and two big coppers hopped down onto the road. Mahoney backed away from them, but the one on the right raised a Taser.

With a pain that was almost physical, Mahoney realised

what had happened and cursed himself for his greed and stupidity. "My money. You took it."

"What are you on about," Lynch said. "What money?"

Mahoney panicked and turned, but, before he could even think about running, he saw that Lynch had moved across to block his way. He tried to step around him, but Lynch moved with him so there was nowhere for him to go.

"You fucked me!"

He heard the whoosh as the Taser discharged and felt a sting as the probes pierced his trousers and the skin on the back of his thigh. The device crackled, and the searing electric shock that followed made it feel as if every nerve was on fire. His muscles convulsed, his legs buckled, and he hit the ground, his breath stolen away, the rough pavement cutting into his cheek. He could taste the dirt mixed with the coppery hint of blood from where he'd bitten his tongue.

The current stopped, leaving him with an overwhelming weakness. His body was a lead weight.

"Detective Sergeant Mahoney," a woman's voice said, "you're under arrest on suspicion of corruption. You have the right to remain silent. Anything you say from now on can be used against you in a court of law."

105

Shay opened the door to his car, got in and opened the glovebox. He kept his own pistol there: a Glock 19 that had never been fired. He checked it was loaded and ready and then adjusted the rear-view mirror so he could see back to the door. Gallagher's Rolls-Royce was still parked five cars over, and there was nothing to suggest that he had left anyone to keep an eye on it. He would've thought he was safe here, that Shay wouldn't do anything as brazen as make a move on him now, in a place like this, but Shay was past caring. He had already given the order to up the ante, and now he was going to up it again. Billy had made the first escalation with the hit in the hotel that had killed Colm, and now Shay found himself wondering whether Coffey's treachery might be traced back to Billy, too. Why not? Coffey makes himself rich, and Charlie Gallagher gets the push into the American market that had been earmarked for Farley. The more Shay thought about it, the more credible it sounded. He screwed up his fists and ground his knuckles into his eyes. Gallagher might have had the upper hand before, but not now. *No.* Not now and never again.

His phone rang. He picked it up and saw that it was his mother.

"Where are you?"

There was fear in her voice. "What is it?"

"Where are you?" she repeated.

"At the venue—why? What's wrong?"

"The police," she said. "They've arrested everyone."

"What?"

"They were waiting for them. Pulled them over, searched them, found the guns. They got all of them."

Shay slumped in his seat.

"They knew," she said. "They'd been tipped."

"By who?"

"I spoke to Mitchell, and he told me they've got a recording of you talking about going after Billy."

Mitchell was a friend of Shay's mother from years back, and he had a son in the police who had been persuaded to provide information from time to time. "What recording?" Shay said. "Where?"

"All he said was that someone called the police and said they had evidence that there was going to be another shooting. The police went for it."

Shay put his hand to his head as he remembered something. "Shit."

"Have we got a rat?"

"I don't know." His head was swimming. "Maybe."

"You listen to me, Shay Dillon. You need to get out of the city. It's not safe for you now. They'll be coming for you, too. Leave with the rest of the crowd and get on a bus and get as far away as you can. You..." She paused mid-sentence.

"Ma?"

"Bollocks," she said.

Shay heard the sound of a heavy impact, of splintering wood and then a loud shout of *"Police!"*

"Get out of the city," she said before the line went dead.

Shay saw movement behind him, and when he looked in the mirror, he saw Gerry Kelly, Billy Gallagher and Charlie Gallagher.

He'd get out of the city, but not right now. He had something to do first.

106

Gerry Kelly held the door open for Billy and Charlie and then led the way across the parking space to the car. Billy was still buzzing after what had just happened. The knockout had been *so* unexpected as to have taken him completely by surprise. Charlie would never admit it, but Billy suspected that even *he* had written off his chances, especially after he had spent most of the afternoon in the boot of Blair's car. The whole thing was just so stupendously random, and, after the chaos that had accompanied the botched shooting of Frank Rickard at the Southside and Blair forcing the early release of Cara Dillon, it felt as if he had finally had a little bit of luck. Perhaps now was the time to take advantage of that. Blair himself needed to be found and punished for his impertinence. And there was the matter of the Dillons, too. Eileen Dillon was a vindictive old bitch, and Shay Dillon was a vicious upstart with no respect for his elders and betters; mother would be dripping poison into her son's ear, and the son would act on it.

Perhaps he should get out in front of it all and act first.

His long tenure in a business not famed for longevity was due, in large part, to a willingness to strike first. He had learned that lesson in Crumlin as a boy, and it had always served him well.

"Come on now, Dad," Charlie said. "Tell me the truth—you never thought I had a snowball's chance, did you?"

"You had a puncher's chance."

"And *what* a punch," Kelly said, a little drunk from the whiskey he'd been nipping from the hipflask in his jacket pocket.

"It's like I always said," Charlie said, rising to the theme. "I don't care who you are: I land my uppercut and you're going down. No exceptions."

Billy wished he'd had the faith to put proper money on his boy. He'd seen the odds from the bookies in the concourse as they made their way inside, and he could've made a killing. Never mind. The end of the fight had been spectacular, and the Americans loved a knockout artist; there would be a contract from them now, and who knew what would flow from that. He'd always wanted to go to Vegas, and this would be the perfect opportunity.

"Hey."

Billy stopped and turned.

It was Shay Dillon.

He'd been hidden behind one of the cars, and now he was approaching them, a pistol held in his right hand.

"Shay," Billy said, "you all right?"

"Aye," he said. "Never better."

Billy gestured down to his hand. "You won't be needing that, then, will you?"

"I think I will," he said, raising his hand so that Charlie and Gerry could see the gun.

"Come on—don't be daft. Put it away."

"'Put it away'?" He laughed. "Are you serious? After what you've done?"

"Put it down, son."

Shay shook his head in mock incredulity. "You killed my brother, you piece of shit, and that was just the start."

"No, I didn't. That had nothing to do with me."

"Don't *lie* to me!"

Billy looked into Shay's face and knew he was in trouble; his eyes burned with hatred and an unhinged quality that said anything was possible. Billy had always seen plenty of Shay in himself as a younger man, and, knowing that— knowing he was ruthless and amoral, just like he was— meant that he felt fear at what might happen now. He felt the first rush of fear that an evening that had become so heavy with optimism was about to take a hard left turn into something else entirely.

Gerry raised his hands. "Come on, Shay. You don't need to do that. Put it down. Let's have a chat, see if we can't work it all out."

Dillon didn't put the gun down. He switched his aim, pointed the gun at Gerry and pulled the trigger. The report was loud in the enclosed space, the echo bouncing back at them from the concrete. Gerry clutched at his chest, looked down at the blood that was already blooming through his white shirt, and then dropped to his knees.

"'Let's have a chat'?" Dillon said. "'See if we can't work it all out'?"

He fired again. Gerry toppled onto his side and lay still.

Charlie froze.

Billy stepped in front of him.

Dillon turned and took aim at Billy again.

Billy raised his hands. "It's not too late—"

The gun fired for a third time.

Billy had never been shot before. He'd always thought it would feel like a sharp, swift pain, but it wasn't like that at all. The bullet punched into his stomach with an overwhelming shock, a white-hot burn that took his breath away. It felt like his body was folding around the point where the bullet went in, as if drawn by some horrible magnet. Everything became distorted and warped: the world spun, and the ground rushed up to meet him as his legs gave way. Sounds became muffled, as if he were underwater; the murmur of voices and the wail of a siren blended into a dull, monotonous drone.

He clutched his stomach, his hands coming away slick with blood. It was warm and sticky, seeping through his fingers. It wasn't just the sight of it that terrified him. It was the understanding of what it meant; his life was draining out onto the grimy concrete.

"Dad!"

He felt hands on his shoulders and looked up into Charlie's face.

His breath came in shallow gasps, each more effortful than the last. His heart pounded, each beat sending a fresh wave of agony coursing through him. It was a strange, twisted duality; the pain was both distant and unbearably present.

"Dad!"

He was vaguely aware of his son, his face just a pale blur against the grey concrete. He could see his mouth moving, but his words were lost to him. Darkness crept into the edges of his vision, and the cold, hard truth settled within him: he was going to die.

107

The road to the railway station was bounded to the north by the Liffey. Milton turned into the car park and found a spot near the doors where he could leave the car. He waited a moment, pausing so he could acclimatise to the surroundings in the unlikely event that there was anyone here who might be looking for him or the girl in the back seat. It was late now, and, although the station was still busy with people, there was nothing to suggest there was anything for him to be concerned about.

He opened the door.

Maria told Cara to wait for a moment and got out, too.

It was warm outside, but there was a humidity in the air that presaged rain.

Maria came around the car's bonnet so that she was alongside him. "Is everything okay?"

"It's fine. I just wanted to be sure."

"You think they'll be looking for us?"

"The Dillons and the Gallaghers? No. They'll have other things to worry about." He glanced over at a Garda officer who had just emerged from the entrance; the woman straightened out her belt and made her way in the direction of the river. Milton watched her go. "The police, though? It's possible. You should be getting on your way."

She bit her lip. "And afterwards? Do you think I could go back to the hotel?"

He shook his head. "I wouldn't. The police will be all over it after what happened. They'll look at everyone. They'll find out you're not supposed to be here, and you'll be deported."

She sighed. "That's what I thought."

"Do you have any friends you could go and stay with?"

"Not in this country. I have a friend from Rio who left when I did."

"Where's she?"

"It's he, actually—in Amsterdam."

"There you are, then—Amsterdam would be better for you than Dublin."

"And you? It's not safe for you, either."

"I have a couple of things I need to do, but then I'll be going, too."

"Why not come to Amsterdam with me?"

He gave her a gentle smile. "That's not a good idea. I'm not the best company."

"Why are you so hard on yourself? You say these things, but I look at you and I don't think you mean them."

That caught him short, and he wasn't sure what to say.

"You look sad, John. You smile"—she pointed—"like *that*, but it is a sad smile, not a happy one. When someone is happy, you can see it in their eyes. I don't see it in your eyes. I don't think I've ever seen you happy."

I don't have much to be happy about.

"Where are you?" Milton asked.

"Outside the arena."

"Can you get eyes on him?"

"Yes."

"Find him, but don't engage. He's headed my way."

108

Shay knew he had to run.

He was going to put as much distance between himself and the arena as he could. He'd left the parking area and gone back into the building, picking a way through the warren of corridors until he was able to push through a door that led to the main concourse, where the spectators who had just watched the fight were slowly filing through the exits. He would normally have been impatient with being caught up in the throng, but not now. It was perfect: a crowd of hundreds—thousands, perhaps—into which he could melt, just another spectator waiting to start the journey home.

Everyone was talking about what they had just watched. No one seemed able to credit what had happened to Farley, and all seemed to agree that the result was a stupendous upset that would stymie any hopes of a successful career for him in the States. Shay waited for someone to argue that Farley must have been drugged, that there was *no way* a fighter as good as him could've fought as badly, but no one did. Maybe it wasn't as obvious as he thought. Maybe they thought it was a bad day at the office or that Farley was ill. Shay would make sure they tested Farley's blood, though, and, when they did, everyone would know.

And he would find Coffey, too, and force him to confess.

Who was he kidding?

He realised, with a sick feeling in his stomach, that he was looking to a future in Dublin and seeing himself in it. That was naïve. It was stupid. He'd just shot and killed two men, with Charlie Gallagher as a witness. There'd be cameras in the car park, too, so the police would have first-hand testimony and evidence of what he'd done.

He was in a *world* of trouble.

And he had no choice: he was going to have to disappear.

He and Colm had put together a plan for that, months ago. It was something they'd done because their mother said it was sensible, that they needed something in their back pockets should anything ever go wrong. Neither of them had ever really thought it was something they'd actually have to put into action. They'd laughed about it then; it didn't seem so funny now.

Shay exited the arena and turned south, walking down to the river and then turning west. He heard the sound of sirens, but it faded behind him as he followed North Wall Quay. The Liffey lapped against the concrete embankments to his right, the lights of the city reflecting across the surface with a shimmering glow. The stretch ahead was studded with architectural tributes to Dublin's recent modernisation: sleek glass structures, like the towering Convention Centre, shone in the night, while Price Waterhouse's headquarters stood as a symbol of the city's economic growth. The modernity of the Docklands merged with the charm of the old city as he approached the hulking silhouette of the Custom

House. Shay ignored it all; his focus was on getting to his destination without being found.

He reached the junction with Capel Street and turned north. The address he wanted—Dublin Luggage Store— was just before the junction with Mary Little Street, pressed between a sandwich shop and a shuttered business advertising Eastern European groceries on its awning, and opposite Slattery's Bar. The business was open late, and Shay could see a clerk flicking through his phone while he waited for something to do. Shay took out his wallet, pulled out the notes that he kept in the cash pocket, and then scrabbled inside it until he found the scrap of paper with his receipt.

"I need the bag with this ticket," he said, handing the receipt to the clerk.

The man looked at it with sullen disinterest before ambling through to the storage area at the back.

The plan was simple: he'd get his go-bag and then grab an Uber to take him south to Arklow Marina, where he'd charter a boat to take him to Holyhead. The harbour there was quieter than Howth and, given that it was used mostly by leisure craft, very unlikely to be a place the authorities would look. He'd go to Liverpool and hide out with an old friend of his dad until he could work out what to do next: most likely, he'd book a private plane to take him to Mallorca, where he could lie low for as long as it took for the heat to die down.

"Here you are."

The clerk put the rucksack on the counter. Shay unzipped it and peered inside: there was a passport, a change of clothes, a new phone with an unused SIM and several thousand euros. He zipped it up, slung it on his shoulder and went back outside.

He turned, intending to head south to pick up a cab,

when he ran into a man coming along the pavement in the opposite direction. He was compact and sinewy, his head crowned by a wild thatch of dense, unruly ginger hair. His cheeks, marked by time-worn acne scars, were framed by deep-set furrows running along the sides of his nose. His skin was pale, and he, too, had a large rucksack slung over his shoulder.

Shay stepped right, and the man mirrored him.

"Get out of the way," Shay muttered.

"Keep your hair on," the man replied.

Shay stepped around him and went south, aiming for Ormond Quay. It'd be easier to get a cab there; he'd be out of the city and on his way to the marina in no time.

109

Lilly was on the other side of the street and watched as Ziggy Penn shared words with the man who had just come out of the left luggage facility. The two of them blocked each other's way on the path; the second man looked irritated, his anger flaring as Penn said something to him before they finally managed to pass.

Lilly was on foot. Two and Three were nearby, while Number One waited in a car. Penn's behaviour had been erratic. He had followed Jimmy to the fight at the arena, but, upon its conclusion, had abandoned him. Instead of maintaining his surveillance, he'd hurried along the river to Capel Street, his phone in his hand the whole time and his attention focused on the screen. It looked as if he was following someone, although there was no way of knowing who that might be. They'd been careful with their surveillance, but Penn had been too engrossed in what he was doing to pay them any attention, and it had been easy to tail him without giving themselves away. Lilly had half-expected him to go into the large pub on the corner, hoping that perhaps he was headed there to meet Milton, but he and a half minutes when he was in his prime, but years had passed since then; he was fit, but not as fit as he had once been.

He pressed his earbuds into his ears more securely. "Update?"

"Still on Capel Street, headed back down to the river."

Milton had memorised the map and knew that Capel Street led onto Ormond Quay and the Liffey Boardwalk. Dillon would be able to get a taxi there. They'd still have the signal from the tracker, but how long would it be before Dillon discovered the device and dumped it? If he did that before Milton could get to him...

No.

Milton wasn't going to let it happen.

"There's a cab coming," Ziggy reported. "He's flagging it down."

Milton sprinted harder, his lungs burning and sweat stinging his eyes.

S hay saw a taxi and flagged it down. The driver spotted him, flashed his lights and pulled over, coming to a halt on the side of the road on Grattan Bridge. Shay adjusted the rucksack on his shoulder, waited for a gap in the traffic, and then crossed over.

The driver wound down his window.

"Where to, mate?"

"Arklow."

The driver sucked on his teeth. "That's the best part of ninety minutes. It won't be cheap."

Shay had neither the time nor the inclination to negotiate. "I'll give you two hundred—that enough for you?"

"I'd need a bit more."

"Three, then," he snapped. "Okay?"

"That'll do." He pressed a button to unlock the door. "In you get."

Shay paused for a moment and looked to the west where the river wound its way to Temple Bar. He had good memories from the time he'd spent there: nights out with his friends as a young man and, latterly, the thousands of euros made from the tourists and locals who flocked there. He loved his city and hadn't thought he'd ever have to leave, but things had changed, and he was out of options. He'd come back when things were quieter, but, for now, he had to go.

"You getting in or not?"

Shay reached for the handle, but, before he could open the door, he heard the roar of an engine and looked up to see a police car racing across the bridge towards him. The car skidded to a halt, the passenger-side door opened, and an officer got out.

Shay backed away.

"Shay Dillon?"

He looked left, to the opposite bank, and saw the blue lights of another car as it raced down Ormond Quay.

"Shay Dillon," the officer said, "I'm arresting you on suspicion of murder. You do—"

Shay turned in the other direction and ran. If he could get across the bridge and onto Essex Quay, then he might be able to lose them in Temple Bar. There were places he could go where he could hide out, lie low until he'd worked out another way to get to Arklow.

He looked back to see whether the officer was giving chase and crashed into someone coming the other way. He tripped and, unable to put out his hands to break his fall, slammed into the pavement hard. His head bounced off the paving slabs, the impact heavy enough to dim his vision. His consciousness returned to the shriek of pain from his shoulder where it had popped out of its socket. He felt a knee in his back and then gave a yell of agony as someone yanked both arms behind his back. He felt cold metal around his wrists and heard a click as the cuffs were fastened, the catch nipping his flesh.

"Shay Dillon," the officer started again, "I'm arresting

you on suspicion of murder. You do not have to say anything unless you wish to do so, but anything you say will be taken down in writing and may be given in evidence."

Shay managed to look up enough to see the man with whom he had collided.

"*You!*" he spat.

It was Blair. He was out of breath and sweating, but it was him. Blair backed away, saying something to the officer still pinning Shay to the ground.

"Settle down, sir," the officer said.

"Get off me!"

Blair stepped to the side and continued on his way, but, as he did, he looked down at Shay and—unmistakably—winked at him.

And then he was gone.

"Shit."

"Don't panic. Don't react."

"That's easy for you to say. How'd they find us?"

"I don't know." Milton kept his gaze out over the water. "But it doesn't matter. They're here—that's all we need to know."

"What do we do?"

"We split up. They might not know about you, and, even if they do, it'll be me they want. Get away from here, get out of the city, out of the country, then hide."

"What about you?"

"I'm going to run. I'll make contact when it's safe."

Milton pulled out the phone, hung up the call with Ziggy, put it away again and surveilled the immediate locale to the east of the bridge: he could see the Millennium Bridge and, beyond that, the modern buildings of the Docklands. He rested his hands on the cold stone balustrade, then stepped away and turned to the south, ready to retrace his steps. Dillon was still struggling on the ground, the officer using his weight to hold him down while the driver of the patrol car came over to help.

Milton crossed over to the other pavement.

He noticed the others now: a man and a woman who had been on the same side of the Bridge as him, and who crossed over to block him. They moved with the coordinated precision of trained agents, their attention focused on him and him alone.

He looked back: Lilly Moon had crossed over, too.

They had him penned: two ahead and one behind. They'd all be armed, and they'd have transport nearby.

He looked back to the police, but they were too busy to pay any attention to what was happening, and he doubted whether they would be able to help.

He was on his own.

The newcomers stopped. Milton was close enough to see them now: the man had close-cropped hair and chiselled features with a stern and focused expression; the woman had vibrant blue eyes and porcelain skin and a cascade of wavy, ash-blonde hair. Her right hand was inside her jacket; Milton knew she'd be holding a gun.

"It's over," the male agent said. "Let's not cause a scene."

"Maybe I want to cause a scene," Milton said. "What would you do? Shoot me on the street?"

"I'd rather not."

Milton nodded back in the direction of the two officers. "Not with the police just over there. I can't imagine London wants me enough to cause a diplomatic incident."

"Best not to underestimate how much London wants you. Not after what you did."

Milton's adrenaline spiked, but he held himself under control.

The woman touched her ear with her free hand; she'd have a receiver there.

The three of them were keeping a careful distance. Milton didn't doubt they would use force if he gave them no other choice, but they'd know his record and that he could make it difficult for them. On the other hand, there were three of them—at least—and Milton doubted he'd get far even if he did manage to escape them for the moment.

There was only one way out.

"All right," he said.

The female agent with the pale skin kept her hand inside her jacket. "You'll come in?"

"Do you have a car?"

The male agent turned his head and spoke into a throat mic. "Two to One. He's coming in. Over."

Two's attention was distracted, the woman was too far away to stop him, and Lilly Moon had retreated to an even warier distance.

Now or never.

Milton put his hands on the parapet and vaulted over it. The world slowed around him, the skyline tilting as he cut through the air. He hit the water with a loud splash. It was as cold as ice, the sudden immersion driving the air from his lungs. The water swallowed him; the world above grew muffled and faded; the shouts of onlookers distorted into incoherent echoes.

Milton fought the shock of the sudden cold and forced his limbs to move, kicking hard with the current. He stayed beneath the surface for as long as he could, allowing the Liffey to carry him away to the east. His lungs burned, and he held on for another stroke, then broke the surface to gasp for breath. He turned onto his back and looked back at the bridge. Moon and the others were there, staring down at him; he wondered whether they would jump in, too, but they didn't. The male—Number Two, he thought—broke away from the others and hurried to the north bank. The women went south.

Milton rolled onto his front and stroked, ignoring his waterlogged clothes and cutting through the water. The water pressed in from all sides, hurrying him away.

PART V

116

Lilly Moon looked out of the window at the entrance to the hotel. A taxi had just arrived, and a man and a woman stepped out, waiting for the driver to get their cases from the back before wheeling them up the ramp and into reception.

Lilly had been here for six hours. The others were here, too; One was hidden around the back, watching the rear entrance, while Two and Three had taken rooms as guests, hoping they might find something inside that would give them an idea where Milton might have gone.

They'd found nothing.

Lilly had known they wouldn't.

She knew it was only a matter of time before they were recalled to London. They'd stayed in the city after Milton had eluded them, but she knew it was a fool's errand. They'd had the drop on him and had squandered it. Milton had thrown himself into the Liffey, and, although they had tried to find him, they'd failed. Group Two discovered how he had evaded them the following day: the crew on a party boat travelling in the opposite direction had notified the police that a man had hauled himself up on deck and then disembarked when the boat reached the dock. Footage obtained from a business at the end of the pier confirmed what they had feared: a comparison with Milton's file confirmed it was him. They lost him after that.

Their focus on Milton meant they'd lost Penn, too. Milton had obviously warned him, and, with all four agents converging on the main prize, their consolation had also given them the slip. Lilly knew the two of them would be together, and knew that the trail had gone cold. Milton would have been careful before; he would be paranoid now. They had been given the opportunity to bring him in, and they had blown it.

They were back to the start.

117

Maria reached into her bag and took out the envelope. She laid it on the table in the airport restaurant and watched as John ran his finger under the flap to open it. He tipped it so that the passport inside slid out onto the table. He picked it up and thumbed through it, examining it page by page.

Maria had been surprised when he had called, and even more so when he told her he needed her help. He'd asked whether the man who had helped her get into the country could get him a fake passport. She'd been taken aback by his request and asked why he needed it; he said she'd been right in what she'd said, that it *would* be a good idea for him to get out of the country and that Amsterdam was as good a place as any. The only problem, he said, was that his passport was still at the hotel and he didn't feel safe in going back to collect it.

She had called the man, and he had told her it was possible, but that it would be expensive: five thousand euros. She had doubted that John would have that kind of money but, to her surprise, he said that he did and that he was happy to pay. The money was transferred into her PayPal account right away, together with the photograph of himself that her man required. She collected the document the next day and had made her way to Cork and the airport. He had been waiting for her, just like he said he would be.

John finished flipping through the passport, scrutinised his photograph, and then laid a finger on the page with his details. "Henry James?"

She frowned. "Is that a problem?"

"No," he said with a smile. "No problem at all. Just a coincidence—I seem to favour literary pseudonyms."

Maria had kept a low profile after taking Cara to her mother's house. She had read the reports online and had seen that the girl's uncle and grandmother had been arrested in the aftermath of whatever had happened at the hotel. John had explained that Cara's mother, Clare, had been bullied into giving up her claim to custody, and that what had happened since would greatly strengthen the case that the girl should be with her. There wasn't anything that Maria could do to make that prospect more likely, but she had still felt a little catch in her heart when she handed the girl over. She had invested a lot in securing Cara's safety, and, without that to occupy her thoughts, she realised that there was more space for her to fear for herself. She knew John was right: the situation at the hotel had made it difficult for her to stay in Dublin, and moving on to somewhere new made sense. That he would come too had made the choice even easier.

"Thank you," he said. "I doubt it was easy to get this."

"Five thousand will buy a lot," she said. "You still want to go to Amsterdam?"

"Why not?"

"Have you been before?"

"I have, but not for a while."

She gestured to the security lines behind them. "And getting through won't be a problem?"

"It'll be fine," he said, closing the passport and then tapping a finger against the red cover. "Your friend is good. This looks fine."

"It looks real."

"Real enough."

She smiled inwardly. There was something about him that filled her with confidence. Nothing seemed to faze him; she remembered the way he had taken charge on the night of the shooting and how he had stayed the course through everything that had happened afterwards. Maria was a strong, independent woman, and she didn't need a man to look after her, but all of this had been crazy, and there was something reassuring about how he had dealt with it. He wasn't as easy on the eye as some men she had been with, but none of them had made her feel as safe as he did. She didn't know if there was a romantic spark between them, but that didn't matter. It would be fun to see if anything could be kindled.

"I'm going to get a coffee," he said. "Do you want one?"

She shook her head. "I'm fine," she said.

"Something to eat?"

"I'm fine. How long is it until the flight?"

John checked his watch. "Just under an hour. Wait here. I'll be back in a minute."

118

The Starbucks was at the intersection of two wide corridors. Milton went inside and, without stopping, went through to the opposite exit, stepped through and kept going. He picked up his pace, uncomfortable with being here any longer than necessary. He reached the main doors and left the terminal. He looked up, saw the hire car that Ziggy had arranged, and got in.

"All good?"

"Go," he said.

Milton felt terrible about deceiving Maria, but he had no other choice. It would've been selfish to go to Amsterdam with her *before* everything that had happened, but now—now that he knew the Group was close, that they had been close enough to touch—it would've been the height of irresponsibility.

He couldn't do that to her.

He wouldn't.

That didn't mean that he felt any better about his deception, but he'd been left with no other choice. His passport was still at the hotel, and there was no way he was going to go back there to collect it, or any of his alternatives. He had to leave the country, but, to do that, he would need fresh papers. Maria had told him the night after the shooting that the smuggler who had brought her into the country could arrange fake passports; Milton didn't have any other contacts in Dublin to help and, even though Ziggy might have been able to arrange something eventually, it would've taken time that Milton didn't have.

"Did she come through?" Ziggy asked him now.

"She did," Milton said. He pointed ahead. "Drive."

Ziggy nodded, looked over at Milton, but said no more. He knew Milton well enough by now to know when he didn't want to speak. He put the car into first gear and pulled away, heading south to Ballygarvan and then west towards the harbour. Milton's plan was to buy tickets on the ferry to Roscoff and then, when they reached France, to find a place where they could lie low while Ziggy tried to find anything that would help him locate Nikita Yevtushenko. Milton knew the Group had found him through Ziggy, and that meant that they must have found him through their observation of Jimmy Moon. He had hoped that he might get to Lilly Moon and then persuade her of the good sense in a confession that would be exculpatory for him, but that avenue was now closed off.

His remaining option was the most dangerous: find the only other living witness to her crime—Control—and bring her back to London.

He looked at his watch. He would've liked to find a meeting, but they were all in the city and he didn't have time to fit one in before the ferry sailed for France. It felt as if he was on top of a high wire, stranded between where he had started from and where he wanted to go, the wind buffeting him and making each step more difficult than the last. He could find somewhere in France, he supposed, but then caught himself: was there really any point? What chance did he have of finding Yevtushenko in a war zone? What chance did he have of persuading him to help locate Control and then making his way through Siberia to find her? Ziggy would of course offer to help, but Milton wouldn't put him in harm's way. He was going to have to manage this by himself and, despite all his experience, he couldn't help but think that this was a trip from which he would not return.

"Milton?"

"Yes?"

"You're a million miles away—we're at the ferry."

Milton looked out onto Lough Mahon and the ferry that would take them from Glenbrook to Carrigaloe.

"You still want to do this?"

He nodded. "Let's go."

ABOUT MARK DAWSON

Mark Dawson is the author of the John Milton, Beatrix and Isabella Rose and Atticus Priest series.

For more information:
www.markjdawson.com
mark@markjdawson.com